P9-DTO-611

DAW BOOKS PRESENTS THE NOVELS OF MARSHALL RYAN MARESCA

THE VELOCITY OF REVOLUTION

Maradaine

THE THORN OF DENTONHILL

THE ALCHEMY OF CHAOS

THE IMPOSTERS OF AVENTIL

Maradaine Constabulary

A MURDER OF MAGES

AN IMPORT OF INTRIGUE

A PARLIAMENT OF BODIES

Streets of Maradaine

THE HOLVER ALLEY CREW

LADY HENTERMAN'S WARDROBE

THE FENMERE JOB

Maradaine Elite

THE WAY OF THE SHIELD

SHIELD OF THE PEOPLE

PEOPLE OF THE CITY

THE VELOCITY OF REVOLUTION

MARSHALL RYAN MARESCA

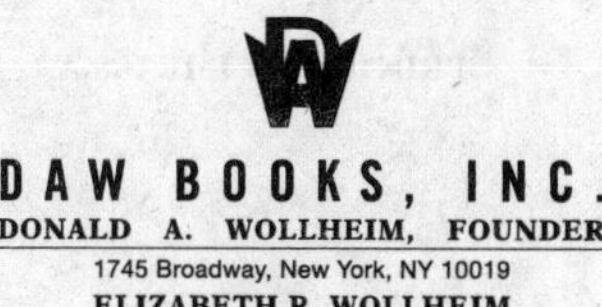

DAW BOOKS, INC.
DONALD A. WOLLHEIM, FOUNDER
1745 Broadway, New York, NY 10019
ELIZABETH R. WOLLHEIM
SHEILA E. GILBERT
PUBLISHERS
www.dawbooks.com

Cover illustration by Matthew Griffin.

Cover design by Katie Anderson.

Edited by Sheila E. Gilbert.

DAW Book Collectors No. 1875.

Published by DAW Books, Inc.
1745 Broadway, New York, NY 10019.

First Printing, February 2021
1 2 3 4 5 6 7 8 9

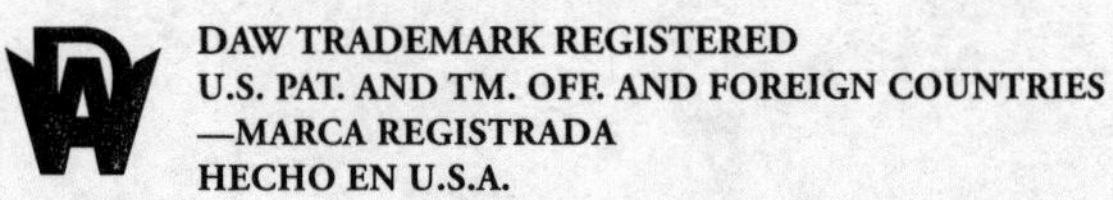

THE VELOCITY OF REVOLUTION

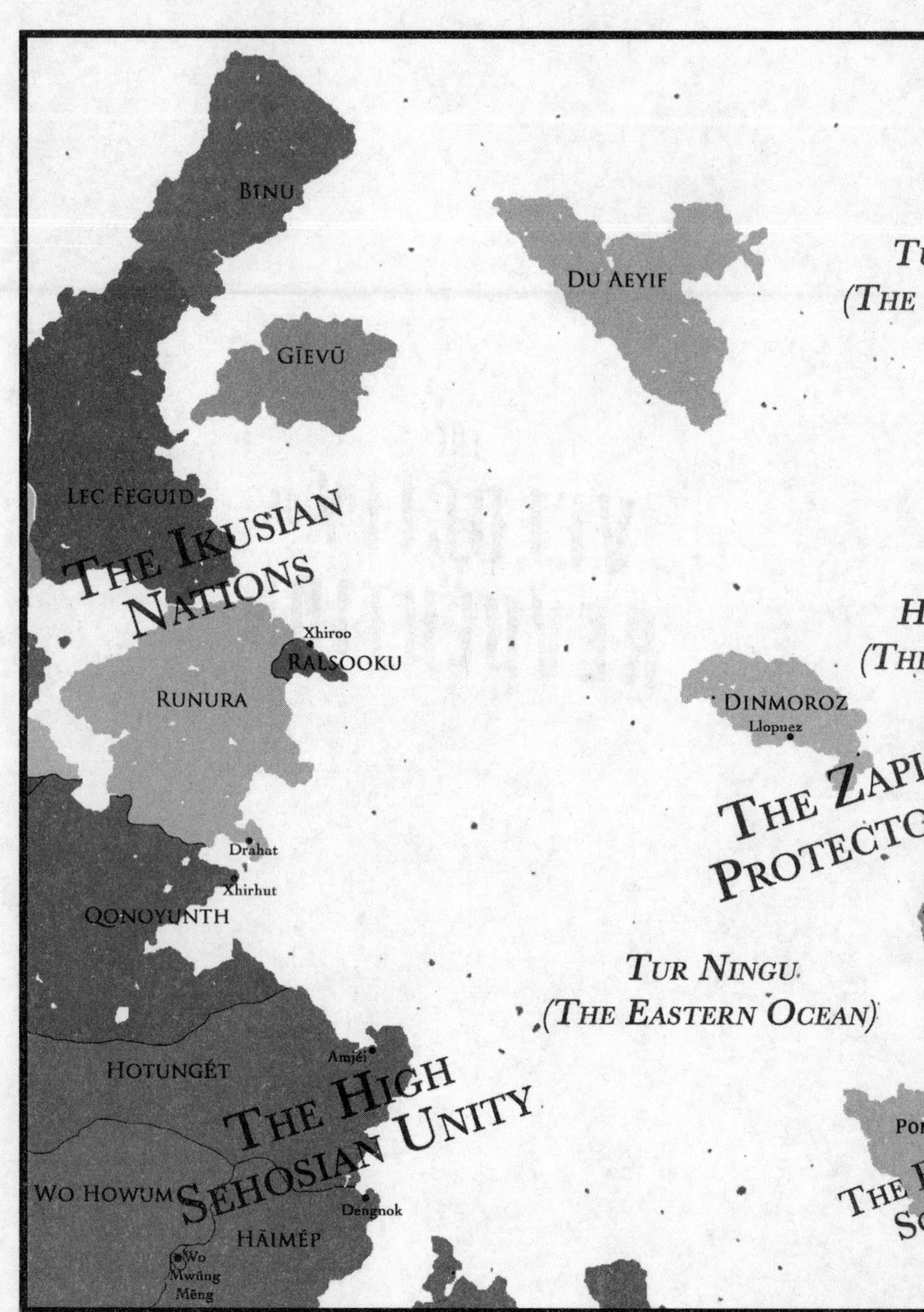

Binu
Du Aeyif
Gīevū
Lec Feguid
The Ikusian Nations
Xhiroo
Ralsooku
Runura
Dinmoroz
Llopuez
Drahat
Xhirhut
Qonoyunth
Tur Ningu
(The Eastern Ocean)
Amjéi
Hotungét
The High Sehosian Unity
Wo Howum
Dengnok
Hāimép
Wo Mwūng Mēng

ÉKE
OCEAN)
POMARJUNGKHU
HOBĂLAIF
KLALARSÅNG
SEMÓ
ND SEA)
THE OUTHIC
STATES
HEMISHUEK
RELOUMENE
Dumamång
GINIĀS
ES
Dutstu
INOGOZ
DIASEWSH
Lubemeu
Ziaparr
Nejandra
HOLY VAILIC
KINGDOMS
IKRIBA
TUR SUWING
(THE BURNING OCEAN)
Gazamai
REPUBLICS OF
ERN ZAPISIA
NORRONDE
OLLAZNUL
PUEZON
ZUIRHAN
DIDIZOYON
CILLÚN

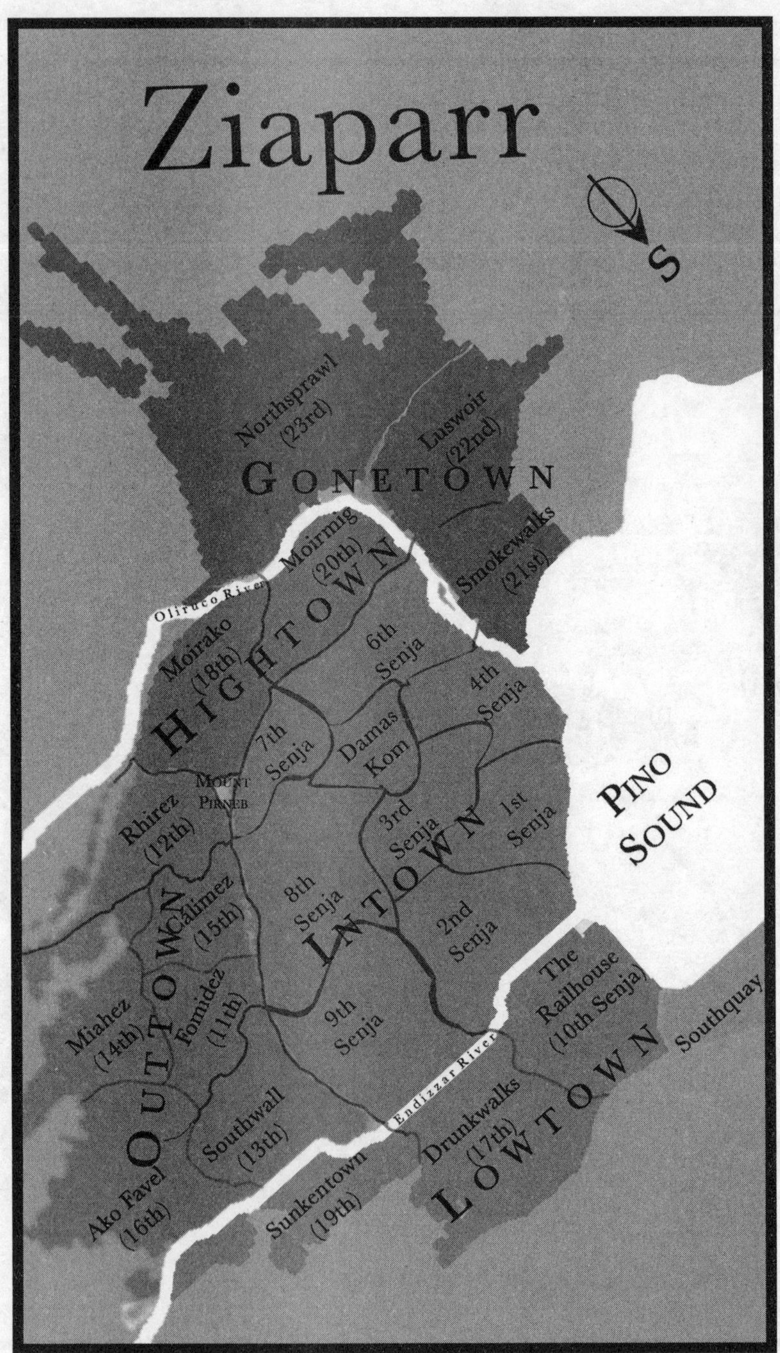

Ziaparr
S
Northsprawl (23rd)
Luswoir (22nd)
GONETOWN
Moirmig (20th)
Smokewalks (21st)
Oliruco River
HIGHTOWN
Moirako (18th)
6th Senja
4th Senja
7th Senja
Damas Kom
Mount Pirneb
PINO SOUND
Rhirez (12th)
3rd Senja
1st Senja
INTOWN
Calimez (15th)
8th Senja
2nd Senja
OUTTOWN
Fornidez (11th)
Miahez (14th)
9th Senja
The Railhouse (10th Senja)
Southquay
Endizzar River
Southwall (13th)
Drunkwalks (17th)
LOWTOWN
Ako Favel (16th)
Sunkentown (19th)

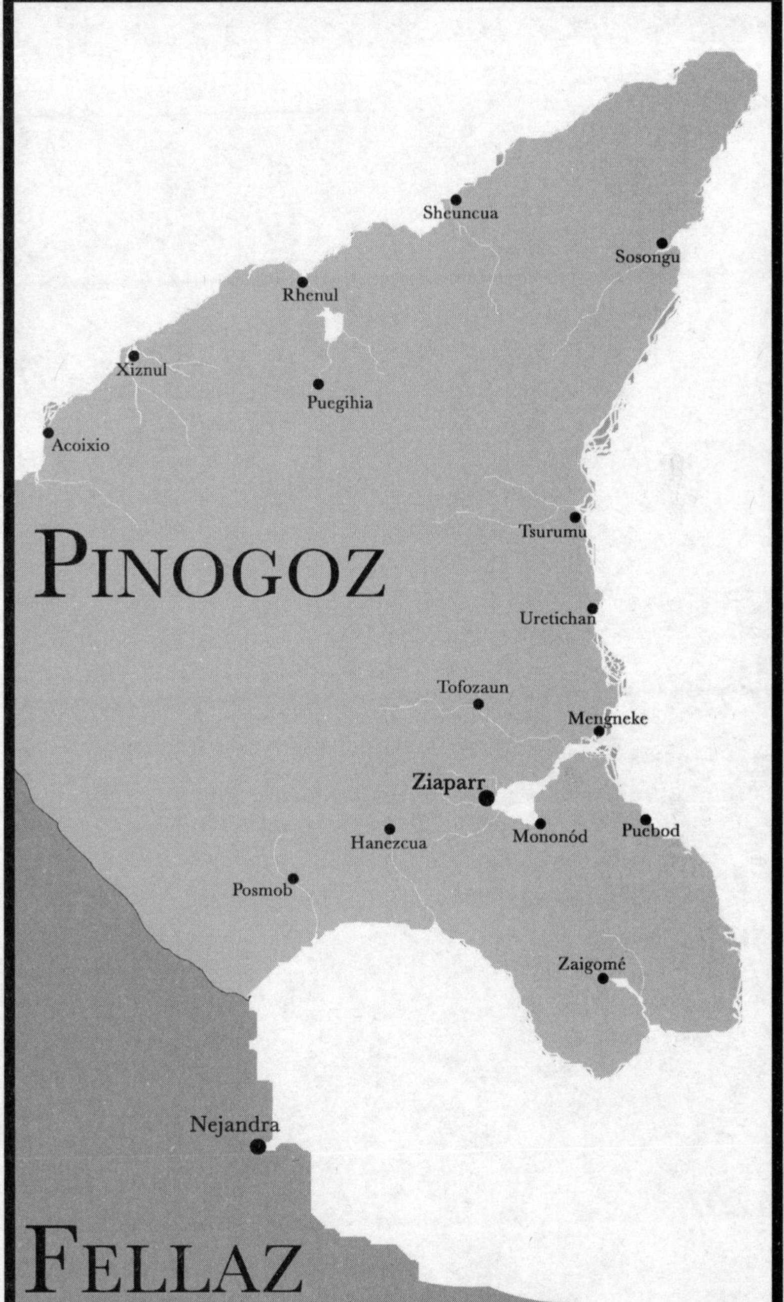
Sheuncua
Sosongu
Rhenul
Xiznul
Puegihia
Acoixio
Tsurumu
PINOGOZ
Uretichan
Tofozaun
Mengneke
Ziaparr
Hanezcua
Mononód
Puebod
Posmob
Zaigomé
Nejandra
FELLAZ

THE CASTES OF ZIAPARR AND PINOGOZ

Llipe (jyee-pay): The uppermost caste, of Pinogozi people whose bloodlines are almost entirely of Sehosian or Outhic descent, especially descended directly from one of the original Sehosian Prime Families from the initial colonization of the Zapisian Islands. The upper class of Ziaparr, living and working entirely in the inner senjas (Intown).

Rhique (rhee-kay): The lesser overcaste, of mixed-race people of primarily Sehosian or Outhic descent, with a minimal amount of local Zapisian parentage. The middle class of Pinogoz, living and working throughout the city, especially the outer senjas of Hightown and Lowtown, and with limited access to the senjas of Intown.

Jifoz (hee-fahz): The undercaste, of mixed-race people of primarily Zapisian heritage, with some Sehosian or Outhic parentage. The working class of Pinogoz, living primarily in the run-down outer senjas of Outtown.

Baniz (bah-neez): The lowest caste, people of entirely Zapisian descent. The underclass of Ziaparr, forbidden from living within the city limits without special dispensation, crowded into the ruined slums of Gonetown.

Zoika (zoh-ee-kah): The honorary caste of "respected foreigner"—tourists or officials of the occupational oversight government. Allowed residence in the Intown senjas, especially the governmental center of the Damas Kom.

OPENING HEAT:
THE SIPHON RUN

1

The steel cruisers are out tonight, my friends. Boys and girls get something thrumming between your legs, and find communion with your spirits. Faster, faster, let the speed fill you, and chase down the night. Rattle some cages!"

The cool alto voice crackled through the tinny speakers of the transistor radio dangling over the kitchen stove. The message was just a brief interruption of the usual bullshit, and then with a burst of static, the prop broadcast kicked back in.

"—doing YOUR part for the war efforts, paying back the debt we owe—"

Nália Enapi tuned that out. Same old bullshit she heard every day, every sweep, without fail. The important thing was the interrupting signal.

"Was that for you?" *Queña* Povo asked. He and the cousins, about to sit down to their rationed portions of rice and beans, all looked to Nália. He lowered his voice. "Was that her?"

"Yeah," Nália said, pushing her bowl to one of the cousins and getting up from the table. "Got to ride."

"Don't bring that back here," Povo said. "We can't risk it."

"I know," she said, grabbing her denim coat. "This is just on me." She went out the door.

Of course Povo couldn't risk it. He—not actually her uncle, nor were his kids her cousins, but they were family enough—was *baniz* caste. Trying to pass as *jifoz* caste like Nália. Living illegally in Outtown with forged identity cards. Castejumper. An offense that would get him a life sentence in the Alliance work camps. Nália wasn't going to bring trouble on him or his kids.

And the trouble was out there. She had barely gone down the steps from the *fasai*—the room above the machine shop she shared with Povo and the cousins—and walked across the street to the phonebox when a pair of Civil Patrol came right up to her.

"You got cards, *jifo*?" one asked. Like most tories, he was *rhique* caste.

Bootlickers working for the Alliance nucks, privileged due to having only a little native blood in their veins.

She produced her identification. Her cards were legitimate, but that didn't stop these tories from squinting at them and holding them up to the sodium streetlight. "Where you off to at this sweep?"

"I got a call to make," she said, pointing to the phonebox.

"Calling for *myco*?"

"Just calling a couple lovers for tonight," she said. "Can I go?"

They scowled but handed her the cards back, waving her off. She hurried over to it, waiting for them to be out of earshot before dialing in her exchange. They had already found another *jifoz* to harass. As the call rang through, her eyes focused on the prop poster plastered on the wall next to the phonebox. Couldn't round a circle in this part of town without seeing one of them. This one had three folks in coveralls building a warplane, with PAYING IT BACK painted along the bottom. Someone had scrawled *"nix xisisa"* across it. She knew only a few words of old Zapi, but she knew that. *We have paid too much.*

"Well?" the woman said when the call connected. Nália recognized the voice—Nic, the woman who had recruited her. Her only contact with the cell so far.

"The message came," Nália said. "This is Nália."

Nic sighed. "Did you already park your cycle?"

"In the alley as usual," she said. The alley led behind the machine shop, and that was where she always kept her baby, so she could see it through the dirty window next to her cot.

"There's the taco cart at the mouth of the alley. Get yourself a nice dinner, and your date tonight will meet you."

Her date. As in her partner for the job she was about to do.

"And then?"

Nic had already disconnected.

Nália glanced about to check again for tories—they were gone for now—and made her way to the cart, sweet smells of pork and corn roasting wafting into her nose. Her stomach growled in anticipation of the rare treat of Ziaparr street tacos. Normally she wouldn't dare the extravagance of even an ear of grilled corn. Not with the small amount of extra coin she earned on top of her ration chits.

If the job went well, she was promised coin to spare and a place in the cell. That money could help Povo and the cousins a lot. If it didn't go well, she'd likely be tethered by the tories, so she might as well have one last decent meal.

"Two sweet pork," she told the cart chef. "And an ear."

"You want the *raina* on that ear?" he asked. He took a good look at her, and nodded. "Yeah, you want the *raina*."

He was right, she wanted the spice. He could plainly see she was *jifoz*, like him. Not that any overcaste *rhique* or, spirits forgive, conceited *llipe* folk would be buying street tacos in the Miahez neighborhood, unless they were the posers trying to act authentic. But even they wouldn't come dressed like she was, cycle cat style, in hard raw denim, stained with grease and oil from engine work.

"That's nine and two," the cart chef said as he handed her the corn.

"I got it." A slick young man with smoky dark eyes came up and handed coins to the chef. "And a pair of tang chicken for me."

"I don't need some—" Nália started.

"You're Nália, right?" he asked. "Enzu."

Her partner for the job. "Where's your cycle?" She greedily bit into the corn, slathered with spices and salt and lime, pure joy on her tongue.

"Down the alley, like I was told," he said. "Yours the cold blue 960?"

"Yeah," she said.

"Style, girl," he said with a disarming smile.

The radio dangling over the food cart, this one playing some old Intown brass, crackled out again, and the cool woman's voice came back in. "*Spirits and skulls on the dark ride, friends. The time is ripe.*" Static again, and the music went back on like nothing had happened.

"That's the signal," Enzu whispered, nudging her on the arm.

"What is?" Nália asked as the cart chef wrapped up sweet spiced pork and onions into tortillas, slathering them with roasted tomatillo sauce.

"On the radio," he hissed. "That's Varazina. She's calling to us."

"Now?"

"*Now.*"

Nália grabbed her tacos from the vendor and ran down the alley slope to the bottom of the step, where her Puegoiz 960 was leaning against the cracked concrete wall. The blue and chrome beauty could clock nearly one-fifty kilos per sweep, and that was with cornering the curves of the aqueducts. She figured on a straight run, she could hit three hundred. Nália had worked with the cousins to crank its engine power so it ran like a 1296. When Nália was sitting on her 'goiz, she was lightning on two wheels, she was fire and steel powering through Ziaparr streets.

Of course, she rarely built up much momentum before reaching a patrol checkpoint.

Pausing before getting on her cycle, she took a bite of her taco. Savory pork and spicy tomatillo created an explosion of alchemy on her tongue.

"Hold up," Enzu said, catching up to her. "I like the hustle, *zyiza*, but there's a reason for the tacos."

"Because they're delicious?" Nália asked through a mouthful.

"Yeah," he said with a far too pretty smile. Back in the sodium light of the alley, Enzu looked like he might be a perfect example of *jifoz* beauty: dark eyes—that lit up with every one of his smiles—which complemented the tawny bronze of his skin. His black hair was slicked back, like how most of the *jifozi* cycleboys would do it, and his dark denim slacks and jacket hugged his thin frame. Nália was wearing the same thing, of course, but the curves of her hips strained the copper rivets holding the pants together. The cousin who had passed them on to her had been a skinny rail. "But that's not all of it."

He opened up a small leather pouch and sprinkled a bit of powder on her taco.

"We need to run on the *myco*?"

He nodded. "You've ridden on it before?"

"Yeah," she said, hesitant to take a bite. Everyone she knew had tried the magic of the *myco* with some willing flesh. She wasn't opposed to doing that with Enzu before the night was over, but his expression told her that wasn't what he was thinking. "Oh, you mean on the cycle. No."

"Be ready," he said, sprinkling some on his own taco, and then biting into it. "When you get up to speed, that's when it really kicks in."

She finished the taco, disappointed that it now had a slightly bitter aftertaste. Getting on her cycle, she asked, "Where's the run?"

"Just keep up," he said, getting on his own Ungeke K'am. A Sehosian cycle, which seemed like treason to Nália. It was all compact and polished casing, no style or character. It was elegant, but it wasn't beauty like hers. His looked like it had just rolled out of the factory, no personality. No love. That said, it had more power and speed than a regular 'goiz 960 ever would.

But Nália wasn't riding a regular 960, and she sure as shit wasn't a regular rider. She kicked the engine on, a glorious roar of petrol and steel that echoed through the alley. Putting on her helmet, she said, "You're going to regret that one."

"I better," he said, kicking his cycle up. His purred like an angry cat, ready to pounce. Not bothering with a helmet, he was down the alley like a bullet.

Nália was not about to let herself get outridden by any fool on an Ungeke, and she cranked the throttle to rush after him. Out of the alley, she chased him around two curves, dodging cable cars and trucks round the circles through the Miahez neighborhood. She hit cruising gear as she caught his tail. He roared up Avenue Nodlion, weaving in between the idling autos that lined up for half a kilometer for their petrol ration from the fuel station at the circle. She was going to burn through a quint of her month's supply on this raid tonight, so she needed it to keep her riding tight.

She needed this to pay off. For herself, for Povo and the cousins.

And, in some small way, for all their freedom.

Enzu signaled he was dropping right, which made no sense, since there was no turning circle coming up. Then he swerved off the road, through a bombed-out empty lot, and fell out of sight. She had no idea what crazy shit he was up to, but she was committed now. She followed right after, loose gravel in the lot flying behind her as she cranked her cycle into racing gear. If he can do ninety-six kilos across this lot, she'd do one-oh-eight.

The heat from the engine crept into her thighs as she crested over the bank at the edge of the lot, and the ground dropped out beneath her. She fought the urge to brake and pull back, and she saw Enzu hurtling down the dry aqueduct gully that divided Fomidez from Miahez. Under the bridges, under the checkpoints. And he was really racing, nearly one-twenty. She wasn't going to be shown up. Not here, not tonight.

She landed hard, wind racing as the cycle threatened to skid out underneath her. She leaned left, pulling herself up and revving the throttle hard. One-eight kilos, gear shift. One-twenty. One-thirty-two. Passing gear. Closing the distance to Enzu.

Then he was there. On her bike with her, his arms wrapped around her waist.

And she was on his, holding on to him.

"What?" she shouted, almost losing her cycle as they went into the dark of the water tunnel.

"Keep with it," he whispered in her ear. "Keep your velocity. That's what powers the *myco*. Pulling us together."

Then it was her on the Ungeke, him on the 'goiz. No, she looked over her shoulder to see herself on the 'goiz, charging through the water tunnel like a bullet from a gun. She was on the Ungeke, but she was Enzu. And Enzu was her. And she was also still holding on to him from the back of the cycle, and being held.

All while hammering around the curves of the aqueduct gully.

She had had a few rides of the *myco,* usually while bedding down some piece of pretty flesh who had done the same. Sex on the mushroom was a trip—every touch linked bodies, sensations reverberating, nerves firing together. Feeding off each other's pleasure.

But nothing like this. That was a pale echo, a memory of touch compared to this.

"Too much!" she shouted. She let go of the throttle and let herself slow down to a stop. Still herself, still on the 'goiz. Enzu passed her, then slowed and turned around, stopping in front of her.

The intensity faded, but she could still feel him. His heart beating in his chest, his pulse racing, the rumble of his engine between his thighs.

"It's all right," he said. "We're synced for now."

"For . . ." She wasn't sure which mouth she was talking out of at first. "For how long?"

"Hard to say," he said, idling his cycle and getting off. "The speed, that's what binds us. The faster you go, the stronger the bond. More intense, and you can feel each other even when physically apart. It lasts longer too, maybe all night? Maybe longer."

"I don't know if I like you that much," Nália said. "Why are we doing the run this way?"

"So we can do everything we need to as one," he said. "And even then, it's going to be hard." He moved closer, gingerly touching her hand. The sensation was electric, a circuit closing in her body as she felt every inch of him, become her. "Are you all right?"

"It's . . . it's . . ." She closed her eyes and let herself flow into it. Like when she rode her cycle. Revving the throttle, being one with the machine. Faster, faster, faster, filling her spirit with the thrill of speed.

Her eyes were closed, but she could still see. See herself, through his eyes.

She opened her eyes. "I've got a handle on it, I think."

"Good," he said. He looked up at the railbridge spanning over their head. "Because the job is going to come thundering through here, and we need to be ready. Ready to race?"

She smiled, and powered up her engine again. "Always."

2

Enzu tossed her a pair of packs that were stashed away in a sluice, then grabbed a pair more. "Good, the other crew did their jobs."

"What's the play?" Nália asked. "You done one of these before?"

"Twice," he said. "Strap that onto your cowl. Hurry up."

She was going to ask why, but then she felt it. Or more correctly, felt what he did, and knew what it meant because he knew. Not quite reading thoughts as words—she didn't think the mushroom could do that—but she *knew* because he did. The low vibration from the railbridge. The train was coming. She strapped the packs onto the back of the cycle and got on, kicking the engine back to life.

He did the same, roaring off, and she was already with him without even moving.

"Come on!" he said in her ear, holding on right behind her. She still needed a swipe to find herself, remember where she really was on her own 960 and not with him on the Ungeke K'am, even as it was racing away.

She revved up and shot off. She knew what she needed to do now, because he was already—she was already—doing it: cranking hard as the aqueduct curved and banked, ramping up the side with a hard throttle and gear shift. The train was thundering overhead, going just as fast as they were.

Enzu—she felt it as if it were her own body, but still him—hit the ramp and flew high, leaning hard as he reached the apex of the jump to land on the train tankcar with a jarring slam, braking before he went flying off the front of the tankcar.

He nailed it perfectly, and the fear, the thrill, the rush of it all surged through her body as well as his, just as she hit the ramp the same way on the 960.

She didn't land clean, slipping the wheel and sliding to the side of the tankcar. But as she braked and skidded to the edge, he was there, grabbing her arm and locking his foot under the walk rail. She felt his ankle wrench, his shoulder pop, felt the pain as if it were her own. She recovered from the slip and pulled back to the middle of the tankcar.

She would ask if he was all right, but she knew, she felt it: He was fine, he would walk it off.

Nália righted herself on top of the train, getting her cycle in place on the top. Enzu was already at work, taking off the packs.

"Now?" she asked him, screaming over the racing winds of the train.

"We hope none of the nucks in the train noticed us, or tories saw us jump. Get the siphon going. I'll reach out."

He hadn't spoken, not with his actual mouth. Instead, it was the manifestation of him that was right next to her, whispering in her ear. His actual body tossed her the pack off the back of his bike and stood at the front of the tankcar, which thundered along the track above the winding streets, toward Ako Favel. She knew the track—of course she did, she had lived with it over her head for so many years—knowing it would curve hard in two kilos. One swipe away, at best.

"Right," his manifestation whispered as she unpacked the siphon hoses and canvas bags. "Get braced for that. The pass is after the curve, as we go down along Southwall." His body lashed their cycles to the top rails of the tankcar.

"Got it," she said out loud, though she wondered if she really needed to. She opened the hatch at the top of the tankcar, and the hard, volatile scent of the petroleum inside crawled up her nose. Sweet and rich, by her spirits, she wondered how many kiloliters there were in there. Fuel for so many cycles, autos, and trucks. Enough for everyone she knew to drive all the kilometers they'd need for the rest of the year. Spirits watching, probably every *jifoz* and *baniz* in Ziaparr. A shit of a lot more than the drops of ration they'd normally get.

Instead this was headed for the railyard, to then get loaded in tanker ships. Fuel to serve the tanks, planes, and cars in the Alliance's wars. Fuel for the Eight Nations.

But barely a drop for the Pinogozi people. While the world drank deeply on their oil, they were thirsting for the blood of their own land. At least the *jifoz* were. The *rhique* dogs and their *llipe* masters were given more fuel, more food, more everything by virtue of their blood. Shit-mouthed guzzlers, the lot of them.

She felt Enzu reach into the speed of the train. That was the only way she could describe what he did—it was as if the very velocity of it racing along the track became a part of his mind, and from that his own eyes and ears expanded all around him. She could feel it as well—as they came up to the hard curve, there were trucks in position on the road that ran parallel to the track. Each truck had a driver in the cab and someone else in the bed. She could feel they were part of the same vibration, all the crews lightly in sync. Not the same intensity she and Enzu were sharing, but a faint touch of matched frequency.

In the train, bursts of static. Nucks—Alliance Guard—working the train, standing guard. Farther out, she could feel tories on the road, hitting her senses with that same crack of static. Not tuned to her or Enzu. Not their allies.

The train hit the curve, and Enzu grabbed hold of the top rail of the tankcar. Nália did the same before she went flying off, but also stayed focused on her task. She hooked one of the canvas sacks to the top rail, and let it unfold over the side of the tankcar. She then dropped the siphon hose down into the sweet, golden nectar. Enzu skittered over to the edge of the tankcar, grabbing the other end of the hose. He sucked on one end, and in a moment, spat out the rush of petrol that hit his mouth. Nália felt it burn in her mouth and throat as it hit, as if she had sucked it out of the hose herself.

Enzu jammed the hose into the nozzle of the bag, and it started to fill with fuel. Nália got to work unfolding and hanging the other bags.

"How much?" she asked, this time having the sense to ask with her mind, the part of her that was wrapped close to him, whispering in his ear.

"Each bag holds sixty liters," he said. "We want at least twelve bags. Fifteen, if we can."

Just a shave off the top of this tankcar, but it would mean so much to the mission, to everyone in the crews, and the movement—the revolution—behind it all. Hopefully this would prove that she deserved to be with them, that she had the skills and the drive.

They worked quickly, starting another hose siphoning, getting the bags filled. As they did it, she felt the trucks drive up parallel to the train, and at the speed they were going, Nália brushed on the wavelengths of the drivers and the catchers in each one, enhancing her sync to their minds. Not the same degree that she had with Enzu, but enough to feel where they were, feel how ready they were.

"Now," Enzu whispered in her ear. She went to the first bag, now full, nozzles sealed. She unhooked it from the safety rail—spirits, it was heavy—and locked eyes and sync with the catcher in the bed of the first truck. He was a real bruiser, with arms like the tires on the truck. She threw the bag, full of precious fuel, to him, and he was right in place to catch it, despite the heavy wallop of it. He strapped it down in the bed. Sixty liters secure.

They kept that up until the first one had six full bags in the bed, and they started to work on the next one. Two bags in, and then Nália felt a hard burst of static hit across her skull.

She reached out and felt it. Tories on cycles, racing up the road behind the trucks.

Enzu had felt it as well, and he gave a signal to the truck drivers. Throwing the last full bag down, he started tossing the empties and the hoses off the train.

"There's no turnoff for another kilo. The trucks are dead targets unless we draw off the tories."

Nália understood. The trucks had the petrol, they had to get back. She and Enzu could be the hares that the dogs chased. They could afford to get caught, if it came to that. What mattered was the fuel.

She unstrapped her 'goiz 960 and kicked it up.

"Let's give them a race."

3

Nália wished she had a handcannon strapped to her thigh right now. The tories were racing up on their cycles, ready to crack every one of them and haul them down to the 9th Senja in shackles. A couple of shots from the nine-piece she kept under her cot would do the job quite nicely.

But the orders from Nic had made one thing clear: Do Not Go Armed. If she had brought her nine-piece, there would be no chance she'd get brought into the crew. The job was to get the fuel and get out, and it was likely to go bad right now.

"Yeah, it might," Enzu whispered to her. Her thoughts must have been plain to him. "Which is why you don't want to get caught with a gun. It'd be the difference between a clang and a hang."

That was an odd way to put it—she'd never heard that idiom—but she understood. Plus, it wasn't like the tories would hesitate to pull iron on a *jifoz* girl if they thought they were going to get some back. She had known enough folks who caught a slug just for holding something that looked like a handcannon.

He kept whispering. "Stay with the trucks, get them to the turnoff. I'll dust up the tories and keep them off your wheels."

Nália revved her engine and launched off, kicking herself up as she went off the edge of the tankcar. She landed next to one of the trucks with a hard jar, but the 960 took it and went like a shot once she touched dirt. Povo's son Nezzu had rebuilt the shocks, and done a beautiful job of it. Nália couldn't ask for better.

She was with Enzu when he landed, but while she stayed with the trucks, he fell back and stopped, spinning his back wheel to kick up clouds of dust and dirt. Then she felt the jagged lines of the tories—three of them on cycles, slow down as they hit those clouds. Enzu dropped his cycle down into the gully, through the aqueduct, and off at high speed. Two of the tories went after him, while the third stayed on the road, on her trail.

Then Enzu faded from her—probably too far away for her to still feel, same with the tories on his tail. She only had the taste of the truck crews, a vague feel of sync with them, not the full body connection she had had with Enzu. She almost felt empty from his absence, at least for a moment. But she didn't have time to think about that. There was the tory to knock off their trail. She had to draw him away from the trucks.

She had a plan, but she had to let the drivers in the trucks know. If the speed made the mushroom stronger, and they were all rolling with the train, was that enough? She tried to push herself to them, touch them each a little stronger, like the connection she had had with Enzu.

That push was all it took—she found herself in the cab of each of the trucks. All the trucks at once. Surprised and disoriented—she was in four places at once, while still riding her cycle—she didn't waste any time.

"Turn off your lights," she said to them. "Keep them off through the turnoff, until you're back on concrete."

Each of them complied as she let herself snap back completely into her body. She dropped back behind the third truck. That last tory was racing up close. All she had to do was draw them off for a few minutes, let the trucks get away.

She revved her engine, loud as thunder, as the trucks turned off in the dark. As the last one turned away, she could feel the tory crackling up on her, headlights shining on her back. Up to racing gear, throttle cranked, she swung off the road, under the pylons holding up the railway. Faster, faster, she weaved her way around the metal and concrete, knowing the tory was trying hard to stay on her.

But she could feel him, all static and jagged lines. Just like she had been in sync with Enzu, the tory—so intent on stopping her—was so out of sync with her that she felt him with as much intensity. She could feel his desperation, feel him struggle with every curve and weave.

He wasn't anywhere close to being the rider she was.

She cleared the next pylon and took a hard left, almost scraping the ground with her knee as she leaned with the turn, and then dropping into the aqueduct.

The tory didn't make the turn. He spun out and went down in a tumble.

The truck crews faded from her senses, but the last thing she felt was them reaching a paved road, lights on, joining the wind of normal traffic. Made it.

She howled with joy as she sped down the aqueduct, through one tunnel and out the other end. Laughing, she came to a stop and powered down her 960.

They pulled it off. Liters and liters of petrol, all away safe. She leaped off the cycle and jumped up and down in pure exhilaration. They had pulled it the fuck off.

She hoped Enzu had made it as well. He'd better have. She was so buzzed with the thrill, not to mention the rush of the *myco,* that she wanted the release of a ride with him, especially if they stayed synced to each other for it.

If not, she'd find some other willing flesh at the carbon hut near her *fasai*. It'd be a shame not to have Enzu, though.

She took a moment to catch her breath, but she knew she needed to move. She could still feel the crackle of that tory, under the rails. He might get back on his ride and catch up and—

A cycle roared out of the tunnel, coming right between her and her own 960. Before she even knew what was happening, the rider was off the cycle, boots on the pavement, gun drawn.

Black coat. Hard leather uniform. Heavy iron pulled on her.

A tory. Not the one who had chased her. He was still a kilo away. Where did this one come from?

"On the ground!" he shouted. "Hands spread, touch nothing!"

Staring down his handcannon, she knew she had no choice.

She held out her arms, fingers spread wide, and got on her knees. As she lay face down on the ground, he grabbed one hand and clapped the shackles on it.

"Consider yourself detained," he said as he finished locking her down. "Expect to face punitive action in response to your criminal acts."

"Not the first time I've heard that," she muttered.

He hauled her up on her feet. She now got a good look at him. Light, tawny complexion, with cool, cruel eyes and hair cut far too short. Of course he was *rhique*. Most of the tories were; traitors to their own blood and people. "Do you have your cards, or are we also going to charge you with failure to carry?"

"Of course I do," she said. Like she would ever try to go about without her identification. Like you could even walk three circles in Miahez without a tory asking for a card check, or even get into the senjas without it.

He shoved his hand roughly into her pocket and pulled out her cards. "Nália Enapi, *jifoz*, residence assigned to the 14th Senja."

Like anyone called Miahez anything but the 'hez.

And, fortunately, the residence listed on those cards was her old room in the factory dormitory. Nothing in those papers to lead back to the *fasai* above the machine shop and, thankfully, Povo and the cousins.

"Do you have work papers to enter the 19th?" he asked her.

"Is that where we are?" Nália snarled.

"You're just making it worse for yourself," he said. "Precinct violation on top of the other charges. I would hate to be you right now, Nália Enapi."

4

Nália had her fingers inked and her face plated, had her denim and boots taken, and every crevice of her body probed and checked to make sure she wasn't hiding a weapon. The tories then left her, alone, in a concrete cell with no bars or windows of any kind—just a hard, heavy door. The gray prison gown they gave her did nothing to cut the chill.

The first part of all of that was typical. She had been hauled in by the tories before, usually for something like carrying an expired card or fare-jumping the cable. The full ritual of plating, inking, and probing was the way it went. But after that, she was always put in a holding pen with fifty others, one big cage where they'd have to all eat, sleep, and shit in front of each other. Then after a day or so, released again.

This clearly was leading to a different kind of lockup, not just a few nights at the tory center in the 9th Senja. She didn't know how this would go, but more likely than not, a train ride to Hanez Pen. Or maybe something worse; she had heard stories of the work camps. But she had thought that would mean being hauled in front of a justice bench, not locked in a concrete room.

She didn't know how long she had been in that room—no way to get a sense of time in there. She was starting to think they had forgotten her when she felt something pull at her.

A hard yank brought her out of that room and into another. No, this was the mushroom sync. She was still in the concrete cell, but also in the other room—well lit, table, comfortable chairs. Two nuck officers—the kind with long leather coats and wide ties, instead of the black tory uniforms you saw on the streets—stood over the table. Over Enzu.

Enzu sat at the table, looking distressed, sweaty, pale.

Very pale in the light.

"Enzu?" she asked.

He looked up and met her eyes.

"How—" he said out loud. Then he shook his head.

"What's the story, Hwungko?" one of the officers asked. Strong accent. Nália wondered where he was from. "Who are you talking to?"

"Nothing," Enzu said.

"Hwungko?" Nália asked. It was very uncommon for a *jifoz* to have a Sehosian familial name. It might have been illegal, she wasn't sure.

But there wasn't a single *jifoz* she had met who had a Prime Family name.

"Nothing, I—" he stammered, trying not to look Nália in the eye. She could feel him pushing against her. "I wanted to know how long this is going to be."

"Shouldn't be too long," the other officer said. "We made the call twenty swipes ago. Unless you think she'd let you stew for a while."

"No, no," Enzu said. "I just—can I get another sparkling?"

"Sure, sure," the first officer said mockingly. "I mean, you want to feel refreshed when she gets here."

"Please," Enzu said.

"The shit is this?" she shouted at him.

She knew, she knew even if she couldn't believe it. She didn't see it from the beginning, but she should have. She let it all cloud her—that pretty smile, the fact that he was on the ride with her, that he could ride as well as he did. She thought he was like her, that he was with her.

The Ungeke K'am should have made it obvious.

Now, in the light, seeing his boots, his denim pants and coat—all spotless, not a scratch or tear. Like they were fresh off the shelf.

A woman came in—gray at the temples of her dry, thin hair; cool and light complexion; waistcoat and robe of painted purple silk. Head to heel, pure Sehosian.

"What has my nephew done now?" she announced, staring hard at Enzu.

"I'm sorry, *sedsa*!" Enzu cried.

"You're sorry?" Nália shouted at him. Only he could hear her, of course, and he cringed away from her.

Enzu was a *llipe*. It was plain as the sun now.

"I'll be taking him home now," the woman said.

"We're going to have some questions, Councilwoman Hwungko," the first officer said. "We've had the courtesy of waiting until you arrived, but we need—"

"Thank you for your diligence, gentlemen," the woman—the shit-filled councilor! —said. She wasn't just an overweening *llipe*, she was one of the traitors collaborating with the Alliance overseers. "I'll be taking him home. You can question him there, tomorrow, with our counsel present."

"Of course," the tory officer said. "We'll call your office to schedule it."

"You're going home while I'm locked in a box here!" Nália shouted. "Just like a *llipe*, act like you own everything!"

"I'm sorry!" he said. "You were supposed to get away!"

"Who are you talking to?" the councilor asked.

"Is he on the *myco*?" the first officer asked. "Is he bonding with someone?"

"You would dare?" the councilor asked. "You foolish, insipid idiot, Enzúri."

"Oh," the second officer said. "That *jifoz* cat down in lockbox."

"I didn't want you—" Enzu cried.

"I'm sure you didn't," Nália snarled. She wanted to be sick. She slammed her fist against the hard wall. Make herself hurt, make him feel it.

"All the more reason to get him away from here," the councilor said. "I appreciate you both dealing with this with discretion."

"Of course, ma'am," the first officer said. "We're all striving together to build a better city and nation. We can't do that without good people like you."

"Thank you," she said coldly.

The first officer helped Enzu to his feet. "Make sure your friend knows you've been a big help, Hwungko. And she's going to help us, too."

"What does that mean?" Nália asked.

"I'm sorry," Enzu said again before his aunt grabbed him by the collar of his denim coat and pulled him out.

"And dressed like this, like you were some common *jifoz* trash," the councilor said as the connection faded, and Nália found herself just in her cell, alone again.

REFUEL: NEWSREEL

Thank you for joining us at the cinescope this evening for our feature presentation of The Beaches of Ikriba, *a glorious epic of the Second Transoceanic War, brought to you by the Alliance Ministry of Entertainment! Starring Hodesat Tibog and Xang Xewung, the biggest cinescope stars on two continents! We hope you enjoy this grand and accurate depiction of the events of the war.*

But before we start, let us extend our thanks to the great Alliance of Eight Nations. The greatest good this world has ever seen, made possible due to the great treaties at the end of the Second Trans! They are making the world a greater, stronger, more peaceful place.

For example, the Office of Alliance Oversight is helping build the nation of Pinogoz and the capital city of Ziaparr into the great, modern nation we all know it can be. We all know that this beautiful island country, with its simple, native people, has thrived over the years as it was supported by the Sehosian Empire, and then later by Outhic nations like Reloumene and Hemisheuk. We wept as it weathered repeated devastation in the Second Trans, and cheered as their Prime Families, descended from old regal houses of the empire, tried nobly to rebuild. Then this poor nation suffered further tragedies under the tyrant Rodiguen.

And the Alliance was there for the people of Pinogoz in the Great Noble War! They came, dedicating personnel and resources to the very important task of ousting Rodiguen and his corrupt regime, stopping his reign of terror before he could launch his doomsday weapon.

Now the Alliance overseers have been there: rebuilding the city, rebuilding the country, getting the people on their feet. They're working with the Prime Families to oversee a provisional government, and they're getting the nation ready to finally have free and open elections.

The Alliance has done so much, so it's good that the people of Pinogoz are happy to work to repay that debt! They're growing food, making steel, and drilling for the precious oil found in such abundance in their lush, fruitful land.

And they are tightening their belts, rationing themselves in their own use, so even more can go to our efforts in the Third Transoceanic War.

Working together, the people of Pinogoz can repay their debt, and all of us can make the world a greater, stronger, more peaceful place!

Now to the cinescope . . .

FIRST CIRCUIT:
THE PATROL ASSIGNMENT

5

Wenthi Tungét waited patiently outside the investigators' office, as he had been told to do, even though it had made him nervous. He had never been called up to the third floor before.

He was the only one up here who was Civil Patrol—the fledgling local police force—as opposed to Alliance Guard officers. All of them *zoika*—the honored foreigner caste. Folks from the High Sehosian Unity or Outhic nations like Reloumene or Hemisheuk, mostly. In his mind they were all looking at him as if he was intruding.

He was, even if they had ordered him up here. The first floor was for the Civil Patrol, who were almost all *rhique* and assigned to street duty, mostly in the senjas of Outtown, Hightown, and Lowtown. Only in the past couple of seasons had anyone in Civil Patrol been assigned to work Intown. Those assignments went to the non-officers of the guard—the "nucks"—who also handled the checkpoints between senjas.

And the third floor was for the offices of the high officers from the Alliance Bureau of Welfare. The guard leadership, and the investigators who handled the deep crimes: murder, robbery, caste and ration violations.

A *llipe* woman came hustling out of one of the meeting rooms, almost dragging a young man behind her. They went through so quickly, Wenthi didn't even get a good look at them, though he was certain he had seen them before. Despite being *rhique*, he had spent much of his youth in *llipe* circles. Whoever they were, Mother knew them, and they knew Mother, surely.

Two investigators came out of the meeting room, chuckling and patting each other on the back. One of them took note of Wenthi and came over.

"You are the one who caught the girl, right?"

"Yes, sir," Wenthi said. "Wenthi Tungét."

"Tungét?" he asked, raising an eyebrow. "As in—"

"My mother," Wenthi said. No need to belabor the obvious question.

"And you're here working patrol? Interesting." The investigator shook his head, as if in disbelief. "And good job at that, son. Quite good. Did you know that tonight is the first time we've actually caught any of those *jifoz* petrol thieves alive in the act?"

"I did not, sir."

"I mean, we've had a few like that one—bored *llipe* kids who want to 'do something' or some bullshit, am I right?"

"I don't know about that, sir," Wenthi said. He had no idea what point this investigator was leading to. "I just ran down the girl on my cycle, and caught up to her when she clearly thought she had shook me."

"That's just it, Tungét," he said. "Every other time, they have shook patrol. I have to tell you, some of us up here were starting to think you Civil Patrol folk weren't actually trying. A little look the other way."

"No, sir," Wenthi said. "I chased her down and had her tethered."

"And good work," the investigator said. "Restored our faith in you folk. Thanks to you, we have a real shot to get some answers, find our way to the center of this thing."

"The center?"

"Son," he said, putting an arm around Wenthi's shoulders, "you think a bunch of organized robberies of petrol off a series of trains isn't organized from a center? It goes deeper, Tungét. Deeper."

"That makes sense," Wenthi said. Though nothing they had been told on the first floor by the Alliance supervisors had made it clear it was anything other than cycle gangs stealing fuel. Did they think it was something bigger? What exactly?

"That's the kind of thinking we like to see up here, Tungét. You are exactly what we need more of. You the only *rhique* boy who can get it done? Somebody is gonna have to step up, be a leader. Can you encourage the rest of your compatriots to get on it?"

"I can do that," Wenthi said. None of the local Civil Patrol had been promoted to leadership yet. He could prove he deserved to be the first.

"Good. Keep riding hard, catching these scoundrels, bring them in. The more you get, the more we can interrogate."

"And put an end to the petrol robberies?"

"Hopefully. And more, if it comes to it. Again, good work." He looked at his watch. "About seven on the fifty. Your stint is about to end, right?"

"Yes, sir. Ready to sign out for the night."

"Well, get out of here. Celebrate with your cadre, hmm? You've earned it."

He slapped Wenthi on the chest with familiar congeniality, which was a bit odd since Wenthi didn't even know this investigator's name. Or much anyone's name up here. Other than Lieutenant Yitsemt—the languid Reloumene officer who gave out the stint assignments and collected reports—the patrol riders rarely saw anyone from the leadership. Let alone formed a friendly rapport.

"Yes, sir," Wenthi said, and made his way to the stairwell as quickly as he could.

6

Heard you got a petrol thief, Tungét," one of the late stint riders called as Wenthi came into the uniform room. The room was filled with Civil Patrol officers coming off the night stint and more coming on the late stint, same as it was every night at seven on fifty.

"Nice catch!" Hwokó said, grabbing Wenthi by the front of his uniform. She pulled him close to her. "How you thinking of celebrating?"

"Getting every late-stinter coming off shift to jump into his bunk?" Paulei suggested. Paulei Jéngka had been Wenthi's riding partner on the night stint for the past season, and friend, lover, and compatriot since training cohort. Paulei was a good cop, the kind of rider everyone in the late stint cadre wanted by their side, especially when patrolling the upper senjas. He was also the one most everyone wanted to meet for drinks after shift, and whatever followed.

"That sounds promising," Wenthi said.

"Mmm," Hwokó said, giving him a playful slap. "Shame I'm double-stinting, or I'd join you all."

"They did say I should celebrate," Wenthi said. "Up on third."

"What?" Minlei said as she changed out of her uniform into her civilian slacks. "They call you up there? And you weren't in trouble?"

"Some vesti just wanted to praise me," Wenthi said. "Though—" He wasn't sure how to put it.

"What's up?" Guand asked.

"Nothing," Wenthi said, swallowing the uncomfortable comment the investigator had made about thinking they were letting the thieves escape, looking the other way. Surely none of them here were doing that.

"Well, thank spirits someone is doing their job." Whoever said that—a late sweeper Wenthi didn't know—knocked Paulei on the arm.

"Wait, wait," Paulei said. "Let me tell you, because, yeah, I fouled it up."

"Heard you slid your cycle, Jéngka!"

"Slid it hard," Wenthi said. "I'm amazed his leg isn't torn up."

"It is!" Paulei said, taking off his uniform pants. Sure enough, his tan, muscular leg was scraped, though the damage didn't look too bad. Paulei was laughing and showing it off to everyone in the room. "But hear it. Radio calls that a couple *jifoz* had torn through the 14th, probably checkpoint jumpers. We're on Outtown patrol around the 17th, you know, rounding the circles like any night."

"Get to the damned point, Paulei," Hwokó said as she put on her uniform coat.

"The mouth on her," Paulei said teasingly.

"You like my mouth, Jéngka."

"You sure you're not *jifoz*, Hwokó?"

"If anyone's got a *jifo* greasehead, it's Tungét," Hwokó said, roughly rubbing Wenthi's head. "Tell the story."

Wenthi chuckled and went to his niche while Paulei went on. It wasn't the first time Hwokó—or anyone else in the Civil Patrol—had made such a comment about his hair. He didn't mind most of the time, and he had had a good shift, so he wasn't about to let Hwokó ruin his mood. He changed out of his uniform and put on his civilian duds. He was hardly that stylish in his dress, but he cut a good figure in his lime-green pegged trousers and wide matching tie and suspenders. Paulei, in the midst of his recounting Wenthi's arrest for the night, was still in his cotton top and briefs, not in any hurry to finish getting dressed. Not that Wenthi or anyone else in the room minded the delay.

"So we charge after this wildcat on her 'goiz, and she's weaving and curving around the pylons, doing at least 120. Crazy one, she is, and I can't keep up with her. She whips around one pylon and drops into the aqueduct without so much as a gearshift. I blow that turn and skid along the gravel. You're lucky you still have a partner, Wenthi."

"Am I, though?" Wenthi teased back. "I mean, you were kind of useless tonight."

"Knock him, knock him." Hwokó laughed as she got her boots laced up.

"Fair, boy," Paulei went on. "I mean, I'm on the ground, next thing I know, the cat is off like a shot, and boom, Wenthi is down in that aqueduct in highest gear, off down that tunnel. I manage to get on my feet and haul my cycle back on its wheels, and my radio buzzes. Here's this boy, cool as a Hemish winter. 'Hey. I got shackles clapped. Call me a roll.'"

Everyone laughed, even though it was only because Paulei had made it funny.

"Hey, come on," Wenthi said. "It's not like Minlei and Guand didn't bring in their own catch."

"You didn't hear?" someone answered. "That fool was a *llipe*. That catch is getting tossed from the files."

"What is a *llipe* boy doing on a siphon steal with a bunch of *jifos*? Doesn't he have something better to do?"

"Don't the *jifos*?" Hwokó asked.

"Don't you?" Wenthi shot at her. "Don't you got a shift to ride?"

"Spirits, he's in a shitty mood," Hwokó said. She left the uniform room, as did most of the other late shift riders.

"Hey," Paulei said, coming over to Wenthi and reaching out to caress his face. "You did good. We finally got shacks on one of those fuel thieves."

"Yeah," Wenthi said. Paulei had that look like he often did after a shift, like he wanted to go back to the dorms and blow some steam, either the two of them or whoever else was available.

"What are you looking for tonight?"

"I just figured the hero deserved a reward," Paulei said with a devious smile. "Or, like Hwokó said, you're in a mood. I know how to fix that. We could rope whoever else is around?"

That did sound like a good idea. Wenthi was certainly for heading straight back to the apartments and getting comfortable with Paulei. Even though doing so in headquarters was frowned upon, he kissed Paulei quick, to let him know he wasn't blowing him off.

"Let's get home, figure it out there, deal?"

Paulei winked. "Deal."

7

The KT dormitory was a nondescript building in Circle Kãtaum in the 9th Senja, just one round from Guard and Patrol Headquarters, and three floors were dedicated housing for Civil Patrol. The rest of the building housed students at Ziaparr College and other *rhique* who were working with Alliance Oversight to rebuild the city. It wasn't luxurious, by any means, but it was comfortable enough. The facility was well staffed with a kitchen open the full ten sweeps, as well as cleaning and laundry services, so none of them needed to worry about those details.

Wenthi and Paulei were the first ones from late stint to come home, at least from what they saw. Most people, it appeared, opted for a stop in a club or carbon shop first.

"Good evening, Mister Tungét, Mister Jéngka," the front manager said as they came in. "How was your day so far?"

"Fine, fine," Paulei said as they made for the elevator.

"News, mail, calls?" Wenthi asked.

The manager presented a slip to Wenthi. "You did receive a call. She left that exchange for you."

"Thanks," Wenthi said, just as one of the building support staff—a maintenance man, Guiho was his name—came up from the back entrance.

"Guiho—" the front manager snapped. "Late again. You are supposed to be here at seven on fifty, and—"

Wenthi stepped up. "Oh, he wasn't late."

"Mister Tungét, you could see he just came in—"

"Right, but he was coming up just as we arrived, and we asked him to check something on our cycles for us. Didn't realize he needed to check in first."

"Oh," the manager said. She nodded her head appreciatively. "Thank you for letting me know. Carry on, Guiho."

"Yes, ma'am," he said. "And thank you, Mister Tungét."

Wenthi smiled and gave him a small salute before joining Paulei on the elevator. As soon as the doors closed Paulei grabbed him and kissed him.

"Why'd you do that?" Paulei asked.

"Do what?"

"Lie for that *jifoz* fellow for being late."

"Guiho's a good sort. And he *has* checked over our cycles before."

"Oh, right."

"And he's coming in from, where, the 14th? With all the checkpoints, you know how long that must take. Any little thing could make him a few minutes late. Why not help him out?"

Paulei laughed as the doors opened on their floor. "You are too good, you know that?"

"I've heard something to that effect," Wenthi said as they approached their respective rooms.

"I am going to take a quick shower," Paulei said. "And see if anyone's around I can recruit to join us in celebrating your success. I think I hear Cinden and Peshka in their room?"

"Good idea," Wenthi said. Cinden and Peshka were essentially a bonded couple, sharing a room, even if they hadn't formally affirmed that and they were not planning on having children any time soon. Despite that, they were usually quite enthusiastic to join their fellow patrol officers in bed, separately or together. "I'm going to make this call."

Paulei kissed him again. "See you in a minute."

Paulei went into the baths, while Wenthi went over to the hall phone, calling up the operator.

"Exchange?" the operator asked.

"One-Basten-Five-Three," he said. The exchange was to the 1st Senja. Wenthi wasn't sure who would call him from there. It rang through.

"New Renbahd Hotel," a mildly accented voice said upon answering.

"Hi," Wenthi said, not sure what to make of it. "My name is Wenthi Tungét, I got a message to—"

"Yes, one moment," the person on the other end said, and there was a click of another ring through. Then another answer, and a woman with a stronger accent.

"Yes, yes?"

"This is Wenthi Tun—"

Sounds of the phone receiver being fumbled were heard, and then a very familiar voice on the other end.

"Wenthi!" Lathéi said. "Thank spirits you called back. I was getting worried I wouldn't hear from you in time."

He was shocked that his half-sister was there, on a local call. She was at school in Dumamång across the ocean.

"What are you—"

"Season classes are done and Mother made a frightful stink that I must come home. You know how impossible she can be."

"All too well," he said.

"Exactly. We were just about to head out into the nightlife—"

"We?" he asked. "Who was it who answered—"

"I want you to meet her. I want to see you. Come out and meet us."

"Now?" he asked. "I just got off my stint, and—"

"Wenthi, I have not seen you in a year and a half, and I will not have you pull some lame story about being tired when all you're going to do is fool around with Paulei or someone else in your cadre."

"Paulei," he said.

"Well, bring him along. We're going to the Fire Chile in the 3rd. We're leaving now so don't dawdle."

"But—"

"See you there." She hung up, and as was Lathéi's way, had assumed he would be there because she told him to.

Which he would.

Paulei came out of the baths, damp and wearing just a towel, and looking far too pretty for Wenthi's heart to take.

"Not seeing anyone else around, but that's fine," Paulei said. He nodded toward Wenthi's door. "Shall we?"

"Can't. Lathéi got into town tonight, insisting I come out to meet her. You want to join us for a drink?"

"Really?" Paulei said. A flash of different emotions passed over Paulei's face. He was clearly disappointed, but he was also almost as fond of Lathéi as he was of Wenthi. "I mean, I don't know if I've got the ration points for any place where she would be willing to be seen with us."

"I know I don't," Wenthi said. "But still—"

"No, yeah, would love to see her. Did she already finish Uni?"

"Finished for this season," Wenthi said. "Two more years to go. Mother wanted her home."

"Right," Paulei said, giving Wenthi a kiss before going into his room. He left the door open as he dropped the towel and started dressing. "Can't disappoint the great lady. Yeah, let's do it."

8

The Fire Chile, a brass club in the 3rd Senja, wasn't *llipe* exclusive, but fancy and expensive enough that it might as well have been. Getting into that part of the 3rd meant going through three card checkpoints. Fortunately the Alliance Guard working the checkpoints respected their Civil Patrol badges and cycles while checking their identity cards. The Alliance folks had usually been pretty cooperative with local patrol, especially in terms of caste-wander carding, but sometimes there was a hard-ass who would hold up any *rhique* crossing senjas at this hour. If they had crossed one who wanted to make trouble, Wenthi still had familial dispensation.

Even Alli nucks would think twice before crossing Wenthi's mother.

They had little problem, though, since they weren't going into the Damas Kom or anywhere near the estates or embassies in the 1st, 2nd, or 7th. The 3rd Senja was posh and expensive, but plenty of *rhique* lived there, especially the coat-and-hats who worked the Intown high-rises and the white-phone jobs.

They parked their cycles at the bottom of a sharply inclined alley before making their way up the winding steps around the street curve to the club.

Coat-and-hats were the type who filled the brass club. Scores of well-dressed men and women laughed and drank and danced to the blaring horns of the brass band. Full suits with high waists and wide legs, long coats with wide lapels and grand shoulders, vests buttoned tight and pinching waists. Most of them in bright reds and purples, limes and ceruleans. And, of course, the wide-brimmed and feather hats that had been the look in the Sehosian Unity a few years ago, and the style had now filtered down to the Ziaparr *rhique.* Wenthi had a couple back at home, but they were hardly practical to bring on a cycle. Instead, Paulei and Wenthi had narrow-brimmed hats, the type affectionately called a doorcheck hat. Not particularly fashionable, but certainly better than being outside without a hat like some *jifozi* lout. Might as well be wearing grease-stained raw denim slacks and jackets.

He spotted Lathéi at a table up on the balcony overlooking the club, sitting with another woman who was either *llipe* or a foreigner. Very fair, in hair and complexion. Neither of them were dressed at all like the rest of the club. They wore tight-fitting coats and skirts, double-buttoned from neck to knee, in muted taupe and aqua. Neither wore hats, which five years ago would have been scandalous for a lady to do. It was still quite frowned upon. He was surprised Lathéi even dared.

He went up the spiral staircase to reach the tables on the balcony. A muscle-armed goon stood at the top—swarthy, dark, surely *jifoz*, like the servers and the dishwashers certainly were—held out his hand to them.

"Gents, you can't come up here. These tables are reserved."

"My sister is over there," Wenthi said, pointing over to her.

"I'm afraid—"

"Lath!"

She noticed him and ambled over, touching the custodian on the shoulder with her gloved hand. "They're my guests, thank you," she said. She handed him a sixer bill and waved him away. She took Wenthi's hands and pulled him toward her.

"Look at you, boy," she said, sounding just a little odd. "I mean, you didn't even *try* to match the style of the place, and I respect that, I do. You would thrive in Dumamång. Thrive!" She gave him a bright smile, showing off her painted lips and perfect teeth. Her attention then turned to Paulei.

"Oh, my faith, Paulei," she said. She took Paulei in a strong embrace and kissed both his cheeks, leaving the mark of her paint on him. "I suggested Wenthi drag you along, and I am so glad he did. You'll want to meet Oshnå. You both will."

Wenthi figured out what was odd about how she spoke. She had almost, but not completely, lost her Pinogozi accent in exchange for a Hemish one. Of course, she had been at university in the Hemish capital for two years, but it still was startling.

As she led them over to the table, it was clear why the balcony was so coveted and exclusive. Up here, the music could be heard, but not so loud to prevent conversation. Plus it had an excellent view of all the folks dancing on the ground floor.

"Oshnå," Lathéi said as they came up. "This is my *half*-brother Wenthi, and his very good friend, Paulei Jéngka. Boys, Nieçal Oshnå."

She extended her gloved hand to Wenthi without standing up. "Charmed. And yes, I am from *that* Nieçal family."

Wenthi had no idea what that meant, but took the hand and kissed it, nonetheless. Paulei did the same.

"So are you at school with Lathéi?" Wenthi asked as he sat down.

"I'm obliged to be," she said. "Though since we're on break, I decided that Dumamång is just so dreary in this season. And Lathéi is always going on about the food and the color and the absolute *charm* here in Ziaparr, how could I not come?"

"This your first trip trans-ocean?" Paulei asked.

"First trip to any of the Zapisians. When I was a little girl we took a steamer to the Unity, trains to Wo Mwung Meng, the whole bit. This must have been in, I guess thirty-seven? Little bit after the Great Noble ended. Of course, *no one* was going to travel to Zapi around then, am I right?"

"Unless you lived here," Paulei said.

"Oh my faith, I'm sorry," Oshnå said. "That was thoughtless, thoughtless.

I mean, especially here, right here, you boys must have grown up right in the middle of it."

"I don't really remember," Lathéi said. She was only five when the Great Noble War ended, of course she didn't. And her tone made her real message clear, to change the direction of the conversation immediately. Wenthi couldn't blame her there. He still remembered the worst of it, what the two of them went through during the war, and there was no need to dwell on that horror.

"We need drinks," Wenthi said, signaling a server.

"Don't worry about them," Lathéi said. "You're on my ration tonight. Both of you."

"Very kind," Paulei said.

The server came over, "And what will you be having?"

"She and I will be having another glass of Relomé Blush," Lathéi said. "And these two brutes will probably want carbon and rum."

"Yes, carbon and rum," Wenthi said. If Lathéi was paying, might as well go all in. "Dark Shumi for the carbon, please."

"Dark Shumi and rum as well," Paulei said.

"Well, wait," Oshnå said. "If that's what the locals drink, I want the full experience. So same for me. And you."

Lathéi rolled her dark eyes. "It can be sickly sweet, but fine. We'll do it proper for you. Four Dark Shumi with rum, thank you. And a plate of tacos for the table. Fruit pork and Ureti beef with rajas. Do you want the corn?"

"I want everything," Oshnå said.

"Four orders of the corn, and load it with that spice. The *raina*?"

The server looked hesitant. "If the lady wishes, but perhaps on the side?" She glanced at Oshnå. "It's not for all tastes."

Lathéi scowled. "Sure, that's fine."

"While we wait," Paulei said, getting to his feet. "I think the music is calling to me. Miss Nieçal?" He held out a hand to her.

"I have no idea how to dance to this," she said.

"You're in luck," he said with far too pretty a smile. "No one does."

She took his hand and they made their way to the spiral stair.

Wenthi moved his chair closer to his sister.

"So how long is she staying?"

"Probably for the whole break," Lathéi said. "Don't worry, she's rented her own hotel suite in the 1st with a view of the harbor. I mean, of course I offered to have her at Mother's house, and of course Mother would have opened her doors to her, but Oshnå wanted to have her own space." She looked down to the dance floor. "You should let him know he's not fucking her or me tonight."

"No?" Wenthi asked.

"Faith, it's a whole thing in Hemisheuk, you can't imagine. I made so many people mad in my first season. You fuck anyone and they act like you already have a union, and everyone gets angry if you fuck someone else without formally ending it with the first, and everyone expects, what's the word—fidelity. I got called things you can't even translate. Madness."

"Sorry," he said. But that brought up more questions. "So, do they only fuck in pairs there?"

"Only," Lathéi said with a sigh. "The idea of a group? They would die. Die. I suggested it once, it was like I suggested eating children."

"Sounds strange," he said. There was hardly a person in their patrol cadre whom either he or Paulei hadn't bedded, either individually or together. On their dorm floor, while everyone had their own beds and rooms, who was where on any given night was always fluid. The Hemisheuk method sounded stifling.

"I've managed. And since fidelity matters to Oshnå—and I do care a lot for her—I'm respecting that for her sake."

"If that works for you," he said. "How was the steamer trip here?"

"Terrible," Lathéi said. "I would have *far* preferred to stay in Hemisheuk for the duration, but Mother *insisted*. I got a cable from her every day until I got on the ship, and then once I boarded she actually used the radio to make sure I was on."

"I didn't know," Wenthi said. "I'm not in the house. I've barely seen much of Mother all year."

"But you are going to be coming by, right? I can't take Mother on my own, and I'll only submit Oshnå to so much of her."

"Aleiv is there."

"She's a child," Lathéi said.

"So were you not long ago."

"Hush," Lathéi said. "But, please, try to be around."

"I do have shifts to work."

She sighed. "Fine."

She looked like she was about to say something more, but the server arrived with the drinks. The server put four tumblers on the table, each with a few ice cubes and a finger of rum. Then she put four glass bottles of Dark Shumi, all still capped. She then took a moment, waiting for Lathéi to give approval. Lathéi touched one bottle, sweating with condensation and a hint of frost, and nodded her head in approval. The server produced a bottle opener from her apron and opened up each bottle, each giving off a crisp fizz of carbonation being released. She offered the caps to Lathéi, who indicated to leave them on the table.

The server handed the first bottle to Lathéi. She took a sip and, again, showed her approval. The server took the bottle back and poured some of the Dark Shumi into one tumbler, expertly managing her pour to keep the carbonation head under control. She did the same with the other three bottles and tumblers, then left the bottles on the table with the remainder of the sweet carbon.

Wenthi took a sip, letting the sugary sweet notes of caramel and vanilla and hints of orange, cinnamon, and other spices glide over his tongue. It was rare nowadays that he had the luxury of a Dark Shumi, usually getting the cheaper—but nowhere near as good—Arlacasta or Fusdaful. But the taste brought him right back to being twelve years old, right after the Great Noble ended. He and Lathéi and Mother, after separation and camps and hiding and exile, had finally been able to return to Ziaparr, to her grand new house in the 2nd Senja, with its own refrigeration and freezing appliances, and the pantry was stocked with Dark Shumi. He had drunk so many in the first weeks that he nearly got sick—and Lathéi did—but at the time they were not sure how long it would really last.

"Stop," Lathéi said.

"What?"

"Dwelling on the bad days," she said. "Like I said, you should come to

Dumamång. It's gorgeous, it's got no haunted memories, and Mother can only reach you via cablegram."

"For one," Wenthi said, taking another sip, "I'm not looking to escape Mother."

"That's what's wrong with you," Lathéi said, accompanied with a trill of laughter.

"For another," he said pointedly, "unlike you, I can't just go to Hemisheuk." He loved that Lathéi never denigrated him or belittled him for his *rhique* status, but more often than not she just plain forgot that he didn't have her privileges.

"If I petition for permanent residency, then I can sponsor you," she said.

"If and if," he said. "Besides, I actually like my job. I'm good at it."

"You can drive cycles anywhere," she said.

Paulei and Oshnå came back up, both looking a bit winded, Paulei with a hint of a limp. Perhaps pushing his scraped-up leg was a bit too much. But "a bit too much" was how Paulei lived his life.

"Now, perhaps I'm missing something," Oshnå said as she sat. "But if I was dancing with him, why was every other person trying to jump in and dance with the both of us? Weren't we claimed?"

Wenthi had no idea what she meant, but Lathéi laughed. "No, no, I've told you, that's just . . . it's not a thing here. Unless you're in a binding, no one is locked to a partner here."

"Binding is . . . like married?"

"Mostly?" Lathéi said uncertainly. "It doesn't mean the same thing in Pinogoz as it does in the east. Frankly, by our rules here, you and I are bound."

"Interesting," Oshnå said. She sipped her drink. "Oh, my, that's a delight and more."

"Isn't it?" Paulei said.

The server came back with plates of tacos and ears of corn, with bowls of spice garnish on the side.

"Are you ready for this?" Wenthi asked.

"Everything," Oshnå said. "Whatever this city wants to throw at me, I want a taste."

"Everything?" Wenthi asked. "Because Lathéi told me—"

"Oh, she made a scandal her first season, let me tell you," Oshnå said. "She does not like the rules of polite society in Hemisheuk."

"But you do," Lathéi said.

"I do," Oshnå said, with an odd expression. "But we're in Ziaparr, and the rules are different here."

"Are you serious?" Lathéi asked.

"Maybe," Oshnå said in a way that made Wenthi think she was trying to seem open-minded, but had many reservations. "In fact, do you know where we can get your mush—"

"No," Paulei and Wenthi said in unison.

"Don't even finish that thought," Paulei said.

"That stuff is dangerous and illegal," Wenthi said. "You don't know how many stories we hear about people being carted to the hospital—"

"If not the morgue."

"Their faces locked in a blissed-out rictus."

"They're patrol," Lathéi said gently.

"Just having it, that's three years in penitence," Wenthi said.

"All right," Oshnå said. "I had heard stories about the famed Pinogozi mushroom bliss, but if you say it's too dangerous."

"Very," Wenthi said. His heart was racing at just the suggestion. Didn't she realize? She had heard the stories, and she wanted to try it? Didn't she know about Nemuspia? Or what Rodiguen had tried to build? Wenthi remained astounded that people ever tried the mushroom for pure recreation. Didn't they know?

It was a mind destroyer. As a schoolboy, that point was made decidedly clear by several teachers. It was driven home with photoplates and cinescopes of the aftermath of the Nemuspian Atrocity at the end of the First Transoceanic, where weapons made from the mushroom had been deployed, leaving the entire populace of the far continent mindless beasts.

A horror.

Lathéi must have noticed his panic, as she took his hand and squeezed.

"Never mind," she said. "Let's get more drinks. We're celebrating."

"More drinks," he said, forcing himself to calm down. "It's been a good night."

9

Wenthi had stopped at one carbon and rum, at least in terms of the rum, as had Paulei. The same could not be said for Lathéi or Oshnå, who each had several. Both of them were giggling and stumbling as they left the club, the last to leave when the doors were shut at nine on the naught.

"How do we get home?" Oshnå asked. "I mean, the hotel called me an autotaxi before—horrid drive—"

"I don't know why they even bother bringing autos to the central part of the city," Paulei said. "The streets aren't made for it."

Oshnå looked at the curving alley, with its sharp drop as they made their way down to where the cycles were parked. "I might get sick from all these curves and winds. Don't you Pinos believe in straight lines?"

"You've had too much," Lathéi said. "We need to get you to your hotel."

"Well, get me an autotaxi," Oshnå whined, waving her hand to the green car winding through the tight street ahead of them.

Wenthi and the others laughed at that, pulling her back into the alley.

"You never want to just hail an autotaxi," Wenthi said. "Have one called from your hotel in the 1st, sure, because they know who to call. But on the street? At this sweep? Anyone could be driving."

"Yeah," Oshnå said, stumbling through a bit of a slur. "But this is a safe neighborhood, right? No . . . what do you call them . . . banzi here?"

"*Baniz,*" Lathéi said. She helped lead the pale girl down the next curving alley slope, guiding her to the walking steps. "Probably not, but you have *jifoz* who work here, and they're nearly as bad. They have to get a work permit to come in here, of course."

"So what's the—"

"I've heard stories. They'll patch together cars, paint them green, and dolly up fake papers, all so they can grab rich, drunk folks and rob them blind."

"And worse," Paulei said. "Heard it too many times."

Lathéi snapped her fingers, pointing at Paulei. "Yeah. And a *zoika* girl like you stands out."

"Like you don't," Oshnå said. "Well, I'm not going to walk to the 1st Senja."

"No, we'll get you there," Wenthi said. They had come up on the spot where he and Paulei had parked the patrol cycles.

"What, on those?" Oshnå asked. "Are you crazy? Are they crazy?"

"It's what they do," Lathéi assured her. "They're cycle cops."

"No, no," Oshnå said. "These streets are crazy enough."

"Let's show her it'll be fine," Wenthi said to his sister. He gave her his helmet as he mounted, and she got on behind him.

"Really," Lathéi said. "Best way to get around."

"I will likely vomit," Oshnå said, joining Paulei on his cycle.

"I can take it," Paulei said. It would hardly be the first time they had been vomited on by someone who had had a few too many rums.

Wenthi kicked his cycle up. Patrol issue Ungeke K'au, high-quality Sehosian engineering. One of the better machines on the market. Not quite the Ungeke K'am, or the Reloumene Maherœk 500. He had gotten to try a 'rœk once, and that was nothing short of divinity between his legs.

With his sister holding on, he cranked up the throttle, up the hill as the road curved around a statue of General Esobåk, an Alliance hero of the Great Noble, and then split into a main road up toward the Damas Kom, and a narrow fork down the hill. Wenthi weaved to one side of a trio of cars—all but stopped on this street as the first one tried to park—and then darted around a traffic circle to pop down into the tunnel leading to the 1st Senja.

If they had taken an auto, they would have had to have gone around the long way, probably gotten stuck behind three snarls, and taken an entire sweep to get Oshnå where she was staying. Between that and petrol rations, he honestly didn't understand why anyone chose an auto over a cycle. Of course, truck drivers had no choice; they drove those to haul cargo. But to just get through the narrow streets, the wild curves, the rising hills, and sudden drops of the Ziaparr streets? The cycle was the only way to go.

He revved it up a gear, seeing that Paulei and Oshnå were right on pace with him, racing through the Bidsaip Tunnel at a speed that would be dangerous if the two of them hadn't been old hands at this sort of thing.

A hard horn wail came up from behind them. Two others on cycles behind them, blue and white uniforms with full mask helmets. Alliance Guard. Wenthi yielded to one side, giving a hand signal for them to pass, but as they reached the end of the tunnel to emerge in the 1st Senja, the Alli nucks pulled parallel, making it clear they needed to pull to the side.

"What's going on?" Lathéi asked as he braked to a stop.

"Probably just want to give us a bit of grief," Wenthi said. "Maybe we buzzed past a checkpoint. Shouldn't be an issue."

The two nucks came up, lifting up the visors of their helmets. Both of them looked full-blooded Sehosian, which wasn't that different from Paulei or Lathéi.

"Where you racing to?" the first one asked. She gave Lathéi an odd look. "And I'm going to have to see some cards."

"Of course," Wenthi said, handing over his identity card. Lathéi did the same. "Did we miss the checkpoint for the 1st Senja?"

"I'll ask the questions," she said. "Like why is a *rhique* patrol officer riding a student through the tunnels, especially one who's *llipe*?"

"She's my sister," Wenthi said.

"Half-sister," the second nuck said, throwing Wenthi's card back at him. "You're not on duty. So why are you riding around after nine stint?"

"Is there a problem with being out late?" Lathéi asked. "I thought curfew locks were lifted years ago."

"Hush, miss." The first frowned. "And those two? Also mixed-caste siblings?"

"No, he's also an officer in the Civil Patrol," Wenthi said. "And she's from Hemisheuk."

"She's got all her travel papers and entry documents," Lathéi added.

"I'm sure," the first nuck said. She pointed at Paulei. "You planning on fucking her? Last thing she needs is you putting a *rhique* baby in her."

"I will report you!" Oshnå shouted.

"No, don't, don't," Paulei said sharply. "Leave it."

The first one glared back at Wenthi, and then Lathéi. "Same mother?"

"That's right," Lathéi said. "Angú Tungét?"

The nuck looked back at Wenthi. "So did she start with *jifoz* trash to have you, and then get her senses on with her father?"

"Do you know who our mother is?" Lathéi snarled.

"If she has *rhique* and *llipe* children, she sounds like a dirty castejum—"

That got Lathéi's blood up. "You will regret that, when she gets word—"

"Can we move on?" Wenthi asked quickly, not wanting this to escalate further. Though it was clear this nuck was one of those Alliance types who took blood caste very seriously. "You can see our family name on our cards."

"They can," the second nuck said. He waved to Paulei to drive off. "But your sister will have to find her own way. We've got a call to bring in one Wenthi Tungét to the Damas Kom on sight. So you better come with us."

Lathéi got off the cycle and gave him his helmet. "This is probably Mother's doing."

"Can you tell me what this is about?" Wenthi asked the nuck.

"No," the first nuck said. "But we'd rather you come quickly and easily."

"Of course," he said. He gave a glance to Paulei, who signaled that he would take care of Lathéi, make sure she got home all right. Paulei was already on the radio, calling for an escort support. He had it covered. Wenthi put on his helmet and started up his cycle again. "Lead the way."

10

The Damas Kom was the administrative center of Ziaparr, the heart of the capital, where Sehosian modernity and Reloumic ingenuity melded with Pinogozi style. In the early dim of dawn, the electric lamps along the streets still brought a majestic, ethereal glow to the buildings, monuments of stone and glass.

Wenthi rode flanked by the two Alliance nucks, stopping at the checkpoint to enter the district. Even the nucks had their cards checked. *Zoika*, just like almost everyone in the Damas Kom. The Alliance Oversight governors administrated the rest of the country from here. The Alliance Oversight Occupation had done incredible work, rebuilding the city and the country since the war, just like they had throughout the Zapisian Islands. Most of the Zapisian nations had now elected their own local governments, and a couple had become full members of the Alliance. Pinogoz would be holding elections soon enough. Soon all the work the Alliance Oversight had done with the Provisional Council would pay off.

The sun was coming over the horizon, down in the bay, as they parked their cycles in front of the Bureau of Welfare. From here, near the top of the hill, the view to the water was spectacular, as the roads of the first four senjas spun and curved below, circles filling up with the traffic of the morning activity. Radio speakers on the corner, tuned to Alliance Voice 930, rang a chime with the time, followed by the announcer's voice.

"And that marks zero sweep zero, brand-new day. It's the twelfth of Komu, year aught-aught-forty-nine of the High Sehosian Unity, and we welcome you to this new day. We hope you have a joyful and productive day. All A and B ration cards with serial numbers ending in three can be validated today, so make sure to fuel up and stock your larders. Rationing helps us all pay the debt we owe to the Alliance for all their generosity in these trying times. We'll be playing a selection from the recordings of the Hāmzhe'oki Orchestra in a few swipes, but first the news. Victory in Ikriba as—"

The Bureau of Welfare housed the central body governing the Alliance Guard as well as the city Civil Patrol. Wenthi had only ever been in front of the building once before, on the day he had been sworn into uniform. He and his fellow cadets—the first cohort of local law enforcement officers under the Oversight—had been marched in, in crisp red dress and coat uniforms, standing in formation at the bottom of the steps. The city elite were on the top steps, in front of the high pillars, in sight of the statues on the roof: heroes of the Second Transoceanic and the Great Noble. The high captain of the Welfare Forces gave a speech—newscasters from all five radio networks were on hand to broadcast it—of how proud he was to induct the first cohort of local, Pinogozi nationals to help the guard protect and serve the city, and the great precedent it would set.

That was three years ago.

Now there was no ceremony, just Wenthi being led—more manhandled, as the rough lady insisted on holding his upper arm as they went up the steps—inside the building.

"What's this?" the desk clerk in the lobby asked as they came in. Unlike the nucks, who were clearly Sehosian, the clerk had the sallow, pale complexion of one of the Outhic countries. Probably Reloumic.

"We heard the points to bring in Wenthi Tungét. This is him."

The clerk looked puzzled, and then opened up a log book. "Yes, all right, a points was called out to all hands to find and call in with *Officer* Tungét. You didn't signal back you had him, did you?"

"We thought the call was to bring him in."

"I mean, yes, but . . ." The clerk sighed. "My apologies, Officer Tungét, for any misunderstanding."

"Am I not needed?" he asked.

"You have been summoned, but—" He crossed over and pulled the nuck's hand off Wenthi's arm. "There was no need for them to treat you like a hostile."

"I mean, he's a *rhique.* Do we really take that chance?" the nuck said.

The clerk sighed. "He's a sworn patrol officer, and a well-*regarded* one at that. Officer. *Tungét.*" He really stressed Wenthi's family name as he ticked his head in disappointment. "Please, one moment. You two, report back to your section chief, and I will be marking you as well." He went back behind his desk as the nucks went off, both of them glaring at Wenthi as they left.

The clerk plugged in a connection on his hardline switchboard, holding a headset over his ear. "Hello, yes, this is Mister Lächisec up front. I have Officer Tungét here. He should—yes, of course."

He disconnected the switchboard jack and stood back up. "I need you to go down that hallway, all the way to the end, and then take a right until you reach a door marked 'baths.' Go there."

"You need me to go to the baths?"

"That's what I said."

"Of course." Wenthi was about to go, when he added, "Those two officers who escorted me here? Needlessly aggressive."

"Indeed, I saw how they treated you," the clerk asked.

"Yes, but I don't care about that. They were crude and unseemly to both my sister—a *llipe* woman, Lathéi Tungét—and her guest, a Hemish woman named Nieçal Oshnå. They seemed to think that just because they were in the company of two *rhique,* they did not deserve the courtesy of their station."

The clerk nodded. "I'll pass that along. Now go." The clerk waved him away. "With some haste."

Wenthi followed directions to the baths, surprised that there even was such a thing here. He thought these were administrative buildings, offices for the people running the city and the country. But maybe that's why they had such things within the building: They were too busy to leave for personal matters.

He had been expecting a small, functional bathing chamber, but instead found a wide garden, open to the sky but walled on all sides. Stone tile floor, surrounding the hot spring pool in the center, with wooden benches and bamboo stalks around the perimeter, with shower heads lining the wall. Wenthi instinctively took his boots off. While he had not been to one of these in some years, he still knew the etiquette. He left them and his hat in a niche by the door and went farther in.

There were four other people in the chamber—two in the spring pool, and two standing at attention at the benches. The two at the benches were clearly the bath servants—older women whose dark skin and hard features made Wenthi think they might be *baniz*, but they had to have been at least *jifoz* to be eligible to work in this district. They stood silently ready, rough sponges and buckets of water in hand.

The man in the spring was swimming unflaggingly, hard laps through the steamy water, while the woman soaked at one corner. She took note of Wenthi as he stepped over to the pool's edge.

"So you're the one," she said coolly. Wenthi knew he had met her before—she was a *llipe* woman of clearly pure Sehosian descent. Surely one of the Roots of the Prime Families. He must have met her when he was much younger, still accompanying Mother to events. If that were the case, it would have been at an occasion when she was fully dressed, jewels adorning her features. With her naked in the bath, he had no context to place her. As with many women with Sehosian features, she had a certain ageless quality. She might be his age, or his mother's, or even older. Of course, her age didn't matter right now: Even having been ordered to come, he was intruding on her space simply by being *rhique*.

"I was told to come here," he said deferentially. "Officer Wenthi Tungét, though I'm not in uniform."

"No need," she said. "Have a seat. He's finishing up."

Wenthi took a place on one of the benches as the man swam eleven more laps. Once he completed the last one, he emerged from the pool, wiping the water off his face. Only then did Wenthi realize who the man was: Tiré Sengejú, the High Captain of the Welfare Forces. Wenthi instinctively got to his feet as the lean, naked man finally turned his attention to him.

"Ah," Sengejú said with a nod. "You must be Angú's boy."

"Angú Tungét is my mother, sir," Wenthi said.

"Yes, yes," Sengejú said, giving the slightest gesture to one of the bath servants. She came over silently and began soaping his body with her sponge.

"We hear you had quite a good catch last night, Wenthi," he said. "Nabbed one of those fuel-thieving rebels."

"Well done," the woman said, still luxuriating in the water.

"Did you know when you caught her she was using the *mycopsilaria*?" he asked.

"Not explicitly, sir," Wenthi said.

"She was," he said. "As was her accomplice, who was also caught last night."

"I had heard that there was a second arrest, sir."

"There was, which created . . . complications. What I'll tell you must remain confidential, Officer Tungét."

"Of course, sir," Wenthi said.

"Her accomplice was a young man named Enzúri Hwungko. Does that mean anything to you?"

Hwungko, like Tungét, was one of the Prime Families. A line that could be traced to the old Sehosian Empire's initial arrival in Pinogoz.

Context. The woman was Ainiro Hwungko. The Root of the Hwungko Branch of the Prime Families, and councilor in the Provisional Government Congress.

Just as Mother was for the Tungét Branch.

And she was the woman he had spotted leaving the third floor.

"Of course, sir," Wenthi said.

"Of course," Sengejú said as the servant scrubbed at his back. "Needless to say, a certain degree of delicacy had to be undertaken. The family was deeply saddened to hear that one of their own had fallen in with this absurd rebellion."

"Mortified," *Senia* Hwungko said. "My nephew always had a head full of nothing, and he's proven it beyond doubt."

"Of course, he will be sanctioned," Sengejú said. "But he has confessed a few intriguing points, which gives us . . . a unique opportunity. And that's where you come in, Officer."

"I am here to serve, sir," Wenthi said. "What do you need?"

"This boy is lovely," Hwungko said.

"What do you know of the *mycopsilaria* mushroom, son?" Sengejú asked.

"It's dangerous, of course."

"It is," Sengejú said. "It's also powerful. We've known the rebels and undercastes insist on using it, but we've now learned that's why they are usually so hard to catch."

"What?"

Hwungko answered as she got out of the pool, her servant immediately approaching. "They say using it expands their senses. Enzúri admitted—"

"He took it?" Wenthi asked, and then quickly bowed his head, hoping to not offend with his interruption.

"I felt the same way," Hwungko said. "Sickened. That he sullied himself, and spirits even know in what other ways."

"Ainiro," Sengejú said sharply.

She sighed, continuing. "But he used it, and he *claimed* that when they did, they could feel law officers and alliance patrol at a distance. Knew they were coming, and thus got away."

"That didn't seem to be the case, *senia*," Wenthi said. "At least when I caught her."

"That's apparently just it," Sengejú said as he strolled over to the showerhead. "They didn't sense you."

"I'm not sure what that means, sir," Wenthi admitted.

"We aren't quite yet, either, Officer," Sengejú said as he started to rinse the soap off his body. "But we want to explore an idea that you could be used against the rebels. We've tried to get officers to infiltrate the rebel cells before, never to any success. They're always found out. We want to do further tests, but we're thinking, maybe you won't be."

His servant turned off the shower and started vigorously toweling him dry.

Wenthi wasn't sure what to make of this. "I'm always willing, sir," he said. "I'll confess I don't understand this business with the mushroom and expanded senses, but I'm here for my duty, whatever you say it is."

"Good, son," Sengejú said. "You understand this isn't going to be working a shift, but rather you will be fully embedded in this role. You will be gone from your home and family for several weeks, even seasons."

"I'm here for my duty, sir," Wenthi said.

"New cards, new identity. Reclassified as *jifoz*."

"That is the challenge, isn't it?" Hwungko said, her voice almost a cat's purr. "Finding someone who will be loyal, but can plausibly pass as *jifoz*. But that's definitely you, isn't it?"

Wenthi took that in. Was Sengejú trying to frighten him? Test him?

That pause must have looked like hesitation, as Sengejú went on, giving only a hint of a glare at *Senia* Hwungko. "Now, we are looking for officers of note within the patrol. We need to identify the people who can step up, be part of the leadership. A young man with your drive, your loyalty, and your name, if we're being honest—you could be an excellent candidate to be promoted to the leadership."

"Someone needs to be the first, after all," Hwungko said.

"I understand what it'll take, sir. I'm not wavering. If living a few seasons as a *jifoz* lets me get in with the rebels, stop their vandalism, I can do that. Whatever you need." Was that what they wanted to hear? Was that the commitment they wanted him to give? Fine. Given. He had become an officer to prove his value, to help the people of this country. He'd gladly do what was asked.

"A loyal boy, indeed," Hwungko said, going over to the showers with her servant in tow.

"Good," Sengejú said. His servant brought over his dress robes. "Go home, put your affairs in order. We'll be expecting you at the 9th Senja tomorrow at zero sweep on the naught."

"Sir," Wenthi said with a quick bow of his head. Nothing else needed to be said, as he knew he should quickly retreat, put his boots on, and leave the baths. He had been told to go, and there was no call for him to linger. His mother had taught him well enough over the years to know his place.

11

Wenthi left the Damas Kom on his cycle, given a cursory check of his cards once again when passing the checkpoint. He rode with the flow of morning traffic as he wound his way through the 3rd Senja, avoiding the urge to weave and whisk his way around the autos and sedans. At this hour, of course, the streets and traffic circles of the 3rd Senja were so choked, even a corn-burning motorwasp couldn't find a hole to weave through, let alone Wenthi's Ungeke K'au.

He wasn't going to be able to take his cycle on this assignment. Would he need to garage it at the headquarters? At his mother's? Would Mother want it in her garage with her shiny Kosopém sedan? Would her driver know how to take care of it?

Maybe he should leave it with Paulei.

After the expected checkpoint stops from the 3rd to the 8th, and then the 8th to the 9th, he stopped at the Circle Omes petrol station, where his ration card would be accepted today. Since it was his day, he should top off, regardless. Once he was able to get in line, it only took about ten swipes to get up front. Cycle lines went faster than autos or sedans, and *rhique* could use most of the pumps. Even still, he let a couple *jifoz* cycle-couriers go ahead of him. They surely were on the job, needing to get rolling again as soon as possible. Wenthi knew that, despite the things Lathéi and Paulei were saying last night, most of the *jifoz* working Intown were good, decent folk. Hard-working people, like all the staff at the KT dorm, usually on a tight schedule. Every swipe of the clock hand mattered. All he needed to do was go back to the dorm, eat something, and sleep for a couple sweeps. He could wait a bit longer for fuel.

Topped off, he made his way home, through the weaving streets and tunnels. Part of him felt that, if he was going to go on an infiltration mission, for who knew how long, he should make the most of the day, but he was just too tired. He pulled up to the KT dorm. Guiho ran up to him as he powered down the engine at the cycle post in front of the building.

"Hello, sir," Guiho said to him. "Do you need me to take your cycle into the covered park? Or shine it up?"

"No, no," Wenthi said. "But thank you."

"No, thank you," Guiho said. "I—I can't afford to—"

"It's fine," Wenthi said. "Where are you coming in from? The 11th? 14th?"

"Ako Favel," Guiho said. "The 16th Senja."

Wenthi rarely rode patrol out there. Worst part of Outtown. That had been where the largest of Rodiguen's purge camps was, as well as his city garrison, and it was bombed the hardest during Great Noble. Still not rebuilt in any way. A complete disaster.

Wenthi slipped a couple coins to Guiho. "Yeah, maybe polish it. If you get the chance."

"Thank you, sir,"

Wenthi went inside, and realized he was more hungry than tired, and went to the cafeteria. As he came in, Paulei ran up behind him, grabbing him in an embrace.

"Everything all right?" Paulei asked.

"Fine, fine," Wenthi said. "I . . . they want me for an infil mission."

"Really? With?"

"With those petrol-stealing cycle gangs."

"Huh," Paulei said. "Strange way to ask you."

"Everything fine with getting Lathéi and Oshnå home safe?"

"Yeah, fine. I radioed Hwokó to come out and help ride them home. Oh, did you see this?"

He handed Wenthi one of the morning newspapers. Someone had gotten a tinplate of Lath and Oshnå at the Fire Chile, with him and Paulei slightly out of focus on the side. The article was headlined LATHÉI IS BACK IN TOWN, DRESSED LIKE A DUMAMÅNG STAR.

"The press always loved her," Wenthi mused. "She does tinplate pretty well."

"That's some truth," Paulei said. He touched Wenthi's chin. "Your mother did make some beautiful kids."

"You're a little too built up, friend," Wenthi said. "I need to eat something before I do anything else."

"Fair," Paulei said. "So let's—"

Before he finished that thought, the desk manager ran up to them with a yellow cablesheet.

"Sorry, Mister Tungét," she said, a little out of breath. "This cable just came for you, declared urgent."

"Who would send a cable if it was urgent?" Paulei mused.

Wenthi already knew the answer to that, and glancing at it confirmed the answer.

COME TO THE HOUSEHOLD IMMEDIATELY. —MOTHER

12

Still hungry and tired, Wenthi rode to the checkpoint between the 9th and 2nd senjas. He knew better than to make his mother wait, and the checkpoint stop was always at least a little trouble.. How much trouble, depended on who was working the checkpoint.

"Not working today, Wenthi?" Oswai, one of the regular *zoika* officers at this check, said as he pulled up. "Didn't think you beat patrol folks got many days off."

"Today's special," Wenthi said, handing over his identity cards as a matter of course. He knew Oswai, but not the other one.

"Does he have a work pass for the 2nd?" the other asked.

"Nah," Oswai said. "Family disposition. *Rhique* with a *llipe* mother."

"Huh," the other officer said, glancing at Wenthi's cards. "I didn't think the 2nd had family privileges, even for that." She took another look. "Oh, Tungét. I didn't realize *llipe* meant . . . yeah."

Wenthi was long used to it. In the seven years since he had to leave Mother's household and get residence in a district that his caste was authorized for, he had faced frequent questions and challenges crossing into the 2nd Senja. By now, most of the folk working the checkpoint knew exactly who he was.

Being a cycle cop helped. He was almost never given too hard a time when he was in full uniform.

Didn't change the fact that it was a fair amount of hassle to visit his mother.

He passed through and turned down the winding slope into the 2nd Senja, which dropped low into the river valley as the Enidizzar flowed into the bay. The last turn popped back up onto the hill where Mother's household had an overlook of the water.

Wenthi stopped outside the bright blue wooden gate and rang the bell. In a moment, Isacha was opening up the gate.

"Hello, Mister Wenthi," he said, his voice a creak. He was an old *baniz* man, and normally it would be impossible for him to work in the household. But he had been in Mother's employ for as long as Wenthi could remember. Possibly before the end of the Second Transoceanic. Mother had spent quite a bit of clout to keep Isacha around. Except for the time he and Lathéi were separated from Mother during the Great Noble, Isacha had been a fixture in Wenthi's childhood.

"How's the house?" Wenthi asked, getting off his cycle and walking it into the wide parking way in front of the household. As usual, it was impeccably kept on the outside: green grass neatly trimmed, the garden bordering the walkways blooming with cacti and succulents, all perfectly organized to complement the house itself—bright peach walls of smooth-plastered stone, with marigold ceramic tiles for the roof.

"It's quieter, Mister Wenthi," Isacha said. "Though Miss Lathéi came in about a sweep ago. I'm certain she's asleep."

"I envy her," Wenthi said. "I could stand to do that, myself, at least a sweep. Would my old room still be available?"

Isacha looked a bit nervous. "I would have to confirm with *ya senia*, sir."

"Of course, of course," Wenthi said. "I don't want to put you out or anything. Is she about?"

"The back terrace," Isacha said. "Take the garden path around."

Wenthi knew the way, and of course everyone would follow protocol.

He would come to the household, but never come inside until his mother explicitly asked him in. As was the way. Mother insisted on all the rules of caste etiquette when Wenthi came, even though no one but family and staff were around. While she never voiced it directly, Wenthi sometimes wondered if she resented having a *rhique* child.

The path led him around to the back of the house, to the back terrace, overlooking the walled-in property garden and pool, and beyond that, the vista of the harbor. The crystal blue of the Pino Sound shone off the morning sun, as grand Pinogozi tankers headed out to sea with Alliance corvette and submarine escorts.

Angú Tungét, Root of the Tungét Branch of the Prime Families, councilor of the Provisional Government Congress, sat at the head of the glass table, coffee in one hand, cigarillo in the other. Wenthi walked up from behind her and kissed her on the cheek.

"Morning, Mother."

She looked up at him with cordial warmth. "Wenthi," she said coolly. "Thank you for responding with such promptness. I'm glad you're here." She gestured for him to sit.

"Today's going very unplanned," he said as he took a seat.

"I have heard," she said. She gave a small snap to Zoyua, the tiny *jifoz* woman who had served the house for the past eight years. Zoyua silently brought over a cup for Wenthi and poured the coffee for him. "Are you hungry?"

"A bit," he said. He knew she would find it rude if he said he was ravenous.

"Bring him some fruit and *cohechas*," she told Zoyua as the woman spooned a small amount of sugar into Wenthi's cup. As Zoyua reached forward with the sugar, her arm stretched out of the sleeve of her violet pullover, showing the old, twisting scars that Wenthi knew covered the entire left side of her body. She was one of the few to survive the bombing of her village, which had been utterly destroyed in the bombing campaigns near the end of the Great Noble. She was very fortunate to have survived, and fortunate that Mother had always taken good care of her.

As much as Mother frustrated him, Wenthi had to admit she was always very good to her staff.

"Right away," Zoyua said, and she slipped into the house through the back door to the kitchen.

"I have heard," Mother said once Zoyua was gone, "that they are giving you a very important assignment."

"I'm kind of amazed they've done so much so fast. No one must have slept last night."

"Certainly not in the Hwungko households," she said. "Such indignity they must feel. Did you see Enzúri when he was arrested? Do you know him?"

Wenthi had not. "I don't think we were ever cohorted together. I think he's more Lath's age."

"Perhaps so."

"And he wasn't the one I arrested. I brought in the girl he was working with. I had no idea about his part of it until a few swipes ago." Though now he remembered that he had seen Enzúri and *senia* Hwungko on the third floor.

"Of course," she said. "But I'm told they have quite a few hopes for you. This is an excellent chance to impress your superiors, Wenthi, as well as the governing board."

"I hope to live up to their expectations," he said.

"We are working very hard to get this country on its feet, Wenthi. Part of that involves having an independent law-keeping organization, and our people in charge of that. That it might be someone like you . . . that could be very important."

He stirred his coffee, not sure how to respond. He wanted to believe that she wanted what was best for him: promotion, authority, a strong career. But he couldn't help but feel that he was just being used as a pawn in her political ambitions.

She took a pull off her cigarillo. "I am worried about what this is asking of you, though. You'll have to live as a *jifozi*. You didn't take it very well having to live as a *rhique*."

"That was seven years ago, Mother," he said, sipping at the sweet, hot coffee. Far better than what they had at the headquarters. "This is a very different situation."

"I just worry," she said.

"It's not like I'll actually *be* a *jifoz*," he said with a light chuckle. "It's just an assignment, papers to cover the identity and such."

Mother watched him with dark, piercing eyes for a long while, and took another drag of her smoke. "It's all just papers, of course. What are they putting on yours?"

"Pardon?"

"I mean, if they're making a false identity for you, I'm curious if you know what it's going to be. They could hardly put Wenthi Tungét on a card that says you're *jifoz*. That wouldn't be credible, would it?"

"I hadn't thought about it," Wenthi said. He hadn't had much time to think about any of this yet. "I suppose whatever they decide. Covert Operations has protocol, I'm sure."

"Foolishness," she said with a scoff. "If . . . since you're going to do this, you need to have a name that means something, that will . . . have weight. It can't be just any name."

"I'm sure—"

Zoyua came back out with a tray and brought it to Wenthi. As she placed the plate of sliced mango and piña in front of him, Mother looked at her pointedly. "Zoy, remind me of your siblings' names."

Zoyua shook her head. "Yes, *senia*. There's Onicé and Eriva, and with my papé there's Sanlí, Leoza, and Davillo, and with mamé there's Yeñi and Nolu."

"Those are the ones still alive."

"Yes, *senia*."

"And how many side-mothers did you have?"

"Three, *senia*."

"Side-fathers?"

"Four, *senia*. No, five."

"And side-siblings? Cousins?"

She put the plate of *cohechas*—poached eggs over black beans spread on thick bread, dotted with salt and grated cheese—in front of Wenthi. "Oh, *senia*, I would have to think to count them all."

"It's fine, Zoy. *S'enj*."

Zoyua bowed her head and went off.

"What was that?" Wenthi asked as he took his utensils up to stab each piece of fruit.

"You need to remember, boy," she said pointedly, "that among the undercastes, families spread wider. They all have people. *Baniz* rarely even bother to formally Bind, they just all pile up in houses together."

"I'm sure—" he started to say.

"You just take any old name, try to pass yourself off as *jifoz*, they'll sniff you out. Wonder who your people are, where you came from."

"They'll probably give me an identity from Uretichan or one of the other northern cities," Wenthi said. "So I wouldn't be expected to have people in Ziaparr."

"That won't—" She sighed, shook her head. "Don't you worry about it. I'll make some calls."

"I wish you wouldn't," he said as he took a bite of the *cohechas*. Fantastic as they always were. "We've agreed—"

"Letting your career alone is one thing. I've done nothing to influence anyone, and you've earned every accolade on your own. Even if people do still call me to an annoying degree whenever you as much as scrape a knee."

"Mother—"

"But I will not sit by and let some minor bureaucrat get you killed for not knowing better. I will make some calls."

Angú Tungét had spoken, and Wenthi knew better than to argue.

"I have been up through the night," he said. "And given all that's going on, I would be honored if I was able to sleep here a few sweeps."

"Of course," Mother said. "When you finish eating, you can go and use the *oxué* near the kitchen. I'll make sure the bed is made up for you." She extinguished her cigarillo and finished her coffee. "And, of course, you are welcome to the house today."

She kissed his forehead as she got up, and went inside. He knew, through the years of doing this, that much of the ritual of him entering the house was simply the semblance of propriety, following the rules of society for whenever a *rhique* came to a *llipe* house, even if it was his family home. Mother never actually refused him entry.

But he was offered a bed in the *oxué*—the servant room—instead of his old bedroom.

He took his time eating the fruit and *cohechas*. With this assignment, it'd probably be some time before he ate like this again.

 13

Wenthi woke up, not sure of the time. The sun was still up, streaming through the window of the *oxué*, strong enough that there was no getting back to sleep. While he was asleep, someone had slipped in and taken his clothing—appropriate for late evenings in the city, but not for daylight hours—and replaced it with clean linen slacks and shirt. The shirt was one with short arms and several pockets on the front, the preferred fashion for older gentlemen with larger bellies and fewer responsibilities. The straw hat completed the look, and made it clear these clothes had been Oscéi's. Aleiv's father. Wenthi and Oscéi had, at best, tolerated each other's presence during the time he had been Bound with Mother, and Wenthi did not miss him one bit when they announced Disunion. He wondered why clothes had been left behind.

Putting the clothes on, though, did spark some of Wenthi's earliest memories, from the years these styles had been in fashion. Wenthi had only vague images of those days, he had been so young—before Rodiguen, before the Great Noble—but he had memories of bright, sunny days in the city circles, bustling with happy people, dressed like he was now. He remembered his mother—or his idea of what his mother was like when she was his age—in bright silk dresses and rounded caps. Celebration and flowers. Flowers everywhere.

"Where is the supper?" a young voice pierced through the air. "I have arrived, and where is the supper?"

Wenthi left the *oxué* and went through the kitchen, where Zoyua, Eunitio, and Izamio were putting together plates of seasoned fish and grilled vegetables. A tinny radio played a traditional Pino song, one older that Wenthi's mother. He gave them a friendly smile as he passed through, out to the dining table, where Aleiv, dressed in her school knee-skirt and blazer, paced about.

"What were you doing in the kitchen?" she asked. "Why are you even here?"

"Don't be rude, Ale," Lathéi said. She was on the other side of the room slouched in one of the lounging chairs, clear carbon in one hand. "Tell Wen it's good to see him."

"Why are you wearing Oscéi's clothing?" Aleiv asked.

"They were left out for me," Wenthi said.

"You aren't having supper with us, are you?"

"I've not been invited," he said.

Lathéi got to her feet and glided over. "I would invite you myself, but I've already used mine for Oshnå."

"No worries," Wenthi said. "Were you two all right? I know Paulei got you home, but—"

"All fine. Though that whole incident was unacceptable."

"The nucks were out of line," Wenthi said.

"What, did they arrest you?" Aleiv asked with a sneer. "Did you get called for breaking curfew or checkpoints?"

"He's patrol," Lathéi said. "He gets dispensation."

"Why haven't they served supper?" Aleiv said, walking away from them both. "Probably waiting for Mother to ring the bell. I'll go find her." She skulked off.

"This is what you're leaving me with, Wen," Lathéi said. "A whole season of this."

"Work," he said. "It's important."

"Yes, Mother told me, and then she made me listen to the radio with her for a sweep. All sorts of horrors about the scourge of insurgents, attacking trains, sabotaging fuel rations. All they're doing is hurting everyone."

"I know," Wenthi said. "That's why I'm taking this assignment."

"Not fair," she said. "Barely got to see you. Even if you're dressed like a character in an old cinescope."

"I haven't been to the scopes in a long time," he said.

"If we had time today, I'd take you," she said. "All the more reason to come back to Hemisheuk with me," she added in a lowered voice. "All the best ones are made there."

"If you say so," he said. Though he truly had very little interest in going to any of the Outhic nations, even with Lathéi.

Mother came down with Aleiv in tow. "We should ring the bell. Is your guest here?"

"She's taking an auto, so she should be here shortly."

"Slowest way," Wenthi muttered.

"Wenthi will join us for supper, yes?" Lathéi asked.

"I'm afraid not," Mother said. She came up to him and kissed his cheek. "I hope you rested, love, but you will need to move along."

"So soon?" he asked.

"I've received some calls," she said. "Nothing you need to worry about, but they—" She hesitated. "There have been some new developments, and with that, a grander opportunity. They'll need you at the headquarters as soon as you can be there."

"Oh," he said. "Do you know what—"

She came over to him and rested a gloved hand on his cheek. "Just promise me you'll be careful."

"Of course, Mother, but do you know—"

Her hand was trembling as she pulled away. "You shouldn't waste time and get moving. That was made clear."

"I should get back to my apartment—"

"Yes, you should," Aleiv said.

"Peace, Ale," Lathéi said.

"They said as soon as you can," Mother said sharply. "I'll send someone around to your place to take care of your icebox, cables, any other loose ends."

"And my cycle?" he asked.

"Have someone bring it here, and we'll keep it in the garage."

"Thank you," he said. He kissed his mother on the cheek.

Lathéi grabbed him in an embrace. "Not fair," she whispered in his ear.

"Nothing is," he said. He let go and looked to Aleiv. "Try not to miss me too much."

"Don't get killed," she said. "Or Mother will be impossible. Can we start supper now?"

"Yes," Mother said, squeezing Wenthi's shoulder one more time before sitting at the table and ringing the bell next to her place.

Wenthi knew what that meant, what was expected of him, so with a last wink to Lathéi, he went back through the kitchen, past the hallway of the *oxué* and pantries, and out the delivery door.

14

Wenthi arrived at the headquarters of the 9th Senja and was ushered quickly down into a sub-basement he had never previously gone to. He had worked at this house for three years, and he had always assumed that these levels were for evidence storage or files. Instead he was placed in an odd white room, where a pair of nurses proceeded to wordlessly undress him, prod and probe him, and draw an absurd amount of blood.

Then they left him alone, in far too cold a room to be sitting on a metal table while nearly naked.

Nearly a sweep passed before anyone else came in, a pale older woman whose flaxen hair was streaked with gray. "So, this is Officer Tungét." Her Reloumene accent was uncommonly thick, so thick he had a hard time understanding her.

"That's me, ma'am," he said.

"Yes, promising. Promising." She looked through a folder of tissue-thin mimeotyped pages. "Twenty-seven years old. Born right here in Ziaparr. Interesting, interesting. Very healthy, very healthy, good." She grabbed his jaw and leaned in, inspecting his face. "And you were classified *rhique*?"

"Yes, ma'am," he said. "My mother—"

The woman chuckled. "I know all about your mother, young man. All about."

"What is that supposed to mean?"

She looked at the mimeotype. "The bloodwork is very promising, yes. Very interesting. Your father?"

"What about him?"

"Who was he?"

"Died in the Second Transoceanic."

"A soldier?" she asked, raising an eyebrow. "Or a casualty?"

"Soldier. Died on the beach of Hessinfoth," Wenthi said.

"Interesting. That isn't listed in your file," she said.

"Did you serve in that war?" he asked. She looked like she would have been prime fighting age at the end of Second Trans. She easily might have been in in the Reloumene Sovereign Order, piloting a laufmobon bomber or gunning on an umshpri single-prop. "You look like you could have been airguard."

"Oh, I served, young man," she said. She stepped back and took a case out of her pocket, taking out a tightly rolled cigarillo. "Served then, served again, and am serving now. Believe me." With unsteady hands, she lit the cigarillo and took a long draw on it. "And you are as well, serving the city, serving the country. Proud boy, yes?"

"I suppose," he said.

"You caught the *jifozi* girl, yes? She was riding the *mycopsilaria*, wasn't she? And yet you slipped under her senses." The word "slipped" danced off her tongue, like that very idea delighted her.

"That's what they say."

"Remarkable." She drew another breath of smoke. "What do you know of the local *mycopsilaria*, hmm?"

Everyone was asking him that today. "It's dangerous, but plenty folks—undercaste, mostly—use it for sex."

"Yes, that is the main use here, isn't it? A little taste, link up your senses with a willing partner. Or two or three. Very intense, I see the appeal." She said all that with a dead affect, and scoffed. "Imagine, the very hand of god, being used for shadow puppets. Foolish waste."

"It's foolish, yes," Wenthi said. "I'm well aware of the dangers. You can lose yourself into it. Too much, you go all the way into yourself, into the other person, and both of you become shells, locked into your body. Or a mindless empty."

"Is that what they say?" she asked. She took another long pull, her jaw tightening. "This is what they teach you?"

"Teach us?"

"At your schools here. Or in your patrol training?"

"Yes, of course," he said.

"And you never dared try it yourself? A little taste, see what the fuss is about?"

"No, of course not. We've seen—"

"What?" she asked, leaning in so close the stale reek of her smoke invaded his face. "What have you seen?"

"We've all seen it. In—"

"You're going to say Nemuspia, aren't you? They point to that disaster and say that could happen here. But it wouldn't, of course. *Mycopsilaria nemuspiana* is completely different than your strains here," she said, her voice rising, her accent harsher.

"I—"

"You know *nothing*, boy!" she shouted, her sallow, blanched face quickly turning red. She stormed out of the room.

The nurses came back in, with several Alliance Guard officers, including a lieutenant whom Wenthi had seen around headquarters, but had never spoken to. The officers carried a series of wooden boxes and laid them out on another table.

"Officer Tungét," the lieutenant said, offering her hand. She was definitely Sehosian *zoika*. "Pleasure to have you with us. I'm Lieutenant Canwei, I work with Covert Operations. I'll be your immediate superior on this assignment. How much do you know about the situation?"

"I know there have been a string of petrol robberies from the tanker trains, committed by an organized group of criminals on cycles."

"Right," Canwei said. "We originally thought that it was just the work of various cycle gangs, simply looking to score petrol beyond their allotted ration. And as despicable as ration-thieves are—am I right?"

"Quite," Wenthi said. Resources were tight in the city, in the whole nation, and it was important that everyone respected their share. Ration-thieves ruined things for everyone.

"As despicable as they are, their goals are far beyond just stealing petrol. The Hwungko boy told us that it's much more insidious. Several different cycle gangs are cells in a larger organization of rebel terrorists, seeking to destroy everything we've built."

"And that's what I'm going into?" Did Mother know this? Was that why she was troubled?

"Very astute. We need you to get into one of the cells, and from there, find their leader. A woman called Varazina."

"I presume Mister Hwungko didn't give us much to work with in identifying her."

"No," Canwei said. "He's never seen her. Very few have, but they've heard her. She leads from the shadows."

"How does that work?"

"She's able to give orders, coordinating the gangs, by hijacking radio broadcasts. We have no idea how she's doing it."

"Why aren't we finding their frequencies and listening in?"

"That's just it—it's not any one frequency. She's able to cut into any station, and frequency, and send a message. We've got no way to trace it."

The doctor came back in the room, her demeanor noticeably calmer. "And they use the *myco* to coordinate with each other, and sense their adversaries. Quite remarkable."

"Ah, I see you've met Doctor Shebiruht," Canwei said.

"Sheb—" was all he said before the full realization of who this woman was registered. His instinct kicked in, jerking away so quickly he nearly fell off the metal table. "You're telling me she—the monster—she worked—"

"Yes, yes," she said dismissively. "The Mushroom Doctor. The Witch of Reloumene. The horror of two wars. Really an exaggeration, if you ask me."

"Doctor," Canwei said sharply.

"What is she doing here?" Wenthi asked.

"Penance," the lieutenant said. "For war crimes in the Great Noble, she is serving her time here, putting her vast knowledge to use."

"Knowledge of what?"

She went over to the wooden cases. "Of the *mycopsilaria*. I remain one of the world's foremost—"

"Butchers," Wenthi spat. He had heard—everyone had heard—of her horrors, what happened to the victims she experimented on.

"Hardly fair," she said. "Butchers work with meat."

"Wenthi," Canwei said calmly. "I understand your reaction. I do. But the simple truth is, we have a real opportunity with you right now, and with Doctor Shebiruht's help, give you the tools you'll need for this mission."

"What tools?" Wenthi asked. His heart started pounding. What, exactly, were they suggesting?

Shebiruht smiled, looking through the wooden case. "Right now, there's a girl a few doors down who is, astoundingly, still processing an active, hypercharged dose of *mycopsilaria zapisia*, the local variation of the mushroom, and I've been able to isolate the strain. That it has lasted this long, that her receptors are still active, how she hypercharged herself, I do not know, but it is fascinating. Definitely something special about her." She seemed very excited, and her accent grew even thicker as she spoke. "Did you know what you think of as simply 'the *myco*' is actually dozens of mushroom species, each with dozens of individual strains?"

"Doctor, we don't need—" Canwei started.

Shebiruht went on regardless, as she held up a glass vial. "To think, every part of the world could touch every other part. Every mind, every body . . ."

"Doctor," Canwei said sharply.

"Yes," she said, coming back over to Wenthi. "And so many small-minded folk wanted to make it into weapons. Klwaza. Elbavu. Rodiguen. Small, petty folk. How can I use this magic to kill, to control, to subjugate? Your people, at least, use it mostly to fuck better. Still small and petty, but it's something joyful."

"I don't—" Wenthi said, the words barely able to come.

"Yes, you're a good boy, I can tell." She shook her head and glared at Canwei. "What are you teaching them, hmm? About the *myco*, the war? Me?"

"I think he has a fairly accurate picture of who you are," Canwei said.

"Yes, maybe," she said, handing the vial to a nurse. "I may know more about *mycopsilaria* than just about anyone, but . . . that knowledge did not come cheaply. But it makes me useful, so this arrangement—"

"Arrangement?"

"Doctor Shebiruht's expertise remains unmatched," Canwei said. "The Alliance does not throw away useful knowledge."

Wenthi got on his feet. "Give me my clothes, ma'am. I don't need . . . whatever this is to do my job."

"Wenthi, son," Canwei said calmly. "I've given this a lot of thought. You're going to need an edge to succeed. The mission will be impossible without what this procedure offers."

"Procedure?" Never had a word sounded more terrifying.

"You need to get better at explaining things, Lieutenant," Shebiruht said, bringing over two more vials. "Like I said, that girl's connective receptors are still active, buzzing with the *myco zapisia* in her system. We're going to use that. If your blood is any indication, based on my tests, you've got a certain . . . aptitude for what the *myco* offers. A remarkable aptitude, at that. So we'll be using that strain she's on, yes. And then the *14-mycopsilaria outhica* to give you dominion over the bond."

"Dominion?" What was she on about?

"You need to be in charge," Shebiruht said. "This bond cannot be mutual. And then, of course, this very rare *mycopsilaria astiknesa*. Oh, this one is the real secret ingredient."

"For what, exactly?" Wenthi asked as his stomach threatened to crawl out his mouth and run off.

"For the fusion," she said. "Between you and that girl."

15

Wenthi had seen the newsreels and tinplates of Nemuspia. Required viewing in school, and again at the academy. Seen the horrors of the *myco.*

Near the end of the First Transoceanic, General Klwaza of Nemuspian Dominion had warned the world that he would unleash his great arsenal of War-Enders across Reloumene, Hemisheuk, and the other Outhic nations, across all the Zapisian Islands, and then the Sehosian continent. He demanded unconditional surrender. But when he planned to demonstrate the power of his War-Ender, this bomb fueled by *mycopsilarian* magic, something went horribly wrong, and the entire arsenal was released on his own people.

They became mindless horrors, their bodies wasted and withered. It spread across the Nemuspian continent, barely contained by the few remaining forces. Millions upon millions, turned from vibrant, vital people into empty shells that only knew hunger.

All of Nemuspia was a wasteland, thanks to the power of the mushroom. The First Trans ended with the Treaties of Sovereignty, where civilized nations all agreed to ban *mycopsilarian* weapons.

At the height of the Second Transoceanic, when Rodiguen's expansion of Reloumene pushed against the Hemish border, he claimed he had new *myco* weapons that were unlike anything the world had seen. He was defeated and ousted before he could use them, the laboratories and factories dismantled. He fled to Pinogoz with his family and inner circle, forced his way to power, and had restarted his *myco* experiments again before he was stopped in the Great Noble. He and most of his inner circle and family had been killed in the final campaign. The remainder of his loyal people were captured and imprisoned for life. That was what the newsreels had reported.

And here was Doctor Shebiruht. The very woman who had been in charge of his *myco* projects in both wars.

"Ma'am," Wenthi asked Lieutenant Canwei as he got onto the gurney. His heart was pounding, but Canwei seemed so certain. She was his superior. She, and Captain Sengejú—he had to know, right? He had mentioned the *myco* in their meeting—they signed off on this. "You're certain we can trust her on this? Trust . . . using the *myco*?"

Canwei nodded and leaned in close, lowering her voice. "The truth is, these rebels use the *myco* without a second thought. It's why they've been impossible to catch, really, until you. You. You'll be our secret weapon." She clapped Wenthi on the shoulder congenially.

"How?"

"People can't hide who they are when connected on the *myco*. But if you are already melded with that girl, the girl who is part of the rebellion, then you will be able to. You'll be able to hide who you are within her."

"Yes, but—"

"You're worried about the risks."

"You know what happens. The comas, the deaths . . ."

"Somewhat overstated," she said. "Our discouragement campaigns lean on the sensational. As distasteful as I find her, the doctor is an expert in usage, dosages. It will be safe."

"But—"

"And as troubling as it is—I do understand your misgivings, Wenthi, about the doctor, about using the *myco*—we need to match them weapon for weapon. These rebels aren't just nuisances stealing a bit of fuel to run their cycles and trucks. They are insurgents, looking to undo everything people like us have been building here since the end of the war. Your mother's good work getting this country on its feet. Our part in the war effort."

"Yes, of course."

"You're scared," Canwei said. "I don't blame you. It's a big risk, I won't pretend it's not. We wouldn't ask this of you if it wasn't about the very security of the Alliance and the war effort."

Wenthi let that sink in. He had still been thinking this was a normal patrol infiltration assignment, busting up a cycle crew of petrol thieves. The real scope of it was settling in his belly. "Are you sure I'm your man for this?"

"I am," Canwei said. "I am sorry this is all a rush, but Doctor Shebiruht says we must act while the *myco* is active in the girl. But the rest of this will be handled clean and tight down the line, all right?"

"All right," Wenthi said, swallowing his fear. He was needed. Everyone—Canwei, Sengejú, Mother—was saying how important this was for the nation. How important it was that he did it. That only he could do it. He had to believe them. He had to try. "Let's do this."

The lieutenant snapped her fingers, and the nurses wheeled his gurney out of the room, then down the hall to another room with a series of complicated locks.

"They call this the 'ice room,'" Shebiruht said as Wenthi was wheeled in. "It's not a proper name, but it does serve a function. The walls have a breed of *mycopsilaria sehosi* growing in the panels. That would block any further connection she would have with someone she had synced with earlier. Antipathetic energies, the *myco* breeds have."

"Why are you talking to me, Doctor?" Wenthi asked. "The lieutenant says we need to use you, so I'm fine, but I don't need to hear you speak."

She looked at him with an odd regard, raising an eyebrow. "Try to open your awareness, Mister Tungét. It will help you with the process."

They locked the gurney in place, right next to another one, occupied by the woman he had arrested the night before.

"The shit is this *gobra*?" she snarled. "What are you doing?"

"Oh, she's a yeller," Shebiruht said. She took out a stopper and put a few drops in her eyes. She blinked a few times then took a good look at the girl. "Oh, look at all that. Isn't it glorious? How much *myco* did you take yesterday, Miss Enapi?"

"I—what? I'm not—"

"There's no harm in answering, girl, it won't change your outcomes. In a few moments, you will fall into a deep coma, and then you will probably never open your eyes or leave this room again."

"What?" She turned to look at Wenthi. "You're the tory who nabbed me."

"And now you're paying for your crimes," Wenthi said. "You should be happy it's a *myco* coma instead of a lifetime in penitence."

"Crimes?" she shouted. "What you are all doing is a crime. What you've been doing. And you!" Her arms shot up toward Doctor Shebiruht, but only came up a few inches because of the restraints. "I know who you are. I know what you did."

"Yes, I'm sure," Shebiruht said. She took a syringe and shoved it in Enapi's arm. "I did so many things, which is why we're able to do this to you."

Enapi thrashed on her gurney for a moment, her jaw clenching, before she collapsed down, still.

"Ready, Mister Tungét?" Shebiruht asked, taking out another syringe.

"Does the answer matter?" He was holding down the fear, the nearly overpowering need to bolt from the gurney and out the door. He was serving the patrol, serving his country, and he would do what he needed to do, not thinking about the syringe full of poison that this depraved madwoman was holding. He didn't listen to that clawing panic at his heart as she approached.

"No," the doctor said, taking hold of his arm. "But I do strive to be polite to all my subjects. It is the very least I can do. Try it sometime."

She pushed the needle into his arm, and his veins caught fire. The fire ran up his arm, filled his chest and then crushed its way into his brain, knocking him into the dark.

He roared out of the dark, out of the tunnel, stopping his cycle right on the mark and drawing his weapon as he dismounted. Standard training, perfect executing. The girl was there—typical jifozi *girl, dark hair, darker eyes, tawny copper skin. Dressed like all the trash in Outtown, dirty denim jacket and pants, stained and fraying.*

"On the ground!" he shouted. "Hands spread, touch nothing!"

She looked at him in confusion. "We did this before."

"On the ground!" he shouted, even though he felt the doubt. Where were they? Where had he just been? Not on his cycle. He had—

She looked at him and took a step forward. "We did this. I should consider myself detained, right?"

"Step back," he said.

"Or you'll what?" she asked. "You already arrested me. We're . . . already here."

Gun still on her, he reached out and grabbed her wrist. "You can consider yourself—"

"Detained," she said. "Expect to face punitive action in response to your criminal acts. Damn, man, think for yourself for once."

"You—" he started, but as he tried to turn her around to force her to the ground, his hand wouldn't move. It was stuck to her wrist. "You will—stop that!"

"Stop what?" she asked. "Get your hand off me!"

He pulled his hand away, but their flesh had melded together. Tendrils came out of his hand, wrapping around her arm as they also snaked their way up his. Vines circled and ensnared them both.

"You let me go!" she shouted.

"I can't!" he said. "You're doing this!"

"No, I'm—"

"—not, you are!"

She was pulled into him, her body crashing into his chest. The flesh of her arm melted into his hand, and the whole of her body slid over him. Her flesh seeping into his.

"What—"

"—are—"

"—you—"

"—doing, tory!"

He shouted that, his mouth, his body, which was also her. She had folded entirely into him, her words her mouth her spirit her everything embedded in his flesh

"No!" she screamed with his mouth. "Let me go!"

Then the tunnel opened up again and the darkness took him.

REFUEL: BROADCAST

You've been listening to Call Sign ZPR 1140, broadcasting news and entertainment for the city of Ziaparr each day and every day. The time is five sweep eighty, and we hope those of you who've been working all day are on your way home to a pleasant evening, and we hope those who work through the night are off to a productive start. Traffic is choked in the 7th and 8th Senjas, and the checkpoints from Intown to Outtown are backed up, especially at the Uzena and Mixala crossings. Those will hold up at least half a sweep, so plan accordingly.

On world news, Alliance Forces report they have liberated the town of Gazamal on the southern coast of Ikriba, where they have been greeted with joy and celebration by the locals. Alliance soldiers returned their joy with open arms and baskets of canned goods—goods like Nimefaid tinned meat. Whether it's pan fried in a tortilla for breakfast, or chopped into your dinner of beans and rice, there's nothing quite like Nimefaid. Use your meat ration points on Nimefaid, and you'll get more meat with every point! The hungry people of Gazamal were as thrilled as you are every time you crack open a can.

Alliance Forces report that this victory puts us one step closer to releasing the iron grip the despotic Ikriban Council holds over their oppressed people. Alliance soldiers have made camp in the lovely town, and are eager to take their campaign to the next stage. Remember that we are doing our part—every can we save, every scrap of iron we rework, every drop of fuel that we can send to aid the effort brings the world one step closer to peace! We're happy to work to pay our debt, as we give with an open hand.

And for some local color, Alliance Guard reports there was quite a dustup in the 14th Senja, as their investigators have worked tirelessly to find the ringleaders of a shoplifting scheme that was stealing dry goods from local vendors throughout the outer senjas. The guard, with the assistance of the dedicated local men and women of the Civil Patrol, executed several warrants on twelve people, arresting Felita Mereto, Marin Mereto, and Anninia Mereto, amongst others, all jifozi *caste. Anninia was the supposed brains of the operation, and she had run from patrol, finally caught hiding in the home of Miss Niliza Dallatan, a name our listeners have heard time and time again in the crime report. As a result of the raid, cloth, rice, and corn flour, valuing up to fifteen thousand ration points, were recovered. I'm sure our listeners are happy to hear of their recovery, for they know the Maretos and their accomplices—*jifozi *all—were stealing from their pockets as much as from the local vendors. We at ZPR 1140 are all glad to hear the goods have been recovered and hope that the* jifozi *neighbors of the Maretos learn that crime hurts all of us, especially you. But they have been caught, and once the hospital releases all the Maretos, you can be assured they will be tried and sent to Hanezcua Penitentiary where they belong*

We'll be playing a selection from Ngei Zhiun's Fourth Symphony, as performed by the Orchestra of the Union Order, brought to you by Oalka Coffee. When you need that rich, strong flavor, you need Oalka . . .

SECOND CIRCUIT:
RENZI LLIONORCO

16

Wenthi startled awake to the loud drone of engines. Deafening.

He was strapped in a seat. Roaring in his ears.

Her screams—Nália Enapi—in his ears.

Where was she?

Where was he?

He realized there was someone else in another chair, across from him, also strapped in.

"Officer Tungét," she shouted over the roar. "You all right?"

"I—what is going on?"

"I was told you'd be disoriented," she said. "It's Lieutenant Canwei. Do you remember what happened yesterday?"

"Yesterday," he said. The words eased into his brain amid the echoes of extra voices bouncing around. His eyes focused on Canwei.

"I wasn't sure if you would wake up before we landed."

"Landed?" he asked. His head was still thrumming, and the roaring around him didn't help.

"We're in a four-prop flyer, about thirty klicks outside of Hanezcua. We land there and then you'll be put on a prison transport train back to Ziaparr. The story is you've just been released from Hanez Penitentiary and are being shipped out for relocation. That should give you cover to get yourself situated in your new identity."

"New—" The words bounced around in his head. "Sorry, I—I'm a little . . ."

"I know," she said. "I'll try to explain the magic bullshit they did to you best I can. Shebiruht was able to forge an extended, long-term *myco* sync between you and Miss Enapi—the woman you arrested?"

"Right," Wenthi said. The obvious question came up through his cloudy brain. "Why?"

"You're going to be trying to infiltrate people who regularly use the *myco* with each other, to coordinate, to communicate. You needed—how did Shebiruht explain it?"

Shebiruht. The Mushroom Monster. The Witch. She had done this.

"You're going to need a shield to protect your real self in those connections, when you use the *myco* in the field."

That brought Wenthi back to the present moment, giving him a better sense of where he was. Sparse cargo hold, metal walls, porthole windows. This was the first time Wenthi had been in any sort of flyer, and the sudden realization that he was high in the air made his stomach jump. He dared a glance out the porthole, but all he saw besides the thick white-and-gray of cloud cover was the wide metal wing and two whirling propellers. The only other person here besides him and the lieutenant was the pilot at the stick.

"Why would I—" he started, then understanding came. "I'll need to do the *myco* with them to join in, to fit with others."

"Precisely," Canwei said. "This sync with Enapi, Shebiruht says it'll act as a magical mask you can use to protect who you really are. When you *myco* sync with someone else, it will make you 'feel' like Enapi does, or is supposed to. Plus you should be able to access some of her memories, her instincts, which will help you blend in with your new identity."

"New identity." That was something he could latch on to. "I've got the gist, you'll load me on the train, so when I get off at Ziaparr everyone will think I've just been let free with the rest of the new releases."

"You've got it," she said. She handed him a few cards. "Those identify you as a *jifoz* named Renzi Llionorco."

"All right," he said. They clearly chose "Renzi" because it was the local version of his Sehosian name "Wenthi." He'd learn to react naturally to that quickly enough. But "Llionorco" was an odd choice, putting him in mind of Mother's warning. "Do you know how they chose that name? The family name, specifically."

"That stuff came from above me. Usually for something like this, they choose a name that had a lot of casualties in the war. That way when people ask who your people are, you say they died in the bombings of Second, or Great Noble. Bombings are a good one to use, they never ask follow-ups."

That sounded like it came from experience. "You did this before?"

"Four seasons in deep with some smuggling crews in Xaopan. But those folks were just working the docks, bringing in contraband. Nothing like this, with the mushroom or rebellions."

[Revolution.]

That didn't quite come from Wenthi's own head. It was like a radio that hadn't landed on the station, half heard through the static.

"So we'll be on the train together?" he asked.

"Once we land, I treat you like a prisoner, and bring you to the trainyard. I'm gonna be a bit rough, fair warning."

The four-prop suddenly bucked, jerking him to the side.

"Lot a wind!" the pilot shouted.

"You all right?" Canwei asked, reached out to him.

"Get your hands off me, tory!" he snapped reflexively, though he immediately wondered why. He had never said something like that before.

"Good," she said. "Like your instincts. We'll keep that up as we get on the train, and no one will doubt you."

"All right," he said. "So I have my papers and new identity, what's my next step when I get back to Ziaparr?"

"Establish yourself in a *jifozi* district. Ideally one of the patches in the 14th Senja."

[Miahez.]

Wenthi shook that off. "And then work to find my way into one of these rebellion gangs. Use this . . . connection? . . . with Enapi to guide my way."

"Right. The bosses are hoping that you're going to know who to find, where to go. From there, your goal is to get in deep enough to meet Varazina, or at least someone high up enough in the inner circle to reach her."

"These are cycle gangs," he said. "I'm going to need a cycle. I presume I'm not going to have a patrol-issued Ungeke."

"Of course not," she said. "When you get off the prison train back in town, you'll be issued your personal effects. Well, the ones listed under Renzi Llionorco."

"Which are?"

She looked at her files. "Looks like a pull shirt, denim coat and slacks, helmet and a Puegoiz 960."

[What color?] Still so much static.

"What color?" he asked, echoing the voice in his skull.

She glanced at the file again. "Cold blue and chrome."

[Mine!]

That hit him hard and clear, like an anchor pulling him down. The radio fully tuned.

"Yeah, that's mine," he said. "I mean, that's Miss Enapi's. Is that wise?"

"It's available. It's not like you can ride a shiny factory-fresh Ungeke."

"All right, that makes sense. If I have that cycle, I can use it and hopefully get in with the same people that I—" He shook that off for a second. "That Miss Enapi was in with."

"You all right?" she asked.

"I feel—" He tried to find the words for what was going on. "I feel like part of me is still left on the ground, in my gut, pulling me down. I'll be honest, I'm not sure what part of that has to do with the 'sync' they did to me, and what's just being in the flyer."

"Ten swipes to ground!" the pilot shouted.

"Thanks!" Canwei shouted back. "When we land, you take a few to get your bearings. There's a cooler box in the back with a couple tortas—achiote pork and pickled onion—as well as a Dark Shumi. Take your time with that, and then we'll shackle your wrists and ankles, and load you in a truck to the train depot. From that point on, you are Llionorco, and I'm going to treat you as such."

"Got it," he said.

"People ask, you were in Ward Eight at Hanez. Everyone in there was in solo lock, so no one would be able to claim different."

"Strap up!" the pilot shouted.

The roaring props sputtered and thundered, as the flyer broke out from the wall of white. Out the porthole, the gray and brown city lay below, a sprawling metro belching flame and smoke. Hanezcua was an industrial town, where they refined the raw crude from the oil plains between here and Ziaparr. Filled with steel refineries, machine plants, and assembly factories. They made the Puegoiz cycles here, the Kathia autos and trucks, not to mention the gunrollers and bombers that the Alliance was using in the war.

The ground came up faster and harder, making Wenthi's stomach drop and heart hammer like a raildigger. With a jarring slam, the flyer lurched back. Wenthi almost puked all over Lieutenant Canwei.

"On the ground," she said. "First one's always the hardest."

"Nah!" the pilot shouted. "It's the *last* one that'll always get you."

Canwei unbuckled herself as the flyer rolled to a stop, and then got Wenthi out of his seat. Only now did he realize he was wearing a white prison gown.

"Eat up," she said. "I mean, take your time, but we do have a train to catch."

17

Wenthi was slammed into a seat, Lieutenant Canwei shoving her finger in his face.

"Give me an excuse, Llionorco," she said. "Give me any excuse to drag you right back to the hole we pulled you out of."

"Maybe I will," Wenthi said.

"And maybe I'll get to put you on a train right back here," she said. She made a good show of knocking his face, spat on him, and stalked off.

"Nice lady," said the fellow sitting next to him. "You Bind with her for a bit or something?"

"She wishes," Wenthi said. The guy was dark amber-skinned, with an accent that sounded like he came from the outer senjas of Ziaparr. Probably a *jifoz*. "You know how these tories get attached."

"Just don't bring me trouble," he said. "I don't need whatever she has over you to spill over on me."

"I'll ride good and quiet," Wenthi said.

The prison car was filled with amber- and copper-skinned people, all in white jumpsuits. Most of them thick-haired, swarthy beards on the men. *Jifoz* and *baniz*, clearly. Wenthi wondered if he stood out as a *rhique* compared to them. Not that he was going to make a scene comparing his tawny-bronze arm to the man next to him. But the papers he now carried said he was *jifoz,* so he doubted any of them would question it.

Guards came through and checked the shackles of all the prisoners. It seemed a bit odd to Wenthi, given that everyone here was probably coming to Ziaparr for release. There wasn't a penitentiary in Ziaparr, just the holding jails in various headquarters. Nothing for long-term prisoners, so they were being sent to freedom. He wondered why they even bothered shackling at this stage. Trying to escape or run now seemed absurd.

Of course, these men and women hadn't exactly made smart choices up until now. So perhaps it was best to prevent temptation.

That thought made his stomach turn. These people didn't have choices. They were desperate, did what they had to do to stay alive, to keep working, to feed their families. They had been punished for that. Most of them had probably been targeted by the patrol for being *jifoz* or *baniz.*

"No," he said out loud. That wasn't true. He knew it wasn't true.

"I thought you'd be quiet," the man next to him said.

Wenthi sneered at his seatmate. "Don't give me reason not to."

But he fought back against the thought that percolated up. No, Patrol didn't target the undercastes. Crime was more common in the senjas where they lived.

[Because that's where people are the most desperate, asshole.]

That thought hit hard. That wasn't him, that was Nália. Her emotions—roiling anger at the guards, rage over the shackles, the pity and fury looking at the sallow faces of underfed prisoners—all bubbled and churned within him.

He closed his eyes and pushed those feelings down. What had the mad doctor said? He was supposed to dominate the link with the girl. Her emotions shouldn't rule over him. He had an assignment, and he would perform his duty, but he would not be ruled by the emotions of a silly young woman with aspirations of revolution and liberation.

Rebellion. Even her words were seeping into his thoughts. He had to reclaim control.

Two guards came through the prison cabin, one with a clipboard and the other an inkpad. They spoke briefly to each prisoner, quickly working through the room. Eventually they reached Wenthi's bench.

"Name?" they asked the man next to him.

"Cerlos," he said. "Beniché Cerlos."

The one with the clipboard flipped through pages. "Is this a work release?"

"Is that what it's called?" Cerlos asked. "I served my time."

Clipboard turned to his companion. "I'm not seeing it on here, so mark him black."

The guard with the inkpad stamped it and put a black mark on Cerlos's hand.

"And you?" he asked Wenthi.

"Llionorco. Renzi Llionorco."

"Here it is," the guard said. "So nice when they get the paperwork right."

"It helps," his friend said. "What's he get?"

"Blue," the first said. "This guy is going home."

As the guard stamped Wenthi's hand with a blue spot, Cerlos grew agitated.

"I am going home," he said. "I did my time. I should get the blue."

"You're not on the list," the guard with the board said.

"No, I am going home. My son, he—"

The guard knocked Cerlos across his face with the clipboard. "You're not on the list. And you deserve the black." He glanced at Wenthi. "You gonna be a problem, Llionorco?"

"I'm going where I need to be," Wenthi said.

"Good," he said, and the guards moved on.

So whatever the black mark meant, it wasn't release. Wenthi glanced around. Most of the hands he saw were marked black. Hardly anyone on this train was going to freedom.

Another emotion from Nália. He tamped down on that, thinking of a box, with a lid and a lock, and put her feelings inside it. The people who were going free, and there were a few with the blue mark, were the ones who had served their sentence. The rest had surely been put on this train, marked black, for good reason. He didn't know what, and neither did the silly girl trying to needle her way into his skull.

Nália. Her name was Nália Enapi.

And his was now Renzi Llionorco. He kept repeating that in his head as the train fired up and started to roll.

18

The train had thundered through the night, but the lights in the prison cabin stayed on, though flickering and weak, the whole time. There was also a radio speaker, crackling out hourly news and prop broadcasts about victories in Ikriba and Runura. "We are fighting on for the good of the Alliance, to stop the next Rodiguen before they gain too much power. We fight now so there shall be no more Transoceanic Wars, for we are united in strength and peace."

Wenthi tried to sleep, but found only fitful dozing and troubled dreams. Dreams of the crowded 16th Senja—the Ako Favel—where there were no roads, just bombed-out patches where ramshackle homes made of scrap metal were crammed on top of each other. He wandered from there to the 14th Senja—but in his head he kept calling it Miahez—all of it nightmarish but also familiar.

He woke with the train whistle blowing hard and sharp, morning daylight smashing through the windows into his skull.

"Welcome to Ziaparr, those of you that are staying," one of the guards shouted. He held a heavy baton, while the two behind him carried heavy rifles. "This is how it's going to work. All of you will stand up, and we will unshackle you each in turn. You step out and follow instructions as given by the guards outside. You will not speak, you will not question, and you will not disrupt the order of things, else example will be made of you. Have I made myself perfectly clear?"

None of the prisoners responded.

"Good. Now, stand up, and we will get you unloaded in a decent and orderly manner."

They went through each row of benches, unlatching the shackles and leading them out of the car. After several swipes of this, the guards got to Wenthi's bench, letting him and Cerlos up at the same time and leading them out.

Out in the depot—exactly where in town, Wenthi wasn't sure, probably in the 19th Senja—another set of guards glanced at the ink on their hands. "Blue, over there into the hut for release process. Black, follow them onto the trucks."

"Am I being released?" Cerlos asked. "Is that where the trucks are going?"

"No," said the guard. "Get over there."

"It's a mistake!" Cerlos shouted. "I'm supposed to—"

That was met with a rifle butt across his head. Cerlos crumpled like a street puppet with its strings cut.

"You got a problem?" one guard asked Wenthi.

"To the hut?" he asked. "Heading over."

He walked over, noticing most of the prisoners coming off the train were being loaded into trucks, including Cerlos, being dragged over there by two guards. Only a handful were coming into the hut with him.

"Name?" a bored-looking guard asked as he approached.

"Llionorco," he said. "Renzi Llionorco."

The guard looked through her files, then got up and went into the back room. She emerged a moment later with a crate.

"Llionorco, Renzi. Personal effects. Go in that niche over there to change, then come sign out for final release."

Wenthi took the crate and went into the niche. He stripped out of the prison whites and started to put on the provided clothing. Hard, raw denim pants, once dark blue, but with black stains and more than a few white distress lines and impending holes. He pulled them on, but struggled to button up all the brass buttons.

Which was odd. They were his. They felt like his.

Except they weren't. They were Nália's; that's why they were tight on his waist, loose on the hips. The pull shirt and denim jacket fit decently enough. He was about the same height as her, if not quite as curvy.

The boots he barely managed to get on. Those were too damn tight.

The rest of the personal effects included a cycle helmet, keys, and ration cards to go with the ident cards he had already received as Renzi Llionorco. He pocketed those—

Something felt wrong.

He switched pockets, putting the keys on the left side pocket, cards on the right. That's how they were supposed to go. He wasn't sure where that came from: Nália's own memory, or just that the pants had white lines of wear that matched the shape of the keys in the left pocket, and the square outline of the cards on the right. Apparently Nália was so habitual, she had worn patterns in the pants.

He came back with the crate.

"Sign here," the desk clerk said, handing him a paper. "Here's housing vouchers, since you have no residence or kin listed. Failure to find housing and employment to pay rent within twenty-five days will result in immediate return to prison."

"Right," he said. "Anything else?"

"You have the keys to the cycle?"

"Yes," he said.

"It's parked in the holding lot at Circle Uilea, by the 14th Senja headquarters. Here's a claim ticket. Holding lot closes at five sweep on the naught, so you better get over there. Failure to claim your vehicle before end of day will result in it being sold to auction."

"No!" he shouted, though that came more from Nália.

"Don't shout at me," she said. "You best get moving."

"Yes, ma'am," he said. He left the hut out the front door, now as Renzi Llionorco, newly released prisoner. A few of the other releasees came out with him.

"Where you headed?" one asked him. About Wenthi's age. Pretty, muscular boy in a swarthy, *jifozi* way.

"14th Senja," he said. "Got to get my cycle."

"You're lucky they held it for you. Most folks get it auctioned straight off."

"Is that how it goes?" Wenthi asked. "First time for this."

"Third."

"Third?" Wenthi asked, hoping he sounded impressed. "How'd you manage that?"

"Tories, always on me, you know?" The man said it like it said it all. "Did you get a bed tonight with your cycle, or you need one?"

"I was planning on working that out after I got my ride. Housing vouchers."

"Housing vouchers are shit," the guy said. "Ain't hardly a place that'll honor them. I know a spot in the 'hez that you can use them at."

"If it's near Uilea, perfect."

 19

The Patrol Center for the 14th Senja—

[Miahez.]

—for Miahez loomed over Circle Uilea. It stood on a steep hill, which dropped down to a fenced concrete lot, right before the circle.

"Shitting eyes all over us, huh?" Wenthi's new companion asked.

"Always watching," Wenthi said. They approached the lot gate, manned by a pair of black-uniformed patrol.

"Well, look who it is," one of them said, putting his hand on his baton casually. "It's Nasty Ren. Thought you were out of my hair."

It was Paulei putting up a good show.

"I know you, friend?" Wenthi asked.

"Oh, I know you," Paulei said. "I was on patrol in Tofozaun a couple years back when you pulled that business." He came in close to Wenthi, grabbing him by the lapels of his denim coat. "You now in Ziaparr?"

"I'm just here for my cycle."

Paulei turned to the companion. "And you're his friend? He your new muscle?"

"That's Mad Pack Parnez," the other one said. Wenthi didn't know her. "How's your sister, Parnez?"

"Partinez," Wenthi's new companion said quietly.

"Whatever," the female officer said. "You two came to turn yourself in or something?"

"Save us a bit of trouble," Paulei said.

"Hey, I'm a freewalker," Wenthi said. "Unless you want to make some business to haul me in over."

"Maybe I do," Paulei said.

"Then do it," Wenthi said. "Else give me my cycle."

"Ease down, Jéngka," the lady said. "You got an impound claim?"

Wenthi handed over the ticket. Paulei snatched it from her hands. "I'll take him. You keep an eye on this one."

"I'll keep both," she said. Paulei grabbed Wenthi's arm and dragged him through the gate onto the lot.

"You all right?" Paulei asked.

"Glad to see you," Wenthi said. "This all went—"

"Way too fast," Paulei said. "Yeah. Why is that? I wasn't briefed on anything other than a temp assignment out in the 14th while you were going under. I'm your point of contact out here."

"How is that supposed to work?"

Paulei handed him a slip of paper. "Memorize this exchange. If you need me, find a coinphone and call it. And if you can't talk openly, give an address, and I'll show up to 'arrest' you. What can you tell me about your mission?"

"Try to get in good with the insurgents who are robbing the fuel trains. Headquarters think they're part of a larger organization that are dangerous to the safety of the nation."

"They're probably not wrong," Paulei said. "I'm gonna push you now so they see."

"Do it."

Paulei shoved him hard, knocking Wenthi to the ground. Wenthi jumped up and shook an angry finger at Paulei. "I think that looked really good. You tell whoever at headquarters that I'm going to need a few days just to find my feet in all this, especially with what they did to my head."

"Your head?"

"Why they had to do this in such a rush. They wanted to do it while that girl was still tripping her *myco*. I've got, like, her in my skull."

"I don't get it," Paulei said.

"Same," Wenthi said. They walked up to a night-blue Puegoiz 960. "But I'm following orders. This the cycle?"

"It is," Wenthi said. A surge of joy and pride burst forth when he saw it. From her, a love for this specific machine. "She's really into this 'goiz junkbash. She made that abundantly clear."

"So, what? She's talking in your head?"

"More emotion than words. I'm still trying to get a handle on it."

"But why?" Paulei asked.

"So I can pass as *jifoz*, I guess. Especially if I use the *myco* with them."

"If? Or when?"

"There's really no way to get in and avoid it," Wenthi said. He sighed. "This whole thing, I agreed to it because the lieutenant said go, so I did. But my head is a mess. The worst part—"

"It all sounds terrible."

"You know who did it? Shebiruht. *That* Shebiruht."

"What?" Paulei's eyes went wide. He looked sick for a moment, which Wenthi completely understood. It made him sick to think of that woman even touching him. "Didn't they, like, execute her after the war?"

"Apparently not. But that's why I don't know what exactly to make of this thing they did to me."

"But they wouldn't have done it if they didn't think it was necessary," Paulei said weakly. "Right?"

"That's what I'm telling myself."

"You need me to do anything?" Paulei asked.

"Just keep your ears high," Wenthi said. He went to get on the cycle.

Something stopped him. A feeling—no, a need. Nália's need to just admire the cycle, drink it in. No, that wasn't quite right.

She needed him to do it.

"You're kidding," he muttered.

Wenthi had never really looked at a Puegoiz before. He had always thought them—like all locally built vehicles—far inferior machines compared to the Sehosian Ungeke line, or the masterful engineering of Reloumic cycles. Those were pure power, sleek lines of metal that looked like they had been birthed into the world as perfection. Every rivet, every piece would lock together in a symphony of machinery that rendered the marvel of its engineering invisible.

This Puegoiz 960 was nothing like that at all. The engine elements were open and exposed, hoses and dual exhaust pipes running along the chassis, gears and chains for all the world to see.

But it shined glorious chrome on those exhaust pipes, which popped against the deep blue of the fenders and seat, which were all embossed with the sunburst logo of the Rhixan Engine Company, and the 960 etched on the gas tank.

And that engine—he saw Nália's memory of rebuilding it, swapping out the three-cylinder of the 960 for a 1296's inline-four, with the hand-rigged rivets and tinstraps keeping it in place. It shouldn't work, but he knew that it did, and beautifully.

Wenthi got on the cycle, unlocking the starter with the keys.

The engine purred to life, that purr growling its way to a roar. Oh, that was delightful. For a moment, he wasn't sure if he was the one happy about it, or Nália, but it felt real and genuine to him.

"I'll be in touch," he told Paulei.

"Be careful" Paulei said. Raising his voice, he added, "And I better not be catching you pulling any business!"

Wenthi kicked the 'goiz into gear, and with a touch of the throttle was off like a shot. Faster and harder than he expected. He almost threw himself off and nearly skidded out correcting himself. He reached the gate and yanked the brake to a stop.

Even with Nália's memory, he wasn't ready for a 'goiz 960 to have that kind of power.

"Partinez," he said to his new friend. "Get on. Let's get out of here."

"Damn right," Partinez said, getting on the back of the cycle and holding on to Wenthi's waist.

They roared off; this time Wenthi knew what to expect from the cycle. This time, he had it under his control. It felt natural. Like his.

If he could do the same to Nália herself, he would be fine.

"Where we going?" he shouted over the wind.

"Spin the next circle out to the left, and wind up the hill to the temple."

"We going to the temple?"

"Nah, that's just the easiest way to find *Urka* Dallatan."

That was a name Wenthi had heard before. The "Aunt of the 14th Senja" was downright notorious.

Good a place as any to start this business.

 20

The road curved in three pins up the hill, so steep Wenthi thought the cycle might flip back with a rider hanging on. But he gunned it up while lowering the gear, burning more fuel than he would have liked to get up to the temple. As he reached it, two autos—both junkers that dated to Second Trans—buzzed around the curve, astounding him that they were able to get that kind of speed on the incline. He was amazed either of them had that kind of engine power, given that both cars looked like they were held together with paste and hope.

"You all right?" he asked Partinez. The man clutched tight to Wenthi's waist when the autos buzzed by.

"Just spooked me," Partinez said as Wenthi pulled onto the curb. He hopped off the cycle to stand in the shade of the temple. "You think they were racing?"

"Be a waste of fuel," Wenthi said. "You burn enough getting up the slope. I wouldn't want to do it if I didn't have to get up here."

"Yeah," Partinez said. "This patch of the 'hez is a pain to get to, but that's part of why the *urka* likes it up here."

"This is your patch, not mine," Wenthi said. Not Nália's either. She lived at the bottom of the 14th, on Street Farama. He shouldn't go there at all, he knew. He had her clothes, her cycle. Her neighbors would smell him out quick. No damn good. Canwei had acted like it was a perfect choice, but riding this cycle could be an issue. He needed to think up a story if someone recognized it. And if he knew anything about cycle cats, they would.

"Where are your people?"

"Not here," Wenthi said. "I had family in Tofo before the purges—"

"Yeah," Partinez said. "So why come to Ziaparr now?"

"I wasn't given a choice," Wenthi said. "I got put on a train and brought here. I'd prefer to take my cycle and ride out to Tofo, but right now I'd run out of fuel before I got to the Southway. So I'm here for now."

"Feel you," Partinez said. "Second time out of Hanez, they released me to Uretichan. Hated that town."

"Never been," Wenthi said, glancing around the street. Other than the temple—which was a stone fortress looming over a small, quiet zocalo of cart vendors—it was all squat, crumbling houses and shops, crammed on top of each other with narrow stairwell alleys plunging down between them. The one road with the dead-eye curve was the only one an auto could get through up here, as it wound around the temple and split into a fork farther up. There were no proper places to park, but quite a few autos and cycles were on the curb, wedged in wherever they would fit. "I suppose I can just leave the cycle here."

"Probably," Partinez said.

Wenthi locked down the engine and pocketed the keys.

"You got any coin on you?" Partinez asked.

"Just the ration cards and housing vouchers."

"Shit," Partinez said, glancing over to zocalo. "That taco cart is lighting up my nose, and I'm ravenous."

"Same," Wenthi said. He hadn't eaten anything since the tortas on the four-prop, and that was yesterday.

"Let's see who's cooking it," Partinez said.

"Don't we need to—"

"It'll wait," Partinez said. "My stomach won't."

They crossed up into the zocalo, passing the carved niches in the temple wall with the usual skull-face spirit icons and flower garlands around tin-plates, clearly from a few generations back, of people dressed in traditional clothes from before even the First Trans.

There was almost no one in the zocalo, save the cart vendors themselves, and three old *jifoz* folk dozing lazily on the cobblestone.

Towering over the zocalo, almost as high as the temple, was a grand bill-board on a giant pole—every temple in Ziaparr, even the solemn, dignified ones in Intown, had a grand pole in front of the doors—with a bright representation of several Ziaparrian people of each caste, standing together with broad smiles. "HAPPY TO PAY THE DEBT! GRATEFUL FOR OUR FREEDOM! GIVE WITH AN OPEN HAND!" There were plenty of posters just like that in Intown, but none of them had been as defaced and vandalized as this one had. The faces of the *llipe* and *rhique* folks on the poster had been shredded and defaced. And the words "*nix xisisa*" painted across the official text.

[We have paid too much.]

Partinez's face lit up as they went to the taco cart, where a weathered woman was grilling onions and chiles and greasy cuts of meat over coals.

"Lajina," Partinez said. "I hoped you were still here."

"It's always me here," she said tartly. "Where else would I be? Where were you, hmm?"

"Hanez," he said gravely.

"I thought," she said coarsely. "You look awful. Too skinny."

"Help me out about that," he said.

"What you got?"

"Nothing but vouchers right now," he said. "About to see *urka* about a place to sleep, but we can't do that if we faint first."

"We?" she asked. She pointed her tongs at Wenthi accusingly. "I don't know that one."

"Llionorco," Partinez said. "He's all right. Off the Hanez train like me."

"At least you got off the train," she said. "Llionorco. You from here? You got people?"

"No, ma'am," Wenthi said. "Unless you count him."

"Help us out, *zyiza*," he said.

She scowled, but pulled a piece of meat off the grill and dropped it on her board, slicing it with practiced, racing movements. In moments, she had two pairs of tacos rolled, filled with meat, chiles, onions, and spiced tomatillo.

"I'll put credit onto Miss Niliza," she said as she handed them over. "You best hope she's in a mood to deal with you all."

"*Runjé*, Lajina," Partinez said. "Saved lives, you did."

"Thank you, miss," Wenthi said.

"Just eat and shut your mouths."

Wenthi bit into the first one, and maybe it was just because he was so hungry, but the flavors exploded in his mouth, a joy he was not expecting. Even though the cut of the meat was greasier than he cared for, it still was smoky and spicy and everything he needed right now.

Or was it Nália who felt that?

He wasn't quite sure. He certainly had never *loved* a street cart taco like that before.

"Come on," Partinez said while he was eating his. "Blue house across the street."

Another junk auto—this one with half sedan parts, and no hood covering the engine—whipped around the dead-eye curve in front of the house. They both waited for a moment, finishing the last bites of taco, before they carefully crossed.

The blue house had a wall with an iron gate, and a small garden beyond the wall before the house proper. This house stood out on the street for that; most of the rest seemed to just have a broken wooden door, cloth curtain, or some other thrown-together measure to separate the inside of the house from the street. This was easily the nicest place in this patch. That made sense—from what Wenthi had heard, Niliza Dallatan was a queenpin in these parts, her fingerprints on quite a few robbery rings and shakedown gangs. Of course she lived better than her neighbors.

As they approached, a trio of dogs came racing up to them, barking and jumping all over each other.

"Hey ladies," Partinez said, holding his hand through the iron bars. "How are you, yes? Are you good to your auntie, yes?"

The dogs scrambled over each other to try to lick the taco grease off his hand, and then started growling and nipping at each other.

"Who's out there?" a woman called out. "Who's got them riled up?"

"*Urka,*" Partinez called out. "It's Anjedaro."

"Daro!" The woman came out of the house proper to the gate. She was a small woman, about Mother's age, perhaps a bit older, with a similar pudgy figure hidden in a loose blue day dress. Her dark hair was sun bleached and streaked with gray, her rich complexion leathered and lined, her dark eyes partly hidden by thick, brass-rimmed glasses. "How is it you're here, I've not seen you in, I don't even know how long, it's been at least a year, and look at you, so skinny, where have you been, you haven't come around, oh, that was right, you were arrested, of course, *xo mirod*, what barbarity, that's where you have been, I have missed you—yes, yes, calm, calm, away—come let me look at you." All those words fired out like an autogun in the few seconds she took to walk from the door to the gate, shoo the dogs to the side, and open the gate. Wenthi wasn't even sure he heard them all.

"Missed you, too," Partinez said, taking the short woman into a warm embrace.

"Well, I'm glad you're here. Did they have you in Hanezcua again? Spirits watch over, that is no place for a body, but look at you, you look good and strong, if too skinny. But I know what you need. Good meal, good bath, and good fuck, am I right?"

"You are," Partinez said. "Though Lajina gave us a couple tacos to start."

"To start, but that's just a start." She grabbed Partinez's face and pulled it down to meet hers, kissing him on the lips. "She put you on my credit? Fine, fine. Let's get you inside, it's so good to see you, oh—" She looked at Wenthi for the first time. "Who's your friend? Is he who you're going to fuck?"

"Not yet," Partinez said, though his face told Wenthi he wasn't against the idea. Wenthi hadn't given it too much thought, though he certainly hadn't minded double-riding the cycle with him. "We just met after the prison train, but he needs a place to stay and—"

"Oh, yes, the housing vouchers. I cannot believe they are even bothering with those things, almost no one but me is going to even take them, and I only—but it doesn't matter. Doesn't matter. Let me look at you." She came closer and peered at Wenthi up and down. "You are a handsome one, aren't you, though? If he doesn't fuck you, I will. Unless you'd rather fuck Lajina. Lajina!" She shouted across the road to the zocalo. "Do you want to fuck these boys who just got out of prison?"

"I'm working!" Lajina shouted back as her only answer.

"She's busy. Maybe later. Whatever you need, though, any friend of Daro is—what was your name again?"

"Llionorco," Wenthi said. "Renzi Llionorco."

"Renzi," she said. "That's a pretty name for a pretty boy. All right, all right, come in here—mind the dogs, don't let them in the street—let's get you all set up."

"I, uh, have a cycle," Wenthi said. "Should I leave it there?"

"Oh, spirits, no, don't leave it there. Some auto will rip around and clip it. But you have a cycle, that's good. Are you a good rider?"

"Pretty good," Wenthi said.

A wicked grin crossed her lips. "I bet you are. Oh, my spirits, you are pretty." She grabbed both sides of his face and kissed him. "So good looking, such a good match for Daro—no Pathé, not in the street—" One hand moved like lightning and grabbed one dog as it darted out. "Bring your cycle down the drop alley, right over there. I've got space in the back shed down there. Close it up in there and come up through the dirt door. Come on, Daro—get Bisque there—let's get things started. I have rice and some cold chicken and we'll get the water going—I'm so happy to see you and I already like this Renzi friend of yours, we'll get you both set up very nicely, I've got rooms to let out for each of you, or one for both if you want, though we'll figure that out—"

She and Partinez went inside as her rapid-fire monologue continued, escorting the dogs into the house with them.

Wenthi didn't quite know what he was expecting from Niliza Dallatan, the crime queenpin of the 14th Senja, but it certainly was not all that. He dashed across the street—checking for anyone careening around the corner first—and went to the cycle. He unlocked the engine and put it into zero gear, then pushed it back across and down the steep alley next to the house. No need to waste any fuel for this.

He would need to get more fuel soon, and that was the key to the assignment. Once he was well established here—and he seemed to be on the start of a good road for that—he would ask questions about getting more petrol than his ration card allowed. That, hopefully, would lead him to the train robbers, and from there, to the—

There was a flash of memory—Nália's memory—of a denim jacket. An image of a flaming fist embroidered on the back. A woman's face, mouth and nose covered with a bandana, eyes dark. A hint of a name. Nic?

As soon as those images flashed through his mind, a flurry of angry emotions came up from Nália. She had let that slip, and given it to him. Something to work with.

Wenthi chuckled to himself, but almost slipped down the slope, nearly losing control of the cycle. It was absurdly steep, and he focused on holding it steady while minding every step until he reached the bottom. As Miss Dallatan said, there was a back shed, and a screen door leading into the basement of the house. Both were just open—no locks or latches engaged. That was surprising.

He rolled the cycle into the shed, taking a look around to see what else she had in there. Tools, chairs, boxes, various odds and ends. Some of it was probably contraband or stolen goods. So many reports of recovered goods, of cracked crime circles, involved properties she owned. It stood to reason she would have that here in her shed.

And she let a stranger just come in unsupervised.

A stranger she had welcomed into her home, with no hesitation.

That was not at all what Wenthi had expected. But it would, hopefully, make his job easier.

He closed up the shed and went in the house, climbing the rickety wooden steps. He emerged into a common room where a large metal tub was prominently in the center. Partinez, already stripped to the waist, was pumping water into the tub while eating a chicken leg. Now that Wenthi had a good look at him, he was decidedly fetching. Lean body, strong arms, piercing dark eyes.

"Are you going to bathe first?" Wenthi asked.

"It doesn't have to be first," Partinez said, putting down the chicken leg. "The tub is pretty big."

"That it is," Wenthi said, taking off his jacket and undershirt. "I mean, I know Miss Dallatan suggested it, but I didn't want to presume."

"Presume away," Partinez said, getting closer to him. "I spent four seasons in the solitary cell."

"Yeah," Wenthi said, wrapping an arm around Partinez's skinny waist. "I imagine that's leaving you pretty anxious."

"That's one word for it," Partinez said before putting his mouth on Wenthi's. This kiss was hard and rough, which Wenthi welcomed, grabbing Partinez by the belt loops of his denim pants and pulling his hips toward him. It was immediately evident that months in Hanez had left Partinez more than ready. Partinez's hand slid down Wenthi's body and caressed his crotch.

"Not wasting any time," Miss Dallatan said. She came into the room carrying a loaded tray, which she quickly put down. "Whatever you need, go ahead."

Partinez turned to her. "You want in on this?"

"That what you want, Renzi?" she asked. Partinez looked at him with expectation.

A pang of guilt washed through Wenthi—he knew neither of them would be interested in him if they knew who he really was. But he was here for a reason, and part of that was to fully insinuate himself into this part of the city, get people to know and trust him. He had to play the part as best he could.

"I'd be honored to have you join us," he said.

"I knew it was going to be a good day," she said, rubbing her hands together. She took one vial from the tray and sprinkled the powder on her tongue.

The *myco.*

Wenthi had known this would come up, but he didn't think it would be this soon. He bottled down the fear, all the stories he had been told in school about what the mushroom would do to one's brain. There was no way to object without giving himself away. His heart had already been pounding with excitement, lust, and fear melted and swirled into each other. He almost froze from panic.

It's fine.

A surety, a calm, surged from within him. From Nália. She had done this. She had done this many times.

It's fine.

Miss Dallatan came over to them, and her blue dress was off by the time she reached them. She took Wenthi's face in her hands and kissed him deeply, traces of the bitter mushroom dancing over his tongue. As the sensation filled his mouth, she kissed Partinez as well.

Her hands quickly found their way to the buttons of Wenthi's pants as

Partinez resumed kissing him. She started kissing Wenthi's chest as she got his pants off, and then helped Wenthi do the same to Partinez.

All the while, Wenthi was filled with warmth and connection—feeling her hands on him, her hands on Partinez, feeling himself through her hands, his lips through Partinez . . .

He stepped back, the entire sensation far too intense at first.

"It's been a bit," he said.

"I can feel that," Partinez said, his hands—which Wenthi felt as his own—caressing Wenthi's arm. "We can take our time, I think."

Miss Dallatan grinned. "I definitely want to take my time with you two." She took both their hands—Wenthi's touch extended beyond his own hands, through her, through Partinez, their hearts drumming in a syncopated rhythm with his own—and led them to the tub. "Let's get into the water, and into each other, and we'll get everything out of your systems."

21

Wenthi had dreamed as Nália.

He dreamed of racing on the 960, through the streets of Miahez. He dreamed being in her body as her legs hugged the cycle, shifting gears and going faster and faster, alongside the train tracks. Then he was her, in the bathtub, with Niliza and Partinez, kissing and touching and tasting. Then he was her, alone with him, the two of them, bodies intertwined, climaxing together—

[Disgusting.]

Nália's voice woke him around dawn, in Miss Dallatan's bed, his naked body curled into hers and Partinez's. Last night's adventures had gone from the bath to the sitting room, included a brief interlude where Lajina from the taco stand stopped by to make sure things were well in hand—which they definitely were at that point—and finally ended in Miss Dallatan's bed with all three of them spent, exhausted, and satisfied.

He hadn't had a night like that since the one after he'd been sworn into the patrol. He and Paulei and several others from their cadet class had cracked open a cask of rum and let their passions take them until sunrise. It was the traditional way to celebrate, after all; to feel that your brothers and sisters in uniform would be joined with you in heart and spirit and flesh.

Not quite the same as fucking two people that he'd just as soon as tether up and send to prison.

But that night was nowhere near as intense or as powerful as the one last night, and that had been due to the mushroom connection. It had faded while they slept, but Wenthi still felt a certain shadow of the sensation. Like Partinez and Miss Dallatan had been part of his own body, limbs that had now gone numb. It was a bit disconcerting to be just himself in his own body now.

Himself and Nália's buzzing thoughts, at least.

It was easy to see why the *myco* was so dangerous. The desire to do it again, to feel that extension of himself, that was powerful. He understood why so many people had fallen into the trap of taking too much, losing themselves to bliss.

Now he had the guilt of enjoying it so much. That, at least, overcame the fear of it.

Partinez definitely had quite a lot to work out after his time in Hanez, and now in the clear light of morning, no longer drunk on lust and climax, Wenthi's thoughts drifted to what Partinez had been arrested for to be locked in solitary at the penitentiary. For that, the Civil Patrol and Alliance Guard would have to have considered him violent and dangerous. The patrol officer at the impound lot knew him, had issue with him. That pressed more guilt into Wenthi's thoughts.

This was the assignment. Insinuate himself within the criminal circles of the *jifoz* in Ziaparr. Get into their lives, become a trusted friend. He hadn't expected to be this insinuated this quickly, but it was a good reminder of what this assignment was going to take. He would have to be deceptive. He would have to engender trusts that he was, at the center, violating. He would have to form close, intimate bonds that would allow him to get closer and closer to the cycle gangs—the flaming fist image he saw was part of that—and, ultimately, Varazina.

Though last night certainly was an *incredibly* enjoyable way to start that process, even if it was with people who were unsavory criminals.

It was also a reminder that he would have to cross very hard lines before this assignment was done. He would definitely have to use the *myco* again, connect with more minds and bodies, and use Nália as the shield to protect himself. It was clear that part worked.

Canwei had said Nália would be like a mask, but she was more like a filter in the moment. From what he could tell, all of his sensations and emotions in the moment, Partinez and Miss Dallatan felt, just as he felt theirs. But his fear, his sense of duty, his awareness of what he had to do for the mission—that didn't reach them, instead being covered by Nália's presence.

Like a perfume. He smelled like she ought to. So they had no sense of who he was, or what his true intentions were.

[Betrayals all around.]

Nália's voice, clear as daylight. Maybe she had managed to assert her will forward while he had slept. He was still waking up. He shoved her thoughts down into the darkness in the back of his head.

He slipped out of the bed and went to relieve his bladder, which was what had woken him up in the first place. When he finished and returned, Miss Dallatan was sitting up, awake.

"Well, that was certainly something," she said with a yawn. "I'm amazed you're on your feet."

"Never was a late sleeper," Wenthi said. "And I suppose I should make myself useful, hmm? I think there's some cleaning up to do in your main rooms."

"I imagine so," she said. "I'll get to it in due course. Though I should find you two proper places to bed down first."

"Not here?" Wenthi asked.

"Oh, no, boy," she said with a chuckle. She got out of the bed and trotted over to the water closet. "I do think you're both very nice but I relish not having anyone underfoot. But I've got a couple empty *fasai* up the curve that you two can take."

"Separate?" Wenthi asked. Not that he wanted to move in with either of them—he was going to need his privacy—but he had to act like Renzi Llionorco.

"Oh, definitely. You're going to need address cards for whenever they check you, and if two bucks straight out of Hanez shack in at the same *fasai*, the tories will notice and be more up your ass than either of us were."

"Good to know," Wenthi said, though he could hardly believe that. He never heard of anyone going after people just out of prison just because they stayed together.

She came out of the water closet, covered in a colored wrap. "But leave me those vouchers before we go up there. Damn near worthless for what they're supposed to be, but I can get something out of them."

"Why are they worthless?" Wenthi asked.

"Because to claim them, you have to register yourself as a licensed renter, that you own the property and have the right to rent it out, and that takes papers and cards and coin switching hands in the offices in Intown. And ain't nobody who's gonna do that bullshit also going to rent out a space to someone fresh off the train, hmm?"

"Except you."

"Oh, I ain't claiming them proper," she said. "But I know a fellow who knows people, and I'll get paid."

Wenthi didn't like the sound of that, but he kept it off his face. Renzi Llionorco wouldn't care. "I just want to make sure it's all fair for you."

"Thank you," she said. "Your people teach you to make coffee? Find your pants and get on that."

"Yes, ma'am," he said with a chuckle.

His pants, as well as other clothes, were on the floor where he had left them, next to the tub still filled with tepid, grungy water. He got dressed and went to the kitchen, finding everything he needed to make coffee. This was not a skill he had acquired until late in life, and the style of pot was not one he was familiar with.

But Nália was.

Her muscle memory took control for a moment as he prepared the pot and got it percolating, all before he realized that he really didn't know what he was doing.

Without any thoughts of hers bubbling to the surface.

He had pushed her thoughts down, kept her silent. He hadn't yet had a chance to really delve into her, figure out what she knew, how that could help him. He hadn't figured out how to use this connection he had been shackled with.

He hadn't had much chance to breathe on this assignment yet, get his footing about anything.

He could feel her pushing on him, like she wanted to speak, but he wasn't letting her. That's what that monster Shebiruht had said—he needed to have dominance.

He had lost dominance when making the coffee. She had taken control, at least the memory of her. He had used her skills, but not felt her intent.

Had that happened at all in the escapades of last night? Had taking the mushroom opened up her connection to him somehow? Had he tapped into Nália's knowledge or skills? He had felt that she had found Partinez as attractive as he did, and in some odd way she enjoyed the events as much as he did.

[You're an asshole.]

That was far clearer than he ever wanted. Instead of trying to lock her back down, he shot back at her.

What's your problem?

[You're an asshole.]

I'm doing my job.

[Your job is being an asshole. These people welcome you on a lie, and you glance around looking for ways to arrest them.]

Do you have something helpful to offer?

[Why would I help you?]

The sooner I complete this assignment, the sooner this bond is severed. I would love to get you out of my head.

[Same.]

So, we have a common goal.

[Do we, tory? As much as I hate—hate—being stuck as a passenger in your skull, at least in here, I can make your life miserable.]

You're only talking because I'm letting you. I'm going to get what I need from you, regardless.

[So why are you talking to me?]

Why was he? That was a good question.

Because I'd like it to be easier. I'd like to be able to report that you cooperated, they should go easy on you.

[Go easy on me?] This was followed by some creative profanity in Old Zapi. **[Do you think they're going to do anything but keep me locked in this box? Provided I can even wake up from this nightmare.]**

Why wouldn't you?

[Please. We both heard the stories about Shebiruht. We know what she did.]

This isn't like that. She's working with the government—

[She always did, tory. Just like you've been—]

Shut your shit up.

And with that, he shoved her down so deep that he couldn't even feel her push. That's where she could stay for now.

"Coffee ready?" Niliza asked as she came in, now fully dressed.

"Yes," Wenthi said. He went over to fetch it for her.

"No, I can get it. I don't need to be preened over." She poured herself a cup and sat at her table. "Now, I've got *fasai* for you around the curve. You'll be above the crystal shop, and that's run by Isilla Henáca and her boys, and sometimes her sister Anizé. Anizé also helps with things in the candy shop, and if you need a ride to carry something she's got a truck. She won't let you borrow it but she'll probably drive you wherever if she's not busy."

"I don't think I'll need—"

"Look, you don't have people, so let the Henáca family be your people, hmm? I'll be here, of course, but I've always got things going on. I don't want you to know only about me. And I'm going to put Daro in his old *fasai* above the carbon shop."

"You've been very kind," Wenthi said. "I don't know how to thank you."

"You ever been out of the pen before, Renzi?"

"First time."

"Yeah, you need people. And Daro made you his people by bringing you here, so you're here in this patch, these are your people. Wasn't it like that where you came from?"

"Not hardly," he said. "Everyone just kept their own."

"That's no way," she said. "But also, the tories will be coming to check on you. Check your papers and cards, check that you're working, that you're not, you know—"

"Being a crook again?"

She scoffed. "You're a *jifo* living on Street Xaomico in the 'hez. They'll treat you like a crook, regardless. But you don't want to get tethered up again, right?"

"No, ma'am."

"Don't you call me ma'am again; you've had your cock in too many places to do that. *Urka* Nili is just fine."

"If you say so."

"I most definitely do," she said. "And I'll take those vouchers, and I'll be asking you to earn your keep as well."

That was promising. He leaned in. "What will you need?"

"Well, you've got a cycle, which is huge. I can definitely find some small delivery work for you, if you can zoom these streets. You should start to learn them so you can get about."

That wasn't something Wenthi knew too well. He knew Intown well, and the parts of Lowtown where he was often assigned to patrol, but the 14th—

Miahez

—Miahez wasn't one he knew beyond the major streets and traffic circles. He touched his thoughts into Nália's, and was hit with memories and familiarity with several of those streets, as well as parts of Ako Favel, and flashes from the *baniz* slums of Gonetown up north.

"I'm a quick learner," he said.

"Real good," she said. "How are you on the cycle?"

"Pretty good," he said.

"You ever race?"

That was an odd question. "Never really tried."

"Folks do like to see a race, is what I'm saying. There's opportunity in that."

"Race where?"

"Plenty of places. Spirits, half the junkers that crack around the curve here are racing each other. If you want to try, you can easily get a chance. Some coin or ration chit in that."

That sounded like a good way to get his head cracked open on the pavement. "I think deliveries and such will be fine."

"All right," she said. "I will definitely have some of that for you as well."

She sipped her coffee. "Now go get Daro out of my damn bed. He's sleeping like the dead and I don't want him there all morning."

22

The crystal shop was little more than a concrete hut with a handful of shelves, loaded with jewelry made from local geodes and onyx, and the candy store next to it wasn't much bigger. Neither shop had proper doors, just wide archways with wrought-iron gates. It was around the curve beyond the temple—the temple was easily the most prominent structure in this patch of neighborhood—where Street Xaomico forked into two rustic roads, each barely a car-width wide. The candy shop faced out to one fork, the crystal shop to the other. Both shops were run by the two Henáca sisters, Isilla and Anizé.

When Niliza brought Wenthi over—with the three dogs in tow—the sisters spoke with Niliza with a clipped reserve. Wenthi presumed they didn't like Niliza or him.

Isilla Henáca sat on the lone stool in the crystal shop. She was one of those women whose age was impossible to gauge, somehow both youthful and weathered at once. She had to be around the same age as Niliza, since two of her sons—there were at least four—were about the same age as Lathéi. Those boys had been loitering about, and once Wenthi came over, they wandered over to the carbon shop—Partinez had headed over to the apartment above it with only a few terse words—and loitered in front of it. Instead Anizé, Isilla's sister, sat on the curb in front of the candy shop. She had that same sun-weathered look that Isilla had, which made her appear nearly *baniz*. She might have been *baniz*, though they weren't supposed to live in the 14th. Maybe she had a family exemption because of Isilla. Or maybe she was caste-jumping.

He could feel Nália growling at him for thinking that.

Wenthi pushed that aside. He had far more important things to do than bother over tethering a caste-jumper in the 14th. If she was, she'd get caught soon enough.

After a quiet exchange with Niliza—all while Anizé glared at him silently—Isilla came over to him.

"You want the room?" she asked coarsely. "It's a shitty room."

"It's fine," Wenthi said. "Happy for anything."

She stepped out onto the walkway and pointed up to the door above the shop. Just a door, three meters up. He realized the only way up was to climb up the iron gate.

"The stairs broke a while ago, so it's a *fasai* for a young man," Niliza said.

"It's shitty," Isilla added. "But if Niliza says it's yours, you have it."

"Thank you," he said. "Should I go up now?"

"If you want. Nenli went up and swept it a few days ago, so it's ready."

Wenthi climbed up the gate, and with a bit of a balancing act, was able to get the door open and step inside.

It was a room barely wider than twice his armspan, with a stained straw cot against one wall, and a metal bucket to piss in. There was no window, no other exit, besides the elevated door. Musky, damp odors filled the place, and there were spots on the wall that made it clear the tin roof leaked. A knotted rope was coiled up by the door, so at least getting back down shouldn't be too hard.

It was, as she said, shitty. But it would do.

He went back to the door, and he saw at least one interesting advantage. From up here, he could see most of the action on Street Xaomico, the zocalo, the carbon shop, and the little plaza next to it, and the window to Partinez's spot above the carbon shop. That last part might not be something he'd take advantage of any time soon—his gut said Partinez didn't get attached to repeat lovers—but it was good to know.

But from up here, he could see everyone in this patch, and from what he had already observed, no one would question him loitering about doing nothing. He could keep watch over the whole patch from up here easy.

All he had to do next was find a coinbox to check in with Paulei, and figure out what, exactly, Nália knew that he could use.

"This is fine," he called down.

"You need anything else right now?" Niliza asked.

"Not at the moment," he said, kicking the rope out the door. He scurried down to the ground. "I appreciate you all helping me out."

"Sure," Anizé said. "You any good in the kitchen?"

"Not very," Wenthi said. "I mean, I can cut stuff up all right."

"Then you can come help me make supper," she said. She pointed to the stairs going above the candy shop to the apartment up there.

"You get settled, get to know all of them," Niliza said, kissing him on the cheek. "I'm probably going to have some delivery work for you in a day or two, so stay sharp."

"Yes, *urka*," he said.

"Good, good, come on girls," she said, shepherding her dogs back toward her house.

"Hey," Isilla said, pointing a weathered finger at Wenthi. "I know she really likes to fuck, and she thinks everyone likes to fuck as much as she does. Don't be expecting that with us, hmm? Or my boys. That's why you stay up there."

"I had no expectations," Wenthi said.

"Good," Isilla said. "Last one she put up with us was like an alley cat."

"Exhausting," Anizé said. "I didn't cry when the tories took him back."

"You get a lot of freewalkers staying up here?" he asked. "Partinez seemed to think this street was the place to go."

Isilla shrugged. "Niliza likes her strays."

"So does she have a whole gang of them?" he asked.

"You'll probably find out," Anizé said. "Come up and help me. Watch both shops, Isilla."

"Shit yourself," Isilla snapped back, getting on her stool again. Anizé went up the stairs, giving no impression that she took her sister's retort as a refusal.

Wenthi's attention went back to the street, and the two autos that roared up around the curve, and then four patrol on cycles ripping up right behind. They were really buzzing, easily in passing gear, if not racing, but those Ungeke cycles weren't made to push that hard uphill, not in this heat. As the autos split off on separate routes at the fork, one of the cycles coughed and sputtered with smoke. He lost control and spun into the plaza next to the carbon shop, sparks flying as metal skidded across stone. Two of the cycle officers split off, staying on the racing auto, while the last one came to a screaming stop. He was on his radio, calling in a Seven Code as he ran over to his partner.

Wenthi's first instinct was to run over, see what they needed. The one who skidded might have snapped a bone, and his partner would probably need help before the wagon came. Where was the nearest hospital, or even wagon bay, in the 14th? There might be a few medics at the ready in the headquarters down in Circle Uilea, but the closest hospital was in the 12th.

He wanted to help. But Renzi Llionorco never would.

The officer got the cycle off his partner, got it kicked up back on its wheels. Smoke kept pouring out of it. The one who had crashed slowly got up. He wasn't too badly hurt; at least he was able to limp his way over to one of the tables outside the carbon shop. The other one barked a few things at the proprietor.

Then a handful of boys—*jifozi* kids, no older than twelve—started laughing, pointing at the smoking cycle. Both officers were on their feet, charging at the boys. The one who crashed grabbed the lead kid by the neck and threw him to the ground. The other snarled and snapped at the rest, reading them all that they could be brought into headquarters to get tethered, inked, and plated.

These kids should know better.

[Better than what?]

"Rude little shits," he muttered. "Just like you."

Nália didn't respond. But he could feel her burning with rage—rage at him, at the officers across the street, rage at the whole city. He sent his own rage back at her. He was already very ready to finish this assignment and be done with her.

All that must have been plain on his face, as Isilla looked at him, and then at the two officers slapping the kids. "Yeah, bunch of shitting assholes. Don't do anything stupid to get tethered all over again."

"No," he said. "Thank you, again. I'll go help your sister."

Hopefully he wouldn't be stuck here very long.

23

The next few days were spent settling into the routine of being Renzi Llionorco. He got to know Isilla and Anizé, and Isilla's sons Mando, Nenli, Oscez, and Tendiz. He was invited to meals with them regularly, though Anizé took his food ration cards in exchange. The meals were meager offerings of tinned meat, canned chiles, undercooked beans, and rice that had gone sour, but Wenthi knew Renzi would never complain about such dishes.

A point Nália would often remind him of when his concentration lapsed and she was able to bubble up to pester him. She teased him that he had grown up with his mother's servants, that even now with a patrol dorm in the *rhique* 9th Senja, he had *jifoz* servants taking care of meals and cleaning. She told him he'd never gotten his hands dirty once.

Go shit yourself. I actually lived through Great Noble. Where were you when Rodiguen was building camps? When the city was being bombed? People marching and starving on the Burning Road? I actually lived that.

[People are still living that shit, tory. And shit yourself, I was born in a purge camp.]

And I was a child in one. Just me and my sister, and you have no idea what it took to keep her alive in there.

[Because she's *llipe*? Oh, poor thing suffered once.]

Does that mean she—a toddler—deserved to have her head smashed in like so many threatened? To be starved?

Nália was quiet for a moment. **[No, of course not.]**

And we lived like that, just the two of us with whoever we could get to take care of us, for two years until the war ended. First in the camps, and then wandering the ruins of the Smokewalks after a bombing raid wrecked it.

[So you know. And yet you're blind to what's still happening here.]

He had learned how to keep her in a box, how to dip into her knowledge and skills. He hadn't cracked into her real secrets yet; she was able to keep that boxed from him. He spent most nights on his mattress focusing his thoughts on breaking through her defenses.

The days, he learned Street Xaomico. He chatted up Lajina at her taco cart in the zocalo, Mister Jendix at the carbon shop, Mister Osceba with two daughters and the mechanic shop at the bottom of the alley. He met "Doctor" Ojinzen, the holy woman of the temple, who tended to the spirit icons, and was also a regular lover of Miss Dallatan. He met the boys who liked to loiter in front of the carbon, the old men who spent the day dozing in the zocalo. He met every dog of Miss Dallatan and all the other neighbors. He met the cat that had no owner, but always managed to be in his apartment at sunrise.

Miss Dallatan gave him a few jobs for coin, which was good, since all his food ration cards were going to the Henáca family. Not that coin did him any good in getting petrol for the cycle. No amount of coin changed the fuel ration card, and his was pitiful. The jobs were mostly delivery—a bundle here, a package there, nothing that seemed explicitly illegal from what he could tell—but the tank of the 'goiz 960 was getting light, and he wasn't going to be able to put anything in it for several more days.

No wonder Nália had gotten into the petrol thieving racket. She needed to keep her own tank full.

When his ration day came up, he drove down to the fuel station at the bottom of the hill, at Circle Hiatea, with its statue of the Sehosian general of the same name prominently displayed in the center. The *jifozi* line was immense, though the pumps for *rhique* and *llipe* sat unused. He waited in line for an hour, until the service attendant came out and said the *jifozi* line was shut down. No more fuel rationed out to them.

While waiting, after thumbing through a magazine that gushed over Lathéi and her fashion choices, he had chatted up a pair of young *jifozi* women—real cycle cats like Nália, decked out in tight-riveted raw denim pants and jackets, shaded visors, and painted helmets. When the petrol station worker announced ration was used up for the day, the cats said they knew another one in the 12th that they could try. He rode with them to check it out, only to be stopped by patrol at the other side of the circle. They checked everyone's cards and declared they had no cause to cross into the 12th unless they had legitimate business there.

Fortunately, one of those patrol officers was a fellow named Andorn, from Wenthi's cadet cohort. Wenthi gave him a wink as he told them they were getting courier jobs with a shop in the 12th, and they would get their transit cards soon, but they needed to fuel their cycles here to be able to work. Andorn clued in, and told them they could pass, but not before giving Wenthi a clap across the head and telling him not to think he was getting away with any bullshit.

They were able to fuel up—or at least half the tank, since that's all he was rationed—and get back into the 14th without trouble. The girls mentioned a party out by the trenches in Ako Favel, and that gave Nália a moment of panic. Wenthi went out there with them, hoping it would give him some sort of lead to the cycle gangs and the petrol thieves. These ladies seemed like the type to be involved in that.

Instead it was just a burned-out lot, with cheap carbons, decent corn, and a loud band of guitarists and fiddlers. Wenthi soon found himself whispering to his spirits to send the patrol to bust it up. Those whispers were answered around seven on the fifty, as a dozen patrol cycles came roaring up. He got grabbed by a pair of patrol, who gave him a few smacks and threw him down, kicking him in the dirt a few times. The kicks weren't too hard—again, Andorn was in the group, and had obviously cued them in to make a show of it. It probably looked good for anyone who noticed, but it still stung. Someone threw a carbon bottle that cracked one of the other patrol across the head, and most of the group ran off after them. Andorn stayed behind for a moment.

"Assignment?" he asked in a low voice.

"Yeah," Wenthi said.

Andorn gave a fake kick. "That'll probably help you out. Good luck." He dashed off.

Wenthi got on his feet and stumbled over to his 'goiz. One of the girls was by her cycle, kicking it up.

"You all right?"

"I'll make it," he said as he got on his cycle. "But I'm gonna roar out of here."

"Same," she said. "See you on the stone." She jetted off, ripping through the lot so she could kick a wave of dust up at some of the patrol before flying away.

Wenthi didn't waste time getting out. Not that it would matter. It was clear this assignment was going to take as long as it would take.

24

Twenty days had passed, and the Garden Season of Komu passed into the Autumn Season of Tian. This usually meant the heat breaking, cool winds whipping through the streets. But this year, it was still damned hot. Wenthi had mimicked the other *jifoz* on Street Xaomico during the day, often walking about in cottons with his arms out, if not shirtless, and definitely no hat. That part was the strangest for him to get used to. Some of the other fellows occasionally wore a beat-up head duster or wide-brim, but it was hardly common or custom in these parts. Not wearing a hat was how to pass as a *jifoz* in this part of town.

Wenthi had known that was the custom; he had seen it plenty on his patrol cruises. He had seen it as a sign of how the people in Outtown had no manners. The *jifozi* who worked Intown always were respectful, but here? It wasn't done. So he didn't do it.

When running on his cycle—which was less and less often, given the status of his fuel tank—he would just wear Nália's denim coat with nothing underneath. That was a look that Partinez and quite a few others seemed to like, so he kept it up. It felt odd and uncomfortable, but it was befitting Renzi Llionorco.

He had nothing lined up for the day—*Urka* Nili had no deliveries, and he still had no line on the petrol thieves. He climbed down to the street, planning on heading to the coinbox outside the carbon shop so he could make a check-in call to Paulei, and then sit out front with Partinez and the Henáca boys, see where that led him today.

The curbway outside his apartment was lined with dry flowers, forming a path down the street, across the zocalo, and into the temple. Anizé Henáca was the only one in the shop, which was odd for this time, and she was wearing a bright blue wrap dress with a woven green shawl. Also, she was hardly minding the shop, instead her focus was on a dingy mirror as she put up her hair in complicated braids with dried flowers entwined in them.

"What's going on?" Wenthi asked.

"Morning," she said absently. She turned to give him a brief glance, and he saw half of her face was painted with a white skeleton pattern, like the spirit icons in the temple niches, with accents of red and purple around her eye. "That's what you're wearing?"

"For what?" he asked.

"Didn't you—you met Osceba, right? Narli Osceba, the one with the engine shop at the bottom of the alley?"

He had, briefly. Tendiz Henáca had mentioned that Osceba and his oldest daughter worked on cycles if he ever had a problem. "Yeah, in passing."

"Well, today's the Spirit Dance for his youngest daughter, Ziva."

Memories flooded up, not his own. Images of Nália, when she was fifteen, in a white dress, flowers of every color crowning her braided hair, her face painted and jeweled. Her uncle—really just the father of the family she lived with—walking her on the floral path to the temple, while one of the neighborhood women took her mother's role of wailing. Her Spirit Dance.

That stirred his own memories. Lathéi at fifteen, in a white dress, while her father led her in with other young men and women from her cohort and their fathers. Led into a ballroom for a presentation, before the heads of the prime families of Ziaparr, so each of them could be blessed. Wenthi had only watched from outside the ballroom, forbidden from entry.

When Wenthi had been fifteen, Alliance troops were the only thing marching through the streets of Ziaparr, maintaining discipline and order. Strict curfews and travel restrictions. No one celebrated in public that year, especially not the shameful *rhique* son of one of the city's Prime Families.

"Are you all right?" Anizé asked.

"Sorry," he said. "Just thinking about . . . it doesn't matter. I didn't know about it. I'll get out of your—"

"What, you aren't going to come?"

"I don't know Mister Osceba or his daughter . . ."

"*Urka* Niliza should have told you, given you . . . right, she wanted us to be your people. Never mind. You're part of this street, you should come."

She sighed. "Go to Mister Anlezri's *fasai* round the street and tell him I said you need to borrow something for the Spirit Dance."

"All right," Wenthi said, though he had only met Anlezri—an old tailor with bad eyes—a few times at the carbon.

"Then come back here and I'll paint you to be my escort. Better you than a nephew, after all."

"All right," he said. While Nália's memories gave him some sense of what was happening, what to expect, elements were still a bit fuzzy. Best to go along.

Anlezri's shop was closed—almost everyone's was today—but he opened up when Wenthi knocked.

"Llionorco, hmm?" the old man asked. "Am I in some trouble?"

"No," Wenthi said. "Anizé Henáca sent me to borrow something for the Spirit Dance? I don't have the right clothes."

"Oh, yes," Anlezri said with his eyes brightening. "You're lucky you caught me. Come in, come in." He led Wenthi into his dim shop. He rummaged through a few boxes.

"Thank you, I don't want to—"

"No bother, no bother, this is important," he said. "Are you escorting Anizé?"

"That's what she says."

"Lovely woman she is. You thinking of fathering with her?"

"I hadn't specifically," Wenthi said.

"I would, were I your age," he said. He let out a deep sigh. "I wasted too much time, you know. Only fathered one boy. He would have been a few years older—it doesn't matter. But I never got to walk a daughter to her dance. Think about that, Mister Llionorco. You should have fathered a child or two at your age."

"Not in this city," he said, finding a tearful choke coming to his throat. He wasn't even sure where that rush of emotion came from.

Nália. Thinking about her father. Arrested when she was a girl, she never saw him again.

"Here," the old man said. He came over with plain white linen slacks and vest. "Very respectful."

On Anlezri's prompting, Wenthi stripped off his denim and put on the linens. He was about to ask about shoes, but he was stopped by a flash of Nália's memory. Her uncle walking on the flowers in bare feet. No shoes.

"Nice," Anlezri said. "I'll hold on to these things so you have to come back for them."

"Fair," Wenthi said.

"You better hurry," Anlezri said. "Bells will chime in half a sweep."

Wenthi went back to the crystal shop, where Anizé had finished her hair—which was an astounding spectacle of braids and flowers and purple ribbons decorated with geode crystals. She was quite stunning.

"Very nice," she said. "Hands."

Taking her meaning, he presented his hands to her. She went to work painting skeletal bones on his hands. "You've not had many of these, have you."

"Where I grew up, we . . . we lost a lot of our daughters and nieces to the purges, you know?"

She nodded sagely. "Our side-brothers were conscripted into the army. Didn't make it. In this patch, we . . . we all have our people but we know we don't all have people. And I have nephews but . . . no nieces. No daughters ever."

"Ever?" he asked.

"Did that old knocker ask if you were going to father me any children?"

"He mentioned it."

She chuckled ruefully and put down her brushes. "You're welcome to try, but you won't have any luck." She raised up her blouse to show her belly, with a jagged scar tearing across it. "Just so you don't get any expectations."

"What happened?" he asked as she dropped the blouse. She went back to work painting his hands.

"My own souvenir from when they bombed the city. Shrapnel tore through me. Still have a piece in there, doctors said. Said I was lucky to survive it. Spirits of Apeilla and Ivala were looking over me." She pointed to the top shelf, above the crystal displays, where a small altar with two old tinplates sat with skeleton icons.

"They were?" Wenthi asked as he took a closer look at the women depicted in the tinplate. Two hard-looking women, definitely *baniz*, dressed in tie-up wraps he had only seen in history books. The tinplates had probably been taken during the height of the Shattered Dynasties.

"Great-great aunts," she said. "Watched over my mother and her mother. Both of them had no children, so . . ." She shook her brush at him. "Always honor the childless aunts, my friend. If you have any, put them on your shelf, one way or another, and make sure they are not forgotten."

Wenthi had had no aunts. Mother had no siblings, full or half or of any kind. She barely had any history that she spoke of at all. Sometimes it seemed like her life began as a young woman when the Second Trans ended and he was born. All she had been, all she ever was, was Angú Tungét, the sole matriarch and representative of the Tungét Root in the Prime Families, the lines from the noble houses of the Sehosian Empire who first colonized Pinogoz.

"Did I touch a spot with that?" she asked.

"Thinking about my mother," he said. "She . . ."

"You don't have to tell me," she said. "I run my mouth too much. My sister always says so."

The temple bells rang out.

"We should be ready," she said. "Come on out."

On the street, people came out of their shops and homes, all dressed in what were likely their nicest clothes. Isilla Henáca and her boys had dresses, stoles, and vests of the same blue and green as Anizé wore. The boys had the same patterns of bones on their hands and arm that had been painted on Wenthi, and Isilla had half her face painted similar to Anizé.

Glancing back at Anizé, Wenthi understood the distinctions of the skeletal designs on each of their faces. They were evoking the great-great aunts in the tinplate, Apeilla and Ivala.

As the crowds gathered on the curb, a young woman in dark denim stalked down the street on the floral path, singing out with a haunted voice. Wenthi knew the tune—Zoyua and the others had often hummed it while working in Mother's house—but he had never heard it sung with heart-rending anguish. The young woman was a figure of mourning—her face painted mostly black instead of white, and the flowers in her hair were decidedly dead.

[She mourns the end of youth. A mother crying that her child is now grown.]

"Is that the mother?" he whispered to Anizé. The woman seemed too young to have a daughter who was grown.

Anizé whispered back, "Older daughter, Ajiñe. Their mother . . . isn't around. So she's playing the role."

[Just like me. How many mothers actually get to wail for their child's walk in this city?]

Then Ziva Osceba came into view with her father guiding her arm, and she was a vision. Her dress of red and violet was resplendent with flowers, including a long cloak woven of living vines and flowers that trailed behind her. Her face was painted in a full spirit mask, white bone and black eyes, dressed with red and violet stones on her brows and cheeks. What stood out stronger than anything else was her crown.

The crown had been sculpted from steel and chrome—clearly scraps from Osceba's shop that had been lovingly repurposed and crafted into something beautiful—dressed with flowers to the top of its high peaks, towering almost a meter above her head.

And she walked, holding her head with serious dignity, until they reached the temple doors. The people of the neighborhood all followed behind, walking with the same deliberate pace. Some raised their own voices, joining Ajiñe in her lamentation.

Ajiñe reached the temple first, opening the doors carefully for Ziva as the young girl approached, her pace remaining steady.

"Take your last steps as a child," Mister Osceba said as they reached the doors. He released her arm as she went up the steps into the temple. As she went in, Ajiñe removed her shoes—she had been the only person on the street wearing any—and placed them at the top of the temple steps. Then she began to clap her hands: a hard, repeating staccato rhythm, which everyone else in the zocalo matched. The clapping built up, louder and faster. Wenthi joined in, partly from instinct of Nália's memories. He had never seen this, not up close, but he knew exactly how it needed to go, what would happen next.

He had seen all this before, of course. He had seen the painted faces, the floral dresses, the clapping and coming dance. He had seen it from his patrol cycle, cruising through the Outtown senjas. Putting out the call to disperse.

Even as he clapped, he felt the urge to join in clashing with the shameful need to break this up. Instinct kept telling him this was blocking the streets, disrupting the neighborhood, creating a nuisance. This display didn't need to be so . . . public.

Ziva emerged from the temple and stepped into her sister's shoes. Ajiñe took the crown off her sister's head and unhooked the floral cape, letting it drop to the ground. She kissed Ziva on the cheek, leaving a black mark behind, and whispered something. Ziva giggled and descended the steps with confidence. She reached the crowd and quickly grabbed the hands of two of the young men—one of them Mando Henáca—and pulled them into the center of the zocalo. Clinging to their skeletal hands, she spun and danced to the clapping rhythm. Now the singing became loud and joyful to match the rhythm.

Wenthi joined it, as he knew the words, even though they were in Old Zapi.

Nália knew the words.

She dances with dead ones.

They will watch her every day.

Her steps are always guided.

The path she walks is guarded.

She will join them too someday.

Then Anizé grabbed his hands and pulled him into the zocalo, and everyone in the neighborhood—everyone—seemed to join in on the dance.

Everyone danced, hands together, laughing and singing, and Ajiñe ran down the steps into the zocalo and swept her sister off her feet and held her in a tight embrace. Everyone cheered.

Then the radios—all the radios on the food carts and vendors in the zocalo—turned on, speaking all with one voice.

"Street Xaomico dances with the spirits of tomorrow, and the dead smile upon the faithful. But cold eyes are coming to see, roaring up to the top of the mountain. Be missing, be missing."

Immediately, Ajiñe put her sister back on the ground. "Go," she urged her. She looked to the rest of the people of the neighborhood. "Tories are coming, go."

People scattered, dashing off into their shops and homes. All of the Henáca family poured into their crystal shop, pulling down the iron grate. Several went into the carbon shop. Ajiñe went into an alley. Ziva ran up the steps into the temple, grabbing her flower cloak with her. Wenthi followed her, picking up her crown as he went in.

From the inner chamber of the temple, he looked back to the street. Rounding the deadeye curve: three Civil Patrol on cycles. They stopped in front of the zocalo and glanced about for a moment. One of them put in a call on his radio, and in a moment, there was a static burst of response. All three turned around and rode down around the slope.

Ziva was clutching Wenthi's arm, but she released it once the patrol cycles were out of sight.

"Sorry, sir," she said.

"It's all right," Wenthi told her. He handed her the crown. "Didn't want you to lose this."

"Thank you . . ." she said haltingly. "Mister—"

"Llionorco. Renzi."

"Thank you, Mister Renzi," she said. They cautiously emerged from the temple down to the zocalo, where Ajiñe came running over from her hiding place, her face paint smeared.

"Are you all right?" she asked her sister. "I'm sorry your dance—"

"I danced," Ziva said quickly. "They didn't ruin it."

"You're more forgiving than I would be."

Ajiñe frowned at Wenthi. "You're that new rider Miss Dallatan has. Thank you for helping her."

"Of course," he said. "Renzi."

Before she responded, the radios crackled on again.

"*The wheels need to grind, race for the people! Mud and petroleum will flow where the water doesn't. Spread the truth!*"

"What was—" Wenthi started.

"I need to go," Ajiñe said sharply. "Ziva, get home, see to Papa. I'll see you later. Thank you again, Renzi."

She ran off down the drop alley toward her father's shop.

Wenthi watched after her, making a polite excuse to leave Ziva. He wasn't entirely sure what just happened with the radios or anything else, but he was certain that wherever Ajiñe Osceba was going could lead him to the people he was looking for.

25

Ajiñe Osceba was a cycle rider.

Her cycle was like nothing Wenthi had seen, junked and bashed together out of parts from so many different models, it was entirely its own. It made Nália's 'goiz 960 look like it had come straight from a factory.

There was a spot outside the carbon shop, a little plaza that overhung the dirt alley behind the Street Xaomico houses, from which he could watch the Osceba shop without looking conspicuous. From there, he could also watch most of the comings and goings on Street Xaomico, the zocalo, and the carbon shop.

He sat on the ledge of the low stone wall, sipping at a Malkeja Dark carbon—all sweet and no taste, but dirt cheap—while she tuned and tweaked her cycle. His own cycle was parked in the plaza, and he sat with his helmet and goggles perched on the wall next to him. The couple of times anyone asked—mostly Henáca boys—he told them he had a delivery to make when he got a signal. They took this with deep understanding.

It was funny—he clearly looked like he was up to no good. If he, on duty as patrol, had seen a *jifozi* sitting on a wall, next to a cycle while dressed in unwashed denim, he would have immediately been on alert about them. In an Intown senja, or even parts of Outtown like the 11th or 12th, someone would have gone to a phonebox to call patrol on him.

In the 14th—**Miahez**, Nália's voice reminded him—they seemed to know he was up to no good, but accepted it as the sort of "up to no good" that they approved of. He was more than a little fascinated by how they had embraced him—for all they knew, a hardened criminal who would happily rob or assault them—with warmth and fellowship. But had he come here as a patrol officer—a pillar of community, law, and peace—he would have been reviled. If they knew who he really was, they would reject him.

But Renzi Llionorco, criminal scum, ex-prisoner? Welcomed to homes, tables, and beds.

He wondered how much longer he'd have to be here. He missed his own room in the 9th, missed Paulei, Minlei, Guand, Cinden, and Peshka. Even Hwokó; she was fun, even if brusque and abrasive. He missed Lathéi so much, more than a little mad that by the time he finished this mission, she might already be back in Dumamång. She, at least, he saw on the newsstands, as she regularly made the covers of newspapers and magazines as a fashion icon.

He even missed Aleiv, the little brat.

Ajiñe rolled her cycle up the alley steps to the street. It was nearly five sweep on the naught, the sun starting to set. He got on his own cycle, kicking up its engines just as Ajiñe was starting her own, so she wouldn't hear. Hopefully, she would lead him to something that would crack everything wide open. Find the petrol thieves, find the mysterious Varazina—that was her voice on the radio, surely—and then he could go home.

She rode down the streets, through the curves of Xaomico, down to the bottom of the gully. Wenthi followed, keeping enough distance that she wouldn't notice, and once they went through Circle Uilea there was enough other traffic that he could blend in, but not so much that he would lose her.

She rode out to the Ako Favel—the 16th Senja—the only part of Outtown more run-down and broken than the 14th. The neighborhood had been an army garrison during Rodiguen's reign, and had taken the brunt of the bombing during the Alliance assault. Now it was a *jifozi* slum, almost as bad as Gonetown.

Cheap tenements had been half reconstructed out of the barracks. A few excavation machines sat idly in scorched lots; stalled, half-built projects in disrepair. Autos and trucks could barely get through the streets here, rough roads with cracked pavement, or none. The railway and the elevated highways drummed overhead.

Was this how the rebels and Varazina stayed out of the watchful eye of the Alliance Guard and Civil Patrol, by hiding in this shithole?

Who even was this Varazina?

[She's the salvation.]

How do you even know that? You haven't met her. She's a voice on the radio.

[But a voice I trust.]

Why? What has she done to earn that trust?

[Besides bringing us together against the Alliance invaders?]

"Invaders" is not true. They defeated Rodiguen and freed us. They're helping us rebuild—

[It's so sad you believe that, tory.]

Wenthi was thinking he'd look conspicuous following Ajiñe here, but they were hardly the only cycle riders coming through the Favel. Several buzzed through, some in groups, many cycles with two riders, or a sidecar. Folks converging on the same place.

He drove up over one ridge, coming up on a channel of the old aqueducts, similar to the one where he caught Nália. This one, also completely dry, had dozens upon dozens of people camped out on the sloping walls, motorcycles of all sorts parked up on the ledges, and more down in the gully of the channel.

Wenthi wasn't sure if it was his own realization or Nália's bubbling up from her experience, but once he saw it, it was obvious. The channel split into two tunnels, one of which curved out to another channel, half a kilo away, and that led to an old war trench that fed back to the tunnel that led to this channel.

A racetrack.

He edged his cycle up to the ledge, looking for Ajiñe and her unique cycle. She had gone down into the gully, joining the other riders down there.

"That's a nice stallion you got under you," one fellow said, coming up to Wenthi. He was with a handful of rough *jifozi* folk, though instead of denim slacks and torn-up shirtsleeves, they were dolled up in suits and dresses from a generation ago. Vintage Second Trans fashion. Wide shoulders, grand lapels, muted colors. But the clothes had clearly been patched up, mismatched, and repurposed. The button-down blouses unbuttoned and tied up at the sternum, exposing plenty of rich skin. All of them sported absurdly wide-brimmed hats, as well as heavy eye-paint, sharp dark lines in cat-points.

It was almost as if they were dressed up as a mockery of prewar, high-class *rhique* and *llipe* fashion, a twisted mirror of the brass club crowd.

"Thanks," Wenthi said. More of them came over, showing their intense interest in his cycle.

"What is he, a tricked-up 1296?"

"He's a 'goiz 960," Wenthi said. Details from Nália's memory flooded in, every upgrade and tune-up. "But with a tran swap to six gears and a 1296's inline four."

"Wild," one of the ladies said. "How fast you clock him?"

The words were pulled from Nália's brimming excitement. "On a straight dry path, if I'm in fire gear and get revs to the white line, he could hit three hundred."

"Fuck," the first fellow said with appreciation. "Course you wouldn't get that down there."

"No," Wenthi said, looking at the curving aqueduct path. The whole thing, it probably was four kilos the whole round, and at best there were about six hundred meters of straight path.

"What could you manage there?" the lady asked. "Like, one-thirty-two?"

"I'd bet a liter he could do one-forty-four," one of the other folks said.

That got Wenthi's attention. "Shit, I could push to one-fifty-six." This brag was pure Nália. Wenthi was shocked the words came out of his mouth. He shoved her back down into the void.

"Five liters says you can't," the guy said, giving a wide, black-toothed grin.

"We betting rations chits here?" Wenthi asked.

"Rations?" the first fellow said. "The shit are you talking? Where did you come from?"

"Hanezcua," Wenthi said. "Most recent."

"Shit," the lady said. "Here, we don't bet on chits on our cards. That's bullshit. You bet with the fuel you got, and down there, you either win or go home empty."

"You what?" Wenthi asked.

"Hey, Paza!" the first guy was shouting. "We got a late entry! This fool thinks his tricked-up 960 can hit one-fifty-six!"

"Wait, I didn't say—" Wenthi started.

"You said it!" the guy said as someone—presumably Paza—came up the wall. "Five liters on clocking one fifty-six."

"I shouldn't—" Wenthi started to say, but then he noticed the racers were starting to get into position. And one of those racers was Ajiñe Osceba.

Paza—an older, portly man who was sweating through his pocket shirt—came lumbering over. "What's this? He a racer? You a racer, boy?"

"I guess I am," Wenthi said. "So let's get me down there."

26

"We've got a late entry!" Paza shouted as he led Wenthi, pushing his free-gear cycle, down the slope. "What's your name, son?"

"Renzi," he said. "Renzi Llionorco."

Paza looked at him for a moment. "You ain't one of old Ocullo's boys, are you?"

"No, sir," Wenthi said.

"Yeah, a bit too pale to come from that *baniz* cock. Come on!" He whistled over to the other race folks as they reached the floor of the aqueduct gully. "Draw from his tank and add it to the prize!"

A couple of folks in denim coveralls ran over to Wenthi's cycle with siphon hoses and opened up his tank.

"How much?" he asked.

"A quint is the entry fee," one of the coveralls said. "We add it to the bladder of the prize fuel."

Wenthi noticed the bladder. No wonder why there were so many racers in this—it looked like a prize of at least twenty liters. Plus the five he had at stake for getting the cycle up to one-fifty-six. After the trouble he had just getting fuel in his tank at all, he understood why all these racers were risking a quint for it. That kind of fuel was more than any of them could hope to get with their *jifoz* rations. Literally what money couldn't buy.

"That's a quint," the other coverall said, expertly stopping the siphon as their container filled without spilling a drop. These two obviously had a lot of practice at that. Wenthi wondered if they were part of the gangs robbing the tanker trains. Between the cycles and the siphoning, the skills were here. However, nothing here clicked with memories or emotions from Nália. This hadn't been her scene.

"How many laps is the race?" he asked.

"Six," the first coverall said.

Six laps, and about four kilos a lap, so he would have to make it two dozen kilos, win the race, hit a top speed of one-fifty-six, and not run out of fuel before he finished. He checked the petrol gauge. He should make it, but he doubted he'd be able to pay the five-liter bet if he failed. Nor would he be able to ride home.

Ajiñe had noticed him, giving him an odd regard. Somewhere between annoyance and curiosity.

"Line up!" Paza shouted. The other racers—about two dozen—rolled their cycles over to a chalk line on the ground. The gully here was only wide enough for six cycles, so they stacked up behind each other in an order that seemed to come from unspoken agreement. Wenthi took position in the last tier, noting that Ajiñe was in the front.

Wenthi looked back to the prize bladder. Definitely more petrol than could be possible from a quint donation from each of the racers. It had to have been acquired through illegal means. So the race organizers were either part of the petrol-theft gangs, or they had a connection. But why would they give fuel away as a race prize?

Why even the race? No one had fuel to spare; it seemed like a waste.

"Mount up!"

Everyone got on their cycles, but still had their engines cold. Helmets and goggles went on, which Wenthi did as well.

"And at the horn!"

Wenthi wasn't sure what the horn meant, and he was more than a little surprised at the answer. The two coveralled folks strutted in front of the cycles on the chalk line, one with a brass trumpet in hand. They unzipped their coveralls and let them drop to the ground, revealing only tight denim shorts and open jackets and, exposing quite a bit of tawny copper *jifoz* skin. Everyone in the crowd—as well as the riders—hooted and hollered as one of them raised up the trumpet and let loose with a magnificent blast.

All the engines kicked up, roaring to life, and all the cycles surged forward as one.

Immediately, three of the cycles in the middle tiers knocked into each other, throwing them off course into the steep wall of the gully, while the ones in front rocketed out ahead of the pack. Wenthi dodged around the crash, weaving past the other racers as he shifted into building gear, then cruising, then passing as he hit the hard curve that led to the first tunnel. It was a sharp right as the gully split into a fork, with the left fork down the dry gully blocked off with wood pallets and concrete blocks.

The tunnel wound and curved like a brass note dance, and in the dark, the only thing Wenthi had to gauge it with was the taillights in front of him. Too narrow to pass, unless he banked up on the sloping wall. Couldn't risk that, not without knowing where he was. Couldn't risk shifting up to racing gear in here, speed topping out at ninety-six. The cycle behind him couldn't pass, just nip at his rear tire.

A screeching crash of metal echoed behind him just as he emerged back out into the open, the second stretch of aqueduct gully. Wenthi gunned the throttle, the rev gauge driving up to a hard six near the white line as he shifted to racing gear, driving to the one-thirties, shifting up to fire. The engine howled as he hurtled down the straightaway, as long as it lasted. Maxed at one-thirty-nine, passing three cycles along the way, leaving behind that follower who wanted to eat his heels.

The straightaway took another hard curve—he knocked back down to passing as he skidded into the turn—then a series of winds he had to zag his way through, sliding up on the aqueduct bank. Ahead of him, at least eight cycles. One of them threaded the needle of skating the banks to pass each one.

Shit, that took brass.

The gully dropped down with another hard right, dropping into the old war trench. It looked like someone had taken dynamite to the aqueduct wall to make the opening, and piled the rubble in the gully path to force the riders into the trench. Here, it was narrow as all get out. Trench walls, where soldiers in the First Trans had bunkered down to hold off Imperial forces—or was it Reloumic?—were at best two meters apart. As the path snaked through, there was no room for error, no chance to pass, and no way to build much speed past eighty kilos.

One cycle ahead must have blown a tire, as it flipped over, sending the rider flying out of the trench. The cycle skidded and sparked as it came to a stop, and the cycle in front of Wenthi slowed to at least sixty to pass in the narrow space left to get through.

The trench then dropped out to a steep hill into the second tunnel. This one didn't weave, but was just one long, hard curve that did a full half circle in the dark. Wenthi pushed hard—this tunnel was wider than the first—and held the turn as he shifted up into racing gear, getting up to one-twenty as the gauges whined. He slipped around the cycle ahead of him just as the tunnel ended, and they emerged back out to the main gully, the shouting crowds.

Six cycles ahead of him, Wenthi pushed it into fire gear. Five laps to go.

27

At the end of the fifth lap, Wenthi had managed to creep his way to the frontrunners, with only two riders ahead of him: someone on a red junk-bashed Ungeke, and Ajiñe Osceba. And with only one lap left, he hadn't managed to crack one-fifty clicks. He couldn't afford to lose the race, especially if he didn't hit that speed.

"You're being too cautious on the curves," Nália said. "My baby can take it."

She wasn't in his head. She was on the back of the cycle, arms clutched about his waist, whispering in his ear with perfect clarity despite the racing winds.

"The fuck—"

"You're going to lose," she said.

"I've got this," he said.

"Then kick up to fire gear and get past that asshole on the junkbash," she said. He hadn't pushed past racing gear on this stretch, and the temperature gauge was showing things were scorching hot. He didn't know how much more the cycle could take if he went any harder.

"This baby can take it," she said. "Let me."

She said that, and in a disorienting flash, she was in front, hands on the bars, gunning the throttle so the revs rammed well into the white. Wenthi was on back, clutching her.

And somewhere in the dark, in the cold, only muffled beeping sounds in the distance.

In the moments it took him to attune and acclimate to what was going on, she had shifted up to fire, gunned her way up the slope, and then slammed back down to the channel in front of the junkbash, speed never dropping below one-thirty as she weaved the curve. She didn't step down to racing gear until she hit the tunnel.

Ajiñe was powering well ahead of them in the tunnel, moving like she was made of light. Despite that Nália pushed hard, laughing as she whipped through the curves that Wenthi had been cautious about.

"Crash!" Wenthi shouted as they fired up to a pile of three cycles all but blocking the tunnel.

"See it," Nália said, banking on the slope of the tunnel, never losing more than a hair of her speed.

She was fucking incredible.

They popped out of the tunnel, Ajiñe half the length of the straightaway ahead.

Nália let loose, shifting to fire and pushing the revs well past the wide. Temp gauge screamed, Wenthi felt his legs—Nália's legs—no, his, only he was on the cycle, only his body—he couldn't keep it straight—singe with the searing heat from the engine. He was sure it would blow any second.

Speedometer kept driving up as Nália closed the distance. One-forty-eight. One-fifty. One-fifty-two.

"You're out of straight!" he shouted. The curve was coming faster than he could imagine, and they were about to taste Ajiñe's wheel.

"Like shit I am!"

Wenthi glanced at the speedometer as she came up to the curve.

One-sixty-two.

Sweet fucking spirits, she did it.

She hit the brake hard, down shifting as they made the turn, dropping into the trench. No place to pass here, and Ajiñe still had that lead. No way to get past her, and every gauge on the cycle was telling Wenthi that the engine was on the verge of exploding. White and gray smoke was already pouring out of the manifold.

"We're gonna blow!"

"I know my baby!"

She didn't let up, staying right on Ajiñe like they were tethered together. As they dropped into the second tunnel, she made her move.

Except Ajiñe was ready. Nália banked up the tunnel way to make the pass, and Ajiñe gunned it and matched the back. Curve for curve, bank for bank, she kept with them and made it impossible to pass.

"Shit!" Nália shouted.

They emerged out of the tunnel, the crowd wild. There was enough space for Nália to push to the left and get around Ajiñe, all while gunning back up to fire gear. Ajiñe didn't let up, even as Nália inched her way up on her.

Both cycles had smoke pouring out, ridiculous amounts.

Nália still pushed. She was relentless.

As she edged up, the half-dressed attendants waved their coveralls like wild.

Ajiñe skidded to a hard stop, and Nália did the same, overshooting the chalk line massively, leaving a tearing skid mark across the floor of the channel.

Soon the other cycles—the red junkbash and the other ones that remained, came screaming down, crossing the chalk line.

"Amazing!" Paza shouted in his megaphone. "By only a tire, the winner is Ajiñe Osceba!"

Ajiñe was off her cycle, which was still smoking, and she grinned maniacally as she took her helmet off.

"And in second, newcomer Renzi Llionorco! Let's hear it, folks!"

The crowd screamed wildly.

"You really did it," Wenthi told Nália.

Except she wasn't there anymore. It was just him, in his body, still sitting on the cycle. He turned off the engine—the damn thing needed to cool, and it was amazing it didn't explode. Probably the only reason it didn't was because it had nearly no petrol left in it.

Nália had fallen back into being just a cold, angry feeling in the bottom of his skull.

Several of the other racers got off their cycle, came and shook his hand, and then went to Ajiñe to do the same. Paza walked over as well.

"I wasn't sure you had it in you, son," he said. "That last lap, though, it was like one of your spirits filled you."

"Something like that."

The pair of suited folks came over to them. "So did he hit it."

"One-sixty-two," Wenthi said.

"How do I know you're not lying?"

Ajiñe came over. "He was gaining on me while I was doing one-fifty-two. No way he could do that unless he was going at least one-fifty-six."

The suited man grumbled. "Fair's fair. I'll go siphon off five liters for you."

He and his entourage wandered off.

"Thanks," Wenthi said. "I wouldn't have had the fuel to get home without that."

"Quite the race you had in you," she said. "And we're both going home with more fuel. Nice."

"You do this often?" he asked.

"Among other things," she said. "Hey, once we're fueled and our cycles cool the shit down, how about we get some tacos and talk?"

28

The crowd slowly dispersed from the aqueducts, and Wenthi was surprised that it didn't involve patrol breaking it up. A few casual questions of Paza and the folks he had won the five liters off of made it clear this was a somewhat regular occurrence. He found it astounding that something like these races, with a crowd of onlookers and a set track, could have been going on without patrol being aware.

Of course, this was on the outskirts of the Ako Favel, at the edge of the city. Parts that had taken heavy fire in the Second Trans, and had been all but obliterated in the Great Noble. Save for the stretch where the rail line came through, he had never been called to ride out here on patrol. No one cared. Maybe someone was slipped some coin or ration chits to not care.

He'd let Paulei know about it on his next check-in.

He was also shocked that, despite the smoke that had been pouring out of the engine at the end of the race, the 'goiz seemed to be in good shape once it cooled down. A piston damned well should have seized, and he had no idea why it hadn't. Or why Nália had been so certain that it wouldn't, that the cycle could handle that kind of abuse.

"If you want, you can use our shop to check your boy out," Ajiñe said as they wheeled their cycles out of the gully and back to the road. "I'm guessing you've got a couple hoses that melted a bit." She leaned in to the 'goiz and sniffed. "Yeah, both coolant and oil."

"I didn't come out here planning to race," he said. "I got kind of pulled into it."

"Yeah," she said, giving him a skeptical look. "We're gonna talk about that, friend. But let's make sure you can get back to Street Xaomico." She knelt down next to his cycle. "Yeah, I see the hoses you blew."

"Shit," he said.

"Are you gonna need oil or coolant right away?"

He checked the reservoirs while she dug in her bag, taking out a roll of tape. They were definitely low, but not completely empty. She finished her work and stood back up.

"That's pretty ugly, but it'll hold you back to our shop. Long as you don't push your boy at all."

"Definitely not," he said.

She looked at him, her dark eyes drinking him in. "Interesting," she said after a long pause.

"What?"

"Come on," she said, getting on her cycle. "There's a good stand that serves all night in Circle Hyunma."

He followed her there, keeping his eye on all the gauges and never daring to go past cruising gear. The 'goiz held up, but he could feel something wasn't quite right, and that feeling wasn't just from Nália's wordless grumbling in the back of his head.

He still didn't understand what had happened with her in the race. Their connection didn't just have intensity, but a real . . . tangibility. Like their bodies were a singular thing, for just a moment. That occluded darkness he felt—was that what she was experiencing, sedated in the ice room? Why had their connection intensified during the race? Was it just her love of the race, the cycle itself? She took control, and she wanted to win as much as he did.

Whatever it was, it had been a strain on her, as she was now all but silent. Just a low rumble of emotion at the base of his skull.

They reached the taco stand—a cart with a wood grill parked under the statue of Hyunma, a Sehosian pilot in the First Trans whose exact significance Wenthi had forgotten after finishing his history courses—where the two cart chefs were still hard at work, and more than a few patrons were eating at the scattered tables about the square. This deep into the night, Wenthi was surprised there were as many people as there were.

"You're buying," Ajiñe said as they walked up.

"Why am I?"

"Because you came in second," she said. "Winners don't buy their own tacos. It's a rule."

"Fine," he said. He did have a bit of coin to spare for it, thanks to Miss Niliza's deliveries. "What'll you have?"

She grinned and leaned over to the cart chef. "What are you grilling?"

The chef launched into it. "We got the sweet pork, the sharp fish, we got the rajas and the Ureti beef and the fruit pork, the tang chicken, the city cheese, the crumbly cheese, we got all the corn, the tomatoes, the chiles, the tomatillos. We got spice and for the salsa, we got the fired red and the burning orange and the sweet green."

"The best damn cart," she said to Wenthi. "Give me a sharp fish, a tang chicken, an Ureti beef, city cheese on all of that, an ear with the raina."

"Salsas?"

"Fired red on the beef and chicken, green on the fish."

"And you, *zyiza*?" the cart chef asked Wenthi. "What are you getting?"

"Sweet pork and fruit pork, both with crumbly," he said. "And a tang chicken with the rajas. Sweet green for all of it."

"No corn?"

"Give him an ear, raina and cheese," Ajiñe said. "He deserves it."

"You're gonna break me," he said.

"I'm gonna help you fix your hoses in my papa's shop," she said. "So you'll be fine."

"Fair."

"What's the name?" the chef asked.

"Llionorco," she told him. "All right, racer, let's sit."

They took a spot at one of the wooden tables scattered around the taco stand in the patch of park in the center of the traffic circle.

"So, Llionorco, what's the story?"

"The story?"

"You following me to the races."

He shrugged, trying to decide the best way to play this. "You caught my eye at your sister's Spirit Dance. You were cool on your toes when the tories whipped around."

"You too," she said. "And you watched over Ziva, and her crown. So I was inclined to think well of you."

"I appreciate that."

"But," she said sharply, "you're also new blood in this city, and you've already made close friends on Street Xaomico."

"I wouldn't say close."

"Your cock has been in at least three people on that street, so that's close enough."

"Are we keeping count?"

"I'm making note," she said. "I mean, Miss Niliza likes you, but she likes a lot of people. You came to our patch right when you got your walking papers from the prison train?"

"Not right to it. But I met Daro on the train, and he said he knew where I could use the vouchers to stay."

"So he brought you over."

"You knew that already," he said.

"I always have my eye open when new meat comes to the patch. Especially when he comes on a cycle."

"That got your attention?"

"A custom tricked Puegoiz 960? Shit, yes. You don't see many of those."

"I suppose not," Wenthi said.

"Llionorco!" the cart chef called.

"Go get our order."

Wenthi went over to the cart, where the chef had laid out the whole order on a tray made out of a hubcap. "I need that back, son."

"Sure," Wenthi said.

He took the tacos and corn ears over to the table, where Ajiñe had acquired a pair of carbons. These were bright piñas instead of a cola, and were probably crazy sweet. Which was fine. She handed one to him as he put their tacos on the table.

"So," she said, picking up a taco, "you come here from Hanez, but you get your cycle back from impound, and settle in on Street Xaomico, in good with Miss Niliza, running piece for her. Not bad for a new bit of meat."

"If you say so," he said. He tucked into the fruit pork first—seasoned with a sweet fruit mash, seared and served with cilantro and onions and the fruit relish, then with a crumble of cheese and the tomatillo salsa. He had had the same taco a month before at the brass club—fancy and highly priced on Lathéi's credit—and had thought that one was astounding. But this taco—this one was sublime in ways the expensive ones could never touch. "Dear spirits, that is so good."

"I told you," she said. "Love this place after a race."

"I can see why."

"So," she said, working on her sharp fish. "Normally I wouldn't give a kilo of shit about some new side of beef, but you've got that cycle, and you showed tonight, you can really ride."

"I didn't win." He took a swig of the piña carbon. A little too sweet, but fine.

"Everyone on that track who isn't me didn't win," she said. "But you came shitting close."

"Close doesn't mean much."

"You won your side bet, aren't going home empty."

"I suppose," he said. He glanced over to her cycle, with the bladders of her winnings strapped onto it. "But you really scored."

"Is that what you raced for?" she asked.

"Of course," he said. "I've been puttering by on my petrol rations. I needed something to make the difference." The fruit pork done, he moved onto the tang chicken. This had been a specialty of Izamio's in Mother's household, and more than a few times Wenthi had sat in the kitchen studying while she prepared the chicken. Marinated in a paste of ground chile, orange juice and zest, garlic and vinegar, it was always sweet and acidic, and that first bite took him all the way back to that. "Wow."

"You've got to stop doing that."

"Sorry, it just made me think of Iza, she—she took care of me a lot when I was a kid."

"One of your side-mothers?"

"Not exactly," he said. "Never knew my father, so, I . . . didn't know any side-mothers either."

"Sorry," she said. "How come you didn't know your father? Did he get it in one of the purges?"

He knew he shouldn't say it, but the truth poured out of him. "Died before I was born, at the end of the Second Trans. My mother, she . . . she never talked much about him. I had side-fathers, of course, but, well, I think he was something special to her."

"Yeah," she said. "My mother, she got taken for the mines during the Great Noble, five days after Ziva was born. My father, he . . . people told him he should Bind up again, but he said he had never broken union with my mother, so it wouldn't be right. Raised Ziva and me in that garage by himself."

"He seems a good sort," Wenthi said. A few more swigs of the carbon to wash down the heat of the salsas. She had devoured all her tacos and was working on the corn.

"But you, you I'm still figuring out, Renzi Llionorco, driving a custom 'goiz 960."

"What do you want to figure out?"

"What someone like you wants," she said.

He shrugged. "What does anyone want? A good meal, a good race, a good fuck—"

"Don't get ahead of yourself here, Llionorco. Like I said, still figuring you out."

"I wasn't presuming."

"Yeah," she said. "So you followed me tonight. Hoping to just peel me out of my denim or something more?"

"What more would there be?" The sweet pork was just as good as the others, if a hint spicier than he expected. He had to wash that one down with the carbon, even if it was sickly sweet.

"That's what I want to know. Are you just a piece of meat, biding his time until he's back at Hanez . . . or are you wanting to be something bigger?"

"Bigger?"

"Or . . ." she said, leaning in, "are you already part of something?"

"What do you mean?"

"I'm wondering if you're a patrol officer working some infil angle."

"That's ridi—" he started to say, but his mouth felt numb, no longer quite obeying him.

"Not that ridiculous," she said. Suddenly two more people were sitting at the table, shoulder to shoulder with Wenthi on either side, pressing against him. The two men from the truck, the ones he made the bet with.

He wanted to say something else in protest, but his mouth and tongue were completely out of his control. Ajiñe, across from him, was becoming a blur, even as the fancily dressed woman from the truck came and took her hand. He tried to stand up, but his legs refused to move at all.

"I'm glad you enjoyed the tacos, Renzi," Ajiñe said. "Because the Fists of Zapi are going to find out what you want, and if we don't like it, *zyiza* . . . that's the last thing you'll ever eat."

REFUEL: MEMORY

Half in the black.

Half in the quiet.

Half in the numb, empty body. Cold room, muted beeps.

Drowning in nothing, with only the tether of a shithole tory as a chance to breathe. Constantly fighting through the dark, dead void just to catch a gasp.

And then the race. The rush. The speed pulling her to him, fully in a body. Fully on a cycle—her cycle, her sweet baby—with the rush in her hair and her heart and throbbing fire from the engine up her legs into her cock.

His. His body.

Not hers.

But still hers, at least for the fleeting seconds of the race. Beautiful, amazing seconds where she and the tory and the cycle were all working together, pushing harder and faster as they closed the inches between them and the frontrunner. Almost won it.

Then the race ended, and as they came to a stop, as the glorious speed faded away, she found herself slammed back down into the void.

Darker, harder, deeper than ever.

She clawed her way up to find, at least, her own body, muted and numb as it was.

In the distance, there was a hint of light, of heat, of motion. She pulled her way through the sickly sweet of the empty void toward it. It must be the tory, the shit that he was. Maybe he was fucking the girl who won. Or fucking Partinez again. Or getting ready to betray them all.

Asshole.

She reached out and grabbed the light and pulled herself to it.

The world exploded.

She was in the bunker, as everything shook again. The next round of bombing had started. It had been relentless. She was huddled under the table, like Mother told her, her sister cradled in her arms.

This time, she was sure, the roof would not hold.

This time, she was sure, Mother wouldn't come back.

This time, she was sure, the soldiers would find them. Maybe the Alliance's. Maybe the tyrant's.

There was no knowing which one would be worse.

Mother had said the 7th Senja was now no one's—they were fighting circle to circle, street to street, inch to inch.

All while the bombers dropped another round of fire and death.

"It's all right, Lathéi," she whispered to her sister, too small and young to understand. She barely understood.

The walls shook again. They certainly wouldn't hold and Mother would never—

Nália pushed back. This wasn't her.

She never knew her mother.

She never cared for a baby sister. She never had a baby sister.

She had been a baby during the Great Noble. Born in a purge camp. Hidden in the floorboards. Kept from the guards. In the dark as the ceiling—the floor—shook with every step.

Everything dark. The void swallowed her again.

Her body being moved.

Not hers.

His body.

In the black.

In the quiet.

Numb and empty.

And no spark of light from Wenthi Tungét, save the labyrinth of horror in his memory.

She reached for it. It was all she had in the abyss of nothing.

THIRD CIRCUIT:

THE FISTS OF ZAPI

29

Ajiñe casually finished the last of her corn while Fenito and Mensi loaded Renzi and his cycle into the back of the truck. Three tacos and an ear, and she was still hungry.

She was almost always hungry, though.

She gave a few more coins to the cart chef. He deserved it just for the tacos, but also for turning an eye from the business of dosing Renzi and taking him and his cycle away. The chef knew the score. He wasn't in the movement, but he had the loyalty. He was as much a proud Zapi as the rest of them, a *jifoz* who knew his home soil.

And he did make damned good tacos.

"Where you want to take him?" Gabrána asked. She was still dressed in her raceside finery, which was a whole thing Ajiñe never quite understood. Most of them looked like frippy fools, just like the Intown *rhique* who wore those clothes twelve years ago. Gabrána loved those outfits, though. Wore them whenever she could, no matter how damned impractical it was. Her wide-brim hat was very cute, though, at least on Gabrána. Ajiñe would never dress that way, not with engine work to do and cycles to ride.

But Gab wasn't one to ride the cycles, even when out on the street for a run. She was brains and eyes.

"Nic is already at the bomb-out in the valley by Street Cohecta?"

"Course she is," Gab said. "So what's the buzz with this guy? What have you figured?"

"Nothing yet," Ajiñe said. "My gut says he's a tory, but that's not what he tastes like. So if he is what he claims to be, he can ride like a dog bites. We need someone like that."

"Sure do," Gab said. "Can I ride your back while they take the truck?"

Ajiñe caressed Gab's beautifully blush-painted cheek with the back of her hand. "Spirits, girl, you know you're always welcome."

"But I always ask."

"That's what I like about you." She gave a little grin to Gab as she went to her cycle, unclipping the tie-downs that held the petrol bladders of her winnings. "I was going to take the Angpica drop, though."

"Because you have to beat them to the spot?" Gab rolled her eyes. "Everything's a race to you."

"Absolutely," Ajiñe said. With a quick whistle, she tossed the bladders to Fenito and Mensi. "So get on if you're coming."

Fenito and Mensi rumbled off in the truck, Renzi out cold in the bed, next to "his" 'goiz 960 and Ajiñe's race winnings. Ajiñe got on her cycle, Gabrána getting on behind her, gathering up her skirt with one hand while wrapping the other arm tight around Ajiñe's waist.

They wound their way through one sheer alley, up to the edge road that had a sharp overlook on Circle Hyunma and that stupid shitty statue. This road was too narrow for the truck, and led up the little mountain in the middle of Miahez, weaving curves the whole way until it reached a fork—one way would take her around the back to Street Xaomico, and the other to Street Angpica that dropped back down hard. Down into the valley below, the worst parts of Miahez that got bombed down in the last war and never rebuilt.

Gab howled with joy as they went over the last crest and dropped down the hill at a ripping pace. Ajiñe kept her cycle in free gear and cut the engine, saving as much fuel as she could. Gravity would do the work, taking them down to the valley faster and faster. Ajiñe had done this run plenty of times, dangerous as it was, but never with anyone clasping onto her back. Gab's grip tightened as she squealed, and Ajiñe couldn't tell if it was out of terror or excitement. Probably a bit of both.

Normally, Ajiñe would let herself fly, but she wasn't going to risk that with Gab on the back. Weight was different, the turns would be as well. She relied a lot more on the brake than she normally would. She still whipped her way down, so for Gabrána it was just as thrilling and terrifying and fast as any ride down Street Angpica ought to be.

They reached the traffic circle at the bottom—which was empty at this sweep—as Ajiñe kicked the engine back to life and flew around it, emerging on Street Cohecta.

"You're crazy!" Gabrána shouted over the wind.

"You love it!"

Two swipes of the clock later, they pulled up in front of the bomb-out. Once a boarding tenement, before the tyrant, before the Tyrant's War—

Great Noble, indeed—before the *baniz* were taken out of here and brought to the purge camps.

Of course, the purge camps were now Gonetown, and there were no *baniz* in this part of the city. At least, not legally. There probably were a few families in one of the abandoned apartments in the bomb-out. But not the one they were using. All the *baniz* who hid out here knew well enough to steer clear.

"It's going to be a quarter-stint at least before they get here," Gabrána said. There were only a few roads that were wide enough for the truck to manage, and they would have to take a roundabout route to navigate to Street Cohecta. "What ever will we do to pass the time?"

Ajiñe put her cycle into free gear and wheeled it into the building. "Like Nicalla isn't already here, and like we don't have work to do."

"Maybe she is, and maybe that doesn't matter," Gabrána said. "You've already got me riled, *zyiza*."

"A quarter-stint isn't *that* much time," Ajiñe said as she locked down her cycle outside the apartment door. A little regretful, but her mood wasn't in the same place as Gabrána right now. "And we've got work to do."

Gabrána sighed. "I suppose you're right." She leaned in close to Ajiñe. "Is it all right if I leave my lipstick on you, though?"

"Always." Ajiñe almost never painted her face outside of ceremonies, while Gabrána never stepped into the street without a fully made-up look. How she achieved that on *jifoz* rations was a mystery. Her lips were always lush, glorious, and red.

"Good." Gabrána hooked her arms around Ajiñe's neck and kissed her, passionate enough to leave her mark on Ajiñe's lips, but controlled enough to not mar her own makeup. The sort of kiss that would normally get Ajiñe's transmission into the same gear as Gab was at, but her head was elsewhere.

The Renzi problem tasked her.

Gabrána must have sensed that. "Let's not dally," she said in a breathy whisper as she pulled away. "Like you said, Nicalla is waiting."

They went inside the bomb-out apartment, where they were greeted by flickering light, tinny radio drama, and the churning drone of the petrol generator that powered the place. Nicalla lay splayed out, face-down on the floor, writing notes in her book while checking a map of the city. She glanced up at them through her carbon-bottle-thick glasses.

"You were kissing in the hallway, weren't you?"

"We considered more, darling," Gabrána said. "But we know how much you don't like that."

"Gross," Nicalla said. This time, she did not add her usual refrain of, "This is where we work, kindly don't turn it into a fuck-den." Ajiñe usually respected Nicalla's feelings in this, but the fact was she—and everyone else in the cell—lived in a tiny *fasai* with several other people. Papa and Ziva, in Ajiñe's case. Having any private space to have sex, especially with the rest of her cell, the people she loved and trusted the most? There were times when it was too tempting to pass up. Especially after they did any job where they were on the same *myco* together, synced up and energized. Nicalla was the only one in the cell who refrained, and she did so thoroughly and completely. Not with anyone in the cell, not with anyone anywhere, as far as Ajiñe knew. For those post-mission celebrations, she tended to intentionally drop her connection from the rest of them.

"We get word of any—"

"No," Nicalla said, pushing herself up on her elbows. "And I'm glad. I hate it when Varazina cuts into my stories to give us instructions."

"Your stories are Sehosian prop," Gabrána said. "I don't know how you can enjoy them."

"I know it's Sehosian prop," Nicalla said. "I can still like them."

Ajiñe knew both of them well enough to know they could go on for some time bickering at each other, and there wasn't time for that. The boys were coming with Renzi, and things would need to be settled soon.

"Clear the floor," Ajiñe said. "And get the chair. We've got a lot to do before dawn breaks."

30

Ajiñe helped Nicalla clear up her work—which was important work, of course. Nicalla kept track of the jobs, listened for Varazina's instructions, knew how to communicate with the other cells. She was the one who recruited new folks. Ajiñe worried that the girl spent too much time holed up in this dusty bomb-out, but she never belittled her.

Gabrána brought out the chair, with its iron shackles welded at the armrests and feet, and further steel reinforcement. She put it in its designated spot in the middle of the floor, quickly latching it into the small hooks they had put into the concrete. No one would easily get out of the chair once they had them in there.

Which is where Renzi Llionorco would be shortly.

"You're sure about doing this?" Nicalla asked. "Usually we recruit with a bit more subtlety."

"You tell me when you see his cycle. I never met the two who got pinched, or saw the girl's cycle. You're the one who said it was a modified bash from a 'goiz 960."

"Yeah, but—"

"It's very simple," Gabrána said, taking off her hat and lying down on the cot they kept in the corner. "We need to check this Renzi fellow out, and I'd rather not waste a moment."

Nicalla's eyes went to Ajiñe. "You think you want him with us?"

"If he's really the person he presents himself as, he'd be perfect. If he's what I think he is, we need to get rid of him now."

"That's the real thing," Gabrána said. "Flush out every tory spy as soon as possible."

"You're wrong, again," Nicalla said. "If we actually find a tory working to infiltrate, we should use that."

"Too damned risky," Ajiñe said.

"And she likes risk," Gabrána added.

The door opened, and Fenito came in with the inert body of Renzi over his shoulder. "Mensi is stashing the truck and will bring the cycle when he comes."

"But you think I'm right about that ride?" Ajiñe asked.

"I don't know," Fenito said as he laid Renzi on the floor. "I mean, yeah, it's a souped-up 'goiz, but—"

But none of them had met the girl who got pinched or had seen her cycle, except for Nicalla.

"Let's not waste any more time," Gabrána said, coming over to Renzi. "He's likely to come to any swipe."

"Right," Ajiñe said. She knelt down with Gab and Fenito as they stripped Renzi's clothes off. No hidden weapons, nothing that was an obvious telltale sign that he was really a tory. Not that she was entirely sure what that would look like. Once they had him naked, they shackled him into the chair.

"These slacks are the real thing," Gab said, sniffing at them. "Old denim, with years of oil and shop work baked into them." Ajiñe took them from her and smelled them, rubbing her finger on the fabric.

"That's true," she said. "But it's not like tories can't get ahold of real *jifoz* oil-cat clothes. All they have to do is steal from the people they lock up."

"And that's what you think?" Fenito asked. "He's a tory, wearing the clothes and driving the cycle of the new girl who got pinched?"

"I think we can't ignore that possibility."

"We probably can't ignore that he's got a gorgeous body, either," Gab said, running a finger across Renzi's well-muscled chest.

"That really should not be a consideration," Nicalla said.

"It's not, truly," Gab said. "If we learn he's a tory, of course, we have to smash in his skull. But if he isn't, well . . . he truly has a beautiful cock."

"Gabrána!" Nicalla snapped.

"Tell me I'm wrong. Ajiñe, you really can't tell me I'm wrong."

"She's not wrong," Fenito said with a wicked smile.

"Stop talking about his cock," Nicalla said. "I am begging to you and the spirits who watch over you, and do *not kneel in front of the chair,* Fenito."

"I'm checking him for scars or such," Fenito said. "I'm not a complete lustball."

"Yes, all his scars," Gabrána added. "He does have a few on his back."

Ajiñe went and looked. There was a patchwork of old scarring, the sort that looked like he had been burned in childhood. Maybe he had been caught in one of the bombing runs.

Fenito had moved to looking at Renzi's hands. "Fingernails are ragged, grease and dirt under them. Not very tory."

"He's been on Street Xaomico almost a whole season. Long enough to grow those out."

"I'm just saying, this guy doesn't look like he's been living a *rhique* or *llipe* life like most tories we come across."

"Right," Nicalla said, coming a bit closer. "But—"

"What do you see?" Gabrána asked.

"Don't you think he looks, you know, almost too fair?"

Ajiñe nodded. "Maybe. Like if he cleaned up, maybe he could pass for *rhique*."

"Some might say that about me," Gabrána said with a teasing tone. She held out her bare arm next to Renzi's. "Pretty close."

Gabrána did have the lightest complexion of the lot of them, and she was absolutely a *jifozi* girl. Renzi was no lighter. Maybe Ajiñe was just being silly. Maybe Renzi was exactly what he claimed to be.

They had to be sure.

"Are you done molesting him?" Nicalla asked. "I really don't need to look at all that."

"Get a handle on yourself," Ajiñe said. "When he wakes up, we're going to ask him some questions, and if we still aren't sure, we're going to do a mushroom test."

Nicalla pursed her lips in a grimace. "How much of a mushroom test?"

"We need to really get inside him, right?" Fenito asked. "So, I mean . . . we might need . . . at least one of us . . ."

"All of us is best," Gabrána said. "Not Nic, of course."

"Thank you," Nicalla said bitterly.

"But we have to presume—as distasteful as this business is—we have to presume if he's a tory spy, that he's at least somewhat expecting to use the mushroom, right?" She looked over to Nicalla.

Nicalla nodded begrudgingly. "Yeah, the Circle Piondo cell had that one Alliance infiltrator who had a few mushroom fucks with a number of them, and they didn't suspect her through all that. Only found her out when they were all connected at once during an after-mission celebration."

"All of them at once was too intense, she dropped her guard," Gabrána said.

"So, is that what we'll do?" Fenito asked, taking off his coat and boots.

"Spirits, the lot of you," Nicalla said. "No, it's better if we all connect with him but . . . we push him, not rape him."

Nicalla had a point. "We don't need to be fucking to make the bonds," Ajiñe said.

"But having all of us in the circuit, all pushing," Gabrána said. "He might be able to hold back against one or two—especially within pleasure—but five? No way."

"Thank you," Nicalla said. "I'll get our mushroom." She went to the cabinets.

The door opened, and Mensi wheeled in the 'goiz 960. "He's not awake yet?"

"You might have overdone spiking his carbon," Ajiñe said. She pointed to the cycle and looked expectantly at Nicalla.

Nicalla came over and crouched next to it. "I mean, bear in mind, I only met the girl once with her cycle, and I'm not the gearfiend you are. But . . . yeah, that looks like her ride."

"That is sketchy," Mensi said. "Didn't you say he just got out of Hanez?"

"That's what I heard."

"And this is his cycle?"

"Rode in on it with Partinez."

Gabrána made a noise of disgust. Partinez was not her favorite person.

"Did you ask Partinez about it?"

"No, I didn't want Renzi knowing we were looking at him at all."

Mensi paced about Renzi. "When I got out of Hanez all I got were the clothes I had when I was pinched. No one I've known who got their free-walking ever got anything more. So how did he come out with a cycle?"

"I'm right, it's suspect," Ajiñe said. "I've never heard that."

"And if we're wrong?" Fenito asked. "If he's not a tory, and he can ride like that? We need someone like him, especially with those new kids pinched."

"Then let's stop talking about it," Nicalla said. She opened up a carbon bottle and spooned a few grams of their mushroom into it. Ajiñe never understood why Nicalla preferred to mix it into a carbon instead of taking it straight on her tongue, but it was fine. Nicalla took a swig out of the bottle and passed it around.

They all took a drink and joined hands, and let the moment take shape.

Ajiñe was holding hands with Fenito and Gabrána, and soon her sense of self spread through their bodies, their heartbeats drumming in sync with her own. Then it went farther, into Mensi and Nicalla, including feeling Nic's nervous breath, the hint of panic clawing up the back of her skull. She knew Nic was *edoromé*—she did not care for this connection or physical intimacy—but despite that, she felt the same love and kinship from Nic that the rest of them shared. Nic wasn't less committed, she just didn't enjoy this.

"Open his mouth," Ajiñe said, taking the bottle. She poured the rest down Renzi's throat while Gab held his mouth open. She ran a finger along his face, feeling that tingle of connection with him feeling herself through him.

Nic's hand instinctively went to her own face. "Let's get this done."

"Right," Ajiñe said. "Cover your faces, friends. Let's wake him up."

31

This was not how they recruited new members for their cell. If that was what they were going to do.

It was how they dealt with traitors and infiltrators. If that was what Renzi was.

He blinked and looked about groggily from the salt pop Gabrána put under his nose. She was now wearing a white skull spirit mask to hide her face, as were the rest of the group. Ajiñe didn't put one on, she knew it didn't matter. Renzi knew her, knew her face. No need to bother protecting herself. But her cell, her dear loves, they needed to stay protected.

Renzi took in his surroundings, and Ajiñe could feel his confusion. And . . . there was another emotion simmering underneath. She couldn't quite get a taste of it. Not something he was hiding, but like it was buried.

Also, he was cold.

He looked down, regarding his naked body and shackled hands.

"You didn't have to go to these lengths to get me naked, Miss Osceba," he said slowly. "I mean, I was already amenable."

"Hush up, son," Gabrána said, running her finger along his bare arm. Pushing her sync up against him.

"What is this all about?" he asked.

"It's about you, Llionorco," Ajiñe said. "We're not sure what to make of you."

"What do you mean to make of me?"

"We've got the questions," Fenito said, taking hold of Renzi's wrist. Nicalla, standing behind Renzi's chair, took hold of his head and kept him focused on Ajiñe.

"All right," Renzi said. His confusion still ran hot, and that had an edge of fear to it. His heart hammered, his breath quickened, and Ajiñe's own body matched the response. But now the undercurrent to his emotions became clear to her. It was an ocean of calm that held him together, cool and collected. "And we're . . . we're all on the same mushroom sync, aren't we?"

"So we'll feel you lying," she said, kneeling down in front of him.

"We'll all feel you," Mensi said, kneeling next to her. The two of them gripped his leg. Now the circuit between them all was complete, like electricity flowing between them all, with Renzi as the resistor.

"I'm not sure what this is all about," he said. "Are you mad I entered the race? That I almost beat you?"

"You know that's not what this is about, Renzi," she said. "But let's start with the race. More specifically, your cycle."

"What about it?"

"Where did you get it?" she asked.

"How did you get it?" Fenito asked.

"I—" There was a hint of hesitation through him. A flash of heat, sweat to his palms. Like he was about to lie, but then the calm washed through again. A decision. "It was from patrol impound."

"So this isn't *your* cycle," Mensi said.

"No, but—" Renzi sighed. "Look, I went to Hanez on a trump up. Someone robbed a petrol shop, shot the clerk. The patrol grabbed me because

I was a *jifoz* on a cycle dressed the same way, so they decided close enough. In a snap, I was pressed and plated and sentenced."

Ajiñe looked to the others reading their eyes and their hearts. They felt what she did, that Renzi was telling something true. They all knew half a dozen people each who had been falsely arrested by tories who just hassled whichever *jifoz* they spotted first, who went to prison for things they didn't do. It happened every damned day. "What does that have to do with this cycle?"

"Getting to it," he said. "Some do-gooder *rhique* lawyer got her teeth in my case and proved that I was innocent."

"How'd you get that?" Gabrána asked.

"She just decided to get into that fight. I mean, there are a few *rhique* who are decent folk."

Ajiñe accepted that. She had heard of a few *rhique*—a few—doing things like that to prove the system wasn't completely rigged against the undercastes. It was bunk, but it at least got a couple innocent people out of prison. Which surely made those *rhique* do-gooders feel happy about themselves. "You didn't ask?"

"I said very little to her besides, 'thank you, miss.' Didn't care why. She got me my walking papers and my property was supposed to be returned to me. As in my cycle."

"That's not your cycle," Fenito reiterated. Despite that, they all could feel Renzi's heart, his lungs, the emotions flashing through him. Annoyance, fear, discomfort. But not deception. If he was a tory, they would certainly feel him crackling against them, like they always did on the street.

"Because *my* cycle was already junked when I got out. Apparently that lawyer made a whole thing that they had to make good on that, that if they failed to do so, it broke faith with honest civilianry—it was above my head, frankly. So she got them to give me something—a cycle that had just showed up in impound to replace mine."

"Do you know whose cycle that is?" Nicalla asked.

"Someone you know, I gather?" he asked. "I mean, it's a great cycle, it stands out."

"Not quite knew," Ajiñe said. "But she was part of what we are. Part of something bigger."

He raised an eyebrow. Curiosity surged through his mind. "Bigger how?"

"We're asking the questions," Gabrána said.

"Was she arrested for sedition or treason or something?" he asked.

Ajiñe stood up and looked him in the eyes. She was satisfied that he was telling the truth. There was no way, with all of them feeling him with the mushroom connections, he could have held it up. Certainly a straight-laced, linen-wearing tory, who never dared use the mushroom, wouldn't be able to do it.

If he wasn't an infiltrator, then she wanted him as an asset.

"Let me ask you, Renzi. You've been to prison. You got set up as an innocent man. So you know how little justice there is for the undercastes."

"I do," he said. "It was bad where I came from, and it's worse here."

"The girl who rode that cycle, she got arrested trying to do something about that. And now you're here, with that cycle, and my spirits would all attest that you know how to ride."

"I do," he said.

"We have a need for someone like that."

"Like what?"

"Someone with skills," Gabrána said.

"And who wants to use them," Mensi added.

"To break the choke the Unity and the Alliance has on us," Fenito said. "And give this country back to the people."

That gave him pause. "And I can do all that by riding a cycle."

"The way you ride?" Ajiñe asked. "Just maybe."

He shook his head. "And that's why you drugged me and shackled me naked to a chair?"

"We had to know if you were the real thing."

"You can feel us back," Gabrána said. "You know we mean it."

"We're very serious about this," Ajiñe said. "The people in this room, but also so many more people in the movement. The question is, Renzi Llionorco, what do you want?"

He looked around at them all. "I think I want to take my clothes and cycle and go home. I . . . I'm not saying no, but . . . I need to really think about this."

32

Dawn had fully broken into day by the time Ajiñe rode back to the family garage. Renzi had agreed to be blindfolded and kept tied up as they took him and his cycle away from the bomb-out. From a safe location in a different ruined neighborhood of Miahez, with everyone else gone, Ajiñe took off his blindfold and undid his shackles, and then rode back with him to Street Xaomico.

"Do you want to bring your cycle into the shop?" she asked him when they arrived.

"Seriously?" he asked.

"I made that offer before."

"Before you drugged and shackled me."

"Still stands."

He scowled, but then nodded. "Not like I don't need to fix those hoses and tune everything."

"I'll help you with that," she said. "Whether or not you want in with what we're doing."

His expression softened. "I appreciate it."

She led him over to the shop, which was surprisingly not open yet. Papa usually had the gate open and was busy working at this hour. Of course, she was usually around to get them all going and open things up at this hour. She unlocked the cast-iron gate and pulled it up, opening up the garage. Renzi wheeled his cycle into one of the work bays.

"Do you want to get started now?" she asked.

"I think we should both get some proper sleep," he said. "Let's say I come back at four on the naught?"

"Lovely," she said. "See you then."

He went off, and she went up the back stair to the *fasai*. He was right, she needed to get onto her bed, and for once she could sleep in it alone since Ziva would be up and about.

Ziva was, in fact, up and about, but sitting on the kitchen floor with Papa, both of them crying.

"Hey, hey," she said, coming over and kneeling with them. "What's going on? Are you all right?"

Papa looked up and a sad smile came to his face. "You're finally home, *doqui*. Did you have a good race? Did you win?"

"Yes, I won," she said. "But what's going on?"

"Just a sad old man," he said. "Nothing for you to worry about."

"Don't do that, Papa," Ziva said. "His rations have been cut down."

"What?"

"They slashed his rations," Ziva said. "Because he no longer has a child to support."

"The shit is this?"

"He got a letter stating that since I've declared myself an adult"—because she had done her Spirit Dance—"I am no longer, legally, a child, and thus not for him to support."

"That's bullshit," Ajiñe said. "So what about your rations?"

"I'm not yet entitled to my own," Ziva said. "The office told me that a fifteen-year-old girl is not eligible for ration benefits because I'm not eligible for work credits."

"That makes no sense," Ajiñe said. "How can you be too young to work but no longer a child?"

"That's what they said, I'm telling you."

Ajiñe was of half a mind to kick in the doors of that office with a wrench in her hand and make them explain it to her. Not that it would help. It made no sense, but nothing the shit-mouthed ration offices did—or anything the Alliance overseers did—made any damnable sense. Yet another kick in the teeth to anyone born *jifoz*.

"We're barely getting by on the rations we get," Papa said. "But you girls shouldn't worry. I will do what must be done." He was always too proud, too ready to kill himself for their sake. He needed to know he wasn't alone.

"No, Papa," Ajiñe said, taking his hands. "We are all in this together. I've got coin right now, and I can get more, and we can make up some of the shortfall with that."

"Coin can't go that far," he said. "And I don't want you to do any—"

"Don't worry about how I get it."

He pulled himself to his feet. "It's my place to worry. I am the parent here. You shouldn't have to—"

"We'll all get through this," Ziva said. "I'll go to Miss Dallatan. I'll earn my—"

"I'll talk to her," Ajiñe said. The last thing she wanted was Ziva taking on underhanded jobs for Miss Dallatan. There would be enough trouble right now, especially since the Spirit Dance had gotten Ziva noticed. They would keep eyes on her, to trap her when she slipped. "I don't want you doing—"

"I don't like either of you—"

"You don't have to protect me—"

"Stop!" Ajiñe shouted. "Papa, just keep running the shop. It will work out. Zi, I will talk to Miss Dallatan about helping get you a job that will earn you proper ration credit."

"But—"

"At least on paper. You're going to want that."

Ziva scowled. "Fine."

"There's a cycle down in the shop, it belongs to the Llionorco boy."

"You talked to him?" Ziva asked. "He's very pretty."

"He is," Papa said. "And that means trouble."

"I'm the trouble, Papa," Ajiñe said. "But he's going to come work on the cycle with me around four sweep. I need to sleep, so one of you wake me at three sweep fifty." She took coins and bills out of her pocket. "Meantime, buy some tacos from Lajina, some carbons and crisp from the carbon shop. We'll figure out ration later."

"What about fuel?" Papa asked.

"That I got covered. And I'll be able to trade some for more grocer ration chits." She kissed her father on the forehead. "We'll get it done."

"You do too much, *doqui*."

"We all do," she said. She peeled off her boots and went into the back. "Now let me sleep a bit."

She dropped down on the bed and fell asleep hard, but then woke up just as fast two sweeps later. A sudden start from a dream where a young *jifozi* girl—a cycle cat in denim on a junkbash—screamed for her to help, but Ajiñe couldn't hear her or reach her. It was far more intense of a dream than she usually had, vibrant and almost tangible, but she wasn't sure what to make of it. Maybe she was thinking about what she was going to do about Ziva.

Shit. She'd go see Miss Dallatan.

She put on clean denim slacks—at least ones that didn't stink of sweat and oil—and tied up the shirt to show off her bare stomach. Miss Dallatan liked that sort of thing. If she needed to mess around with the old lady a bit to get her help, that was fine. At least Miss Dallatan knew what she was doing.

She went down to the street and knocked on the gate, setting off all three of the dogs. She should have expected that. They started barking up a storm, which got Miss Dallatan, wrapped in just a woven blanket, out to the gate.

"Ajiñe," she said, peering through her glasses. "You don't usually come to me in the middle of the day. Something up?" She opened the gate, shooing the dogs back. "You're looking prettier than usual, so you want something."

"Am I that obvious?"

"You're usually as subtle as a brick in the face, dear. Which is what I like about you. Come in."

She closed the gate and brought her into the house. "Did you hear what happened to my father?" Ajiñe asked.

Miss Dallatan went to the icebox and pulled out a couple bottles of Arlacasta. She was the only one on Street Xaomico to have good stuff like that. Ajiñe wondered if she was getting it out for the charity of it, or just as a demonstration of her own wealth and power. It could be either with Miss Dallatan. Either way, Ajiñe took it and savored the sweet, rich goodness.

"Let me guess. They got wind of Ziva doing her Spirit Dance so they cut his parental rations?"

"Exactly."

"And left Ziva with nothing because she's too young to earn her own?"

"You've heard this song before."

"It's been around longer than I have," Miss Dallatan said. "Somewhere in the Shattered years, when this city was under the Reloumene, they made that policy to force undercaste folks into stopping Spirit Dances. Didn't work, but, well, they love enforcing the policy anyway."

"Can you help us?"

"I don't know, what can Ziva do?"

"She's patched up these pants pretty good," Ajiñe said, lifting her leg to show off the patch on the large rip going through the crotch of the pants. She also showed off the hole that Ziva didn't patch, hoping the flash of skin would keep Miss Dallatan's attention. "And she's the one who can cook."

"All right, I'll ask around. Maybe there's a taco shop or meat stand that needs an apprentice. I could get Anlezri to apprentice her at the tailor shop, but . . ."

"But?"

"He does like to have his apprentices watch him touch himself . . ."

"The meat stand would be lovely," Ajiñe said firmly.

"I can—" Miss Dallatan said before her radio went from the Sehosian Orchestra to a cool alto voice.

"No rest for the wicked, dear friends, the trucks are rolling and the people are hungry. Ride hard and fast to feed them all."

Miss Dallatan raised an eyebrow. "Is that what I think it is?"

"Yeah," Ajiñe said. "That was Varazina. She just gave me a new mission." She finished the last of the Arlacasta—not going to waste that—and kissed Miss Dallatan warmly. "Thank you for Ziva."

"I like that girl, and your father." Miss Dallatan grabbed her ass and squeezed. "You're pretty good too. But you've got important things to do. I'll see you later."

33

Ajiñe went down the street to the phonebox, where she passed Renzi walking back up.

"We still on for working the cycle?" he asked.

"You tell me," she said.

"I thought so."

"I need to make a call," she said. "Go over to the shop, my papa is expecting you. Be there in a bit."

"Sure," he said. "Everything all right?"

"I don't know," she said. "Let me make the call and I'll let you know."

He shrugged and went back up.

The phonebox was like most of the ones in this part of town: an ugly steel box with the door ripped off, papered with Alliance propaganda about giving more and paying back the debt—the shit they know about debt?—and then those prop sheets torn and written over.

She got in and called into the switchboard.

"Connection?"

"Fourteen-Atreina-Seven-Seven."

"One moment." The buzz and click of the switchover, and then the ring of the other end of the line.

"Well?" Nicalla's voice on the line.

They all knew that the shitheads, both the Civil Patrol and the Alliance Guard, would listen in on calls, even in the phoneboxes. Not that they knew who was on the lines: Ajiñe was in a public box, and Nicalla's box was rigged up with trick switches so even the shitheads couldn't track it. Nicalla was too smart for them.

Still, they had to be careful what they said.

"I heard our old friend was looking for me," Ajiñe said.

"That's true," Nicalla said. "She was hoping you could do a favor."

"Is it her usual favor?"

"No," Nicalla said. "She was hoping you'd help her with dinner."

That meant food delivery trucks.

"I'd always love to help. Do you think I should invite a new friend for dinner?"

Nicalla paused for a moment. "Yes, I think this would be a good time for him to come."

"Is that you or our old friend saying that?"

"It's my decision," Nicalla said. "And I think it's a good idea. If he's hungry and wants to join us."

"I'm going to go ask him. When should we come over?"

"See you tonight at six sweep on the naught. And make sure you all have clean shirts on."

"I understand," Ajiñe said. There were a number of places around Outtown where they had arranged to meet before a mission. Tonight, it was in the alley behind the laundry shop on Circle Yendwei. "Tell the family I miss them."

An instruction to have the rest of the cell hold back, in case of ambush. She still had doubts about Renzi, and if she was going to bring him in, she'd minimize the risk.

"They'll see you there," Nicalla said. "And everyone will be eager for a taste of what's being cooked up tonight."

"Great," Ajiñe said. "See you tonight."

She hung up and got out of the box fast, walking into the circle grocer across the street, cutting through and out the back of the store. Then up the alley to wrap around her way back to Street Xaomico. An absurd series of precautions, because it was unlikely the patrol were specifically tapping that call. Even if they were, even more unlikely that they also were watching that box, or could send a pair of tories to cycle past it quick enough to see who made the call. But Ajiñe had too much to lose to not take extra care.

She made her way to Papa's shop, where Renzi was already sitting on the ground with Papa, swapping out the burnt hoses.

"He's got a good machine here," Papa said. "Don't know who thought it was a good idea to put an inline four from a 1296 in this—I bet the heat singes your leg—"

"Little bit," Renzi said. "That's why my pants have the mark here."

"But he's a tight machine for a junkbash 960." Papa laughed with approval. "Needs new oil and coolant, though."

"Do you have that to spare?" Renzi asked.

"Not for free, boy," Papa said.

"No, of course," Renzi said. "I wasn't expecting that."

"I'll go fetch it." Papa walked past Ajiñe, tapping her on the arm. "Nice boy."

"Too nice for me, Papa," she said.

"We'll see," he said as he went into the storeroom.

Renzi pulled himself up onto one knee, kneeling next to his cycle. "Something up?"

"Are you good to ride tonight?" Ajiñe asked him.

"There another race?"

"No," she said. "This wouldn't be a race."

"Oh," he said. "Does that mean—"

"Yes," she said. "So . . . are you good to ride tonight?"

"Yeah," he said. "Let's do this."

34

Tonight, they weren't standing on any sort of ceremony. Ajiñe welcomed having Renzi join them for this run—it was a test, of course—but she needed to decide whether or not to trust him. They had come here, to the alley behind the laundry shop, straight from Papa's shop, and he had stayed in her sight the whole time. He hadn't had the chance to betray them yet. Of course, he might have been anticipating that. He had been walking back from the phonebox. Had he made a call? Maybe someone had followed from the shop.

As usual for a run like this, she had her hard denim slacks and jacket, goggles and helmet. Renzi was dressed the same, ready for action. He had asked about bringing a pistol or handcannon, but she had made it clear that was *not* part of the plan. "Pistols give the tories an excuse." She did have *Urka* Quibala's military knife on her hip, though.

"So what are we doing?" he asked.

"I don't know yet," she said.

"You don't?"

"You'll find out when I do, and that's when we move. That's how it works."

"Ah," he said, leaning into the seat of his cycle. "You're still testing me."

"Is that a problem?"

"No," he said. "I mean, I'm testing you all as well."

"Are you?"

He gave her a cocky smile. "I'm still trying to decide if you are just a common gang on a lark, or if you actually are living up to these grander goals."

"And yet you said you were in."

"I'm in for a lark, sure. But I want to find out how deep this goes. Is it just you and your friends taking the mushroom, playing revolutionary, or are you trying to do something real?"

"What are you doing that's real?"

"Me?" He sighed. "Nothing, and that's the problem. I've already been locked up for nothing, though, so if I have to do that shit again, I want it to be for something. So you tell me—not knowing what we're going to do, can you tell me it'll matter?"

She did know the answer to that, and it annoyed her that he was asking. "Yeah, it will."

"So you do know something."

"I know what, but not where," she said. "We do this right, it means the difference between people going hungry or not."

That got his attention. "By 'people,' do you mean your family, or people in a larger sense?"

"Both," she said. She didn't want to talk about her family's situation with him. "What's your food ration like?"

"Not as bad as my fuel one," he said. "I usually eat at the Henáca place with the family."

"And your ration chits?"

"I give them to Anizé." So he knew how to be part of a family, even one he just joined. That was in his favor.

She looked out of the alley, partly to see if she could spot Fenito, or Mensi, and partly to see if anyone seemed to be following or watching them. Neither one. "And you know it's bullshit, don't you?"

"What is?"

"Food rationing," she said. "Fuel rationing. All of it is just an excuse to keep their thumb on us."

"Do you think it's a lie or something? They aren't sending fuel and food to the war effort?"

"I'm sure they are. But why do they send *ours*? You best believe the folks in Intown aren't going hungry or unable to fill their tanks. The overcastes aren't being asked to pay *their* debt."

Renzi frowned but didn't say anything.

She looked out of the alley again. Gabrána was standing on the other side of the circle, looking pretty in her belly-tied loose blouse and tight pants, dressed just like Xang Xewung in the opening scene of *The Desperate Ladies*. Ajiñe had seen it in the cinescopes with Gab at least three times, and Gab had seen it often enough to mouth every line Xang said along with her. Every time they were on a job, if she could, Gabrána would dress exactly like a character from one of her favorite scopes.

Ajiñe never had the heart to tell Gab plain that she would never be on that screen herself. Let her keep that impossible dream.

For now, though, Gabrána was on watch, and any tories who rode past her would assume she was a curbgirl looking to make coin and leave her alone. Ajiñe always felt better on a run if Gabrána was on watch. She always spotted more than anyone.

"Stay right here," she told Renzi, and went out across the circle to Gab.

"Hey, girl," Gabrána said casually. "You looking for a tumble?"

"Maybe a taste for a chit?" Ajiñe said, holding up the coin.

"I'll take it, it's been slow." She took the coin and grabbed Ajiñe by the front of her shirt, pulling her close before kissing her hard and strong.

She slid her tongue into Ajiñe's mouth, and with it, a dusting of the mushroom.

"That's enough taste for you and a friend," Gab said, pushing her away. "All you get for a chit."

"All I need for now," Ajiñe said. "But I might come back later."

She went back to the alley, still feeling the warmth of Gabrána's mouth on hers, and feeling Gab's own mouth, the tight pinch of her pants, the cool breeze on her bare stomach. And the web spread from her—to Mensi on another curb, wearing just an open jacket and denim pants with the top two buttons undone, showing off the tight muscles of his stomach and hips and a hint of what more he had. Every spirit watching over him knew he could work curbboy all night long and make good coin—that was how he always had gotten by—but he was ready for the run.

Fenito was in the truck, nervously tapping his fingers on the wheel while parked in a cracked-up lot next to a demolished apartment. Eyes on the highway passdown. Ready to move. Nicalla was in her listenhole, with radios and a two-way and a hardline and maps of the whole city.

Everyone was ready, save her and Renzi. The mushroom dose was dissolving on her tongue, filling her body and mind with more and more of her crew.

"Are we—" Renzi started as she came back to the alley. She grabbed him by the back of the head and pulled him in for a kiss, depositing the rest of the mushroom in his mouth.

He kissed back, warm and firm and strong and she felt herself kissing him as the mushroom synced his body with her. She pulled away and wiped off her mouth.

"Now we're ready," she said. "Get on your cycle and ride with me."

He got right on, adjusting himself slightly to not hurt his aroused member. Ajiñe always loved feeling that through the mushroom sync. Something so powerful and intense in feeling that arousal from someone else, knowing that she had evoked it.

But this wasn't the time.

She kicked on her cycle and raced it out into the circle, kicking up the loose gravel of the shitty road as she whipped through the traffic and coming out on the street leading toward the highway passdown. She wasn't sure of the timing, but she knew they needed to build up some speed, activate the sync to the next level. She cranked it up to cruising and then passing gear, her speedometer clocking higher and higher.

"Spirits, I love that," Gabrána whispered in her ear, her hands coming around her waist, as if she was on the back of the cycle. "I could live and die a thousand lives and never tire of it."

"Slip onto Renzi," Ajiñe said, and with that she felt herself reach the speed to manifest with him on his cycle while still being on her own. She and Gab were both with him on the 'goiz, as impossible as it would be if they were all there in the flesh. She and Gab melted and intermingled with each other as they clutched on to him. His emotions flowed into them, and fascinatingly, he was completely calm. Like he did this sort of thing all the time.

"Stay cool, pretty boy," Gabrána told him.

"What the shit—" he said.

"This is what happens when you sync and speed together," Ajiñe said. "The faster you go, the harder and stronger it becomes."

"Ease back!" he shouted. "I can't focus on the road with the three of you."

That was odd. Maybe Mensi or Fenito had synced with him as well. "Follow along," she said. "We need you on your game."

He took a deep breath, not easing on the throttle an inch. "Lead the way."

She took a hard curve leading to the highway.

Nicalla was there. "The target is coming in now. Get around to the ramp-up and crank it. You've got about two swipes until it's in position."

Not much time. She shifted up and rocketed down the street, past the passdown and Fenito in the truck.

"Marked you," he whispered in her ear.

"Got you marking me," she told him.

"How are you not losing your damned minds?" Renzi asked, on her back like he was clutching for his life. Amazing how, on the outside, his projection, he behaved like he was almost in a panic, but he still read as completely calm. It didn't make sense. Was the panic an act, even though he was completely in control?

"Focus on your riding," she told him.

"It's handled," he said. "What's the play?"

"Head for the ramp-up, get on the highway, and crank it to your fire gear once you're up top. Then follow me."

"Yes, ma'am," he said, and his cycle surged forward toward the ramp.

She had to admire his enthusiasm. She gave chase and launched up to the highway, putting her cycle up to fire gear.

"That's the target," Fenito said, appearing on her cycle with her, just as he was moving into position from the curb he was pretending to work. He pointed to the twelve-wheel rig barreling down the highway. "Get it off at our passdown."

"What's the play?" Renzi asked.

"Get in front and push it toward the passdown," Ajiñe told him.

"That's a twelve-wheel truck, it'll crash right over me."

"You better hope not."

She gunned her throttle, getting ahead of the truck. On her signal, she and Renzi both swerved in front and tapped their brakes, just enough to make it jerk over one lane, closer to the passdown.

"Now to force it the rest of the way," she said. "Distract the driver."

Renzi whipped back to the side of the truck, next to the driver's door.

"Hey, gorgeous," he shouted. "That's a lot of metal you're steering!"

"The shit is wrong with you?" the driver shouted back. "You trying to get killed?"

The driver's attention firmly on Renzi, Ajiñe dropped to the other side of the truck, matching pace while hopefully staying in the driver's blind spot. She drew out the knife, whispered to the spirit of *Urka* Quibala to guide her hand, and threw it at one of the tires.

It struck true, and the tire blew.

Renzi dropped back as the truck skidded to the side, toward the passdown. It had to go all the way down or hit the divider. With a hard jerk, the driver went for the highway exit.

The back cab of the twelve-wheel tail wagged, clipping the side of Ajiñe's cycle.

She went skidding, and before she was able to get back in control of her cycle, she ramped up onto the divider, and she and her cycle went hurtling through the air.

35

Time stopped as Ajiñe hurtled through the air. She would crash face-first onto the concrete, her cycle on top of her. If she was lucky, she'd survive it with only most of her bones broken.

But then Renzi's hands were there, grabbing hers, pulling her up.

Grabbing the handlebars, twisting her body around as the cycle and she both flew.

He wasn't holding her, though.

He was driving her.

Using her hands, her legs, her weight. She suddenly became a passenger in her own body as he took control over it, spinning it and twisting her and the cycle until she was on top and the wheels were down again.

Then in a breath, the frozen ticks of time slammed back into gear, and Ajiñe landed her cycle with a hard jar on the rail guard; she kept control and dropped down onto the concrete, braking to a stop at the bottom of the passdown.

"The shit was that!" Fenito shouted as he fired up his truck. He took off in pursuit of the twelve-wheel, skidding and racing on the main road toward the traffic circle, Renzi rocketing along with it.

"You all right?" Gabrána asked in her ear.

"Fine," Ajiñe said, downshifting and getting back up to speed. She had never seen—felt—anything like that before in her life. "Get the job done."

"We're ready," she said.

"Renzi?" Ajiñe asked.

"Got it," he said.

Fenito gunned the truck to push parallel with the twelve-wheel, while Renzi zipped and wove around the other traffic to get in front of them both as they hit the circle. Ajiñe lagged behind as she built her momentum back up, catching up with the rest of them.

"Block and blind," Nicalla whispered in their heads, and the full plan materialized for all of them, clear as day in all their skulls.

As one, they acted.

Renzi curved into the circle against the flow, leaning hard into the turn, until he stopped right before the twelve-wheel, blocking the exit. Then he gunned the throttle, kicking up dust and gravel and smoke that filled the circle.

Ajiñe came in behind them doing the same. The twelve-wheel screeched to a horrific stop in the middle of the mess of smoke and debris, with Fenito's truck right next to it.

Fenito jumped out of the truck as Mensi and Gabrána both moved on the twelve-wheel. Fenito, prybar in hand, cranked open the cab door of the twelve-wheel, and in a dash, the three of them pulled the driver out and threw him in the bed of the truck. Mensi jumped into the cab of the twelve-wheel, Gabrána got behind the steering wheel of the truck, and Fenito wrestled the driver down and bound him up.

"Go!" Nicalla yelled to them all.

Renzi took the lead, racing out the circle exit, with Mensi driving the twelve-wheel right behind him, Ajiñe taking up the rear. They flew off down a side road, away from the highway toward the edge of Miahez. Gabrána and Fenito in the truck turned off another fork, heading far away from them.

"Where now?" Renzi asked as they raced away.

"Three-quarter the next circle, then turn into a warehouse with a yellow roof," Nicalla said. "I'm dropping from sync now."

Ajiñe tasted the sour blast of the ipecac Nicalla downed, and with the queasy twist of her stomach, Nicalla puked and vanished from her senses.

"Does she usually do that?" Renzi asked as they approached the circle.

"Most of the time," Mensi said.

Part of why Nicalla did it was because she hated the sync and the intimacy of that contact, but mostly because she was in contact with the other cells. She was aware of information the rest of them—out in the streets for a run, at risk to be nicked by the tories—couldn't afford to know. Nicalla kept people safe by disconnecting from the rest of them.

They pulled into the warehouse—the door was open and waiting—and as soon as the cycles and twelve-wheel were inside, the doors slammed down shut.

A handful of *jifoz* folks were in position, coming up to the twelve-wheel and breaking the lock on the cargo hold. This must be the cell the goods were being passed to.

Renzi parked his cycle and came over to Ajiñe. "You all right? That crash was pretty close."

"It wasn't just close," she said. "What . . . what did you do?"

"I'm not entirely sure," he said. He looked spooked. "It was like . . . you were going to die and in an instant, just for a moment that stretched out forever, I could feel every aspect of you, your body, and . . . I just knew how to move your body to land safely."

"And you did it," she said. "You rode my body like a cycle." She wanted to be mad about it—it felt like a violation—but at the same time, she didn't want to think about what would have happened if he hadn't. She might be a mangled mess of blood and bone at the bottom of the passdown.

"I didn't *mean* to," he said. "I didn't know that was . . . possible. That I could do that to you."

"You've never done anything like that before?" she asked.

He chuckled. "I've never done anything like this before. And that was just . . . I don't know, instinct."

"Yet you managed pretty well," Mensi said as he came over. "So, Renzi Llionorco. Nice riding."

"More than nice," Ajiñe said. "Miraculous."

The members of the other cell cracked open the cargo door. "Perfect!" one of them said.

"What was this about?" Renzi asked.

"See for yourself," the woman from the other cell said. They were unloading boxes as icy mist wafted out of the back of the rig, each of them labeled "LLIPE QUALITY BEEF" or "RHIQUE QUALITY PORK."

"A meat truck?" Renzi asked.

"I told you," Ajiñe said. "This run meant people won't go hungry."

"I expected, I don't know, something more monumental."

"Full bellies are pretty monumental," Mensi said, clapping Renzi on the shoulder.

The other cell crew were unloading the rig, putting the cases of meat onto the back beds of their various trucks. One of them came over with a case.

"Thought you all deserved some of this," she said. "At least one case of the stuff they keep for the overcastes."

"And the rest of it?" Renzi asked.

"We'll get it out there," the woman said. "Take that and roll your cycles out the door over there. Odds are tories didn't track you here."

"No chance of that at all," Mensi said.

"Best take no chances," Ajiñe said. She offered her hand to the woman as Renzi took the case of meat. "Break the cages."

"Open the roads," the woman said back as she took Ajiñe's hand and pulled her in for an embrace. "And ride with faith."

"Every day. Your spirits watch over you."

"And you."

They put the cycles into free gear and wheeled out the back. A quint of a kilo away, they came up on Fenito and Gabrána waiting in the truck.

"The driver?" Renzi asked with concern.

"We dropped them in a ditch a couple kilos away in the other direction. They'll be all right."

"Good," Renzi said. "I mean, they're not the enemy here. Just someone working a job."

"Plenty of people working a job who are the enemy," Gabrána said. She came over to Renzi. "We've not been properly introduced, have we?"

"Are we supposed to be?" Renzi asked. "I got the impression you were all hiding who you really are from me now."

"We've been swimming into each other's heads enough not to pretend not to know each other," Fenito said.

"Plus you all stripped me naked and tied me up," Renzi said.

"How can we make that up?" Gabrána asked.

"Will kisses work?" Fenito offered. "Or are you *edoromé* like Nicalla and you hate that?"

"No, I'm a fan," Renzi said, taking a long kiss from Fenito followed by Gabrána. Ajiñe was happy they were getting along, but she wasn't in the mood.

"We should move along here," she said. She opened up the case of meat—frozen beef, vacuum-sealed in individual packets. She took out a few and put them in her coat pockets, and then handed a couple to Renzi. "He and I should get back home, and the lot of you should get back to your people. Have a nice meal with them all."

"Indeed," Mensi said. "Though someone should bring a couple to Nicalla. This is something she would actually miss out on."

"I'll get on that," Gabrána said. She touched Renzi's chin. "Another time, Llionorco."

"Look forward to it," he said.

The three of them piled into the truck and drove off.

"So did I pass the test?" he asked.

"You did all right," Ajiñe said. Though she still hadn't sorted her feelings about what he had done, even though it had saved her. She had known that speed brought the mushroom connection to another level. Had Renzi somehow unlocked a level beyond that?

"I really didn't mean to . . . take you over like that," he said. "I've honestly never done anything remotely like that before."

"Try not to do it again," she said. "Well, if you're saving my life, I suppose. But not otherwise."

He nodded with a shy smile that was far too endearing. "Should we get these cuts of beef back to your place?" he asked. "I'm guessing your papa would appreciate them."

36

Ajiñe was woken by the radio.

"Time to live on, no regrets. Ride that streak of lightning."

There were times that, regardless of how much she believed in the cause, she wished Varazina would just keep shit in her mouth. No one—as far as Ajiñe knew—had any idea how Varazina cut into any radio, anywhere in the city, or why she only sent cryptic messages to the faithful. Ajiñe often wondered if Varazina saw everything, or at least could see the faithful, and knew where they were and what needed to be done.

And if she did, why the shit she didn't just let Ajiñe sleep.

Ziva, sleeping next to her on the bed, must have felt the same way. Her hand flopped onto Ajiñe's face. "Why does that happen?" she mumbled in her sleep.

"Sorry," Ajiñe said, pulling herself off the bed and stepping over Papa. He had slept through Varazina's radio message. He had lived through the bombings of the Second Trans and the Tyrant's War. He had spent more than a year in a purge camp, gunfire at any hour.

Papa could sleep through anything.

She didn't know what time it was, but it was too dark out to even be zero on the naught.

She stumbled to the water closet, got herself together, and pulled on her denim and boots. Eyes still filled with sleep, she went down the road to the phonebox and called the hardline to Nicalla.

"Why?" was all she asked.

"Big party coming," Nicalla said. "Thundering down the rail right now, and we need every hand."

"How big?"

"Every hand," Nicalla said. "Top of the track."

That woke her up.

"I'll be on it," she said.

She ran back up the hill, over to the crystal shop and climbed up the wall to Renzi's *fasai*. She didn't bother to knock—hard enough while holding on to the side of the wall—and threw open the door to hop in.

"Renzi, we—oh!"

Renzi was already awake, and he wasn't alone. Fenito and Gabrána were both curled up with him on his mattress.

"Hoped you'd show up," Gab said, giving a devastatingly wicked grin.

For a moment she was a little hurt that they hadn't called her over for this party, but she put that down. "Sorry to ruin things, but we just got a calling. Big score, gotta ride now."

"How big?" Fenito asked as he got off of Renzi's cot.

"Nicalla said all hands."

"Why didn't we get the call?" Gabrána asked. She, like Fenito, was already getting dressed again. Renzi was being a bit slower to get his gears shifted to the new situation.

"We've got another run?" he asked. "At this hour?"

"The hour doesn't matter," Ajiñe said. "Do you even have a radio in here?"

"Should I?"

"That's why there was no call for us," Fenito said. He was fully dressed now and came over to Ajiñe. "We're, um, already in sync."

"Hit me," she said. He put a dose on his tongue and came in to kiss her. She welcomed it—she always did from him—and let the magic fill her body and connect it with theirs. "We need to get moving."

"What about Mensi?" Renzi asked as he got his boots on.

"Have to assume he'll get word and meet us," she said. "How'd you two get out here? You have the truck?"

Gabrána shook her head. "Cable cars and walked the hill," she said.

"You ride with me," Ajiñe said, kicking the rope down. "Renzi, take Fenito."

"As you wish," he said.

Ajiñe scurried down the rope, followed by Gabrána.

"I'm a little hurt," Ajiñe said as they went down the alley to the shop door. "You never took a cable car out here to see me."

"First off, you share a bed with your little sister in the same room where your father is on the floor."

"Fair," Ajiñe said. "Not that your—"

"Not that my situation is any better," Gabrána acknowledged. "We take our moments where we get them. And that boy has a room to himself. Fenito and I agreed there was no need to deprive ourselves another night, and we didn't. I'm shocked you have."

"Gab, I'm just tired," Ajiñe said as they reached the cycle. "We're working the shop, Papa's rations got cut. We'd be really drawn thin without the meat from the truck."

"I hear you," Gabrána said. "We've got nine in my *fasai*, with ration cards for only six."

"Sorry." She wheeled the cycle out of the shop to the alley.

"We're all in this for a little more, hmm?" She smiled brightly, but her weariness shone through. Through the sync, Ajiñe could feel it, deep in Gab's bones. "All the more reason to spend my night with some joy."

"I'm all for that," Ajiñe said as she mounted the cycle. Gabrána kissed her—warmly and deeply, reminding her of the memory and promise of something more when the moment was right—and got on with her. They rode down the hill, and as they got to speed, the sync with one other grew stronger. They were fully connected with the boys, cruising down on the 'goiz.

This was peak time to get nipped by patrol, making checkpoints not only between each senja, but at key traffic circles throughout Outtown. They dropped off the road into an empty aqueduct, through the tunnels, to avoid getting spotted, but surely there were a few folks on patrol who would hear the roar of the cycles and come investigating.

There was no way a call of all hands would go unnoticed.

Even still, they were able to cross into Ako Favel without getting nipped, and from there to the racetrack.

"Back here?" Renzi asked as they stopped, noting the large cadre of riders in the aqueduct. "Are we doing another race?"

"I doubt it," Ajiñe said. "If I understood Varazina correct, it's going to be a train run."

"What do you mean? What did she say?"

Ajiñe wasn't sure how to explain it, but Gabrána stepped up. "The orders, the leadership, that comes from Varazina. She sends us messages over the radio. We didn't get one—"

"Because I don't have one in my place."

"She can do it to any radio, any station, they say," Gabrána said. "So that's partly how we find the people to join us."

"That and the questioning," Renzi said. "Shackled and naked."

"You quite liked that, I think," Gab said. "You keep bringing it up."

"The point is, while Varazina is often cryptic in what she tells us—she knows the tories and the Alliance shitmouths are listening . . ."

"Sure," Renzi said.

"You get to learn what she usually means. So if this is a train—"

"It is." Two people Ajiñe didn't know came up: a smooth drink of a man and a smoky-eyed woman, but they gave off an air of authority, both of them about her father's age, but both looking fit and vigorous. The man continued, introducing the two of them. "Casintel and Bindeniz. We're in charge of this run."

"This is very against protocol," Ajiñe said. Names were not to be shared between cells, and each was supposed to be led independently. Another group in charge put everyone in danger. "We're not supposed to all meet openly like this."

"This mission is going to change several things," Bindeniz said. She gave an appreciative glance to Renzi as she went on. "The next petrol tankers are coming racing in, and we're going to get them. This the new fellow?"

"Yeah," Renzi said.

"Word is you're very good," Casintel said.

"We want to see it," Bindeniz added.

"We'll need fill bladders," Ajiñe said. "So we can siphon—"

"Not this run," Bindeniz said. "This is the call, no more catwalking the mission. That train full of petrol tanks is about to thunder into the city, and by my spirits, we're going to take every single drop of it."

37

Ajiñe didn't know how many crews were in play right now. Casintel and Bindeniz barked out orders and positions so quickly, all Ajiñe could really do was note her own responsibilities, and make sure her people were in place to act. Each crew was on their own strain of the mushroom, and then each crew had their Nicalla, and all of them were connected to each other as well. Which meant all of them, taking places along the tracks, getting into position on their cycles. It was the biggest thing she had ever seen the Fists of Zapi try to do.

She wondered why now. Up until this, they had been mosquitos, nipping bits of fuel and food from Alliance transports, taking what they could to make up for the shortfalls of rationing, ease the suffering of the undercastes.

Renzi surely felt her fear and doubt and churning unease in her gut.

"This run is very different than anything you've done before," he said. They were staged in one of the abandoned tunnels, both sitting on his

Puegoiz 960, waiting for their signal to move. Her cycle was with the rest of the cell, on the back of the truck.

"That's the truth," she said.

"We do this," he said, "we follow the plan we've been given, the Alliance, the Provisional Council, the patrol . . . they're going to come down hard. You know that, right?"

"I know," she said. "This is a declaration of war."

"You're all right with that?"

"You aren't? You're the one saying this needed to matter."

Their sync connection was light at the moment, but she felt a conflict brewing in him, like he was having an argument with himself. "It's just I hadn't expected something this big quite so soon," he said.

"Same," she said. "I recognize this is a lot for your second run with us, but . . . you are in, right?"

He was troublingly silent.

"Renzi," she said, placing a hand on his shoulder. "People are counting on us. Plus, you already know the plan."

He looked back at her. "Are you saying you would force me?"

"No, but . . . if you're out, we're going to stay right here, together, until it's all over."

"You don't trust me?" he asked. "Think I'd go to the tories or something?"

"It's not about trust," she said. "Let's say you leave here right now. Let's say you drive off, but the tories spot you and tether you up."

"Then I'm arrested."

"They're doing some dark shit, I've heard," she said. "I've heard stories of what they do when they've got people. Especially to people who are in mushroom sync. A cousin of a friend of mine told me—listen to this shit—that the Alliance and the Provisional Council are keeping members of the tyrant's inner circle around. Alive and well."

"What?" he asked.

"It's what I heard. My friend's cousin has this Intown job cleaning toilets for some fancy set of *fasai* right outside the Damas Kom, and you know who she heard lives there?"

"Who?"

"Doctor Shebiruht. You know, the tyrant's Mushroom Witch?"

Renzi went pale and stammered. "You . . . you've heard that?"

"After the horrors that woman did in the Tyrant's War, after the shit in the purge camps—I've got spirit tins up for an aunt and two side-uncles that she twisted to death—they have her alive and well and living fancy. Probably *still* doing experiments."

"No . . ." he said. "No, that . . . that can't be true."

"I totally believe, if they had you, saw you were still synced, that witch or someone like her could pull all of it out of your head. Just yank that shit out of you. Get everyone you're synced to. Why do you think we're so careful about who knows what?"

"Sure," he said, faltering a bit. "It all makes sense. But . . . but with this . . ."

"You've seen a lot of faces. If they didn't have you in time to stop the run, they definitely would roll through Outtown and tether everyone they could identify."

"Yeah," he said quietly.

"Shit, they'll probably roll through anyway and crack heads open just because."

"No, no," he said halfheartedly.

A buzz flew through her body and his. Train was coming.

"Renzi?" she asked. "We good?"

His response was to kick on the engine and rocket forward.

The train was already racing along the tracks, with other Fists riding alongside in the narrow patch of road at this section. In about five kilos, the tracks would cross over the bridge into Sunkentown, and from there on out, the track elevated. Not much time.

Their target was the third tankcar—there were six in all, each of them carrying approximately 9,600 liters of petroleum fuel. She couldn't even contemplate the madness of this run.

They raced up on the car, as their compatriots each approached their own assignments.

"Get ready!" Renzi rode hard, riding so close to the train tankcar his exhaust pipe brushed against it, sparks flying like a burning tail behind them. Feeling his every motion as much as if she were driving the cycle herself, Ajiñe pulled her feet up onto the seat and stood in a crouch.

"Now!"

He gunned the throttle and bumped up on the front wheel, and in that same moment Ajiñe jumped, flying high enough to grab the upper edge of the train car. She pulled herself up as Renzi spun around and rode off into the gravel.

But he was still right beside her, her velocity from the train and his on the cycle locking them together. The sync loved speed.

"Nice moves!" he said.

"Same," she said. She scrambled over to the front of the car and then down the ladder to the hitch. She could feel that the teams behind her had already done their jobs, unhitching the cars and applying the brakes. Uncoupling the hitch was easy; two flips of the latch and it was done. Immediately her car separated from the rest of the train. Up the ladder to the top again, she dashed to the back.

Something slammed across the side of her brain. That was a feeling she knew.

"What was that?" Renzi asked.

"Tories," she said. "When you're on the mushroom, fully in the sync like we are, it's like you can feel the folks who are at hard angles to you."

"I see their cycles," he said, and the part of her that was with him could see them heading toward the train. "I'll buy you some time."

She kept her focus on herself as he whipped around and careened toward the patrol cycles. She had to reach the brake before they reached the bridge, which was maybe a kilo away.

She climbed down the back ladder as Renzi raced circles around the tories. There were three of them that she could feel, and one of them tried to draw iron while also riding. Renzi wasn't a target they could catch, weaving his way through the gravel yard, taking them farther and farther from the train. Good.

The brake handle was right below her. She dropped down with one hand on the ladder to guide her, and pulled the handle strong and hard. Sparks flew and the train wheels seized, grinding to a stop.

Her job was done. The next part relied on another cell, racing into position. They came driving up, in a small fleet of tank trucks. They must have been working for seasons to get everything together. That must have been why this run was happening now. They needed to hur—

Danger crashed across her skull, but not soon enough. A tory cycle buzzed past her as the rider leaped off it, tackling her and pulling her off the train to the ground. The tory tried to get hold of her wrists as they tumbled together. She wouldn't let him, throwing wild punches to keep him from getting his hands on her, or worse, the shackles.

Then he slammed one foot on the ground, getting his weight on her as he pulled his iron. He didn't quite get it trained on her, so she went for his wrist while jamming her knee into his balls. She didn't get a great grip on him, but was able to knock the gun out of his hands. It skittered to the side, but he remained undeterred.

His fist pounded into her face, dazing her.

"The shit are you doing, *jifo*?" he snarled. "You're shitmouth crazy if you think you can—"

She brought her fist up into his face, knocking him off of her. They both stumbled to their feet as he drew out his baton.

"Now you're going to pay your debt, *jifo,*" he said.

"Hey, tory!"

Ajiñe didn't need to look, because she felt it. She was right there with him.

Renzi had the tory's gun trained on the asshole.

"Don't you even—" was all the tory got out before Renzi fired.

The tory went down in a heap.

Renzi grabbed Ajiñe's hand, and the electric intensity of the shared bond, of being each other, taking each other's hands and being taken at once, hammered through her.

"We've got to—" she started.

He pulled her to his cycle and got on it with her.

"We've got to draw the rest of the tories away, protect our siphon teams until they can get away."

She glanced over to the dead tory on the ground there. Spirits, that really just happened. She would have been tethered and locked away if Renzi hadn't been there.

"Thanks," she whispered.

"Don't thank me yet," he said, tossing the gun away as he fired up the cycle. "Run isn't over until we finish it."

38

The crews had done their jobs, quick and hard, draining the train tanks down to nothing, leaving them empty and abandoned on the tracks. More patrol tories had shown up, but the cycle riders kept them occupied, drawing their attention away from the tanker crews. By the time a real patrol presence had managed to get to the tracks, the tanks were drained and the crews had slipped off into the night with almost all the fuel.

Almost.

They had left behind a bit of fuel, on a patch of concrete a short distance from the scene of empty, abandoned train cars. When the last crew got on their cycles to drive off, they lit a match and threw it at the fuel.

Flaming words greeted the tories that arrived on the scene.

¡Nix xisisa!

THE DEBT IS PAID.

OUR FIST IS CLOSED.

VARAZINA SAVES!

Ajiñe hadn't been able to see it all. She had been on the 'goiz 960 with Renzi, tearing through the streets to keep the tories away until everything was done. When Gabrána, who had been able to watch it all, gave them the signal that the job was done, she and Renzi dropped off the streets into the old tunnels, giving all the tories the slip.

They never had a chance.

Ajiñe knew this day was coming, but she was still astounded it was here. Here heart hammered with fear and excitement and joy as Renzi cranked his cycle to racing gear through the old tunnel under the Ako Favel, coming up near Street Cohecta, not a single tory anywhere in sight. They surely were all swarming around the train site.

She led him to the bomb-out, parking his cycle in a hidden niche before heading in.

"Is this where you brought me the other night?" he asked.

"Fond memories?"

"It had its good points," he said. "So, what we just did—"

"Crazy, hmm?" she said. "Look, I . . . I appreciate what you did there with the tory who was on me."

"It was nothing," he said, his head down. "I mean, him or us there, right?"

"It's not nothing," she said. She put her hand under his chin—his delightfully sharp chin—so she could look him in the eyes. Spirits, Gabrána was right about him. "I know you went to Hanez on a trump up, so . . . I know you've never had to do anything quite like that before."

"No," he said quietly. "But, you know, you can't be squeamish in a war."

"You think this is a war?" she asked.

"I think it is going to be one now," he said. "Up until now, we, the, uh—"

"The Fists of Zapi," she said. They hadn't said the name around him yet, except when he was drugged. He deserved to know, and his eyes lit up at hearing that.

"The Fists of Zapi, yes. You've mostly been just a nuisance to the Alliance and the government and all. This is a new level, and they're going to hit back hard."

"Probably."

"And, are . . . are we ready for that? Like, where did the fuel go? Who's going to keep it safe? Where's it going to go?"

"Too many questions," she said. They got to the door of their hidden apartment. "Today we're just going to celebrate the victory."

"Right," he said. "What do I smell?"

"That is Nicalla cooking in there." She opened the door, and sure enough, Nic had set up a small grill pit with smoldering wood chips and the sweet smell of seasoned meat filled the place.

"We got a win," Nicalla said. "And we have this lovely meat from the other job. I had been marinating it all day, figuring we'd either be celebrating, or it would be a last meal. Either way, worth it."

"Celebration," Ajiñe said, touching Nicalla on the arm gently—all the physical affection she would bear.

"Where are the others?" Nicalla asked. "I dropped sync as soon as the job was done."

"You really are missing out when you do that," Ajiñe said, snatching a sliver of meat off the grill.

"I'm really not," Nicalla said firmly.

"But then you can't do this," Ajiñe said, putting the piece of meat in her mouth and letting the flavors play and dance on her tongue. "What do you think, Renzi?"

He ran his tongue across his teeth. "That's . . . really delicious."

"Indeed it is," Ajiñe said.

"Spirits, what a joy, tasting things I didn't put in my mouth," Nicalla said flatly. "Whatever will I do without this in my life?"

"Nic," Ajiñe said firmly. "I love you, I do. But you're also very boring."

"How I like it. Where are the others?"

The sync with the other three had been faint and fading, but Ajiñe still had a vague sense of them. "They're almost here. And they aren't waiting to celebrate."

"Tell me none of them are trying to drive and fuck at the same time."

"No," Renzi said, and then he started laughing. "They are not trying that."

"What are they doing?" Nicalla asked with an exasperated tone.

"You don't want to know," Ajiñe told her. "They're celebrating a bit early, let's leave it at that."

"Spirits, I don't know how you have that kind of energy," Nicalla said. "I would appreciate it if you all just kept that to a low simmer for an hour or so while we eat and talk about what's next, then I can go and you all can violate yourselves and each other however you like."

Renzi raised an eyebrow at Ajiñe as if to tell her he was more than interested in that idea.

"Simmering it down," Ajiñe said.

"Absolutely," Renzi said as he sat down, but at the same time Renzi—or at least the connection of him—was right behind her, hand on her waist, kissing the back of her neck. *That* Renzi whispered in her ear, "Just a low simmer."

"How are you doing that?" she asked out loud. She had been able to visit and project with the sync when at a high speed, and for a little bit afterward, but she had never known anyone to do it like this, sitting still and calm while their own projection was right there with them.

"Not entirely sure," the real him said.

"Do you mind it?" he asked through the projection.

"Not at all," she said, enjoying the sensation and the secret thrill of it all.

"Good," his projection said, moving around in front of her. "This is really quite fascinating."

"Disgusting," a feminine voice said in her ear as another set of hands went around her waist. "She would nev—"

Then the projection of Renzi vanished, along with those additional hands.

"What was that?" she asked him.

"I don't know," he said. "I've never . . . I've never seen anything like that."

"What just happened?" Nicalla asked.

"Renzi and I are still in strong sync," Ajiñe said. "And for a moment, someone new was with us."

"Like, a stranger slipping into your sync?" Nicalla asked. Her brow furrowed in thought.

"Do you know what that is?"

"I've heard . . . just heard . . . that Varazina can do that. Like she does with the radio, she can slip into the frequency of the sync. She can feel her way in and join you."

"That . . . that must be it," Renzi said. It had clearly spooked him. For a bit, he looked *rhique* pale.

The door opened and Gabrána, Fenito, and Mensi poured in, hands on each other's exposed skin and lips attached to each other.

"Ease it down!" Nicalla said. "I thought you were getting it out of your systems."

"These two were definitely getting it *into* their system," Gabrána said. "And it better be my turn soon."

"Eat and plan first," Ajiñe said. "Then the rest once Nicalla leaves. Out of respect."

"Of course," Gabrána said. She looked to Nicalla. "That's how much I love you."

"Same," Nicalla said flatly. She had taken the last of the meat off the grill, laying it out on a platter with charred onions and chiles and tomatoes and a pile of tortillas. "But let's eat this glory and then—"

The feeling hit Ajiñe hard. Tory angles. Static. From every direction.

"They found us!" she said. "We need to bolt!"

"Shit!" Nicalla said, gathering up her papers. "I can't leave this here, or—"

"Come on," Renzi said, grabbing Ajiñe's hand. "We'll draw them off, the rest of you clear off!"

Ajiñe would normally argue—that was her authority to say, not his—but he was right, and there was no time to waste. She ran out with him and got on his cycle. Spirits, hers wasn't even here. Just one cycle for them to do this.

"Plan?" he asked her as he kicked up the cycle.

"Make noise, get their attention, so the others can get out with Nic's notes and the truck," she said. She wrapped one arm around his waist, and grabbed hold of her knife with the other. She knew she shouldn't want a handcannon right now, but she still did.

"What I was thinking," he said, and gunned his throttle, off like a shot.

Make noise is exactly what he did, revving the engine hard, skidding through the gravel to kick up as much as possible, and squealing the tires as he whipped around corners.

Four tories on cycles came up right behind them, jagged static with them. "You feel them?" she asked.

"Got it," he said. He gunned hard through the Ako Favel, already drawing them more than a kilo from the bomb-out.

"Where are you?" Gabrána, still in sync, appearing behind Ajiñe.

"Coming up on the crossing to Miahez," Ajiñe said.

"We're out of there, I'm not feeling any on our tail."

"They're clear?" Renzi asked. "Then let's scatter these tory shitheads."

He buzzed up one steep hill; over the crest would take them in into

Miahez, but as he started to slow down from the incline, he whipped around and launched back down, right at the tories. The distance closed before Ajiñe was even aware of what was happening, and faster than she could blink, he had weaved in between their formation and went right past them. All of them swerved out of the way, losing pace and balance. She looked back and saw that one of them had crashed into a powerpost, another had just fallen over, and the other two were struggling just to get turned around.

"Nice work!" she said. "Run it up and put some kilos between them and us."

"Yes, ma'am," he said. He knocked it up a gear and wound around another circle to lead to Miahez and Street Xaomico. He whipped through it, getting completely clear as she checked again. No one was behind them.

Then the sharp static hit her hard from in front of them.

"Renzi!" was all she had a chance to say before he came to a screeching halt.

At least a dozen tories in a blockade in front of them, all of them with iron drawn.

"On the ground!" one shouted. "Drop the knife! Hands spread, touch nothing!"

"Too many of them," his phantom whispered to her.

She threw down the knife and stepped off the cycle. He did the same, and in a snap, tories swarmed on them, pulling them to the ground and ironing them up.

REFUEL: MEMORANDUM

FROM: *Overdeputy Cannic Fanzhai, Ministry of Apportionment, Ziaparr Oversight*

TO: *High Captain Tiré Sengejú, Oversight Officer, Ziaparr Welfare Force*

DATE: *06 Tian, High Sehosian Year 0049*

MIMEOCOPY: *Vice-Governor Idanji Nangmai, Provisional Government Oversight*

Ministry of Materials, Ziaparr Oversight Office, Damas Kom

Ministry of Resources, Ziaparr Oversight Office, Damas Kom

Alliance High Command Archives, Wo Mwung Meng,

Ministry of Records, Ziaparr Oversight Office, Damas Kom

REGARDING: *Safety and Security in Delivering Oil Quotas, Fourth and Fifth Season, HSY 0049*

High Captain:

It deeply saddens me to report that we are significantly under quota on refined petroleum fuel delivery for the year to date, with notable shortfalls in the Fourth Season. Furthermore, deliveries to date in the Fifth Season are well below expected levels. This is especially shocking considering it is only the sixth day of the season, but the situation is dire enough that it requires direct intervention.

These shortfalls cannot be blamed on the production end, and our fine allies of the Outhic Military Command who administrate the oil wells and refineries in the Zian or Ureticar regions. They have been performing their duties with admirable zeal. Oil quotas are being reached on their end, when they load it on the trains.

But there have been notable shortfalls when the trains arrive at the port facility. Which means, the flaw lies in transit, and thus is a matter of security and welfare. I understand that we have an insurgency problem in the outer reaches of the city, which the tanker trains must pass through, and part of that problem manifests as petroleum theft. We have deemed a certain percentage of petroleum loss as "acceptable" while the problem was being investigated.

However, in light of the latest action, where an entire train's worth of petroleum was stolen by these insurgents, I must stress we have crossed the threshold into "unacceptable," and demand action be taken in the strictest of terms.

I recognize that the minutia of these matters is not within my jurisdiction, but I have gone over the reports of the latest operation to deal with these insurgents, and, frankly, find them deeply unacceptable. Are we resting our hopes on an infiltration mission carried out by a local Civil Patrol officer, hoping to make his way into the center of the rebellion and root out its leaders?

And more to the point, said officer is the half-breed child of Angú fucking Tungét?

Do you even read your own intelligence reports?

I know I will receive a missive the length of my leg about how we're rebuilding the local government, and that the Prime Families are the best strategy in using the existing infrastructure and leadership and we need to be respectful in how we handle them, and these decisions were made over my head years ago. And, yes, I know several people in the leadership back home really like the idea of a Pinogoz led by the Prime Families just because it harkens back to the Cultivated Roots from glory days of the old empire. She already has too much power entirely because the Wotungét Root still has nostalgic meaning here and back home in Sehosia.

Power that she would have been kept completely away from had there been anyone else with her name left in her generation. Read your own files: The locals were barely able to put a leash on that woman twenty years ago, and I don't see a way to weave this silk in a way that doesn't undermine that and embolden her. If her dark-blooded son succeeds, that will give her further clout, and if he fails and is killed, there's nothing left to control her with.

In short, this is a stupid plan, and I want it on the record that I have stated this is a stupid plan, and it will not be on my head when Alliance High Command is asking why we're failing to deliver entire tankers' worth of petroleum.

Signed,

Overdeputy Cannic Fanzhai,

Ministry of Apportionment, Ziaparr Oversight

(Postnote, not included in mimeocopies)

Tiré—Seriously, I know you like sharing baths with Ainiro Hwungko, but use some common sense and do not let her whisper *stupid ideas* into your head. Try to remember, even though most of the *llipe* locals might look like us, have our old names, and even maintain much of our heritage, *they are not us*. For your sake, friend, I hope this pans out for you.

FOURTH CIRCUIT:
CEREMONIES OF SPEED AND HUNGER

39

"Well, tonight was mostly a disaster," Lieutenant Canwei said.

Wenthi couldn't disagree. "I had no idea until it was too late that 'the next job' would be something of this scale." One of the ice rooms had been set up as a comfortable debrief room, complete with a cot and shower. Despite the shame Wenthi felt about the loss of petrol, he was relieved to be sitting here, drinking a Dark Shumi with the lieutenant, with a plate of pulled pork tortas between them. Wenthi wished he didn't need to be confined down here for the debrief, but he knew that there was still risk of sync connection with the rest of the insurgent cell. Especially Ajiñe, who was being kept isolated in a different part of headquarters. At this distance, she'd easily still feel him.

He could feel Nália, like a shadow looming over him. It was muted, but still there nonetheless. The strange combination of her being so close and yet the layers of the ice room's sync-blocking walls made their connection feel like a numb hand. He was aware of it, but couldn't quite feel it.

But what he could feel from her was both angry and proud.

"That's not your fault," Lieutenant Canwei said. "None of our intelligence indicated this level of escalation."

"I was supposed to be that intelligence, ma'am."

"Not our only source," Canwei said, tapping her nose. "Though that's not something you need to worry about."

"So what's next for me?" Wenthi asked.

"I want to go over the people involved that you do know," she said. "Not just the people in the insurgent cell you've entered, but anyone else remotely connected."

"Sure," he said, grabbing another torta off the plate and taking a greedy bite of it. Spirits, that was good. Not quite like the tacos on Circle Hyunma, which Wenthi was feeling an odd craving for, but it was clear that the Welfare Force had spent a fair amount on not only the Dark Shumis, but tortas from one of the finer restaurants in Intown.

The image of the box labeled "Llipe Quality Beef" flashed in his head.

He wasn't certain if that was a memory of his own, or something provoked by Nália.

That faint echo of seething anger from her was there.

"You all right, Tungét?" Canwei asked.

"Sorry, just . . . lost in the moment of this torta," he said.

"Spared no expense there," Canwei said. "Because—and I talked about this with the high captain—that even though tonight was an extraordinary blow, we're happy with what you have achieved. No one has ever infiltrated these rebels as successfully."

"Because they can feel the tories and—"

"Tories?" Canwei asked with a subtle smile.

"Sorry," Wenthi said. "When you're on the mushroom—"

"You've been careful, yes?" Canwei asked. "I know it's been this risk you've been taking, that you've had to take, but we'd all hate it if you ended up in a burnout ward."

"I've done what I've had to do, ma'am," Wenthi said. "It hasn't been easy, but it's fine. As I was saying, they can sense us when they're on it. Quite easily."

"Except for you," Canwei said.

"I can't answer to why that is."

"And I don't care, as long as it works." She laughed as she picked at her own torta. "But is that why we have such a hard time catching them?"

"When you all approached the hideout tonight, we knew. And I had to all but drive myself into your blockade to get us arrested."

"We did try to catch the others, but they slipped away. Let alone the spanking we got with the train. All we have to show for this venture is arresting . . ." She looked at her notepad. "Ajiñe Osceba, who at most seems a minor player in all this."

"Yeah, she leads the cell, but it's Nicalla who is the actual contact who interacts with other cells, interprets the missions from Varazina—"

"Who only talks on the radio? But *any* radio?"

"I don't know how she does it. Maybe Nicalla does, but I think there're more people between her and Nicalla."

"Then the job definitely isn't over," she said. "Tell me about the others."

"Gabrána, Fenito, and Mensi. Gabrána is the lookout, at least from what I've seen. Fenito drives the truck, and Mensi is a little bit of everything. Whatever needs doing, Mensi does, it seems." He could mention that Gabrána wanted to act in cinescopes, or that Fenito had a back full of scars from getting caught in an explosion as a kid in the Great Noble, but those weren't relevant things that Canwei wanted to know.

"Right. And what about Niliza Dallatan?"

"Nothing, really. I mean, I could tell you a handful of petty crimes she's involved in, but I don't know about her connection to the rebellion."

"Nor these folks you live with. Isilla and Anizé Henáca?"

"They're just hardworking *jifoz*, frankly."

"But they're connected to Dallatan."

"They're friendly with her. But everyone on Street Xaomico is. She kind of runs that patch."

"Good, good," Canwei said. "Good information." She got up and pushed a button on the wall. "So this is the plan. Tonight and tomorrow we're going to comb through the 14th Senja, and just tether up whoever. We need a good show of force after the train, anyway. But that'll give us a good batch of *jifoz* in the holding cells. Sometime tomorrow, we'll add you into the mix of those folks, and then around nightfall, we'll release most of them, including you and Miss Osceba. That way you can still use her to get in deeper, find this Varazina person."

"Sounds good," Wenthi said. There was an odd sense of relief that Ajiñe wasn't going to be kept in lockup. He wasn't entirely sure why he felt that. Probably because he couldn't possibly get any farther without her.

That must be it.

"In the meantime, you can stay here tonight, relax, eat the rest of those. Try to feel like a normal person."

Wenthi wasn't sure how to take that. Being Renzi Llionorco had been tough, living in the terrible *fasai* and managing on *jifoz* rations, but he had never felt like he wasn't still a normal person. That life was as normal as anything.

"Doctor Shebiruht does want to take a look at you, though," Canwei said as she opened the door. Shebiruht, looking as sallow and wicked as ever, especially with the disturbing smile on her lips, was standing in wait there.

"Hello, Mister Tungét," she said, her accent seeming even thicker than before. "We've been having some fascinating readings from our tests on Miss Enapi, and we would love to run a series of tests—"

That was all she said when a wave of emotion—definitely from Nália—hit Wenthi like a truck. Panic. Fear. Rage. So strong, Wenthi couldn't protect himself from it, feeling it just as intensely as she did.

Or maybe he just plain felt it, too, seeing this witch, this monster, looking so damned pleased with herself.

"No," he said firmly. "Get her the shit out of here."

"Wenthi, it'd be best—" Canwei started.

"No," he said again. "I don't want to see her, let alone be prodded and tested by her. Get her the shit out of here."

Shebiruht laughed—she laughed!—and said, "We need to make sure your synchronous bond with Miss Enapi—"

"It's fine," he said. "It's been working perfectly, and I don't need her, don't want her, get her away from here."

"Wenthi—" Canwei pressed.

Then the last person Wenthi expected to see here stepped into the doorway. "My son said to get her away. I suggest you listen to him."

40

Mother waited quietly while Canwei and Shebiruht shuffled out, closing the door behind them. Once they were definitively gone, she let out a deep exhalation.

"Spirits of my mothers, I can't stand that woman."

That nearly broke something in Wenthi. "You knew she was here? That she was . . . that she was . . . what she's doing . . . she—"

"Easy," Mother said, coming up to Wenthi, caressing his cheek. "Of course I knew. It killed me to be . . . weighed down with that knowledge."

"How the shit did that happen?"

"Language, Wenthi," she said, sitting down. "It happened exactly how you imagine it happened. The Great Noble War had ended, Rodiguen was toppled, and she, cockroach that she is, was still standing. The Alliance governments all thought she was far too useful to simply imprison or execute, and they decided, since we're rebuilding Pinogoz, that we'll keep her here."

"That doesn't make any sense."

She clicked her tongue dismissively. "One thing I've learned about the Alliance in my years working with them? They love to talk about their respect for their principles. Their code, their rights, their unimpeachable standards. Then they come up with clever loopholes to work around those things."

"What does that have to do with that witch?"

"If they took her back to the Unity, or Reloumene, or some other Alliance nation, they would be obliged, by treaty and rule of law, to give her a trial, within their system of fairness and justice. And then follow through with the result of that trial. Likely life imprisonment or execution."

"Which she deserves."

"But here's the clever bit, dear boy. Pinogoz is not an Alliance nation. We are simply—what's the phrase the Oversight Board loves to use? 'A burgeoning nation preparing itself for freedom on the world stage.' We don't have a law for how to treat an international war criminal like Shebiruht."

"Isn't making one your job?"

She laughed, dry and hollow. "I don't have an gram of power that isn't granted to me by the grace of the Alliance Oversight."

"You're—"

"I know what you are going to say. I'm the Root of one of the Prime Families, with a seat on the council. Empty thing. Last time that actually meant a damned thing was in—" She sighed, and went over to the icebox.

"When?"

She took out a Dark Shumi and popped it open without a tool. Wenthi didn't know she had that kind of strength in her hands. "Those few years between the wars, before Rodiguen took power. Those were almost good years. Do you remember when we lived in that little green house, in what used to be the 5th Senja?"

Wenthi tried to think back—flashes of incomplete memories. Before the Alliance, before the Great Noble, before the tyrant. The house. Flowers in the streets. Mother on a stage, talking about something with passion and conviction.

That memory held and lingered for a moment, as if it had been picked up and examined like one of Isilla Henáca's crystals.

Nália. Muted but still there on the edge of his awareness. She couldn't quite dig into him through the ice room walls, but she was still there, and she burrowed into that memory, as if to find a hint of whatever Mother had been so fiery about.

But it wasn't there in the memory. He had been so young. The words she had said hadn't stayed, just the emotion.

"Wenthi?" she asked him.

"Sorry," he said. "Memory is a little . . . difficult right now. Thanks to Doctor Shebiruht."

Mother's eyes went wide, angry. "She damaged your memory? I'll—"

"No," he said. "But when I remember something, it—Nália feels it as well. It's disconcerting."

"She's that girl you arrested. They told me—" She choked on the word for a moment, and then took a swig from the carbon to wash it down. "They told me you had some unique connection that they could expl . . . use. And it tied to her."

"I'm tied to her, all right."

"They didn't tell me that. I . . . I'm sorry."

That may have been the first time she had said that to him in as long as he could remember.

"Why did you come?"

"They said my son had come in from his infiltration mission. Of course I came."

"That mission isn't done."

She took another drink, sitting down. "And you've got to finish it, Wenthi. You have to do it spectacularly."

"I was planning on competently."

"And I know you can," she said quietly. "I should tell you that people in

Oversight are livid about the amount of fuel stolen. And they know that you are on this mission, and if you fail, they will use it as a weapon against me."

Wenthi let that sink in, and finally found only one word. "Amazing."

"What, dear," she said, taking his hand.

"I think, for the first time in your life, you actually need me."

The porcelain facade of her face cracked ever so slightly, just around her eyes. "That's very hurtful, Wenthi."

"I know something about hurtful words, Mother."

"Hmm," she said, standing up and smoothing out her dress. "I suppose that's what we earn for our troubles. Regardless, I wanted to make sure you were well, and that you understood how important this mission of yours is for *everyone.* Stay safe."

"Give Lathéi my best," he said.

"She knows she has it," Mother said. "But I'll tell her, anyway. For your sake."

"I appreciate that, Mother," he said. "But now I'm tired."

"I hope you really do appreciate it, my boy," she said. "That you appreciate everything I've done in this world, and will continue to do in the next."

She left, and Wenthi was just alone with his thoughts, which dwelled on what he had done, and would still have to do to finish this.

An ember of self-loathing breathed into life in his heart, fueled with the knowledge of the betrayals ahead. He pushed those feelings down, burying them deep to forget them. But they lingered nonetheless, and he wasn't sure if they came from his own heart, or from Nália.

41

Breakfast—tacos of eggs, beef, and avocado with absurd amounts of cheese and salsa—arrived with Paulei, and Wenthi was thrilled to have both of them show up in his isolation cell.

"How did you—" Wenthi started when Paulei came in with the tray. He couldn't even finish the sentence, instead grabbing Paulei as soon as he put the tray down. Paulei pulled him into a strong embrace.

"Traded a few favors with quite a few people."

"And you're all right?" Wenthi asked, touching Paulei's chest. He hated shooting him, even with a false round and Paulei wearing an armor plate. But the ruse had worked well enough to get Wenthi to that next level of trust with Ajiñe and the others.

"I'm fine," Paulei said. "Barely stung. And I think I missed my calling as a cinescope star, don't you think?"

"Great performance," Wenthi said, accepting a kiss from Paulei before sitting down with the tacos.

"So how has life been as a spy?" Paulei asked as they ate.

"I'm not a spy," Wenthi said. "I'm on an infiltration mission."

"Spy," Paulei said. "You've been handling life as a *jifoz*?"

"It's not great," Wenthi said. "You know how hard it is to get petrol for the cycle?"

"How hard could it be? You get it on your ration days."

"Ration days are half of what they are for us. And you're much more limited with where you can use your card, and most places run out of their *jifoz* allocation by midday. It's very challenging."

"Huh," Paulei said, mouth full of taco. "And you need to go back out there."

"Back to being Renzi Llionorco," Wenthi said. He thought about that for a moment as he ate. "I should have asked my mother about that when she was here."

"She came?"

"Yeah. And . . . maybe it's nothing. But she had made a thing about having the right name when I did this mission. That the wrong name could get me killed. Maybe it's nothing, but I almost have a sense that this name is one she chose."

"Why would she do that?"

"Because she likes to control things," Wenthi said. "That's who she is."

"You get that from her, you know."

"What do you mean?"

"I mean, that's what we do, Wenthi. We try to exert control on this chaotic city. We help keep it in line. Keep ourselves in line."

"It's important work," Wenthi said. "If we don't, we'll never—"

The words froze in his mouth. He couldn't force himself to say anything else, as if his whole body had decided to disobey.

"Never?"

"Be free from those Alliance assholes!"

The words were not his, and once they forced their way out, his body became his again, and he covered his mouth in shame.

"The shit was that?" Paulei asked.

"Nália," Wenthi said. That echo of her had, for just a moment, pushed through the walls of the ice room into him like a bullet. But that was all she had, he could feel, the effort had worn her out. But the fact that he could feel that through the ice walls gave him some concern.

Like their connection had grown too strong.

"You all right?" Paulei asked. "Should I call someone?"

"No," Wenthi said. "I've got her under control now. They'd only call in Doctor Shebiruht and she's the last person I want to see."

"That witch is actually here? In the building?"

"She really is. At least she was last night."

"That's horrible," Paulei said. "If you think you're all right."

"Fine," Wenthi said. "Nália pushed hard for one big punch into me, and that's all she managed. I've got it."

"Speaking of punch," Paulei said. "After you finish eating, there's something we have to do, and you're not going to like it."

42

With one solid punch, Paulei had given Wenthi a bruise and busted lip that looked nasty. It would look good enough for their purposes. Then Wenthi got dressed, got his head back into character of Renzi, and Paulei signaled for two other patrol officers to drag him out of the ice room and throw him into a holding cell with a handful of other *jifoz*. Now out of the ice room, he could feel hints and shadows of Ajiñe in one of the other cells, and the heavy presence of Nália in the back of his skull. One of the patrol gave him another punch—this one completely for show—so the other prisoners in the cell could see it.

Wenthi sat in the back of the cell, waiting for much of the rest of the day. Near sunset, they fed everyone a bowl of cold beans, and then dragged most of them out of the cells and into trucks.

In the back of one truck, Wenthi felt Ajiñe's presence strongly. She was in the other truck. After driving through the city, across a checkpoint into Outtown, the trucks stopped and tossed everyone out in front of the impound lot in Circle Uilea. Once they were dumped out on the street, most folk started shuffling off in every direction, surely anxious to get home. Ajiñe was brushing herself off near the other truck.

"Hey," he called out, moving toward her. He grabbed her hand. "You all right?"

"Yeah," she said, squeezing back. She pulled him close and kissed him, which made him wince. "What did they do?"

"Tried to slap me around and get me to confess to shit I hadn't done," he said.

"What about that patrol you killed?" she asked in a whisper. "I'd have thought they'd hammer you to the floor for that."

"Never asked. Assholes were far more concerned about the stolen petrol, if you can believe that," he said, and he hoped she did. Their sync had faded too much for him to get any read on what she was feeling. "Shows you what they really care about."

"Assholes," she muttered.

"What did they do to you?"

"A little less slap, but the same," she said. "Though apparently all they held me on was a curfew violation."

"Same, thank my spirits," he said. He pointed to the impound gate, where the 'goiz 960 was waiting. A patrol officer he didn't know was at the gate, looking over a checklist. "Hey, that's my ride."

"This piece of shit?" the officer asked. "And you think you get it back?"

"I think it's mine, tory," he said.

"Renzi," Ajiñe said, grabbing his arm. "We don't want another fight."

"I want my cycle," he said. He got up close to that officer. "You going to let me take it?"

"Name?" the officer asked, looking more bored than anything.

"Renzi Llionorco," he said. He pointed to the cycle. "Mine."

She glanced over the checklist. "Fine, you're here." She went into the guard booth, opened the gate, and then threw the keys on the ground. "Get your shit out of here."

"You need a ride?" he asked Ajiñe. She answered by picking up the keys and getting on the cycle.

"I'll drive you," she said with a wink.

He liked the sound of that. He got on and let her take the 'goiz through its paces, flying up Street Xaomico and parking in the zocalo.

"Now?" he asked as he dismounted. "We never did get to properly celebrate."

"And we're not tonight," she said, pushing him away gently as she got off. "I'm going to my place, and you should climb up to your *fasai* and rest. I'm going to just fall down next to my sister in my bed. I'll see you tomorrow." She kissed him on one side of his face to avoid the bruised lip.

She walked off toward her apartment over the shop. Wenthi sighed and closed his eyes. He was exhausted, just from spending the bulk of the day in the group cell. He almost didn't want to bother climbing up into his apartment. He idly wondered whose bed he could try to find his way into, one that didn't require scaling a wall.

"You really disgust me, Tungét."

Wenthi opened his eyes to see Nália standing right in front of him.

"The shit—"

She grabbed him by the coat. "You're standing here in my coat, my denim, riding my sweet baby of a cycle, all so you can betray those people who welcomed you into their hearts? Their beds?"

He knew she wasn't really there but her hands on him felt as solid as anything. How was she able to do that? He grabbed her by the wrists and pushed her off. "The shit are you doing?"

"Telling you how fetid and gross you are, shitmouth," she said. She looked thrilled at what she just did.

He walked away from her, trying to force her back into the dark. "You are not supposed to be manifesting to me."

"Oh, right, I'm supposed to be locked in the back of your skull. That nightmare was what it was supposed to be. I forgot."

He closed his eyes, made himself slow his breathing. He just needed to push her down, put her in check. He didn't need her shitty attitude or opinions, well, ever, and he certainly didn't need her manifesting in front of him like this.

Shitting nightmare.

"Go back to your room," he said as he went up the street toward his *fasai.*

"Not a chance," she said, walking with him. She started to laugh. "That witch thought this bonding would be something you could control, keep me dominated. Keep me down in the abyss of your brain. But she must not have known how speed would affect our sync."

"She must—"

"I mean, you've been syncing with the whole crew over there," Nália said, smug look on her face. "With speed syncs getting stronger and more intense, taking more mushroom the whole while. Did you think that wouldn't affect your connection with me? Break down the walls holding me in?"

"Shut your mouth," he said.

"Not a chance," she said. "Right now my whole world is through you, my shitmouth friend."

"What do you want?"

"Everything you don't," she said. "A free Pinogoz, free and fair for the people born of this land."

"People like me?" he asked as he climbed up to his room.

"You are not—"

"Excuse me?" he asked. "I was born right here, just like you."

"But you're—"

"I'm what? *Rhique*? All that means is I had only one grandparent of Zapisian blood, instead of two or three like you."

"And yet that makes all the difference, doesn't it?" she asked. "The difference between clubs in Intown and going hungry in Outtown?"

"No one's—"

"How many times do you get your papers checked in Intown, hmm?"

"Any time I cross from one senja to the next," he said. "Especially going into the 1st or 2nd."

"And out here? You can barely walk from one circle to the next without getting a hassle."

"That isn't true. Half of Outtown has barely any patrol at all!"

"The part that's bombed-out, run-down, and unsafe?"

"Unsafe because you people—"

"There it is!"

"*Dissidents* like you," he said, stressing the word. "Who make trouble for the good people out here. The patrol wouldn't harass folks like the Henácas or the Oscebas or Lajina—"

"Spirits, you are dense. You've been here with us, living like us. I see it through your eyes *every damned day*. But somehow you don't."

"Leave me alone," he said. "I'm going to sleep."

"Funny," she said, her image sitting on the bed with him. "I don't need to sleep. I don't need to eat or piss or shit or anything since my body is lying in a coma in a patrol headquarters. I'm just here with you with nothing better to do."

She looked at him with a trickster grin, and for half a moment, he was even charmed. "You're not going to hurt me."

"Why not?"

"Like you said, you only live through me. See what I see. Feel what I feel." He pinched his arm.

"Ow!" she snapped. "The shit is wrong with you?"

"We're going to play nice, Nália Enapi," he said. "Because if I'm miserable, you are too."

"Not sure if that's true."

"Don't be such a pain that I call Paulei and have him smother you with a pillow."

"You wouldn't."

"Don't test me," he said, stripping his clothes off. She must have some control over how she appeared to him, wearing her denim slacks and coat, just like when he arrested her. "You coming to bed?"

"With you? Please."

He got onto the cot. "I mean, don't think I don't know what's in your head, either. You've been enjoying the time with Ajiñe's group. Especially Fenito."

"Go shit yourself." She sat down. "I mean, how can you even think about sex with all of them when you'll just as soon arrest them? *Ezodi*."

"It's not like that," he said, bristling at the invective she just used. Bristling because it wasn't a lie: He was fucking without any spirit. Hollow. Or at least in part. He wasn't sure what it was with the crew, what he was doing. Sex was just a way to fit in. To be part of the group, get in closer. Necessary. Part of the job.

"Which is why it's hollow, *ezodi*."

He lay down. "Look, the sooner the job is done—"

She lay down next to him. "The sooner I'm somewhere like Hanez. Probably better than your skull."

He could feel her anger radiating off her, her frustration and pain. Whatever their connection was at this point, she was as open as a book to him, and he couldn't shut her down, or off. He wondered if that was supposed to happen, or if it could be fixed. Maybe Doctor Shebiruht could fix it, but she was the last person he wanted to call on. He'd rather just live with it.

Nália lay there, wallowing in her feelings he felt with her. Anger, pain, fear, sorrow, and . . . arousal.

"Are you turned on right now?" he asked her.

"No. Shut up. No." All her emotions spiked at that.

"You want to fool around?" he asked, if only to needle her.

"That would literally be you jerking yourself."

"Is it, though?"

"Shut your shit," she said. "Go to sleep." And with that, she went quiet.

Which was what he really wanted: to go to sleep. Nicalla said something would happen tomorrow, something crucial. The sooner that happened, the sooner all this would be done.

43

Wenthi woke up eating a taco in the zocalo.

The taco was literally in his mouth, and he was in the process of chewing, while Lajina was talking about meat deliveries and rolling out tortillas by hand.

"Oh, you're finally here," Nália said. Her phantom body sat next to him, leaning against his arm. "You really are a sound sleeper."

"How—" he asked. He still had a mouth full of taco, which he kept chewing and then swallowed.

"Well," she said, getting up and walking about the zocalo. "You fell asleep, very heavy with very smutty dreams about the crew, and Partinez, and me—which, odd, but I get it—and that was nice until it switched into dark stuff with your sister, running through winding alleys while shadows chased you. I wanted none of that, so I . . . pulled myself up and found myself up and about in your body."

"That is unacceptable—" He stopped himself from saying more and looking like a lunatic in front of Lajina, who was still talking about pork.

"Yes, that is," Lajina said. "I tell him, he needs to deliver what I pay for."

Nália chuckled even as she looked over Lajina's grill, the spiced meat sizzling away, the tortillas browning. "I know, very wrong. But there I was, awake with your body, and craving tacos. So here we are."

Despite himself, he was hungry, and the rest of the taco was still in his hand. He took another bite, which was delightfully sharp and smoky. So good.

"That was delicious," Nália said as he finished it.

"Of course it was," Lajina said. "I know what the fuck I am doing."

Wenthi realized Nália had spoken with his mouth. Just like she had taken his body while he was asleep. He had to stop her, protect himself from her doing something like that again.

"Of course," Wenthi said. "It was worth saying, though. Thank you."

"Now that you are done, you should find out what *Urka* wants with you."

That was odd. "What do you mean?"

"When you came up to me, I told you that *Urka* had said to send you to her house when I saw you."

Wenthi chuckled nervously. "Right. I was kind of only half awake when I came out here. This might sound odd, but . . . did I say anything . . . strange?"

"The only thing you said was, 'first two Ureti with extra salsa and cheese.' Which I understand."

"Right, I . . . Sorry. I was still half in a dream about your tacos, I think."

"That's a good dream," Lajina said. "I had a dream about you, maybe later today we make that one true?"

"She does like you," Nália said. "That would be interesting."

"All right," he said, giving her a smile. "We'll see what Miss Dallatan wants of me, though." He left Lajina to her work.

"I don't suppose you'd let me take charge of that experience," Nália said. She was walking with him, sensual thoughts radiating off her. He found himself almost shaking with rage, which he kept tamped down. No need to look like a madman in the middle of Street Xaomico.

"What the shit did you say when I was asleep?" Wenthi said.

"Like she said, I ordered two tacos."

"You cannot—"

"Listen, little flower," she said. "Could I take control of your mouth, say something to get you found out? Yeah, maybe I could. But will I?"

"Will you?" he asked after her pause was too interminable.

"Do you know what they would do to you?" she asked. "If they found out you were a tory officer? They would chain you to the back of a cycle and drag you through the racetrack. Then they'd set dogs on you. And then, if you were very lucky, they would chain your legs to one cycle and arms to another and drive in separate directions. But rest assured, they would play with you for days, Officer Tungét. Days."

Wenthi swallowed hard.

"Sounds like you'd like that."

"I would," she said. "I'd love to see it. But what I wouldn't like to do is *experience* it. I'm not so much of a martyr for the cause to go through that just to rat you out. Not yet, anyway. Maybe you'll prove too horrid to keep safe. So test me, Tungét."

He went to Miss Dallatan's house, knocking on the gate and setting the dogs off. She was outside in a moment. "Took you long enough."

"Got a couple tacos first," he said.

"That makes sense, of course. Sorry, I'm in a bit of a—it's fine. But we've got something real here, and I don't like it when this sort of thing comes in person to my door, you hear? But come in."

"Is this a job for me?" he asked as he slipped through the gate, which he opened just enough to not let the dogs get out.

"Something like that," she said. "Not from me."

In her sitting room were Ajiñe and Gabrána, both looking very serious—if tired—as well as an older gentleman Wenthi hadn't seen before. He had the bearing of the sort of person who was used to being listened to, but he was clearly *baniz*. Rich, dark skin. Heavy features. Wenthi doubted he had a drop of Sehosian or Outhic blood.

"So this is Renzi Llionorco," he said in a deep timber. "We've heard so much about you."

"Can't say the same," Renzi said. "I don't know who you are."

"Mister Hocnupec," he said plainly. "You all are interested in joining the cause of Varazina. Of being inducted into the Inner Circles of the Fists of Zapi."

"Being inducted?" Gabrána asked. "I thought we were already part of it. We've been doing plenty."

"Plenty for the cause, yes. But that is not the same as being inducted. You need to fully understand what you are getting into."

"This sounds like some shit," Gabrána said, getting to her feet.

"Forgive me," he said. "I'm being needlessly obtuse. We've been using secrecy to protect the cause."

"And you're part of this?" Wenthi asked Miss Dallatan.

"Not precisely," she said. "But you know me, fingers in the dough."

"Oh, spirits," Nália said, walking around Wenthi. "You really impressed someone, didn't you?"

"He's here now," Ajiñe said, staring knives at Gabrána. "So can we move on with whatever this is? I presume it's all of my crew that are joining?"

"Being inducted," Hocnupec said. "I'm not being glib when I say that what this involves will change you. You—all of you—will have a choice. You have to choose."

"And if we refuse?" Gabrána asked.

"Gab!" Ajiñe said. "You don't—"

"I have a lot of questions," Gabrána said.

"Like, who are you, and who is Varazina?" Wenthi asked, taking the lead she gave him. "Are you part of the Inner Circle? Are you leading us toward something, a proper goal, or playing games in the shadows?"

"This is no game—"

"Renzi—" Ajiñe started.

"I'm really wondering," Wenthi said. "I mean, you all take mysterious orders from a voice on the radio, with no sense of who she really is, what she's trying to accomplish. Is she on your side?"

"Very rich from you, tory," Nália said.

"Her side is our side," Hocnupec said.

"So say you," Gabrána said. "But he is right. Do we get to meet her? Do we get to ask her questions? Or are we expected to just follow her instructions blindly?"

"You have reasonable questions," Hocnupec said. "Choose to become one with us if you wish, and do that with grace. Or you can keep doing the good work you've been doing for us. We will welcome that. Your free choice is the most important part."

"What an interesting concept," Nália said sharply. "Giving someone a choice."

Wenthi glared at her. "And how do we choose? Do we say yes or no now?"

"Now?" Hocnupec said. "Of course not. You don't know what you'd be saying yes to. No, first you must come with me and learn what we really are."

"Wait, wait," Gabrána said. "What do you mean by that? This is freaking me out. Are the Fists something more than a rebellion?"

"Gab, please," Ajiñe said.

Wenthi was grateful that Gabrána kept asking the questions, because he wanted to ask the same things, figure out where this was going. Her asking kept him from looking too suspicious. But even still, he wanted to be able to get more control over this situation. Hopefully get word to Paulei.

"Much more," Hocnupec said. "If you want to know more, come with me. And after you know, you will have more choices to make." He knelt down in front of her and Ajiñe. "You deserve to know what we are, and more importantly, what you are."

"I'm not sure what that means," Ajiñe said.

Hocnupec held out an open hand to her. "Then find out." She took it, and Gabrána did as well.

"And you, Mister Llionorco?" he asked, holding out his other hand. Wenthi started to reach out, but some instinct held him back.

"This is what you've been waiting for, Wenthi," Nália said mockingly. "You'll be able to crack this whole case and go home. Are you afraid they'll find out what you are?" She came up close to him. "Or are you afraid you'll find out what you are?"

Wenthi took his hand.

44

The cycles were left behind. Instead, Hocnupec had an old military truck—a Sehosian transport rumbler from the Great Noble—

"The Tyrant's War," Nália said absently from beside him. "No one here calls it Noble."

So now she could even pull idle thoughts from him. Wonderful.

The Sehosian rumbler had a tented bed, and with the canvas shut, Wenthi and the others wouldn't be able to see anything of where they were or where they were going. Which was probably the point. Hocnupec gestured for them to get in the back.

"Load in, friends," he said. Ajiñe got in without hesitation, which seemed to be enough to spur Gabrána. Wenthi got in right behind them, not wanting to show any lack of enthusiasm. Wherever they were going, this was the key to his mission. He had already been more successful with infiltrating the Fists of Zapi than any other officer, and that was something to be proud of.

"It's really not," Nália offered.

But if this led to the Inner Circle, the leaders, and hopefully Varazina, then . . . then all this would be worth it.

"I'm starting to think you don't love me, Wenthi," Nália said. "All the pity."

The truck went through the back alley and up and down the hills, twisting through so many curves of road that Wenthi lost all sense of direction. By the time they stopped, for all he knew, they could be anywhere in Outtown, Lowtown, or Hightown. And when Hocnupec opened up the canvas, the surroundings didn't help. They were in a closed garage, with no sign of the outside.

They were led through a dark hallway, down steps into a wide cellar, lit with colored candles. Seated on the floor already were Mensi, Fenito, and Nicalla.

"Now we're all here," Nicalla said. "What took you?"

"Renzi took his sweet time joining us," Gabrána snapped. Her mood could strip paint.

"There's no rush, all will be in due time," Hocnupec said. "Take off your shoes, sit, and contemplate."

They all did, and sat in uncomfortable silence, as Hocnupec looked upon them all with a beaming smile, constantly seeming like he was about to speak but never doing so. Multiple times one of the others—usually Gabrána—looked like they were about to say something, but then Hocnupec's gaze went on them, which was just enough to keep them from speaking up.

Finally, it was Ajiñe who snapped.

"What is this, exactly?" she asked.

"You are here to learn who you really are."

They all turned to the source of the voice—an old *baniz* woman, wearing only a brightly colored woven blanket draped over her body, reminding Wenthi of pictures in the history books from school.

"Who are we really?" he asked.

"You don't want them to know," Nália said, though the old woman had her rapt attention.

She came and sat in the center of them, holding a tray with cups of steaming tea. The aroma coming off them made it clear that it was made from the mushroom—the scent was the same but stronger, richer. Far more potent, most likely.

"And what is that?" Fenito asked.

"This will connect us to each other. Like you have connected before, but deeper, purer. Drink of this, and I can show you my heart, and the heart of the land."

"But who are you?" Gabrána asked.

"They gave me a name when I was born," the woman said. "And the invaders gave me another. But I found a name whispered by the spirits that guided me, and that is what I should be known by."

"Which is?" Fenito asked after an uncomfortable pause.

"Jendiscira."

"Forgive me," Nicalla said. "But that doesn't sound like a Zapi name, or a *baniz* one, or . . ."

"*Baniz*," Miss Jendiscira said with an ugly scoff. "That is another label the invaders gave me. Like they called you *jifoz*. They separated you and yours from me and mine, tried to make you think, thank my spirits at least I'm not *baniz*. All to divide us." She presented the tea tray again. "Take of this, of our land, and we can be united."

Ajiñe took one of the cups and drank it. Wenthi wanted to hesitate, but his hand—perhaps at Nália's bidding—snatched one as well. It went down hot and bitter, and as soon as the liquid touched his mouth, he felt like something was pushing in through his teeth, up his skull. It dropped into his stomach, and the feeling, like a spreading wildfire, went out of his body.

Nicalla and the others took theirs, with Gabrána the last. When they had all consumed theirs, Miss Jendiscira did the same.

"I will tell you the tale my grandmother told me, which was told to her by hers, which was told to her by hers, and thus came before any outsider sullied our land with their ways."

Wenthi didn't like how that sounded, nor did he like the queasy sensation of the room swaying, the candles melting into the walls, fire dancing around them.

"Long ago, there were five sisters who made the world," Miss Jendiscira said, her words turning into shapes that swirled into images around them like a cinescope show. "They cried out the oceans and they reached deep down into the waters to pull up the land, island after island. And they looked upon the land they pulled up, and knew it was beautiful.

"Their ecstasy at the beauty of the land was so great, it filled their wombs, and children sprang forth from them, to become the people of the land. The sisters looked upon their children, these beautiful people, and they said, 'We must give all we can to them. We must tear our hearts out so our blood can bless the land and give them the gifts they need to survive.'"

Wenthi's body was frozen. He couldn't speak, couldn't move—and furthermore, had no desire to do either—as the old woman's story played out in front of him in shadow and fire.

"The eldest said, 'My children must have bounty to harvest,' and tore out her heart and squeezed the blood onto the land, and the corn sprung up from where her blood spilled. She fell and died happy, knowing her children would be blessed with its nourishing riches.

"The second said, 'My children must have strength to forge,' and tore out her heart and squeezed the blood onto the land, and it soaked deep into the ground into veins of iron. She fell and died happy, knowing her children would be blessed with it, to build great things.

"The third said, 'My children must delight with fire on their tongues,' and tore out her heart and squeezed the blood onto the land, and where it fell, the chiles grew, red and yellow and green. She fell and died happy, knowing her children would be blessed with rich flavors to dance in their mouths.

"The fourth said, 'My children must know each other,' and tore out her heart and squeezed the blood onto the land, and where it fell the mushrooms grew. She fell and died happy, knowing her children would use them to join heart and flesh and spirit, and be of one people.

"And the people looked to the last sister, and asked, 'What of you, dear Mother? What gift will your blood bring?' And she said, 'My gift you will not understand, not for many years. I will give you water that is fire, fire that is water.' And the people asked, 'Why do you do this? How will this help us?' As she cut out her heart, she said, 'For you will need it when the world is full of enemies, and they will come for you. My sisters gave you nourishment, and strength, and flavor, and connection, but my gift will one day give you speed.' She squeezed her heart and her blood—thick and black—soaked deep, deep into the ground. 'And when you have that, your enemies shall never catch you.'"

Then the image of the last sister faded, and the black blood rose up from the ground, filling the room, covering Wenthi's face. For only a moment, he panicked as he drowned in the thick black, which then turned into pure darkness of nothing.

He threw out his hand out of instinct and made contact with another. He pulled himself toward the owner of the hand, to that body, wrapping himself around them out of pure instinct, to hold on to something, anything, to survive. Another body wrapped around him, and another, all intertwined and entangled limbs.

Then a sudden clap, and instead of thick, drowning darkness, the room was back to normal, except all of them—Wenthi and all of Ajiñe's crew—were now coiled up in a seven-person embrace with Miss Jendiscira. Ajiñe had her legs wrapped around Wenthi's waist, strong and powerful, while her fingers were buried deep in his hair.

"What was that?" she asked.

"Our story," Miss Jendiscira said. "The story of our people, as our ancestors used to tell it."

"Our people?" Wenthi asked.

"The true Zapi people, native to this land," she said. Her hands grabbed Nicalla's face and Mensi's neck. "Oh, dear children, you never could learn because your stories, your heritage, your very blood is corrupted by the outsiders who came and shat on our land. They steal our food, our iron, our oil . . . but we still have something, children. We have the mushroom to bind us together, and we have the true gift of the last sister."

"That's the oil," Fenito said. "She filled the land with oil, so we could build autos and cycles and trucks . . ."

"And have precious speed," Miss Jendiscira said. "I think you all know—and Renzi truly knows—that the real power of the mushrooms that the sisters blessed us with is unlocked, deeper and deeper, the faster you go."

"That's true," Wenthi said in unison with Nália, who he only just realized was equally entangled with the others. At least, from his perspective, her phantom was. The others gave no sign that they sensed her.

"And that is our purpose," Miss Jendiscira said. "To not only rid this place, our sacred land, of the outsiders who plague and control us, and once again be the rightful rulers, but to reclaim and rebuild the true heritage of our country. Of our people."

"The undercastes are the rightful people of this land," Nicalla said as she pulled herself out from the pile of bodies. "The *baniz* and the *jifoz*."

"Those words hurt us, child," Miss Jendiscira said. "They are corruptions of foreign words, imposed on us by invaders. Do you know how they came about?"

"During the first Outhic occupancy," Wenthi said. "At the end of the empire."

"You seem to be corrupted with their very education, Mister Llionorco, using their terms," she said. "Believe me, I fear for the children raised now. Though you aren't wrong. First the Sehosian Empire came and enslaved us as one of its provinces, and the ruling families of the empire took our people as spouses, lovers, partners. The blood of our people was mixed with theirs. But then the Outhic people came as conquerors, and they hated the Sehosians, hated the mixed children of the Sehosians, and most of all hated the native Zapi people. So they forced us into the castes, breaking us against each other. Even the very words come from them. Did you know that?"

"No," Ajiñe said.

"*Baniz* comes from their word for 'befouled,' and *jifoz* meant 'soiled.' This is what they think of us, child. And we keep using these words today."

"I didn't know that," Nália whispered. "Why don't we know that?"

"That's what they think of us," Ajiñe said. "It makes sense."

Miss Jendiscira continued, "And that is why they keep us under their heel, forcing the people who belong to this land into the most wretched and destitute lives."

Tears came to Wenthi's eyes. He wasn't sure if they were truly from himself or from Nália.

"We were taught that was just how things are," he whispered.

Miss Jendiscira took his hand, holding it tenderly. "What they wanted you all to think. And to separate you from us. You're told that caste mixing is what?"

“An abomination,” Wenthi said.

“When the truth is that you, and the *rhique*, you are the result of our open hearts generations ago. You are all our children.”

“Please,” Nicalla said. “The *rhique*? They all think—”

“They have the blood of this land,” Miss Jendiscira said. “All of us are, to some degree, children of the five sisters, and we must all honor that.” Her gaze was oddly intent on Wenthi. He felt that and had a strange sense that she saw through him, that she knew. She reached out to Hocnupec, taking his hand and pulling him toward her. “Of course, we *baniz*—as much as I hate that name—they are the ones who suffer most, and are the truest heirs of the legacy of the sisters. This fight is for the land of Zapisia, and especially for us.”

“What does this have to do with stealing fuel and food and such?” Mensi asked. “I want to get tories and the other occupiers off my neck, off the necks of my family. I don’t care about myths and blood of the land. That doesn’t help people in need.”

“You’re right,” she said. “So let’s move on. Everyone, shoes back on, let’s get moving.”

“What?” Ajiñe asked. She looked worried, like something had suddenly been ruined. “What are we doing?”

“We’re going to help people, Miss Osceba. So let’s load back into the truck, hmm?”

45

The truck bumped and jerked as it drove, and from under the canopy, that was the only hint Wenthi had where they were. They had left the paved cobblestone or smooth concrete, and were on a dirt road somewhere. His stomach was still churning from the story Miss Jendiscira told them and the visions her mushroom had induced. He had wanted to infiltrate the Fists of Zapi so they could root out the source of the rebellion, quell the problems they caused to the city and the country, but he had not been prepared for the toll it would be taking on him. He didn't need all this infesting his mind, his very soul. Nália—her intangible avatar, only sensed by him—seemed troubled by it in a very different way, as she sat in the corner of the truck in dark contemplation. At least she was being quiet. The last thing he wanted was her chatter.

"You all right?" Ajiñe asked, reading his face.

"Just wondering what the mystery is here," he said.

"You're still in?" she asked.

"Absolutely," he said. He had to keep playing the part. He looked to the others. "You all?"

"I'm not out," Fenito said. "But I'm definitely not all the way in. I was doing this to help people, not join a—" He faltered.

"Cult?" Gabrána offered.

"This was always about faith," Nicalla said.

"But not blind faith," Mensi said. "I don't see what stories about goddess sisters bleeding oil has to do with . . . anything."

"I was thinking the same thing," Wenthi said. He was glad to hear they were at least skeptical. Regardless of the fact that they were thieves who would have to be arrested and send to prison, he had to admit a certain fondness for all of them. And not just because of what Fenito and Gabrána would do with their mouths. "Not that it is, but I just—"

"You still don't get it," Nicalla said.

"Did you know about all this?" Ajiñe asked.

"Some of it," Nicalla said. "This isn't just about faith or belief. It's our history as a people. The land we belong to."

"All of us?" Fenito asked.

"I'm wondering about that as well," Mensi said. "They talked about being *baniz* like it made them more pure or something."

"Is that wrong?" Nicalla asked. "That's what *baniz* are, fully of local Zapisian heritage."

"She's right about that," Wenthi said. "But does that make us less of the land?"

"She said we're all children of the sisters," Nicalla said.

"Yeah," Ajiñe said. "But the *baniz* more so."

"I worry," Gabrána said, "that they don't plan to dismantle the system. They just want to flip it."

"She didn't say anything like that," Nicalla said.

"Yeah, but I wonder," Gabrána said. "In their vision, because I have a grandfather from Reloumene or Renzi's got a Sehosian grandmother, are we not properly Zapi or Pinogoz or something?"

"Pinogoz is a lie," Nicalla said. "That's a shit name from conquerors. It's not who we are."

"But you see what we're asking?" Wenthi asked. "Are we all equals in this idea of theirs? Or are we the lesser, tainted children of the sisters?"

"Especially you," Nália said in Wenthi's ear. "Where would a *rhique* boy with a pure-blooded, Prime Family *llipe* mother and *llipe* siblings fit in the scheme of things here?" She nodded over to Fenito and Mensi. "What would they do to your mama?"

The truck pulled to a bumpy stop. Then the canvas opened up to show the bright light of day, and Miss Jendiscira's grinning face.

"Come on out," Miss Jendiscira said. "Come on, come on."

They piled out of the truck, to a dusty, shattered landscape of broken buildings and ramshackle huts made from tires and corrugated metal. There were people everywhere in the dirt road. *Baniz* people, dressed in little more than rags.

It made the Ako Favel look like the 2nd Senja.

"Where are we?" Gabrána asked.

Nália answered in unison with Miss Jendiscira. "Gonetown."

"You're not serious," Ajiñe said.

"We've crossed the Oliruco, left the bounds of the city, and are looking at Northsprawl."

"Shit," Mensi said.

"That is right," Wenthi said. "What are we doing here?"

"First, you're taking out the crates in these trucks."

A few of the local *baniz*—spirits, these people looked wretched—came over to the trucks with toothless grins, holding open their hands. Those hands, most of them were missing fingers, or had horrifying infections.

Miss Jendiscira came over to them. "It's good to see you," she told one of them. "We've had a good season."

"What are we doing?" Gabrána asked.

"You haven't figured it out yet?" Nicalla asked as she took out the crates. "These people are starving."

"No, no," Wenthi said. "That's impossible, they'd have rations—"

"Rationing is controlled in the city," Jendiscira said. "Where the occupying Alliance government is working with the council, building things, making sure the city is cared for. But this? It's outside the limits. Purely under the Outhic military governorship. No one is watchguarding what happens here. None of the colonels gives a good damn if these people die."

"The rationing is handled completely differently," Nicalla said. "There's hardly a system at all, and these people—"

"Please, please," one of the *baniz* said as she approached them. "Is there medicine? My son."

"Yes, yes," Jendiscira said. "We're getting right on that." She looked at the rest of them. "Come on, daylight is burning."

"What are we—" Fenito started.

"Are you this foolish?" Nicalla asked him. "We've been stealing fuel, food, other supplies. Who do you think it's for? These people."

Wenthi understood, but Nália put it to voice, even if only he heard it. "You're here to deliver it to them."

"Let's get on it," he said, opening up a crate. It was full of military rations—packets of easy-to-transport meals, meant to be delivered to the soldiers across the ocean. He started handing them out to the gathered folks. "One of you find the medicine this woman needs."

"Well now," Nália said as she stayed at Wenthi's side. "You are putting up a good show."

"Shit yourself, Miss Enapi," he said under his breath. He handed out all that he had carried and went back to the crate. "Whatever you think of me, my job is to help people."

"Some help you give."

"I uphold the law," he said. "But this . . . this is a travesty. I . . ." His voice broke.

"You all right, Renzi?" Ajiñe asked, coming over to him.

"Sorry," he said, wiping away the tears at his eyes. "I didn't expect . . . These people are hungry, let's help them."

"Yeah," she said, opening up another crate.

"Very good performance," Nália said. "I'm almost believing you."

"No one should go hungry, not like this," he said. He knelt down in front of a pair of children, no older than he was during the bombings of Ziaparr. "You guys want some?"

"*Gia,*" the kid said in Old Zapi. Wenthi handed over two more meals.

"What do you know of hunger?" Nália snapped. "You haven't gone hungry a day in your life."

"You've been digging around in my head," he said back. "You'll see that isn't true."

Her eyes narrowed in concentration, and flashes of memory rolled out. The days upon days in the bunker. Lathéi crying and inconsolable. The soldiers coming, taking them out of the bunker, being dragged from camp to camp. Held by Rodiguen's forces, that camp falling to the Alliance, then the survivor patch before he and Lathéi were alone in the cracked streets of the Smokewalks . . .

Just a little way to the east, here in Gonetown.

"I'm sorry," she said. "I didn't think you really . . ."

"Because you don't know anything."

He looked to her, but she had gone. Retreated back to herself, still there in the back of his skull, shame burning like a dying ember.

"You all right?" Ajiñe came over, her eyes full of warmth and affection.

"I'm fine," he said. "I just . . . I was thinking about when I was kid, when the war was on, and . . ."

"Yeah," she said. "I'm glad you're here, on board with all this. I don't know if I've made this clear, but . . . I'm really glad you've been with us, Renzi."

"I'm glad I found you all," he said.

"Listen," she said. "Regardless of how the rest of this goes down, I think it's time I climbed up to your *fasai* myself, if you'd like."

"Just you and me?" he asked. He had been trying to ignore how attractive he had found Ajiñe. He had been acting on attraction with all the rest of the crew, for the sake of the mission, for the sake of maintaining his cover. Renzi Llionorco would, of course, fuck all of them because it was expected. Perhaps because he and Ajiñe hadn't yet, he found her all the more desirable.

Which was decidedly off-mission.

But there it was, nonetheless.

"If that's how you'd like it," she said. "I mean, if you really want backup . . ."

"Just you and me is good," he said.

She glanced around at the folks the others were passing food around to. "Do you notice something odd?"

"Like?"

"It's all young folks—hardly any older than Ziva—or very old people. Almost no real adults in this sprawl."

That was true. No one his age at all. "Maybe the ones who can work are off working right now?"

"Maybe," she said.

Jendiscira came over to them, carrying another case. With a slight gesture from her, Ajiñe went back to the truck.

"I'm glad you're getting it, Renzi." Jendiscira said. "Renzi Llionorco. You're not from Ziaparr, are you?"

"No, ma'am. The prison train just released me here."

"And your people?"

"Lost most of them in the purges, or bombings of Tofozaun."

"I'm sorry," she said, though she had a slight smile. "But come. I have something for you to see."

46

Jendiscira led Wenthi down the makeshift alleys between the ramshackle huts. As she walked, she occasionally handed coins to the baniz children that she passed, or took a moment just to touch someone who was sitting on the ground.

"We've been watching your cell for some time, Mister Llionorco," she said. "But it wasn't until your involvement that we knew they were truly ready for induction."

"Mine?" he asked. "Why is that?"

"You are relatively new to using the sacred mushroom, aren't you?"

"Sacred?" he asked

"You didn't realize that?" She sighed as she took a piece of fruit out of her robe pocket and handed it to a child. She knelt down next to them and said, "There's more by the trucks, parked that way. You won't go hungry today."

"I just never thought of it that way," he said. "Growing up, I have to admit—"

"You had absorbed the propaganda, saying how dangerous it is."

"And the stories of—" He almost said Rodiguen, but Nália's mind told him a better way. "The tyrant making a weapon from it."

"All of that was how they tried to control us. For generations they—the Sehosians, the Reloumene, the tyrant, the Alliance, it's all 'they'—have been determined to erase our history, our beliefs, the things that are sacred to who we are. That includes the mushroom, which is at the core of who we are."

"I thought every part of the world had the mushroom," Wenthi said.

"Yes, and each one is special to that land and those people. I don't care about the Sehosian one or Vailic or Outhic, or even what the ones on the other Zapisian Islands are or what they do. They are not for us, our land. Ours contains what is sacred to us, Renzi Llionorco."

"Which is?" he asked.

"When we use the mushroom—especially when the connection is accelerated through speed—we are all part of a greater network. When a few people use just a little and connect with each other for the intensity of lovemaking, they're only brushing against it. When you and your crew use it while also achieving great speed, you feel something stronger, right? You become more of each other, no?"

"Something like that."

"And you come closer, right?" Her eyes lit up as she spoke. "Tell me what happened on the highway."

"I—" He wasn't sure what to tell her at first, but a sudden thrust from Nália pushed the truth to his words. "I took control over Ajiñe's body. She was going to crash, but I could get a handle on her, her cycle, so I . . . just did."

"Imagine that it can do that. Not just feel each other's bodies, but *be* each other's bodies. And maybe, even deeper, the true heart of what it offers is more than any one of us can ever handle. Because that network is vast. I will tell you a secret, Renzi Llionorco."

"All right," he said, not sure where this was going. Any secret she might tell him would bring him one step closer to the center, one step closer to ending this assignment. But as this whole process went deeper into inductions and visions and diving into the divinity of mushrooms and the people of Pinogoz, the more he wanted to extract himself from it.

"Many people believe there are hidden patches all over the city, all over the island, where the mushroom grows, but they are wrong. It isn't patches of mushrooms at all. It is all one mushroom, a singular, ancient lifeform that has tendrils that spread throughout the island. The patches we harvest are the tiny bits that spring forth above the land. It connects us all because it is already part of the very island."

"I'm not sure I fully understand."

"And maybe none us truly do," she said. She reached out and caressed his cheek. "But consider this: the ancient Zapi connected with it, this ancient life, a reservoir of connections and thoughts that we still touch today. Buried within that reservoir is the memory of our people for generations upon generations. Histories, languages, cultures that have been lost to foreign incursion and colonization. But it isn't lost. It remains living memory. We can hold on to that, immerse ourselves into it."

"That's hard to believe. And I do not see how that ties to me joining the cell and how that got your attention."

"We were all connected to you during the meat truck run, and the train robbery. We felt you go farther and deeper in sync than we've ever seen before, Renzi. Briefly, you weren't just feeling what Ajiñe felt, but you truly inhabited her, made her body an extension of your own. You shone brighter than we could imagine. There is something very special about you. And we want—we hope you want—to explore what that means, and how far that can let us go."

Wenthi was more than a little disturbed about this. It sounded like madness, running counter to everything he had been taught about the mushroom and the people who use it. But he couldn't deny the experience he had had while on it, experience they had all sensed.

"And how much of that is because you aren't you, but us?" Nália asked, back at his side.

"It frightens you," Miss Jendiscira said, stopping in front of one dilapidated home. "And I understand that. That's why I've brought you here, so you can see how deep and true the connections between us all can be. Especially in terms of family."

"What's here?"

She smiled and knocked on the empty doorframe. "*Focoiz! Cuthinon Jendi!*"

Several *baniz* youths—at least a dozen—came out, some as old as Lathéi, some still toddlers. Two of the older ones had babies on their hips. All of them were in filthy, hole-filled clothes, most of them with no shoes.

"What what, Jendi?" the oldest looking girl said, passing off the baby to one of the other ones. "You come with the trucks again?"

"I did," Jendiscira said. "And I brought a friend. Renzi, this is Tyeja, and her siblings, halfs, and sides. There's a lot of names and I don't remember them all."

Wenthi offered his hand. "Renzi Llionorco," he said.

Tyeja gasped and then grabbed him in a huge embrace. "*Quid!*" she shouted. "*Nonfuz quid!*" The others all swarmed him with embraces and kisses.

"What?" he asked. "I don't understand what this is."

"You're home," Jendiscira said. "Tyeja and the rest are all named Llionorco."

"Blessed kin," Tyeja said, her eyes filling with tears. She looked to the others. "Go, go, get what's on the trucks before it's all gone."

"I don't understand," Wenthi said.

"I do," Nália said. "Looks like you just got caught."

"I know you don't," Jendiscira said. "But meet your people and learn who they are. We'll fetch you before the trucks leave."

"Let me see you," Tyeja said, looking him up and down. "Oh, you're very handsome, yes. Where were you from?"

"Tofozaun," he said.

"We lost a lot of kin in the wars, some shipped off to Tofo. At least that's what *queña* says. He'll know who your people are. But you are here and we love you."

"You don't even know me," Wenthi said.

"That's the truth," Nália added.

"But you are kin. Come in."

She led him into the dark hovel. It was little more than a shack with dirt floor, ratty blankets on the floor. Wenthi couldn't imagine as many people as he had seen were living there. The only proper furniture was a single wooden chair, where an old *baniz* man sat.

"What's the ruckus?" he asked. He looked up at Wenthi and his dark eyes lit up. "What's this fellow?"

"Miss Jendi brought him, *queña,*" Tyeja said. "He's kin."

"Renzi Llionorco," Wenthi said. He was stuck here; he needed to keep playing the part. "Though I don't know if we are actually family at all."

"Hmm," the old man said with a dark chuckle. "No, you most certainly are."

That was surprising. "I'm not from here, just—"

The old man waved him off. "Tyeja, did the others go to the trucks?"

"They did."

"Go join them, make sure they don't get stupid, hmm?"

"*Gia, queña,*" she said with a bow of her head, and left.

Wenthi looked back to the old man, who had a smile wider than Pino Sound. "Look at you, child. You've done well."

"Sir, maybe you're confused—" Wenthi said.

"Not in the slightest," the old man said. "I know exactly who you are, Wenthi."

47

Nália was cackling, which made it impossible for Wenthi to concentrate.

"My . . . my name is Renzi, sir—"

"Wenthi Tungét," the old man said with a wide grin that showed how many teeth were missing. "How is your mama? Don't listen to the radio much anymore, it's mostly prop garbage from whoever is pretending to be in charge, but last I heard she was doing good for herself."

"How . . . I don't . . . you must be mistaken."

"Hmm," the old man said. "Oh, of course. You're pretending to be 'Renzi Llionorco' for some reason. Some reason that Jendi woman and the rest of her folk probably wouldn't like." He laughed a little. "I tell you, I don't cotton to any of that stuff either. So sit your shit down, Wenthi, I'm not going to turn you in or anything."

"Why?" Wenthi asked.

"Excellent question," Nália added, her joviality diminishing.

"For exactly what Tyeja said, boy. You're kin. Did you not realize that?"

"No," Wenthi said.

"Then why the shit are you using the name Renzi Llionorco?"

"It was . . . they assigned me the name with the identity documents."

The old man chuckled. "Does your mother, by any chance, have some sort of influence over the people who would assign such things?"

"Yes," Wenthi admitted. "Who are you? *Queña*?"

"*Queña* is what they all call me. More or less means 'uncle' in the old tongue. Less accurate for many of them, more accurate for you." He sighed. "And you really don't remember."

"Remember what?"

"Sit, sit," the old man said, indicating he should take a spot on the floor. Wenthi did, and Nália took her place next to him, her face showing that she was as fascinated by this development as Wenthi was. How could a destitute old man in Northsprawl know his mother, claim to be family, know Wenthi? It was beyond understanding.

"So you think you're my uncle?" The uncomfortable truth of what had to be coming crept up Wenthi's spine, and he tried to hold it down. There was only one thing coming that could make even the slightest sense, and irrational panic gripped Wenthi as he fought against the idea of it.

"Think," the old man said with a scoff. "I am, son. Ocullo Llionorco, oldest of seven. They're all lost, including the youngest boy. My brother Renzi. Your father."

He knew that was coming, and still it defied belief.

"No," Wenthi said. "No, that's not—"

"You're his very image, if a bit paler and narrow about the eyes. Your mother's blood."

"Wait, wait, wait," Wenthi said. He didn't want to accept this. "My father was *rhique*, he served . . . he served in the Second Trans and died on the beach of Hessinfoth."

"Your mother told you all that?" Ocullo shook his head. "She always was a storyteller."

"What?"

"Do you know what she was like as a young woman? Do you know what this city was like before the Second Trans landed on our asses?"

"Not really." History books talked about rebuilding the world between the First and Second Trans, as the Shattered Dynasties moved into the High Sehosian Unity. The details of Pinogoz and Ziaparr were glossed over.

"There were a few years, just a few, when I was a young man, where it really looked like this was going to be its own country, with its own identity. And the Prime Families were scrambling to stay in power, and the caste system served their needs. So they cracked down on it even harder, forbidding caste-jumping, caste-mixing, all of it. But before the Second Trans hit our island, there was a movement to abolish the castes, to be one people. Your mother was only sixteen—and the youngest daughter of the Tungét tree—and was already a powerful voice for the cause. And she loved your father."

"My mother?" The idea of her as anything resembling a political radical was beyond comprehension. Especially one who challenged the castes.

"I thought she had taken up with a *baniz* boy as some sort of political statement. Using him as a toy to show off and prove how open she was, and definitely piss off her family. But when I actually saw them together, well, they convinced me they were the real thing."

"So what happened to her?" Nália asked.

"Yes, what happened?" Wenthi asked.

"The Second Trans happened. The whole island became a battleground between the High Unity and Reloumene, and Ziaparr was a critical game piece that kept switching hands. People were conscripted—pressed, really—into fighting for both sides. Renzi and I were both forced to fight. I don't know how he died, exactly—no one does, far as I know—but I do know he never went to Hessinfoth. He died in Ziaparr in the last seasons of the war. And Angú was already pregnant with you."

"Wait," Wenthi said. "If my father was *baniz—*"

"Then you shouldn't be *rhique*," Nália said. "You'd be *jifoz*. What is that shit?"

There was no way Ocullo heard her, but he chuckled like he had just the same. Maybe he understood exactly what Wenthi was asking. "The funny thing is, her family had the intention of disowning her for cavorting with my brother, but they had been killed in some of the final bombings before they had formalized it. When the dust settled at the end of the war, the Prime Families united to maintain some kind of control, some semblance of civility to rebuild with . . . and your mother was the only Tungét left. She dropped her talk of caste dissolution then. And I didn't see her—or you—for years."

"You expected me to remember."

"In the Tyrant's War. Or the Great Noble or whatever shit they call it. You were taken from your mother's bunker, do you remember?"

"It's a blur," Wenthi said. "I remember Mother hid Lathéi and me in there, and we were alone for days and days. Then Rodiguen's soldiers came, and we were at camps, and . . . then when the camp fell, we were alone in the Smokewalks until Mother found us."

"That's how you remember it?" Ocullo and Nália asked simultaneously. Nália reached out and touched his face—spirits, her hand felt so real—and her touch made memories break through like a flood.

The camp. Packed into bunks, everyone sleeping head-to-toe like fish tins. So many people—*baniz*, *jifoz*, *rhique*, all together—with almost no food. Tempers flaring. People screaming. Half the bunkhouse wanted to smother the little girl—Lathéi. Too loud, too needy, too much trouble. Too *llipe*. She'll grow up to stomp us all anyway so do it to her now.

And the old man—the one who looked out for children in the bunkhouse—standing up to them. The words Wenthi had forgotten after all those years. "He is my blood, and she is his blood, and we are all each other's. We'll not turn on them."

The bombing of the camp. Running away, the old man guiding the children away. Getting them safe, carrying Lathéi so Wenthi could run. Hiding in the ruins, gathering cans of food, making sure Wenthi ate. Making sure Lathéi survived.

Then Mother arriving in an Alliance car, with soldiers and officials. Taking Wenthi and Lathéi up in her arms.

Stopping the soldier who was about to shoot the old man.

"He's a friend."

Nália let go, bringing Wenthi back to the present moment.

"You were there," Wenthi said. "I . . . the camp, the Smokewalks, it . . ."

"You were young, and it was all a horror," Ocullo said. "I don't blame you for not wanting to remember."

"Why did my mother lie to me, though?"

"Isn't it obvious, shitface?" Nália asked. "She had to lie about who your father was so you could be *rhique*. Bitch couldn't have a *jifoz* child."

"To protect you, probably," Ocullo said. He reached out and took Wenthi's hand. "Which I did as well, and will keep doing."

"You wouldn't if you knew—" Nália started.

"I'm a tory," Wenthi said. "I'm supposed to infiltrate and take down the Fists of Zapi."

"Hmm," Ocullo said, nodding slowly. "Sounds like you've got a tough job ahead of you."

"You're not going to stop me?" Wenthi asked.

"I'm an old man," Ocullo said. "You'll do what you need to. Besides, Miss Jendi is always talking about how we are of one blood. That doesn't stop being true for you."

Tyeja came in, carrying armfuls of food, fear in her face. "Some soldiers are coming up. You better get back to the trucks, cousin."

"She's right," Ocullo said. "Run off now. Come back when you can, we'll talk more about your father."

"You know who he is?" Tyeja asked.

"I do," Ocullo said. "And I think he's starting to as well."

Ajiñe came up, sticking her head in the hovel. "There you are. Come on, Renzi, we've got to roll. Now."

48

Ajiñe held Wenthi's hand tight and pulled him down the dirt path.

"What is going on?"

"Alliance soldiers," she said. "Not the nucks, but actual soldiers in Reloumene uniforms."

"Yeah, that's who has jurisdiction outside of the city," Wenthi said. He knew from Mother's work that the Alliance stewardship worked to rebuild the cities, to eventually establish the independent, elected government, but outside the city needed more than they had the manpower or infrastructure to handle. So the Reloumene Army handled the countryside, especially getting the farms, mines, and oil fields back into shape after the wars had torn them apart. It took years before they got operations to the point where they could sustain Pinogoz and contribute their share to the war efforts.

"Are they policing?" he asked as she pulled him into a niche between two shanties, pressing her lean, muscular body against him in the tight space.

"I don't know what they're doing, but I'd guess they got word we were here, and came to crack down."

"Let's get back to the trucks."

The trucks weren't where they had left them.

"Shit!" Ajiñe muttered. "Did they leave without us?"

Wenthi noted the tracks in the mud, leading down the road, around one curve through another set of shanties. "That way."

They tracked the path through another row of shanties and huts, no sign of the trucks.

"What are we going to do?" Wenthi asked.

A pair of hands grabbed them both and pulled them into a narroway. Nicalla and Fenito.

"Thank your spirits," Nicalla said. "We thought they had nabbed you both."

"Are they nabbing?" Wenthi asked. "What for?"

"For just being here, I guess," Nicalla said.

"I heard a couple of the kids say something about how they round up for work detail," Fenito said. "When we heard them coming, Miss Jendi went to hide the trucks, and the locals said we needed to hide ourselves."

"Where are we going to hide?" Ajiñe said. "How do we get to the trucks?"

Wenthi looked back out at the wide path—not a proper road, but wide enough for the truck to pass through. "Looks like there's a set of shacks down the way there, big enough for the trucks to fit in. I would bet—"

Gabrána charged over to them all, tears streaming down her face. "They grabbed Mensi."

"Where?" Ajiñe asked.

"Down that way," Gabrána said. "Four of them, taking him toward their gunroller. I'm . . . I'm sorry, I panicked, I was scared, I didn't . . ."

"We need to find him," Ajiñe said. "But I don't see how we can—"

"We're still in faint sync with him," Wenthi said, realizing it was true. He could feel all of them, including Mensi, vibrating on the edge of his senses. "And with each other. That must be how we found each other right now."

"I just ran on instinct," Gabrána said. "And it brought me right here."

"We can't—" Fenito started.

"You all, follow the tracks, get to where Miss Jendi hid the truck, and stay with it. I'll go for Mensi."

"Alone?" Fenito asked.

"There are four of them," Gabrána said.

"If I go alone, the worst that happens is they just have Mensi and me. If we all get caught—"

"I couldn't bear it," Nicalla said.

Wenthi closed his eyes, and dug into himself, feeling the faint whispers of the sync with the rest of the crew. The echoes of Gabrána, Nicalla, Fenito, and Ajiñe right around him.

And Mensi. A quarter mile or so away.

Wenthi started running.

He opened his eyes, knowing Ajiñe was right with him.

"I said—"

"You don't give orders," she said.

He didn't argue, because he could feel Mensi moving. Faster. The speed helped Wenthi lock into Mensi, draw on more of his senses. Mensi was in the back of a truck, shackled with a number of young *baniz*—mostly boys and girls who had just turned old enough to do the Spirit Dance—which was driving away with a gunroller at the lead. Heading north, out of the town.

He ran, and as he ran, he felt more and more of Mensi—the fear clawing at his heart. Fear of where he was going, of never seeing his friends again, of not knowing what would happen.

He ran with his heart slamming, his lungs burning, but he could feel the truck and Mensi getting farther and farther away.

"Renzi!" Ajiñe pulled up on a garbage junkbash cycle, a weak-engined corn-burner. "Get on!"

He didn't argue and she poured off.

"Where did you—"

"I asked and they said yes," she said. "Which way?"

She went fast enough that he could just guide her, connected her with Mensi, feeling him pull on them.

"Can we go faster?" he asked.

"Not much," she said. "This cycle is shit."

"It's the only shit we have," he said. "Drive it to the white."

She gunned the throttle and went off.

"Take that path, and try to cut off the truck from the gunroller," he said.

"You got a plan?" she asked.

"Not at all," he said, pulling her knife out of its sheath.

Ajiñe crossed through the path, across a ramshackle alley, and dropped down another narroway just as the gunroller rumbled by. She darted into the path of the truck, crossing right in front of it.

Wenthi jumped when she did, and the truck slammed on the brakes. He landed on the hood, and holding on to it with one hand, hung the other arm over the side and jammed the knife into the wheel.

The truck swerved out of control, colliding with a corner pole of one of the shacks.

Wenthi held on, but one of the soldiers inside flew through the truck's windglass, while the other smashed into the steering wheel. Wenthi scrambled up the hood into the cab, and drove his fist into the soldier's face, again and again. The soldier sufficiently dazed, Wenthi pulled the keys off his hip and jumped out, around to the truck bed.

"Renzi," Mensi said weakly. "You shouldn't—"

"Let's just get you out," Wenthi said, unlocking Mensi's shackles. He got him out and pulled him down to the ground. "Can you run?"

"Not well," Mensi said. Ajiñe had come back around on the corn-burner.

"Let's go!" she shouted.

Wenthi helped Mensi on the back. "Get him out! I'm right behind!"

She darted off, and Wenthi climbed into the truck bed, unlocking more shackles.

"Go, go," he told the young *baniz*. "Get out of here!"

"Gunroller!" Nália shouted.

Wenthi looked up, and saw the gunroller had stopped and turned its turret toward the truck. Unshackling the last *baniz*, he pulled them off and ran just as the shell hit the truck. The blast knocked them both to the ground.

Wenthi was dazed and addled, not quite able to see or hear or will himself to move.

But yet he was on his feet, running.

Nália. Her head was clear. She got his body back on its feet and ran.

"Do you feel them?" he asked her. "Are they safe?" He was able to take a bit of control back, look over his shoulder. The gunroller was lumbering forth, but this path was one of the few it could take in this maze of shacks and shanties. The *baniz* had scattered and hid.

"This way," Nália said. She willed them to move down through the alleyway, around a set of hovels, and to a bombed-out lot just as the trucks rumbled over.

"Get in!" Jendiscira shouted, barely slowing down. Wenthi wasted no time jumping on and climbing into the canvassed bed, falling down in a heap around all five of his crew. All of them together, safe.

49

The ride home was quiet. Even Nália kept to herself, scowling at Wenthi the whole ride. She radiated anger and confusion, and he felt all that as well. The boundaries between where her emotions ended and his began were unclear.

They were parked at Circle Hyunma, which didn't make any damn sense to Wenthi.

"Why are we here?" he asked Jendiscira as they got out.

"Don't know if we were spotted by the soldiers," she said. "Or if they radioed into the Alliance nucks or Civil Patrol. We don't know if we were followed or watched. So we won't move to the next level of things until we're comfortable. And also until you're comfortable." She guided them over to the taco stand as she talked.

"I'm rather not comfortable with a lot of this," Gabrána said.

"Gab!" Nicalla snapped. "How can you—"

"I have opinions," Gabrána said.

"I have concerns," Fenito said.

"Same," Mensi added. "And I definitely think I earned them after that."

Nicalla's troubled expression turned to Ajiñe. "What do you think?"

"I'm in," Ajiñe said. "But I don't want to impose that on anyone else."

"Let me attempt to put your minds at ease," Jendiscira said. "For one, you are all being invited to be inducted with us to the closer circle. And each of you is free to make your own choice, not contingent on each other."

"So it isn't the whole cell or nothing?" Nicalla asked.

"Of course not," Jendiscira said.

That was good. The induction process would still move forward.

"Oh, that was it, you asshole," Nália said. "For a moment, I actually fell for it. I thought you saved Mensi because you cared, but that was it. You knew if he was gone, the rest wouldn't want to move forward, and you need that, don't you? That's how you get to the Inner Circle. To Varazina."

Jendiscira looked at him kindly. "Renzi, you are being very quiet."

"Because he's still figuring out how to arrest you all," Nália said. "Despite what just happened."

"Sorry," he said. "Between the soldiers and meeting my uncle, I'm . . . more than a little out of sorts."

"They were actually your family?" Ajiñe asked. "That's incredible."

"So incredible he's going to tether them all up," Nália hissed.

"Are we eating?" Wenthi asked. "Can we order and sit? I'm sorry, just, my head is spinning."

"Yes, of course," Jendiscira said. She gestured for them to sit at the table while she spoke to the cart chef.

"You aren't all right," Ajiñe said to Wenthi.

"I'm just ringing in my head," Wenthi said.

Mensi came over and took Wenthi's head with both hands and kissed him. "Thank you, brother. I . . . I don't even know what would have happened if you hadn't been there."

"We're in this together," Wenthi said. "Aren't we?"

"I want us to be," Ajiñe said. "I know that I . . . I need to move forward. Get closer to the center. Push this fight further. But if you want to turn off here, that's fine. All of you, any of you, it's fine."

"Yeah, but," Mensi said. "If, say, just you and Nic go all in, are we still a cell together? What do the rest of us do?"

"New cell?" Gabrána asked. "We find new recruits, or go our separate ways?"

"Or just go," Fenito said.

"I don't want to split the family," Mensi said. That word hit Wenthi in the chest. They were a family, and they had brought him into it.

"I don't either," Fenito said. "But this is a lot more mystical woo and ancient bullshit than I want."

"What do you want?" Nicalla asked. "Do you want a revolution?"

"Yeah," Fenito said. "But . . . what does that mean? What does that mean with the Fists? Do we push out the Alliance? Do we kill the caste system? Do we hold elections? Or do we try to, I don't know, rebuild ourselves into some idea of what Ancient Zapisia was?"

"Is that what you think they want?" Ajiñe asked.

"They talked about this ancient stuff like, I don't know, like it was something better. Like being farmers with spears was more pure than living in the here and now. Some bullshit like that."

"I don't think they're talking about giving up cycles or trains," Ajiñe said.

"But then what are they talking about with that?" Mensi asked.

Wenthi was barely listening to all of this, but words bubbled up from his mind. And he knew they were his own.

"I really wonder, what does this country—call it Pinogoz or Zapisia or whatever—can we even conceive what it should be like without Sehosian or Outhic interference?" he asked. "Is the Zapisia that might have been a goal? Or do we embrace that we have a legacy that is intrinsically connected to our invaders? They may have colonized this place, but we . . . each of us . . . are children of the colonizers."

"What is this shit you're on? Do you even actually mean this?" Nália asked. Her anger at him bled into his own emotions, and he wasn't sure where the boundary between them even was anymore, but the ideas he was having melted into her feelings, creating a strange harmony in his mind.

"I don't care about the Alliance overseers or the Outhic military governors," Wenthi said, surprised by how much he meant it. Or did Nália mean it? "Kick them all out. But if we are a part of something that is going to matter, that is about justice, about law—"

"Law?" Nicalla asked.

"The law isn't for us," Gabrána said.

"No, but . . . shouldn't it be?" He didn't have the words, but the ideas crashed into Nália's emotions and bounced back to him more fully formed. "Let's say for the sake of argument, the revolution is successful. We reclaim this country. What does that look like? What is justice in that country? What is the law there? Who decides what it looks like and how do we make it fair?"

Jendiscira came over with trays full of a wide variety of tacos and salsas. "Those are heady questions," she said.

"But that's right on it," Mensi said, pointing a finger at Wenthi. "He's on target."

"How can we know that working with you creates the better world?" Gabrána asked. "Spirits, do we even know if we can create one? Are we just fighters who never should win the fight?"

"Aren't you angry?" Nicalla asked Gabrána.

"Livid," Gabrána said, smothering her taco with salsa and lime. "All the damn time. I am angry *all the time* about how things are here. Which is why I love what we do, punching in the nose of the Alliance and all the others who have dared grind their boots into our country."

"But does that qualify us to do better?" Jendiscira asked. "Would you feel better if I said I struggled with it?"

"A little," Fenito said between bites.

"This is what I learned today," Wenthi said. "My parents were part of a movement, before the Second Trans came here. To change things, to dissolve the caste system, to try and change all of it. First I've heard of that. Have any of you?"

Heads knocked all around, save Jendiscira. None of them had.

"And I wonder what that world would have looked like. What we would look like if *baniz*, *jifoz*, *rhique*, and *llipe* were all the same."

"There it is," Nália said.

"Even *llipe*?" Ajiñe asked.

"Privileged cocks," Nicalla said.

"Cocks who were born here," Gabrána said. "And in most cases, so were their parents and theirs."

"Do we plan to make a nation that excludes them?" Wenthi asked. "Do we punish them for who they were born to?"

"Like they did to us?" Ajiñe asked, which Nália echoed in near unison.

"Would doing it back be justice?" Wenthi asked. He took up a taco—beef or pork, he didn't know or care. He just needed to eat something.

Gabrána spoke up. "I had a full chart done a few years ago."

"Spirits, why?" Ajiñe asked.

"I wanted to know. I always—"

"Always thought you were light enough to pass for *rhique*?" Nicalla shouted. "Thought you could request a chart and learn you were just enough Sehosian to put you over the line?"

"It turns out my father was *llipe*. I didn't know."

"Some *llipe* are with us," Jendiscira said. "Not inducted into the Inner Circles, but with the cause. The boy who was arrested a ways back. Enzu."

"Shitting traitor, he was," Nália shouted. "Thought he could trick us."

"Was he really with us?" Nicalla asked. "Are any of you? Spirits, I'm not sure what 'us' even is."

"I hope you all are," Jendiscira said. She took Wenthi's hand. "We need your ideals. We need your sense of justice."

Nália scoffed again. "His sense of justice is us all in prison. Or worse."

The radio on the taco cart squelched. *"Justice isn't in the streets, not tonight. Tonight we bring it in, tonight we ravage our hearts, tonight we close our fists. Tonight is united in we, tonight is united in love, tonight is a beating drum of truth. Tonight we come together and welcome."*

Unease filled Wenthi's gut on hearing her voice again. Who was she? Where was she? What did she want?

"Finish eating, children," Jendiscira said. "We'll come together for the last rituals, and you can all decide where you stand."

50

They were brought back to the temple, or warehouse, or whatever it was, where Hocnupec was waiting with several other people—a full mix of *baniz, jifoz,* and even a few so fair they had to be *rhique.* There were a few faces he had seen before, like Casintel and Bindeniz. They were all dressed in simple robes of agave cloth, the sort that Wenthi had seen only in the Great National Museum in the 7th Senja.

"Welcome, children," he said. "You've seen what we do, what we want. Are you ready for us to open our heart to you?"

"You, or Varazina?" Ajiñe asked. "Are we actually going to meet her?"

"You will feel her," Hocnupec said. "We will all feel her and know her. And each other."

Wenthi noticed the answer was a dodge. Why was that?

Nicalla's hand went up. "Does this ritual mean we have to fuck? I . . . I want to be a part of this, with all my heart, but . . . I hate fucking. I really hate it so much."

"Completely?" Hocnupec asked. He looked at the other members around him like he didn't even know how to respond to that.

"We've never inducted an *edoromé* before," Jendiscira said.

"Well, that's what I am," Nicalla said. "And I want to be part of it, but . . ."

"Our induction, our faith, it does involve surrendering to each other, giving ourselves fully. Heart and mind and body in totality. I don't mean to be offensive, but that is how . . ."

Ajiñe stepped closer to Nicalla. "We all love each other, in every way possible, but in this we have always honored Nicalla. None of us could continue with this if she isn't respected here."

"Of course you couldn't," Jendiscira said.

"I won't be dishonest," Hocnupec said. "Regardless of the physicality, the induction will be emotionally intense. There is intended to be joy in release and connection. But if that does not bring you joy, you will not be imposed upon that way. We would never do that."

"And I don't want to be in sync with people who are," Nicalla said.

"She knows how to pull herself out when she wants to," Gabrána said.

"You might find it more challenging in these circumstances," Jendiscira said. "The sync connecting you here will be stronger than you've ever experienced. I want you to understand that if you choose to go forward."

Wenthi saw an opportunity here, and moved up next to Nicalla. "Whatever you choose, I'm with you."

Mensi and Fenito came up to Nicalla and put their hands on her shoulder. "We go where you do, sister."

Nicalla took Wenthi's hand, and then Ajiñe's. "No matter what, stay close to me. I can endure anything if you are with me."

"Damn it," Gabrána said. "All right, all of us together. I would accept nothing less."

"All of us," Ajiñe said.

That worked. They were moving forward now, and Wenthi knew the rest of the cell fully accepted him as part of their family. He would have no problem—

"Betraying them?" Nália asked. "All this, all you saw, all you learned, and you're still gunning the throttle to turn on these people who love you."

"What now?" Wenthi asked.

"Now you can shit yourself until you die," Nália said.

"Now we begin," Hocnupec said. "With fire and iron and connection and speed. And it's time to commune with Varazina."

51

Their clothes had been taken, which Wenthi had expected. Everything leading up to this had told him that at some point in this process, he and the rest would be naked. He didn't object to that—being naked with Ajiñe and the rest of the crew was quite agreeable—but he found it decidedly amusing. It was predictable to the point of absurdity.

Two people came up to attend to each of them, washing their bodies with sponges and cold water. The attention felt respectful and reverent, not spiritless like the bath servants forced to wash High Captain Sengejú in front of Wenthi. No one was flexing power over anyone else, and Wenthi felt equal to the rest of the cell, to everyone in the room.

Nália paced angrily about while the attendants dressed each of them in white robes of woven agave. Coarse and rough, the robes and Nália's attitude. As they were led outside, through the back of the warehouse to an empty lot, Nália started shouting at every other person, screaming for them to notice her, hear her. No one reacted to that.

Wenthi wondered why she didn't try to take his body over, force her words from his mouth. Maybe because right in this moment, he was focused, calm. She couldn't push through that.

Hocnupec presented a mushroom to each of them. Not the dried powder, not the tea, but whole caps. Wenthi took it, and his thoughts were flooded with all the stories from the broadcasts and prop scopes of people who had their minds wrecked by the mushroom, and to see it here in such a pure form made those fears trickle up the base of his skull.

Though he had been on the mushroom all this time. The government had ordered him to use it, to let Doctor Shebiruht—the monster behind the tyrant—use it on him. Was it all a lie? A story to hold people down, to keep them from finding connection or empathy?

"Go on," Nália taunted at him. "Maybe it will shred your brain—both our brains."

Wenthi tried to not pay her any mind, as his attention was far more on the strange thing in the middle of the lot. It was a great circular cage, perched on a gimbal of some sort. Chains led from the cage to three cycles.

"What is this?" Ajiñe asked.

"This is the induction. You will take the mushroom and take your place inside. And then we apply speed and signal. The rest will be what it will be."

"Speed and signal?" Fenito asked. "Meaning?"

"We will spin you faster and faster," Hocnupec said. "Intensifying your connection to us, to the mushroom, to everything. Then Varazina will come to you, as she does, through the signal of the radio."

"So she isn't *here*," Gabrána asserted. Despite all the openness they claimed, they were holding something back. Wenthi began to wonder if they even knew what they were holding back.

"If you wish to back away, that is your choice," Hocnupec said. "It will be honored."

Nicalla swallowed her mushroom and climbed up into the cage. Ajiñe looked to Wenthi for support.

He nodded back to her and took his as she took hers. Then he took her hand and walked into the cage.

Mensi was right behind them, and Fenito and Gabrána followed.

In the cage, there were six rough mattresses in a circle, bolted to the floor, each with a radio bolted at the head of the mattress. Loud static poured out of each speaker.

"Well, this seems pretty obvious," Ajiñe said, lying down on one of the mattresses. Wenthi took a spot next to her, and soon the rest of the group were in position.

Jendiscira came in, her face a picture of blissful calm. "I'm thrilled you've all come this far. I will be clear, this will be like nothing you've known before. I cannot tell you exactly what you will experience, only that your experience will be yours. But you will know each other, the land, everything, deeper and stronger than you've ever known before. May your spirits watch over you, and tell you what you need."

She stepped out, and Nália was there, right over Wenthi's face.

"That mushroom is already doing things, friend," she whispered. "Do you feel that?"

He felt his body spreading out beyond his fingertips, joining with Ajiñe and Mensi on either side of him, as their bodies spread out beyond their fingertips, and his sense of where he ended and they began melted into nothingness. Everything he was fell into the two of them, and then into Nicalla, Fenito, and Gabrána.

And Nália. Dropped in the dark in the ice room. Deep and cold and nothing. As connected as he was to everything out here, he still felt her strongest of all, like an anchor keeping him down.

Nália's phantom hands enlaced with his, her hips grinding onto him.

Then the cycles fired up and started riding, riding in a circle, and the cage began to spin.

Spinning faster and faster, and as it spun, the static grew louder. Wenthi tried to see outside, but everything was just a blur of light and color as they went faster and faster, and the thing that was his own body became just a memory, his sense of self and identity all melting away and merging into his cell. He was Wenthi and Nália and Ajiñe and Mensi and Nicalla and Gabrána and Fenito and the static and the people outside the cage and the land beneath their feet and the tendrils of the mushroom curling and winding through the ground and deposits of iron and pools of oil and the grass and trees and the corn.

And Renzi. He had to keep Renzi in the front. Hide Wenthi away, at the bottom of who he was, keep that deep and secret.

"Bring him out," Nália whispered in his ear. "Let them see the real you."

"Surrender to the truth," Renzi whispered in his other ear.

He looked up to see himself—except not him, fully Renzi Llionorco, the manifestation of the person he was pretending to be. As if the fiction he had created had taken form.

"Surrender everything," Nália said, and Renzi grabbed her face and started kissing her. Renzi and Nália's hands caressed each other as they both mounted Wenthi, hands and mouths and everything until Wenthi was inside Nália while Renzi was inside him.

"I hate you so much," Nália whispered as she drove her hips against him.

"And you hate yourself more," Renzi said as he pushed deeper, biting Wenthi's ear as he hissed at him.

"Surrender," Nália said.

"Give yourself," Renzi said.

"Join us," said another woman. The static took form around them.

And there, in the center of the cage, which was racing in a spin of incredible velocity, but somehow completely still and quiet, stood a woman—tall, gracile, and wearing a crown and cape of living flowers.

Varazina.

Not just a woman but an ancient spirit, and ancestor to all of them, yet living and present and flesh in front of them.

"Come to me," she said. "Be one of all Zapisia, be true to your blood, and be free."

Despite Wenthi's body being entwined in impossible phantom sex with Nália and himself, he stood—another impossibility in the racing, spinning cage—but yet he stood.

Ajiñe and Mensi had stood as well, taking his hands. The six of them were all joined together, a ring of six bodies and one body at once, and they stepped forward as one, surrounding this magical, impossible woman.

Somehow with only two hands she touched all six of them, and in an instant eternity, their worlds exploded.

52

It felt like the release of climax, but stronger and more intense than anything Wenthi had ever experienced.

And it didn't end.

This must be how people lost their mind to the bliss, he managed to think in the small part of the back of his mind, that part he held closed off from everything else. *This is more than anyone could handle alone.*

But he wasn't alone. He was one with the rest of the crew, one with

Nália—he was vaguely aware of sounds around her: machines beeping, concerned voices of nurses—one with Varazina and all the others around them.

All the others—the rest of the Fists. They were all here, together in the cage.

No, they were no longer in the cage, at least as far as he could tell. It was a stone chamber, decorated with thousands of flowers in every color. Green vines snaked across the ceiling, with more flowers growing there, and the floor—

The floor beneath them was soft and pliant, but not quite dirt.

Wenthi knelt down and touched it.

The mushroom. Pulses of energy—beating like a hidden heart within the island—came into Wenthi through his hands and feet, and through everyone else there in the chamber.

The chamber isn't real, he thought.

"We're within the mushroom itself," Nália whispered in reverent awe as her ghostly body shook on the ground in front of Wenthi. If the others could see her, could feel her, they gave no sign of it. "This is where all our minds come together."

"Feel it," Varazina whispered. She was a radiant goddess, naked save for the cascade of flowers that covered her from every direction. "Listen to it all as it fills you."

A pulse washed up through them, and with it, memory. Dozens of generations ago, Zapisian ancestors with stone tools and animal skins. Burning the mushroom in sweet-smelling fires and breathing in the smoke. Communing with the spirits of their ancestors, living memory within the mushroom. Learning the stories, the secrets of the land.

Another pulse.

Time raced by. Temples to the ancestors built. Sages and holy ones climbing up the giant poles, ropes tied to their waists. They coiled the ropes around the top of the pole, and drank deeply of the mushroom brew, then let themselves fly off the pole. They spun through the air, faster and faster, their connections to each other building stronger.

They would take the mushroom and run.

They would take the mushroom and throw themselves off cliffs into the ocean.

Anything, anything, to go faster.

Stone tools became bronze, and bronze became iron.

Cities rose, wars raged. Generations lived and loved and fought and fucked and built and bartered and became a people. Became a Zapisian nation.

Then the Sehosians came.

Another pulse. This one sharp and painful.

They came with great sailed ships and pistols and steel and their hard boot came down on the Zapisian people. They forced the island, the cities, the people, into their image. They brought their laws, their language, their food, their disease, and pushed it all on the people. They scrubbed the temples of all their character, all their purpose, leaving a shadow of its memory behind.

They made a home on the land, made the people into their servants, fucking them and claiming the children as their own.

Then their empire fell. Sehosia couldn't impose itself upon them anymore, though many of their children still lived on the island.

Another pulse.

For a moment, the Zapisian people, mixed and muddied as they were with Sehosian blood, started to find themselves again. They dug into the earth and found the mushroom again and remembered the spirits of their ancestors that used to guide them. They found iron in the ground and made it into steel. They found oil and made it into fire.

And the cleverest ones made the engine. Engines of steam, engines of oil. They built the engines into trains and autos and cycles, and they would race.

Faster and faster.

Another pulse.

It was more than Wenthi could handle. So much at once. He reached out and pulled whoever's hand he found, bringing their body to him. Amid the memory and emotion and connection with the dozens and dozens of faithful Fists and Varazina and the crew, he needed to feel real flesh against his own. Something to anchor himself to his actual body.

The Outhic people came. Reloumene and Hemish and more. They

brought their rules and created castes and declared people as sullied or useless and forced them into camps and divided the city into senjas and . . .

Another pulse.

The wars came. First Transoceanic. Second Transoceanic. Great Noble. Zapisia was fought on. Zapisia was fought over. Bombs from the sky. The island split into two peoples. Fellaz, which would be free. Pinogoz, under the tyrant's thumb.

So many dead.

All blamed for the wars they wanted no part of. Forced to pay a debt they never asked for.

Another pulse.

This one filled with love and joy and pleasure.

A spark in Wenthi's heart that ignited the engine of his soul.

He pulled the bodies closer to him, as they clawed to be one with his flesh. Mouths on his mouth, his chest, his legs, everywhere. Some real, in the room with him. Others elsewhere, the echoes of their psyches joining in the throng of naked bodies grinding and pushing and kissing and exploding.

Wenthi looked up to find Ajiñe's eyes, her body on top of him, him inside of her, and he was as much her as she was him. And they both were each other and one and building toward waves and pulses of greater pleasure. Every body—bodies of people all across the city, secretly united through the network, through the sync of the mushroom, through the spirit of the people.

Faster. And faster.

Wenthi couldn't hold anything back much longer. They were all giving him everything, everything, and there was nothing he couldn't give, wouldn't give to be fully with them.

He looked up to find Nália's eyes.

They bore into him with hatred and ecstasy. As her body—she felt as real as any flesh he had ever felt—pushed against his, he pushed inside her, and her hands wrapped around his neck.

"I hate you so much," she said again through her heaving breaths, edging closer and closer to climax.

He tried to push her off him, but his hands just found other bodies, and she rode harder and harder as her hands tightened around his throat. His body was fire, and nothing could keep it from exploding.

Together, he and Nália went over the edge.

And left his body behind.

REFUEL: VISION

Up.

Beyond.

Together, Nália and Wenthi were one consciousness without form or body. They flew out of the city, nothing but mind and vision.

Across the wide sprawl of shattered land, dry and cracked where water once flowed, where corn grew.

Smoke and steam belching out of great chimneys in the distance, they flew across the plains toward the horror.

It was horror. Deep mines for iron, refineries for steel. People working the machines, digging with their bare hands, bloody and raw. Wearing only rags, with chains and steel collars on the people as they worked. *Baniz* people.

Around them, soldiers—Reloumene soldiers, with heavy guns—forcing them to work. The butt of a rifle slammed against one woman's face when she faltered. A boot driven into another man's knee when he stumbled.

"Get back to it," an officer with a thick Reloumic accent said. "You're behind the quota."

They reached to help the enslaved people, but instead they flew out again, farther to a farm. More *baniz*, sleeping in squalor, the bunkhouse overpacked with bodies and stinking of disease and raw filth. Rats and roaches crawled over them as they tried to sleep.

And the soldiers came in, slamming on the lights. "To the fields, you worthless slugs! You're behind on the harvest."

They had no fist to strike the soldiers, no hand to help the people up. They were nothing, nothing but pain and anger and shame as they flew across more of the wasted landscape, ruined by the Alliance bombs and the tyrant's atrocities.

The oil fields. Great metal derricks, pumping precious blood of the five sisters out of the holy land of Zapisia, while their children—the *baniz* people forced to work at gunpoint. The ones not working not even given the dignity of the bunkhouse, kept in literal cages, locked up like they were wild animals.

"Why are you stopping?" a soldier demanded to a group of workers. "We can't stop the drills!"

"The machines are—" one man started.

"Shut your fucking mouth!" the solider said, and he went over and flipped a switch.

The drill started up, metal grinding on metal.

A spark danced from the drill.

Fire exploded from the ground.

Fire burst forth, covering the soldiers and workers around the drill. All of them screamed in horror, pain, terror—which Wenthi and Nália felt every moment of.

The fire spread. It would soon hit the other wells, spread out of control. To all the derricks.

To the cages.

To the people, trapped.

FIFTH CIRCUIT:
THE VOICE OF THE REVOLUTION

53

Nália slammed back into flesh, the weight and solidity of it making her gasp for air. She reached out and grabbed—she could reach and grab—the person nearest to her. Fenito, whose naked body was curled up against hers. She pulled him close, mostly out of instinct.

"Where are we?" she shouted.

Not her voice. His.

Wenthi's.

"Renzi, easy," Fenito said, pushing back on Wenthi's bare chest. "You're all right."

"No," Nália said as she tried to find her bearings. She flexed Wenthi's fingers, feeling the power of his muscular arms. Sweet air in his lungs. She had been feeling everything through his body since this nightmare began, but now it was different. She was in complete control. It felt like it was her own.

They were still in the cage. It was hard to imagine that they had never really left it. Morning light was hanging overhead. Five of them were naked and clumped together in an exhausted mass where they had all fucked until completely spent. Nicalla sat apart from them, still in her robe, but with a similar blissful calm on her face. Around the cage, the rest of the Fists were strewn around the courtyard, all naked and dozing.

She had seen it. The horror. The suffering. The fire. People were burning. Right now. It was happening right now.

"Get up, get up. Did you see it?"

"I saw it," Nicalla whispered. "Varazina showed us the truth. Of the land, and the memory, and our connection. It was beautiful."

"No, after that," Nália said, pulling herself to his feet. Wenthi's feet. She was still disoriented, his body hers, as real as anything she ever knew.

"After was more than just seeing," Gabrána said.

Ajiñe was on her feet, concern on her face. "Renzi, are you all right? What did you experience?"

Nália took a moment to collect herself, anchoring in Ajiñe's dark eyes.

Renzi. Ajiñe saw her as Renzi, of course. Presumed she was Renzi, and talked to her as if she was him.

She could be Renzi Llionorco.

Wenthi appeared next to her, dressed in his patrol uniform, looking like he wanted a fight. "Stop that right now!"

"I saw . . . everything," she told Ajiñe, ignoring Wenthi. He was exerting pressure on her, the same as he always did when he forced her down. Before his will had been like a torrential storm, tearing into her, but now it was little more than gentle wind. No power over her. "I saw everything, over the whole country. The mines, the farms, the oil derricks, and the people who were forced to work there."

"Oh, my spirits," Ajiñe said.

"I saw all of it," Nália said, glancing at him. "I saw how they were forced to live. How they were treated. Worse than animals."

Wenthi stammered, backing down. "It was . . . a horror. The fire. The locked cages. How could . . . how could anyone . . ."

"We need to move," Nália said, taking Ajiñe's hand as she jumped out of the cage. "Everyone! Get up! Get up!"

Jendiscira, lazily pulling her robe over her body, came over to them. "Calm down, Renzi. You did fine. You are one of us, now."

"No, you don't understand," she said. She could still feel it. Hear the crackling flames. The searing heat. The fear. People couldn't escape. "Something is happening, out in the oil fields."

"We know about the oil fields," Jendiscira said. "The soldiers who abduct the able-bodied *baniz* from Gonetown, they put them to work in the fields, in the mines. It's a horror—"

"It's on fire!" she shouted. "I saw it, there's a fire in the oil fields, and—"

"I'm sure you did—" Jendiscira said. "It is real."

"They're trapped," Nália said. "I'm still there in a way. Still with them." She realized there was a buzz of the sync in the back of his head, with everyone here. Stronger with his cell, but lightly with Jendiscira and Hocnupec and everyone else here, people throughout the city. And the poor, suffering *baniz* across the countryside. All of them were with her. "I can feel all of it."

Jendiscira touched Nália, her weathered hand caressing the stubble on

Wenthi's cheek. Nália wasn't sure what to make of the sensation. "We knew there was something unique about you. Varazina said so. You have a gift with the mushroom beyond the rest of us."

"Listen to me!" she said. "The derricks are burning. People will die. We have to—"

"Have to what?" Hocnupec asked. "Those fields are over a hundred twenty kilos away."

Ajiñe was at her side. "And our cycles can do two-forty on a straight run easy. Maybe even faster. If we go now—"

"Go to where?" Hocnupec asked. "To the oil fields?"

"They are on fire!" Nália shouted, though still no one but Wenthi heard her.

"It's impossible," Jendiscira said. "The highways are patrolled by military forces. Who also control the oil fields."

"I'm sorry?" Gabrána said, coming up behind Wenthi. The rest of the crew were with him, shoulder to shoulder. "I thought we were a rebellion."

"I thought we were the Fists of Zapi," Fenito added.

"I thought we were here to fight those shiteaters," Mensi said.

Nicalla came up, joining hands with them. "Wasn't that the point of all this?"

Spirits, they all loved Renzi.

"That's me," Wenthi pressed.

Who you pretended to be, she pushed back. *But I could really be that.*

"You think you're going to hold my body forever?"

I can be Renzi Llionorco, better than you ever were. To punctuate her point, she pulled Fenito and Ajiñe closer to herself.

"We are fighting them," Jendiscira said firmly. "But we have limits. There are dozens of dozens of dozens of soldiers between us and those fields. Dozens of dozens of ours would die just to get there."

"Dozens of dozens are dying there," Nália insisted. "I can still feel them." It was just a faint shadow, but that connection still held. The screams, the burning flesh, the scent of death, she felt it all.

"We need to go," Ajiñe said.

"We can't do anything for those people," Hocnupec said. "Assuming your visit was real—"

"It is," Jendiscira said calmly, placing a hand on Hocnupec's bare chest. "Renzi is much more attuned to the mushroom than any of us."

"So listen to him!" Ajiñe pushed.

"It's not a matter of believing him. It's what we can do."

Nália couldn't believe her ears, even though they were Wenthi's. "What does Varazina say?"

"The speakers are quiet. She's not saying anything yet."

"Well, let's call her—"

"That is not how it works, child," Hocnupec said. "She leads us in grace. We do not demand of her."

"That sounds like some bullshit," Wenthi said.

As much as she hated the idea of it, Nália found herself agreeing with him. There was something rotten about that.

"You've all been through an extraordinary experience," Jendiscira said. "And we welcome you into the circles with us. But clearly you need some time to process and settle your emotions. It's very normal."

"But—" Nália said.

"Take them back to their hideout," Jendiscira told a pair of people. "Let them calm down, and I'm certain Varazina will reach out to us soon and guide us on the proper path."

54

Nália watched Wenthi's avatar as they all rode in the back of the truck. She knew where his thoughts were at. He wanted to regain control of his body. But he was also tracking their route. Even now, she noticed—and Wenthi noticed as well—there wasn't complete openness with the Fists yet. They were put in the back of the truck, the canvas closed.

"You don't think that's a bit odd?" she asked Ajiñe.

"Maybe a little," Ajiñe said. "But an open truck with the six of us in the bed? Bait for the patrol. Especially with them still riled up over the fuel raid the other night."

"Yeah, I think it's less about keeping things secret from us, and more about being safe," Mensi added.

Gabrána came over, caressing Nália's leg. "You seemed pretty spooked back there. You can talk about it if you need to."

"I want to know what you all experienced," Nália said. "None of you felt what I did. None of you saw it."

"I'm curious what you felt," Fenito said to Nicalla. "I mean, I know for me, it was a full-on fuckfest. All the rest of us were all in it, so was Varazina, so were the old folks of the inner circle. People I ain't even met before."

"Yeah," Mensi said. "It was . . ." He chuckled ruefully. "It was a lot more than I was ready for. I think I . . . I kind of lost myself in the waves and waves of the rest of you. And, honestly, I don't think I'm going to be able to get hard again for the rest of the season."

"Same," Fenito said.

"Renzi isn't having that problem," Gabrána said, her hand moving to Nália's crotch. Which was more than Nália wanted to deal with right now. As interesting as it would be fully engaging in the pleasures of Wenthi's body, in complete control of it, her head wasn't in that.

"Not now," she said. "No, it was the same for us . . . for me. But then at the height of climax—or the apex of the coming upon coming, I suppose—it was almost like I left my body."

"My body," Wenthi said absently.

"But more, it was like I connected to everything, at a level beyond anything I had ever experienced. Like I was in sync with everyone who had ever used the *myco*, and the great mushroom itself."

"The great mushroom?" Ajiñe asked.

"It's all one lifeform," Nicalla said quietly. "It's older than anything else in the world, its tendrils and fibers spreading under the land."

"You knew that?" Nália asked.

"I . . . felt it. While you were all scrumping each other, I was communing with the life force of the mushroom. And Varazina. We were one with the mushroom itself. I've never been more at peace."

"So you didn't feel us all fucking?" Gabrána asked.

"I was aware of it, but I didn't experience it. I was also aware of being something beyond my own humanity."

"But you didn't feel the suffering, the fires, any of that?" Nália asked. "That was just me?"

"Just us," Wenthi said, though he was only giving them a portion of his attention. The truck came to a stop, and she could feel he had mentally mapped out where the Fists headquarters was. She could still lightly feel Jendiscira and the others, and she was certain he could as well. He was taking advantage of the fact he wasn't tied to his body right now, figuring out what his mind could sense when it wasn't held back by flawed, solid flesh.

And most troubling was an odd sense of calm emanating from him. He was ready to wait. But he was also concerned about the fires, and the *baniz* people dying out in the burning fields of oil.

He must have sensed her feeling that off of him. "We could make a call, you know. Send official help."

Nália didn't want to speak out loud, so she sent the thought at him. *Like the patrol would save them. Or the nucks.*

His resolve quavered a little.

Nicalla was going on. "I felt . . . I didn't feel any specific individual suffering. But I did have the sense of pain from everyone out there in the country."

The canvas opened up. "You're all home," the Fists who drove them said. "I saw a lot of patrol out there, more checkpoints than normal. Be careful, maybe lay low."

That riled Nália up. "How can we lay low when people are dying out in the country—"

Ajiñe grabbed her and pulled her into the tenement. "Thank you, we'll be ready when you call on us."

Nália let herself be led inside, but she was still upset. "This is wrong. This is what we should be fighting for, and we're not . . ."

Ajiñe stopped her from talking by kissing her, which reminded Nália of the peculiar sensation of being Renzi, the masculinity of her own mouth and face and hands.

"What was that for?" Nália asked.

"To bring you back down to the ground," Ajiñe said. "I understand you're upset, but . . . if you saw it, surely Varazina did as well. We were all connected to her, communing with her power."

"Did she?" Wenthi asked. "Were we really?"

"What do you mean?" Nália asked.

"We know she sees everything, knows what's going on, which is how she reaches us."

"Oddly singular in direction," Wenthi said. "Did we really commune with her? Or what she wanted us to feel?"

"What was she to you?" Nália asked the rest as they settled into the bomb-out. The crew all looked like they were ready to sleep right then and there, which was understandable. As agitated as she was, the body was tired to its bones. Surely the rest of them were. "How did you see her?"

"Like a human manifestation of the spirits that watch over us," Gabrána said. "A woman of absurd beauty, but—"

"Natural," Fenito said.

Mensi continued. "Like she was one with the land and nature and—"

"Connected to me," Ajiñe said. "Like she knew my every secret and—"

"Loved me anyway," Nicalla said.

Nália had felt all that as well. But yet—

"A little too perfect," Wenthi said. "I was sucked into it as well, but now . . ."

"Right," Nália said.

"But why do you have this deeper connection?" Gabrána asked. "They all said they knew you were stronger with your power, which is strange."

"You took control of my body on the highway," Ajiñe said. "I've never known anyone to do that before."

"I'm not sure," Nália said. Was it Wenthi who was special? He didn't feel like a tory that night he arrested her. He was able to slip under her senses, get right up to her.

"Shebiruht said I was very interesting, too," he said. "But maybe part of it is that it's us, synced and stuck together permanently, with more and more speed. A fluke."

"Whatever it is," Ajiñe said, pulling Nália over to the mattress on the floor where they were all lying down—even Nicalla—"We're happy you're with us. We're all going to do great things together."

The radio sparked on, and Varazina's voice crackled through.

"*Fires are burning in the oil fields. Your people, your blood, your sisters and brothers and cousins, are dying. They are slaves under the boot of occupation, and we will bear it no longer. Rise up, my friends. This is the moment. This is the time. We will bear it no longer. Rise up, take to the streets. Beat back all who hold you down! For Zapisia! For me!"*

"Did she just—" Ajiñe started, but Nália didn't hear any more.

She had felt the charge, the connection that had activated the radio, the signal that brought the voice to them. And she knew—she *knew*—that it wasn't just a message to them. Varazina had spread it wide, talking to every single radio next to every *jifoz* in Outtown. She had just called them to war.

Almost by instinct, Nália reached out and grabbed that charge, and it pulled her senses out with it, bringing the entire city to her.

 **55**

For a brief moment, Nália could see it all. She touched into the signal on the radio, and her anger connected with Varazina, with Wenthi, which charged through the fungal network beneath her feet, like an electrical grid spreading across the country to every city.

She saw the factory workers and prisoners in Hanezcua, the destitute in Tofozaun, the hungry in Uretichan, the dying in the work camps, the angry in Ziaparr. If they were feeling a touch of connection to the mushroom, Nália felt a touch of them.

She heard Wenthi in the corner of her mind. "Like Doctor Shebiruht said, the very hand of god." She tried to push his thoughts away, keep them out her experience, but everything she felt was too intense, too powerful, and she could barely maintain her control over the body. She would not yield it to Wenthi; he could wallow in the shit of his impotence.

The anger in Ziaparr was a fire that burned through Outtown. Hundreds upon hundreds of people, mostly *jifoz*, had heard Varazina, and for them, the suffering of the *baniz* out here was their own. Their fathers and mothers and side-siblings and cousins, chained and starved and burned and killed.

That anger built and broiled, took form. *Jifoz* who had been waiting in ration lines at the petrol station, denied entrance to the grocer, had a patrol officer's finger pushing into their chests, they all, collectively, heard and burned. And burst forth with action.

Sticks and rocks and empty carbon bottles were taken up. Overcastes filling their sedans with petroleum—no wait and no limit—were torn out of their vehicles and dragged through the streets. Shops in the 11th and 12th senjas, boldly bearing signs out front saying *LLIPE AND RHIQUE ONLY*, had windows smashed and doors ripped off their hinges.

Patrol officers were knocked off their cycles, fists and boots slamming onto their heads. If the people caught them, they were torn apart. She saw some try to fight back, hold their ground in the circles they patrolled, but many more raced to the Intown wall, holding lines at the Uzena and Mixala crossings.

It came to Nália in flashes, in waves. She felt the anger, felt jaws snapping and skulls cracking and knuckles bleeding. She saw shouts for justice on Circle Uilea. She saw fires burning on Avenue Nodlion. She saw faces she knew—no, faces Wenthi knew, friends and colleagues and lovers in the patrol—get beaten beyond recognition.

She saw the Henáca boys tearing things up. She saw Officer Andorn bleeding, lifeless, on the ground. She saw Jendiscira and Hocnupec and the other members of the Fists Inner Circle shouting for action, ordering riders and looters toward the railyards, the crossings, the warehouses full of food earmarked for a useless war across the ocean.

She saw Paulei, fearfully trying to guide a pair of *llipe* youths to Hightown before they were caught by the angry crowds. That brought surges of emotions from Wenthi, screaming with no mouth of his dearest friend in danger.

For a brief moment, she felt pity for him.

Trucks were overturned, blood was spilled, and barricades torn down while bullets, bottles, and burning petroleum flew across the city circles.

All of Outtown had exploded.

And at the edge of all that, Varazina, joyful for the chaos.

That last feeling hit her like a brick in the face, snapping her out of the signal. She came back to her own senses, collapsed on the floor of the bomb-out.

All the crew were huddled around her, holding her close.

"He's awake," one of them said. "His eyes are opening."

"Renzi, hey," Ajiñe said, touching her face. "You're all right. Look at me. You're all right."

"I am," she said, trying to get back on her feet. She still had Wenthi's body. He had been pulled along just as she had; he had no chance to reclaim control. Even his phantom form lay on the floor, dazed and unsteady.

"What just happened?" Fenito asked. "You had a seizure or something."

"I connected with her signal," Nália said. "It was liked I reached into her broadcast, and for a moment, saw what she saw."

"Which is?"

"The city is rioting. All over Outtown. Just like she told them to." She realized they were all still here. "You didn't follow orders?"

"You were in trouble," Ajiñe said.

"We weren't about to leave you," Mensi added. "Orders or not."

Nália pulled herself to Wenthi's feet, watching him get up as well.

"This isn't right," he said. "You know that."

"A lot of people are going to get hurt out there," Nália said. "She . . . she was talking about the fires, wasn't she? The ones I saw."

"I think so," Nicalla said. "That seems a good thing to rise up over."

"So she'd rather start more fights than save people?" Wenthi asked. "You felt what she felt. Joy in the chaos."

"This isn't sitting right with me," Nália said.

"How so?" Ajiñe said. "We're listening. I don't fully understand this stronger power you have with the mushroom, but I believe in it."

"And in you," Mensi said.

Nália wanted to cry. First, because of the trust and love they all showed her. But then, because she knew that trust and love was built on Wenthi's deceit. They loved the Renzi Llionorco he had pretended to be. She needed to be worthy of that.

"Think about how this works. It's still filled with secrecy. Still one way."

"No, no," Nicalla said. "We communed with her. We felt her."

"But who *is* she?" Fenito asked. "I mean, yeah, I felt that . . ."

"Bliss?" Gabrána offered.

"Yeah, bliss, and that blinded me to it, but . . . I still don't know anything about her."

"And we don't have a voice with her, do we?" Mensi said. "Like, it's still her broadcasting orders, and we're in the dark."

"What actually changed, with the ritual and the Inner Circle?" Ajiñe asked. "Or was that just a—"

Gabrána fumed. "I said it the other morning, didn't I? No answers, not really. And we're still expected to follow instructions, blindly. They sexed us up just to—"

"A distraction," Nicalla said quietly. "A balm to make us feel like we mattered."

Gabrána snapped her fingers. "Like we have a voice in this. But it seems like we don't, and I do not like that."

A realization came to Nália. What needed to happen. "I want to talk to her," she said. "I want an actual conversation with Varazina."

"That's not possible." Gabrána said. "Right?"

"Maybe it is, for me," Nália said. "I came close right now, reaching into the broadcast. Maybe I just need to amp up my power."

"How?"

The answer was obvious. "Go as fast as possible. I'll get on my cycle, and—"

"Whoa, no," Wenthi said. "You saw what happened with that connection. We do that while riding, we—"

"You passed out," Ajiñe said. "You can't get on a cycle."

"It's just this body," Nália said. She would hardly cry if she got Wenthi killed in the attempt. Worst case, she'd be back in the ice room. "I go fast enough, I leave it behind—"

"I'm a little fond of that body," Fenito said.

"Same," Gabrána said.

"Well, I'm doing it," Nália said as she went to the door. "Unless you have a better idea—"

"Wait." Ajiñe's hand was on her shoulder. "I think I do."

56

This isn't going to be anywhere near as fast as my cycle," Nália said. "I could get over three hundred on a flat highway run."

"And end up a taco," Ajiñe said. "Not gonna let you do that. This is safer, if anything is going to work." She took Nália's hand and pulled her up into the bed of the truck.

They had loaded the mattress in the bed, and Mensi and Gabrána climbed into the back. "If you're going to do this, you won't be alone." They both took a dose of the mushroom.

"I can't ask you—"

"You didn't," Fenito said. "But we're here anyway." He got in the cab and started up the truck. Nicalla climbed in with him, armed with a heavy shotgun and a nine-piece on her hip.

"I thought we never used guns."

"You never bring guns on a run unless I give the order," Nicalla said. "And I'm bringing them this time, just in case."

"In case of what?" Wenthi asked. He had taken position in the bed of the truck. For better or worse, he wanted to do this as much as Nália said, but she knew at least part of his motivation was finding Varazina so he could turn her in. That wasn't going to happen, though, she wouldn't let it happen. She wanted to find out the truth, put some accountability on Varazina for the choices she was making in this leadership. But she still would respect the woman and what she had built.

"So here's the plan," Ajiñe said as Nália lay down. "The three of us are riding back here with you. Mensi and Gab will get in sync so they can stay anchored with you. If you get lost in—whatever it is you're going to do, hopefully they can be there to help you find your way back. Fenito is going to get on the highway and open this truck up like no one's business."

"Gonna really let her fly."

"He's the best one we got for driving the truck. Nic stays in the cab there as an extra pair of eyes, and ready to ride gunner."

"Even with the riots going on, you can bet a truck tearing down the highway will bring patrol raining on us," Nicalla said.

"That it will," Wenthi confirmed.

"If I have to hold them off, I'm ready," Nicalla said.

"And you?" Nália asked Ajiñe.

Ajiñe held up the transistor radio. "Apply the signal. Plus I'll be talking to everyone."

"Always in command," Nália said, cupping Wenthi's soft hand on Ajiñe's face. "Brilliant. Thank you."

Nália lay back and accepted the mushroom-filled kisses from Gabrána and Fenito, and as the truck started rolling toward the highway ramp-up, and they both started caressing her. She wasn't entirely sure if this aspect was necessary for what she was attempting to do, but she didn't object. Though as both of their hands and mouths worked her, the three of them moving into sync, she became more and more aware of how different Wenthi's body was from her own. She wished she could have been able to enjoy the two of them as herself.

Maybe someday.

Ajiñe straddled over Nália's legs and held the radio close as the truck ramped up on the highway. And, as Fenito promised, he tore it up as soon as he got up there.

As soon as he did, the static from the radio hit like a hammer into Nália's skull. She reached out and grabbed hold of it, like it was a chain, and pulled. But it didn't budge. She pulled again, and while its signal, the frequencies, burrowed into her mind, she couldn't get any purchase on it.

"Faster," she managed to say.

"Open it up!" Ajiñe shouted.

"Patrol is already on us!" Nicalla said.

"What are they riding?" Wenthi asked. She felt his hands on her—on himself, oddly—and his strength took hold of the static chain as well.

"What are they on?" Nália grunted out. "The patrol?"

"Looks like Ungeke K'ams," Ajiñe said.

"Can't top one-sixty," Wenthi said. "Get him to go harder."

"We can beat them," Nália said, through her teeth. She felt something tug at the chain—but now she could see deeper, and felt how it wasn't a chain at all. It was a network of tethers, like a spiderweb, all connected. She pulled herself along it, aware of how Wenthi was right there, pulling along with her, the two of them giving strength to each other, and the drive to move forward.

It was like riding a cycle through a storm.

She was vaguely aware of Mensi and Gab, echoes of their body, like a beacon back home as the network spread out in impossible directions. If she didn't have them there, or Wenthi holding on to her, she would have been buffeted out into nothing, flying off into the ether of this connection that both was and wasn't of the mushroom.

She felt it as both. The mushroom, an organic, living thing. It had breath and pulse that fell into sync with her heart—her own heart, still in her unconscious body in the ice room. But then there was the artificial crackling network of the radio waves, interlaced on top of that one. The two vibrations found sympathy, which resonated in her spirit.

But then a wave of emotion—anger, discord—crashed against her.

STOP

Like a brick wall. She would have lost her hold on everything if it wasn't for her anchor points. Mensi and Gab. Wenthi. Her own body.

"Don't listen to her!" Wenthi said.

Don't do this. More pleading than anger. *Let me guide you. This isn't for you.*

With the pleading, direction. Hints of dishonesty. Nália rode along the electric tether of frequency toward it, toward the light.

And it was a light. A shining light in the spidery static, of glory and beauty and unearthly perfection. The face of Varazina, goddess and spirit of all spirits.

Child, your work is not here, she said calmly. *You are not strong enough for this. You are not made for it. You risk being destroyed.*

She wavered for a moment, but then Wenthi's hand laced with her own. Together, they reached out toward this face, and as they did, tiny cracks splintered its perfection.

"Talk to me!" Nália shouted. "Who are you to lead us? What do you want? Answer me!"

I want us to be free. I want us to strike back! I want you to fight those that have held us down! Restore the truth and beauty of Zapisia!

"Who are you?" Nália called out. The storm of the static intensified, and typhoon winds assailed her. She only held firm because Wenthi was there with her, holding her in place, while the distant thoughts of Gab and Mensi kept him in place. That line back to the body, to the material world.

Was that what Varazina was? A spirit that had completely left the real world? Did she exist only within the mushroom and the signal now? Was she everywhere and seeing everything because she was nowhere?

Now you see.

But the cracks in that perfect face had opened into fault lines, through which Nália sensed something else. Something just as real and solid and anchored as her own body.

She pushed forward into the cracks, but intense force and power fired back at her. The signal of it rocketed back down through Wenthi's body in the truck. Pain and shock slammed into him, through Gabrána and Mensi. On the edge of the senses Nália still had in the real world, she felt them both fall out of sync with her, like they had been torn away. The last sensation she had from them was terror and agony.

"Renzi!" she heard Ajiñe call out, so very far away. "Stop it, you have to—"

Nália wanted to tell her no, they had to keep pushing, but she knew she couldn't spare an iota of her concentration. All of what she was had to be focused on getting through those cracks, getting to the truth. It was so close now; it was a taste on her tongue. And the unearthly force pushing back on her, keeping her from that truth, was unceasing. She knew, if she relented now, she'd never get another chance. Varazina would be ready next time.

"Fenito, get off the highway, we have to—"

Wenthi was there. His will pushing with Nália's, fully in sync with each other. He was able to spare enough focus, enough faint connection with his body, to say one word with his mouth, whispered to Ajiñe.

"Faster."

They both felt Ajiñe's tender hand on their cheek, a kiss on their forehead.

"Stay on. Burn the engine out."

A surge of velocity flooded into them, up the chain, strength and power like they had never felt.

Together, Nália and Wenthi sent that speed, that power, at the vision of

Varazina, and like a porcelain mask, it shattered. The spiderweb of static and frequency fell away, leaving them together, in a very real, physical, richly furnished room.

57

"What is this shit?" Nália asked. She didn't even know what she was seeing. In all her life, she had never seen a room like this. She didn't even have the words to describe it, but the right words came from Wenthi.

The furniture—a bed with wooden posts and lace drapery, several cushioned chairs with embroidered pillows, a wooden table with gold and silver inlay—was not of Pinogozi design. Wenthi presumed they were Outhic, likely Hemish or Reloumic. Not a scratch or tear on any of it.

And the room was bright, light and airy due to the grand open window, with a balcony overlooking a view of the Pino Sound, glorious and blue. Nália had no idea where one could even see such a view.

Wenthi knew.

"This is Intown," he said. "In the 1st or 2nd Senja."

"Yes."

They both saw the woman who had spoken, sitting in a cushioned wicker chair on the balcony. Her pale hand reached out and clicked off the radio next to her chair, which had just been playing low static. She slowly got to her feet, picking up a cane as she did, and walked over to them.

Nália didn't understand what she was seeing. Or more correctly, she didn't want to. This woman was milk pale, golden haired. Surprisingly young looking considering how she moved like an old woman. No. She moved like someone who was in constant pain.

"Determined, aren't you?" she asked as she limped over. "I sensed that in both of you. I thought I had it in me to hold you back, but . . . well, here you are."

"Both of us?" Wenthi asked. "You mean—"

“Yes, I’m aware of the both of you,” she said with a disgusted sigh. “Quite the trick you two have been doing. I don’t think Shebiruht even knew what she was making this time.”

“How do you know—” Wenthi started.

“Wait a shitting swipe,” Nália said. “Who is this *llipe*?”

“You haven’t figured it out, Miss Enapi?” she said, limping closer. Then her body shifted, into the flawless image of Varazina—perfect vision of timeless Zapisian beauty—and then back to the golden-haired, broken woman. “I’m who you fought so hard to find.”

Nália couldn’t believe that. It was impossible. Too unthinkable to even put into her own words.

Wenthi did instead. “How is Varazina a *llipe* woman living lavishly in the center of Intown?” he asked.

“Lavishly is a strong word,” she said. “It’s a well-appointed prison, but still a prison.”

“This is no prison,” Nália spat out. She looked around the room, spotting bits of food and luxury that no single person she knew could afford in a year. “Who are you?”

“I told you, Miss Enapi,” she said. “I’m the voice you heard on the radio, who gave the orders. Who touched your spirits and your bodies.” She ran a finger on Wenthi’s chest. Nália felt the charge of connection. “At least, to the extent I could, being kept in here.”

“But always through a mask,” Wenthi said. “Why the deception?”

The woman went over to the bed, her breathing labored. “I think you just have to look at Miss Enapi’s face to see the answer to that. She’s in absolute shock. The horror that a woman like me might be leading their revolution.”

“Like you?” Nália said. “A damned *llipe*? Or not even that? Are you some shitmouthed Reloumene here with our Alliance overlords? Is that what you are?”

“Oh, no, I was born here,” she said. “And to call me *llipe* is fair. That’s entirely why I get locked away in here instead of . . .” She gasped for breath, crawling onto the bed. “I am just as much a victim, though, as any of you.”

“That’s some bullshit,” Nália said.

The woman rang a bell as she struggled for breath. “You’ll forgive me. I had already exerted myself quite a bit before you two pulled that stunt. So I am quite spent right now."

An old woman—a servant, clearly, by the style of her dress, and either *baniz* or *jifoz* by her complexion—came in.

"What do you need, Miss Penda?" she asked.

"Bring me the doctor," the woman said. "I am very shaken right now."

"Right away, miss." The servant left.

"This doesn't make any damned sense," Nália said.

"Penda?" Wenthi asked. "That's impossible."

The woman smiled weakly. "It's not, Mister Tungét, I'm sad to say."

"What?" Nália asked.

"She's not just a *llipe*," Wenthi said. "She's Penda Rodiguen. The granddaughter of the tyrant."

58

Guilty as charged," Penda said.

"No, no, no," Nália said. For a moment, they flashed back to the truck—racing at absurd speeds with a dozen patrol on cycles chasing after them, smoke pouring out of the engine. They couldn't go much longer. Even with the anger building in her, waves upon waves, she forced herself to stay anchored in this shitty palatial suite with the horror of a woman who claimed to be Varazina.

"I often say that myself," Penda said.

"The tyrant and most of his family were killed in the last bombing campaign," Nália said.

"Most," Penda said. "And the rest?"

"They were imprisoned—"

"And here we are," Penda said, waving about the room. "Not the dreary cell in Hanez you imagined—or that we fucking deserved—but yet, my prison nonetheless."

"But how?" Wenthi asked. "Even presuming you are Varazina, why?

Why be her? And how? How could you do what you do on the radios, giving the orders, leading the Fists of Zapi?"

"The answer is coming into the room," Penda said.

With crisp steps, a woman came into the bedroom, addressing Penda with a thick accent. "I hear you are feeling more peaked than usual, dear?"

Nália and Wenthi both knew the monster on sight.

"Rather, Doctor," Penda said.

Doctor Shebiruht came over to the bed and prodded Penda's head, neck, and chest. "You are a bit feverish. What were you doing?"

"Just . . . trying to feel the people out there."

"Absurdities, girl," Shebiruht said with a disapproving click of her tongue. "You were not made for such things."

"So you keep saying, Doctor. But it's what I can do."

"And what I can do is try to keep you alive. Perhaps long enough for them all to see the value you offer. We're getting closer, dear. They'll see."

"Can you just give me my shot and let me rest?"

"You're in a mood, I see," Shebiruht said. "Try not to impose it on the folks in the streets below, hmm? Today is bad enough." She took a syringe out of her bag and injected it into Penda's arm—which was heavily bruised, covered in scars of needle marks. More than Nália could count.

"The shit was that?" Nália asked when Shebiruht left.

Wenthi had his own question. "What did she mean, not what you were made for?"

Penda struggled to sit up in the bed. "The two of you are hopelessly dense. And you don't have too much time. That truck is about to fail and be forced to stop."

"Wait," Wenthi said, and Nália could feel the realizations click in his mind, and as they did, the true horror of it resonated in her. "Doctor Shebiruht came here with Rodiguen, when he took over Pinogoz. Throughout the Great Noble War, they were working on a weapon. A weapon made with the mushroom."

"And that weapon is you," Nália said.

"I can't tell you how many times I've heard Doctor Shebiruht tell me how I am her unappreciated masterpiece."

"How?" Wenthi asked.

"I was built to be a vessel for the mushroom. Injection after injection, experiment after experiment. The horrors you heard of in the camp—yes, Wenthi, I see it in your memory now. All steps she took to figure out how to perfect me." She laughed, a harsh, resentful laugh that turned into hacking coughs. "As if this is somehow perfect."

"Wait a damned swipe," Nália said, realizing what this meant. "If you can sense the both of us, feel what's in our memories, then . . . you always knew he was patrol, infiltrating the Fists."

"And Shebiruht did such good work creating him into the perfect infiltrator. Of course he already had the natural gifts, the untapped potential. Incredible. With your help, of course, Nália."

"My help?"

"You discovered his natural vibration in tune with the local mushroom," she said. "That's what let him arrest you, thus allowing Shebiruht to discover the perfect way to combine the two of you. She doesn't even know the power the two of you have unlocked together. She would be very excited."

"What do you want?" Nália asked. "How could you possibly command the rebellion, be the leader the Fists think you are, while also being . . . this?"

"A pampered *llipe* doll?" Penda asked. "I have spent years trapped in this prison. These apartments and this dying shell of damaged flesh that my own family made me into. I finally—*finally*—figured out the full extent of my power, what Shebiruht made me into, and knew what I could do. What I needed to do."

"Which is what?" Nália asked. "For you to rule over this country like your grandfather did? Another tyrant to take us over?"

"Please," Penda said. "The last thing I want to do is *rule*. I couldn't care less about any of you people, or your rebellion, or your war, or the fucking Alliance and what they hope for. Everyone can rot."

Anger came off the woman in waves as she struggled to get back on her feet.

"I just want the chaos."

Nália stumbled, in as much as her phantom form in this well-appointed apartment could lose her footing. Her senses flashed briefly to the empty dark of the ice room, the screaming chaos of the truck losing ground on the highway, but she didn't lose her place here.

Thanks to Wenthi, who caught her—caught her in every way—and kept her up and present.

"It's all a joke, isn't it?" she asked, half to herself, half to him. "There's no real revolution, no one here to save us. There's just her, another *llipe* tyrant here playing games with us."

"And all of it can burn, for all I care," Penda said. "I won't be a pawn in anyone else's game, when I can be a queen of the inferno."

Nália found Wenthi's eyes, and for the first time, actually looked into them. She didn't see the hard gaze of a dirty tory, burning with contempt for her. She didn't see the indifference she expected.

She saw the eyes of that boy who had his life torn apart by the tyrant. Who took care of his baby sister in the camps. Who went hungry so she would eat. Who pulled Ajiñe back onto her cycle, who saved Mensi from the Alliance nucks.

"They'll do whatever she says," she said quietly. "She doesn't care and isn't who we need and we can't—"

"I can stop her," he said.

"What?"

"Let me, Nália," he said. "Please, let me stop her."

"How . . ." she stammered. "How do I—"

"Please. Let me."

She knew what he meant. And as much as it shattered her heart, she knew it was the only way.

"Do it right, Wenthi," she said.

And she let everything go.

59

Wenthi opened his eyes as the truck skidded to a halt, careening into the barrier on the side of the highway. Black smoke was pouring out of the engine, and everyone was shouting.

"Get ready to hold them off! As long as we can!"

Ajiñe stood protectively above him, nine-piece in hand. Wenthi looked up and saw an entire squad of patrol officers stopping their cycles and taking position around them. They would rain iron on them all in a swipe if he didn't stop things.

He grabbed Ajiñe's leg. "Stop," he said weakly. He still needed to catch his breath, find his place in his own body.

She dropped to one knee over him, still holding up the gun and she leaned down to kiss him. He realized Gab and Mensi were still curled up next to his body, both alive but out cold. He couldn't see Fenito and Nic in the cab, but he could hear them, both shouting about the truck and getting ready to fight.

"Renzi," she said. "Did you do it? Did you reach her?"

"Yeah," he said.

"And?"

"It wasn't good."

"Drop your weapons and exit the vehicle with your hands laced behind your head!" one of the officers shouted. "This is your only warning!"

"Do what they say," he said quickly. "All of you. Guns off to the side, quick."

"But—"

"We're about to die," he said. "And we need to live."

He hoped she understood. He hoped she would trust him. Nothing would work if she didn't trust him.

She threw the gun.

"Lose the iron, Nic!"

Wenthi heard the clatter of the rifle hitting the road.

"What are we doing?" Ajiñe asked.

Wenthi pulled himself up, hands high, lacing them behind his head. "Surviving. Follow along."

"You sure?"

He stepped off the truck, keeping his hands in place. "We're surrendering!" he shouted. "Weapons are gone." Wenthi saw all the patrol officers, iron in hands, all surrounding them. He scanned for familiar faces. Thankfully, there were a couple. Minlei and Guand were in the front. He locked eyes with them, hoping they would catch on.

"The rest on the pavement, face down!" Minlei shouted. "All of you!"

The others all came out of the truck, getting to the ground with their hands behind their heads. On Minlei's signal, patrol swarmed in, grabbing each of them, tethering their wrists and hauling them to their feet. Minlei and Guand took Wenthi and pulled him off to the side.

Nália appeared next to him, tears in her eyes.

"You're sure this is right?"

"Yeah," he said. Guand and Minlei made a show of working Wenthi over while the rest of the crew were hauled out of sight.

"You do it, Tungét?" Guand whispered once the rest were gone. "Did you get what we need?"

"I got it," Wenthi said. "Enough to take all of them down."

REFUEL: REPORT

16 Tian, 0049 HSY

As of five sweep zero, eighteen arrests have been made of key members and ringleaders of the organization that refers to itself as the "Fists of Zapi," a series of terrorist cells consisting of miscreants and agitators seeking to disrupt supply chains, corrupt distribution of rationed goods, and undo the fragile peace of the city of Ziaparr. These arrests include the following key figures:

- Quiva Mascindi*, *baniz*, who had been using the name "Jendiscira" as an alias.
- Bedo Hocnupec*, *baniz*
- Niliza Dallatan, *jifoz*
- Nicalla Menita, *jifoz*
- Otaca Menita, *jifoz*
- Casintel Vaitra, *jifoz*
- Bindeniz Vaitra, *jifoz*
- Ajiñe Osceba, *jifoz*
- Narli Osceba, *jifoz*
- Gabrána Corriba, *jifoz*
- Daro Partinez, *jifoz*
- Isilla Henáca, *jifoz*
- Yenimensi "Mensi" Darabo, *jifoz*

* It should be recorded that both Missus Mascindi and Mister Hocnupec offered significant resistance when attempting to arrest them, and lethal force needed to be applied. Their bodies were, upon request, sent to the research labs in the lower levels.

We have reasonable information that these individuals, as well as several others captured over the course of the unfortunate uprisings in the 11th, 12th, 14th, and 17th Senjas in the past day, represent a sizable share of both the leadership and the rank-and-file of the "Fists of Zapi."

Most notable is the arrest of Penda Rodiguen, *llipe,* who had been the mastermind behind the cult leader figure known as "Varazina." While the full details of how she accomplished this from her placement in the Alliance Notable Confinement Center, we are sufficiently satisfied in her guilt. We are thankful to High Captain Sengejú for arranging the transfer of Miss Rodiguen from Alliance confinement to our hands, and to the work of Councilmembers Tungét and Hwungko for their tireless efforts in convincing the Alliance Ruling Overboard to allow this to be handled by local justice and authority.

This was made possible thanks to the incredible efforts of one Civil Patrol officer who was the lead for a deep infiltration assignment, identifying and directing Civil Patrol to the specific ringleaders and malefactors. We are deeply grateful for that officer's efforts, and they will be rewarded with an extended paid leave before returning to regular duty with a promotion.

This has proven to be a very encouraging venture, and the Alliance Oversight Office has faith that this operation can demonstrate how Pinogoz-local officers could be, eventually, entrusted with leadership positions in the Civil Patrol, as an eventual step for the nation to reach self-rule on an acceptable timetable.

SIXTH CIRCUIT:

THE TRAITORS OF ZAPISIA

60

For three days, Wenthi's mind had been quiet. No more Nália Enapi in his head. No more her controlling his body. No more of her, the constant and aggravating voice of rebellion and revolution, drumming in his skull.

A damned relief.

The silence was uneasy.

Three days ago, he had been brought into the headquarters in the 9th Senja, separated from the rest of the Fists crew, and put into an ice room so they could no longer sync with him. Once there, he delivered his full report, and cycles and arrest buses were sent out to pick up everyone he named. Everyone except Penda, initially, but Lieutenant Canwei said she'd work to make that happen. He wasn't privy to what that work entailed, but Paulei brought him the report that detailed her arrest.

Wenthi had worried that she would be given some sort of pass, like she had been before. He didn't want to know who else was in the Alliance Notable Confinement Center. He knew it would just make him angry.

He already knew Doctor Shebiruht was one of the residents. Who knew what other dark secrets were in there.

He was more than happy that he didn't have to see her again. One of the nurses came and gave him a series of shots, which severed his connection with Nália, and then a bottle of pills they insisted he needed to take twice a day. Canwei told him to take a dozen days to relax and recover. "You've earned it."

He had been in his room for three days straight, fucking half the squad on the late sweep patrol. That had mostly been a core cadre of Minlei, Guand, Cinden and Peshka (always together), Hwokó, and especially Paulei, but several others had drifted in and out of the group over time. Wenthi had enjoyed all of it; it was wonderful to be back home, back with his people, but it felt off. Incomplete. He had gotten used to sex on the mushroom, and the sensation of just feeling in his own body was, while oddly novel, distinctly lacking.

Not that he told any of them that.

He lay in his bed—he was thrilled to be back in his own bed after that horrendous mattress in the shitty *fasai* on Street Xaomico—looking over the arrest report once more. Names he knew, names he gave in his reports. Names that troubled him. He had mentioned people like Partinez and Isilla Henáca in his debrief, but not in the context of being part of the Fists.

Jendiscira and Hocnupec had been killed in the arrests. There was an odd comfort there, that they refused to compromise, refused to go quietly. They'd rather be martyrs than prisoners.

Narli Osceba was another name on the list that hung hard on his heart. He had done nothing, beyond being Ajiñe's father. "You've seen all these people in holding?" he asked Paulei, who had been in a blissful half-asleep state for the past few minutes. Wenthi envied him. Everyone else had been called onto a stint or was recuperating in their own rooms.

"I mean, they don't wear name tags, but, yeah, the cells are packed up right now. Once final judgment comes down, they'll be shipped out, just like they deserve."

"What about Nália?"

"Who?"

"Enapi," Wenthi said. "The girl I caught, the one they synced me with."

"Oh, her," Paulei said, running his fingers on Wenthi's chest. He was already ready for more. How did he do that, Wenthi wondered. "I think she's still in the headquarters. I didn't ask. She'll probably be lumped in with the other judgments."

"Good," Wenthi said, not sure what he meant by saying that. Maybe he figured Paulei needed to hear it.

"You called her Nália?"

"She was embedded in my head for nearly two seasons," Wenthi said. "Hardly room for proper social niceties. Not her style, in any event."

"What was that like?" Paulei asked. He had, over the course of the three days, asked a few gentle probing questions about Wenthi's whole experience, which Wenthi had only ever answered tersely. Paulei hadn't been pushing too hard with those questions, but he would regularly leave a window open for Wenthi to crawl through and talk about it.

"Invasive," Wenthi said. "You know, all those propaganda reels we saw about the mushroom are bullshit. Completely."

"What do you mean?"

"I mean, they talk about how dangerous it is, but it's really not—"

"We've heard all about how dangerous it is."

"Heard, yeah. You ever actually brought in a mushroom burnout? I've been thinking, and I never have. I don't know if I've ever seen one."

"I'm sure I have."

"Have you? I've never had one when riding with you. I can't even recall someone coming off their stint saying they had one. We're just . . . told it's a thing that happens, and we've accepted it as truth."

Paulei frowned, still caressing Wenthi's chest. "I must have."

"I can tell you this, having done the mushroom—"

"How much did you do it?" Paulei asked. "Is this why you need time to get clean? Did you take your pills today?"

"Spirits, yes," Wenthi said. Though he wasn't completely sure. He must have taken it this morning. The past days had been a bit of a blur, but he was nearly certain.

Paulei's voice dropped to a low, horrified whisper. "Is the sex really better on it? Is that why you're talking about it? You want to—"

"No," Wenthi said. "I mean, yes, it totally is, but—"

"It is?"

"You have no idea," Wenthi said. "But my real point is, why were we led to believe it was so dangerous? Especially when the Alliance government is more than happy to use it to suit its own purposes?"

"I don't know," Paulei said, climbing on top of Wenthi. "So are you saying that no matter how many officers we get into this bed with you, it's not going to be like it was on the mushroom?"

"Well, how many are we talking?" Wenthi said, letting himself grin. Letting himself feel happy. "Because I'm willing to make the attempt. You know, for science."

"I do love science," Paulei said, leaning down to kiss him. He climbed off the bed and pulled on a robe. "I'll go knock on some doors, see what we can round up. A lot of people are working double stints, holding back the unrest and mayhem in Outtown."

"That hasn't stopped with the arrests?"

"It's gotten worse. But that means anyone who's off shift and here will have a lot of tension to blow off."

Wenthi lay back on the bed, his thoughts scattered. Thoughts still on the reasons behind making the mushroom illegal, scaring people from using it. Thoughts on the people from Street Xaomico arrested. Thoughts on the idea that there was still uproar in the Outtown streets, that nothing he had done had quelled it. If anything, he might have made it worse, and more riots were coming.

Paulei opened up the door to find someone already there.

"Oh!" Lathéi said. "I was about to knock."

"Didn't think you'd come see us up here in our hovel," Paulei said lightly.

"It wasn't my first choice, but this silly boy has been off his mission for days and hasn't come to see me."

"The fool," Paulei said. "Go in there, it's fine."

"You sure?" she asked both of them.

"I'm off to round up some people to fuck some sense into him, but that will take me a bit."

"It's fine, Lath, get in here," Wenthi called out as he pulled his own robe on. She came farther into the room as Paulei went off.

"I wasn't certain you wanted to see me," she said, coming over to the bed and sitting on the edge. She was dressed in what Wenthi assumed was the high fashion of the season in Ziaparr, her green dress fitting tight at the waist and flaring out at her knees. She wore what Wenthi could only describe as the tiniest hat he had ever seen, pinned to the top of her hair with lace and wisps of ribbon that elegantly framed the sides of her face.

"Why wouldn't I want to see you?"

"Well, you haven't made much of an effort to come out, have you?" she asked.

"You mean come to Mother's house," he said.

"I've been enduring that household all alone."

"With Oshnå."

"Practically alone."

He pointed to the pile of newspapers and magazines on the floor. "Paulei collected those for me while I was gone. It looks like you spent the past season getting your tinplate plastered all over Intown." Society, fashion, and gossip pages were filled with pictures of Lathéi and Oshnå, and every young *llipe* and *rhique* in the city tried to get tinplated with her. He had already seen how most young folk in the 9th were now dressing like she and Oshnå were that night at the brass club.

"I didn't ask to be a style influencer. It's quite annoying."

"I'm sure."

"I wore this hat for the first time today, and five people plated me on my way here. Mark me, brother, you will see this all over town in three days. It's tiresome."

He knew Lathéi well enough to know she was being honest, she didn't relish this sort of attention. "I wonder what would happen if you dressed like I had to this whole time. Boots and raw denim."

"Oh, I could get the whole town dressing like that if I wanted. Phony followers, the lot of them. They were all, 'oh, Lathéi, you and your girlfriend are so elegant, so Outhic, so sophisticated.' It's like no one has ever gone to Hemisheuk before."

"I bet you're ready to go back."

"Quite. And Mother keeps making noises about how my place is here and there is no need to go across the sea again, which is just impossible of her."

"When do you go?"

"Five days," she said, giving a playful slap to his arm. "Which makes your failure to come see me almost unforgivable."

"As long as it's almost."

She sighed. "You look exhausted, though. Was it the assignment, or is it the ongoing celebration?"

"Bit of both."

"I don't begrudge you your fun, but unless you are getting on that steamer with me, I refuse to lose another day of seeing you."

"I can't get on that steamer," he said. "I would have had to apply for travel permits two seasons ago."

"Faith, they make it so hard. Normally I'd say Mother could find a way, but she doesn't even want me to go, let alone let you leave the country as well."

"I think she'd be fine with it."

"Not at all!"

"Lath," he said, "she wants you here because you are the presumptive heir to her place in the Prime Families. The ranking Tungét."

"Like anyone really cares about such a thing," she scoffed.

"Do you want to hear something wild?"

"Always."

"Mother gained her place because she was the only surviving member of the Tungét line, but she had nearly been disinherited. Apparently it was only because the rest of the family was killed in the Second Trans that they didn't have time to remove her standing."

"You lie!" Lathéi said with a laugh. "Wherever did you hear such a thing? Mother has never talked about that. I think she was born thirty."

"Do you remember during the Tyrant's War—"

"The what?"

"The Great Noble," he corrected. "The bunker, the camps? Being lost in the Smokewalks?"

"Only in the vaguest ways," she said. "I remember you taking care of me, if that's what you mean."

"Partly," he said.

"Which is why I want to take care of you now," she said. "And I can. I can take you to Hemisheuk, and I think it would do you a lot of good to get out of this country. At least the city. We could take a train to Ureti for a day or two, live it up—"

"I appreciate that, Lathéi."

"But you don't want to do that," she said, her face sinking a bit. "I get it, I do. Fine. Well, I have one more piece to play, and after that I'll leave you to your celebration."

"I am glad to see you, you know," he said. "It's just—"

"I know, dear," she said, caressing his face with her gloved hand. "Mother is holding a dinner gathering tomorrow night. She has said it is in honor of your success, how the rebellion was quelled thanks to your work, but was very vague about if she intended to invite you."

"First I've heard of it."

"In which case, I am inviting you as my extension. Are your measurements still on record at the haberdasher? You didn't thicken your waist too much on *jifozi* tacos while on mission?"

"No risk of overeating on the mission," he said. She had no idea how hungry the *jifoz* were.

"Good. I'll have a proper suit for this bash made and delivered to you tomorrow—on my account, don't worry."

"So Oshnå will miss the party?"

"Oh, she's coming," Lathéi said. "If I am the heir apparent of the Tungét seat or whatever, I will make a thing of having all the caste-breaking guests I want at a party."

"It won't be trouble?"

"It probably will be," Lathéi said. "But honestly, the idea of Mother hosting a thing to celebrate what you did without inviting you to it? It sickens me. I will not stand."

He smiled. "Hold on to that spirit," he said. "No matter where you go, what position or seat you have. Remember how you feel right now and lock it into yourself, so it can always guide you."

"What a peculiar thing to say," she said, getting on her feet. She leaned over and kissed his forehead.

"I think Mother forgot more about who she was," he said. "What she used to fight for. I don't want you to do the same."

She gave him a peculiar regard. "You have more story than you're letting on. I'll press you on it tomorrow. See you then." She went out the door, leaving it open so Paulei could return with a half-dozen half-naked patrol officers who had just gotten off duty.

"Heard there was a sad hero here who needed cheering," Hwokó said as she threw her blouse on the ground. "Let's get on it."

Wenthi put on a good face and waved them all into his bed. It would be wonderful, of course, despite being stuck in only his own skin.

61

Wenthi's Ungeke K'am was still stabled at Mother's house in the 2nd Senja, so he had little choice but to take Nália's junkbashed Puegoiz

960 to the party. He was surprised that no one had asked him to turn in the keys, and when he pressed, Canwei told him to get the cycle out of the headquarters garage for now. What else would he do but ride it? Even though it looked like junk next to the Ungekes the other patrol who lived in his building drove, he knew what kind of machine it was, how much it was capable of. Still, it did look like an Outtown cycle, which was surely quite a sight when paired with his lime green vest and suspender suit, with violet brim-cap and cravat. It was an odd look, nothing like anything Wenthi had worn before. It was, he suspected, an outfit Lathéi had curated specifically to annoy Mother. That was a purpose Wenthi could respect.

It did look good, in a foppish, young *llipe* sort of way, though the fabric was hardly what he'd call comfortable.

Maybe you got too used to the raw denim against your skin.

For a moment, he was about to tell Nália to be quiet, but it wasn't her thought. It was just his.

That would be what Nália would say, after she mocked him for this outfit.

He was given a bit of a hard time at the checkpoint between the 9th and 2nd Senjas, as there were now double the Alli nucks working the spot, and none of them were the usual familiar faces.

"You're going into the 2nd at this sweep?"

"Invited to an event," Wenthi said. He pointed to his card. "You'll see I have dispensation to cross into the 2nd at any time."

"Don't tell me what I see, son," the nuck said. He peered at the card, held it up to the light, squinted at it again. "What's it say your family name is?"

"Tungét."

"There is that thing at the Tungét home tonight," one of the other nucks said. "A lot of *llipe* Prime folk are going there."

"And this *rhique*, apparently," the one still inspecting his card said. "On a junker cycle, at that."

"Why are you riding that like some *jifo*?"

"Bit of a loaner," Wenthi said. "My proper cycle is at the house I'm going to."

"You're going to a house in the 2nd? Not to work one of the shops?"

"That's right," Wenthi said. "My mother's home."

"Oh, well then," the first nuck said with a mocking tone. "That explains why a *rhique* who leans dark like you has the dispensation privilege."

"What does—"

"I took you for a shop scrub," he said.

"Ride along," the second guard said, opening the checkpoint gate before Wenthi could respond. "Party is waiting."

Wenthi drove in, not sure how he wanted to respond.

There were plenty of sedans parked all along the road to Mother's house, and more inside the gate. Wenthi threaded the 'goiz between them all and parked it next to his Ungeke, leaning against the wall of the grounds in a far corner.

"Hello, Mister Wenthi," Isacha said from the work shack. He was sitting inside the metal structure with the door open. Wenthi had never looked in there before, only now realizing that there was a cot with all the garden tools. Was this where the old man always slept?

"It's good to see you," Wenthi said. "How has the household been?"

"We keep it going," Isacha said. "Though Miss Angú thought I should stay out of sight for the party."

"How long have you known my mother?" Wenthi asked. "Well before I was born, yes?"

"Yes, Mister Wenthi."

"So you knew my father, then?"

Isacha didn't answer, but looked to the floor.

"His name was Renzi, wasn't it? Renzi Llionorco?"

Isacha looked up. "He was a good friend. Your mother would never say so, but she still misses him, I think."

Wenthi moved closer to the old man. "They were part of a movement or something?"

Isacha chuckled ruefully. "We made some noise, not that anyone really cared."

"You were part of it, too?"

"Foolishness of youth," Isacha said. "Every generation thinks they can change things, I think. We tried to tear down the system, decry the castes. All it did was divide the people, open us up for the tyrant to step in. Your father, he had . . . such ambitions."

"Tell me about him."

"Brilliant, beautiful man," Isacha said. "He didn't deserve what they—"

"Wenthi!" Lathéi came over to them. "People heard you had arrived, but you hadn't come inside yet."

"Sorry," Wenthi said. "I was talking to Isacha about—"

"Let the poor man alone," Lathéi said. "Faith knows he's worked enough today."

"Right," Wenthi said.

"Another time," Isacha said.

"Come along," Lathéi said, leading him to the door. "You are welcome to the house."

"Isn't it odd you have to say it every time?" he asked her as they went in.

"It's custom," she said.

The household—at least the grand dining and sitting rooms, as well as the back garden behind it all—was filled with the upper elite of Ziaparr. Almost anyone here who wasn't staff was *llipe*, except for the handful of *zoika* foreigners like Oshnå, who was leaning against one wall quietly nursing a rum and carbon. Wenthi knew exactly who most of the people here were, at least by reputation. Mostly members of the Prime Families, as well as leaders in the city government, the Provisional Council, and a handful of Alliance administrators.

"Great gentles and friends," Lathéi announced as she led Wenthi down the steps to the grand dining room. "You've all been singing praises of what he accomplished, and now he is here with us. My dear half-brother, savior of the city, Officer Wenthi Tungét."

People all looked over to them, and gave a smattering of polite applause, followed by murmurs of discontent. Wenthi had seen those disapproving looks before; they all had opinions about his presence here.

One of them did walk up, though. Ainiro Hwungko strolled up to him, smart and styled in a silk robesuit, with a small entourage of hangers-on walking behind her. "Officer Tungét. It's very agreeable to see you again."

"Councilwoman," Wenthi said with a polite nod of the head. "I'm happy to be seen."

"I was thrilled to see you had been so successful with your mission. I'll confess I was uncertain how you would fare, but you proved quite capable.

We are *all* very pleased with that work, and there will be rewards in due time."

"Thank you," Wenthi said. "Just doing my job."

"Humility is a grossly underrated virtue. It looks quite fetching on you." She turned to her people. "Some of you could stand to take a lesson at this."

"The councilwoman was saying earlier how we need to take advantage of the opportunities you've given us," one of her hangers-on said.

"What opportunities are those?" Wenthi asked.

"Finally revitalizing the outer senjas. Most of the 14th—"

"Miahez," Wenthi said instinctively.

"Pardon?" Missus Hwungko asked.

"In Outtown, they call that senja 'Miahez,'" Wenthi said.

"How very charming," the hanger-on said. "But imagine, most of that area is run-down, never properly rebuilt since the bombings of the war."

"That's true," Wenthi said.

"We could make it into a place proper people could actually live."

"We could what?" His voice went harsher and louder than he had intended, causing that hanger-on to lurch back in surprise.

Lathéi took his arm. "I haven't gotten you anything to eat yet. Terrible oversight."

"One thing," Missus Hwungko said. "Someone has something he needs to say to you."

She waved, and a handsome young man stepped up, his gaze fully on his own shoes.

"Enzúri," she said sternly. "What do you say to Officer Tungét?"

"Thank you for your service," he said quietly. "You've made this city safer."

"Very good, Enzúri," she said. "Now go find me something to drink."

Lathéi said some final pleasantry as she pulled Wenthi away from them toward the banquet table. Wenthi glanced back at Enzúri as he went to the bar. He was the one who had run with Nália when she was arrested. Why had he been part of that? He wouldn't have been unless Varazina had called him, or Nicalla had recruited him. How had he joined in with the Fists that night? Why had he? How had that all happened?

"As much as I delight in tweaking everyone's nose by having you here," Lathéi said. "Let's not actually shout at Mother's guests."

"Sorry," he said. "It's just—plenty of good, decent people are ones who live in Miahez."

"I'm sure they are. Zoyua, could you make a plate for Wenthi here?"

Wenthi put on his best smile and looked at Zoyua, standing behind the banquet table. "Thank you, Zoyua, I appreciate it."

"What you want?" Zoyua said coldly. Mother had clearly spared no expense laying out this banquet. In addition to several Sehosian and Hemish delicacies, there was a wide array of Pinogozi standards: chicken, beef, fish, rajas, cheese, and salsas, and Eunitio pressing tortillas and cooking them fresh on a griddle right there.

"The tang chicken, with the pickled onions and tomatillo salsa," he said. All Izamio's specialties.

In as much as someone could plate a pair of tacos with rage and disdain, Zoyua put together his plate with harsh motions and loud clatter.

"Zoy, are you all right?" Lathéi asked.

"I am fine," Zoyua said crisply. "Mister Wenthi is a hero." She held out his plate with a jerking motion.

"Thank you," Wenthi said quietly, taking the plate and moving away from the table.

"That was bordering on insubordination," Lathéi said. "I'm quite cross."

"Don't make anything like a scene, Lath," he said. "Please."

"It was very rude."

"And it's very possible someone in her family, or someone she cares about, is locked up right now because of me. So let her have her anger."

"You're too kind," Lathéi said.

Oshnå came over, taking a moment to kiss Wenthi on the cheek before kissing Lathéi with a bit more fervor. "This party is the worst, dear."

"It really is," Lathéi said. "I'm sorry about that."

"Apologize to him," Oshnå said.

"I am sorry, Wenthi," Lathéi said.

"It's good," he said. "We're good. Always. You got me out of my room, at least." He took a bite of the taco, and it was excellent, just as he remembered. Izamio's gifts in the kitchen had not diminished over the years.

But yet it wasn't quite as good as the ones from the cart in Circle Hyunma. Somehow they lacked—

He wasn't sure.

Mother came over to them, her face completely unreadable. "Wenthi. I'm so pleased to see you, safe and well. I trust you're eating well?"

"It's all lovely, Mother."

She looked over to Lathéi with a hint of a scowl. "Do you have any further theatrics planned?"

"I didn't know honoring my brother was theatrics."

"It's a matter of appearances. There is a proper way to do things. We don't want to make our friends uncomfortable."

Wenthi couldn't hold his tongue. "Our friends who are here, at least. Friends like Ocullo are quite uncomfortable."

"Who?" Lathéi asked.

Mother took Wenthi's wrist and squeezed. Her eyes flashed with a dozen emotions. "Wenthi, darling, I imagine you and I have quite a bit to speak of."

"That's a bit of an understatement."

"Then let's not make a spectacle of that," she said. "We should go to my study. Come along."

62

Mother's study had always been her sanctuary in the house—on the far end of the upstairs hallway, with a heavy wooden door and cast-iron latch. Wenthi—as well as everyone else—had always been expressly forbidden from going in there when she was working. There was even a dumbwaiter and a pneumatic tube to the kitchen so she could send requests and receive meals without disruption. Wenthi could count on one hand how many times he had even stepped foot in the room.

One side of the room was dominated with bookshelves and a plush couch. Mother gestured for him to sit while she went to the small icebox under the desk and retrieved a pair of Dark Shumis. With practiced ease she poured two glasses with ice and a splash of whiskey and a wedge of lime. Wenthi chuckled to himself at the idea that the staff must always be making sure that she had freshly cut lime wedges at the ready. Nothing too good for the Root of the Tungét branch.

"So," she said as she handed him the drink and sat on the couch as far away as she physically could, "you've remembered Ocullo. I had been thinking you had forgotten about those times."

"I had," Wenthi said, sipping the drink. Perfect and sweetly rich as always. "But then I met him."

That got her eyebrow up. "How did you manage that?"

"Well, like you said, the right name was crucial to the mission. Everyone has people, and by giving me the name 'Llionorco,' folks presumed that he was mine. My shock was finding out he actually was."

"Someone actually brought you to him? Out in the 23rd?"

"Well, given that part of what the Fists of Zapi actually do is smuggle stolen fuel and food to the *baniz* in the 23rd, it wasn't much of a step farther."

"Why do they—"

"Because those people are starving. Ocullo is starving. The dozen kids he lives with are, too. Someone has to take care of them. Spirits of every ancestor of ours know the Alliance isn't. You aren't."

"I am doing what I can," she said, a tremble of anger in her voice. "And I'm stopped at every curve."

"Why did you arrange for me to have my father's name on this mission if you didn't expect someone to make that connection?"

She sighed and took a sip. "Hubris. Vanity. Maybe just to give you a small chance to honor the man you never got to know."

"So is it all true? My father was *baniz*. And you were part of some subversive movement to eradicate the castes?"

"Every generation has their movements," she said. "Then they either fail in their ambitions, or compromise their ideals as they gain power."

"That's bullshit, Mother," he said. "What was your compromise?"

"You hadn't figured it out yet?" she asked. She put down her drink and looked at him, really looked right at him for the first time since they came in here. Her eyes were welling with tears. "It was you."

That was impossible. "Me? How did you—" He was so flustered, he couldn't even figure out what the question he wanted to ask was.

She sat down and took a long slug of her drink. "I'll start at the beginning. Between the first two Transoceanic Wars, it was kind of a magical moment where we really thought anything was possible. We were finally, after generations, our own nation free from the Sehosians and Reloumic and everyone. We had a chance to define what that was going to be. But it was also chaos. The Prime Families, the caste systems, these were structures that already existed. People wanted to fall into them because, frankly, people are always hungry for things to 'return to normal' as easily as possible. Especially people for whom those structures already provided power and comfort."

"Like you," Wenthi said.

"Like my whole family. Especially my grandmother, may her spirit wail in darkness. But for people my age, there was this carefree sense that the old rules didn't have to matter. The castes might still exist, but for us they were just a name to describe ourselves. We lived and loved and celebrated everything together. Ocullo might call it a movement, but it was nothing more than young people who wanted to experience life and have a good time without having to listen to any rules."

"So not a rebellion or dissident group?"

"We weren't actually trying to change anything. Oh, we shouted and made noise, but—" She laughed, hard and mirthless. "Not in any way that would have an effect. I'll hand it to these rebels you stopped; they were active. All we did was decide how the world ought to be, and pretend like we had already done it just by pissing off our parents. Just buzzing on the mushrooms and fucking each other."

"You were using the mushroom?"

"Mushrooms," she said with a firm distinction. "So many people were losing their minds over what happened in Nemuspia, but your father knew differently. He had this whole idea about using the different mushrooms from all over the world, that they granted different abilities in each part of the world, in harmony with the character of their peoples. He was convinced that blending strains could open up new doors in our minds, change the world."

"That sounds like Doctor Shebiruht's garbage."

"She's a monster, but her ideas aren't completely wrong. The . . . the difference between her and your father is he practiced his beliefs with humanity. He—" Her voice caught for a moment. "He talked about helping people be better. He fought against the castes because he believed that people, like the mushroom, could achieve greater things by combining together and unlocking the best of us."

"What does that even mean?"

She reached across the distance and touched his face. For once, for the first time he could recall, he saw love and tenderness in her eyes. "That you, my beautiful boy, are a result of his work. We—we conceived you while using one of his mushroom blends together."

"You *made* me?" Wenthi shouted. "Like I was your science experiment?"

"No, no," she said, gesturing for him to be quieter. "It was never our goal. But when we found out I was pregnant, he had hoped that you would be a stronger, more connected person as a result. But at the end of the Second Trans, when the Unity realized what his work was, they destroyed him, destroyed his work, every trace of it."

"Every trace but me."

"Because I protected you. Haven't you realized?"

"What am I supposed to realize?"

"Why do you think when the war ended, and I was full-bellied with you, I took my place with the Prime Families? Why do you think I made sure you were declared *rhique*? I traded favors upon favors to get people to go along with it. I had to do whatever I could to keep you safe. They wanted me to claim my role as the Root of the Tungét, give the whole system legitimacy. I went along with what they all wanted. If I hadn't . . ."

It made a sick sense to Wenthi, as much as it curdled his stomach.

"Well, now I understand."

"What do you think you understand?"

"The whole time I was on the mission, I had to use the mushroom—"

She gasped.

"Which you should have realized I'd have to," he continued. "But when I did, I unlocked deeper and newer parts of myself, found levels of power no one knew were possible. I had first thought that was because of what Shebiruht did to me, syncing me with the Enapi girl. That our connection had opened new abilities up because we were paired together. But it was me, wasn't it? I had those abilities because you and my father did the same things to me as Shebiruht had done to her victims. Like when she made Penda Rodiguen into the weapon she was. And you knew about that, right?"

"I—" she said haltingly, but Wenthi wasn't done.

"You knew that woman was alive in her fancy apartment prison, that she was made by that witch. That Shebiruht was still putting daily work into keeping her, I don't know, functional? Which let her play with the hearts and spirits of the people who believed in her? And for what, Mother? What goal of yours, what dream did you have for this country that keeping her alive would help? What good do you even think you're doing?"

Mother was very quiet for a long period, and then a weak, hoarse whisper came out. "Did you say Enapi girl?"

Wenthi had no idea why that was what she had taken from his tirade, but he answered. "Yes. The dissident that Shebiruht jammed into my brain, synced me with on a spirit deep level, and messed with every thought with? Her name was Nália Enapi."

Quietly, she said, "Your father worked with a young woman named Zenisa Enapi. She volunteered for a few of his tests."

"Did you know what I was capable of? What Shebiruht was going to do? What this mission would do to me?"

"I didn't," she said, tears in her eyes. "They just said you were perfect and you needed to serve. You represented a potential for leadership in the patrol, so that our people could eventually take charge."

"They do like that line, don't they?" Wenthi said. Not that he believed the Alliance had any real intentions along those lines.

"I was sternly reminded of my duties and kept in the quiet. I pushed my authority as far as I could just getting that name on your papers. Which was just . . . some small bit of rebellion I had left in me. And for your sake, for

Lathéi and Aleiv, for the . . . stability of the country . . . that's all I dared to do."

He remembered something she had said the last time they spoke, of how the Alliance was livid about the fuel that was stolen. It was obvious to him now, so clear he didn't know how he hadn't seen it before. The Alliance went through a pretense of "rebuilding" the country they had devastated in at least two wars, if not the generations of occupation and colonization that had preceded them, but only so they could take the oil. That's what it was all about, all they cared about. Not the people, not the ideals they professed. They kept the undercastes hungry, and the overcastes comfortable, and kept them hating each other, so no one would notice what they were really doing.

He got up and finished the last drops of his drink, then left the glass, still damp with condensation from the ice, on her wooden desk and went to the door.

"Where are you going?" she asked.

"Home, in the 9th Senja," he said. "I would say that's where I belong, but that's a lie. It's all a lie. But maybe the truth will come to me."

63

Wenthi returned to his room, desperate to sleep. He had pushed out any possible bedmates for the night, including, and especially, Paulei, stripped out of the gaudy suit Lathéi had dressed him in, and fallen down into a deep sleep in minutes.

Dreams brought him to Circle Hyunma, the scattered wooden tables around the taco cart, in the shadow of the memorial statue. He sat alone at one table, the scents of the taco cart taunting him despite there not being anyone cooking or serving. At the table farthest away, he could see his compatriots in the Fists of Zapi: Ajiñe, Fenito, Gabrána, Mensi, and Nicalla. They were eating and laughing and talking and touching hands, but everything they did felt muted and far away, like the air between him and them was a thick membrane.

He called out, but they didn't hear him.

He shouted again, but they didn't react.

Then a train barreled through the circle, smashing them and their table, leaving nothing but wisps of smoke in its wake.

"You betrayed them."

He looked and saw Nália, almost hidden behind the statue, almost out of sight.

"I did my job," he said, moving toward her. But as he did, she slipped away. Always staying on the other side of the statue, just enough exposed that he could see the edge of her.

"You betrayed your blood."

"That's bullshit," he told her. "I don't owe anything to blood."

"What do you owe to, then?" she asked.

"If anything, I'm owed," he said.

"You are owed," she said. "*Nix xisisa,* we have paid too much."

"I'm owed explanations. Owed the truth."

"You already know the truth," she said.

"You as well," he said. "And what are you doing with it?"

"Trying not to die," she replied. "What any of us are trying to do. But what are you going to do to survive? Let all of them die? Let me? Let things continue as they are?"

"Are . . . are you really here?" he asked. It occurred to him that this wasn't a dream—he had awareness and agency that he never had in his dreams. "Nália, what's happening?"

"Sinking," she said. She melted into the statue, her body becoming one with the concrete and metal. For a flash, he felt her pain of solid flesh dripping away. Losing herself drop by drop.

"Please, Wenthi."

Wenthi sat up in his bed, covered in hot sweat despite the room having its usual late-autumn chill. He stumbled over to the water tap and drank two glasses before he realized that his bottle of pills sat on the sink. The pills he had been prescribed to complete his disconnection from Nália.

The pills he had forgotten to take when he went to sleep.

He opened the bottle and without hesitation, dumped the remaining pills down the drain.

64

Getting to Northsprawl involved passing through several checkpoints. Wenthi rode through the 9th, 8th, and 7th Senjas, crossing into Hightown through the Mangzei Crossing, winding up and down the hills of Moraiko—the quiet 18th Senja mostly populated by the *rhique* who didn't have Intown living privileges—and stopped at a taco stand to buy a bag full of tang chickens, crispy pork, and Ureti beef. He ate one of the chicken tacos before riding off again—fine, but nothing spectacular—and then went across the bridge, out of the city limits. The whole affair would have been easier if he had worn his uniform and rode his official cycle; he would have had less hassle. But that would have obviated the purpose of going.

No one he was going to wanted to see him as a patrol officer.

Once he was in Northsprawl, though, it didn't matter. He wasn't sure where he was going, and asked one kid if he knew where the Llionorcos lived.

"You are shitting tory?" the kid asked.

"Do I look like one?" Wenthi responded.

"Shit, yes," the kid said.

So wearing civilian clothes had made little difference.

He rode through the dirt streets of the Northsprawl for half a sweep before spotting a familiar face.

"Hey, Tyeja!" he called as he rode up. She was walking out of what mighty charitably be called a carbon shop, wearing a dirty cotton shirt, knee-cut denim, and no shoes. He wondered how she could stand walking here, with the scattered stones and broken glass, with nothing covering her feet.

"Shit," she said as he came to a stop. "What's your roll, cousin?"

"I came out looking for your place, but I didn't know where it was. Been riding about this part of town for a while."

She looked at the bag on his cowl. "What's that there?"

"Tacos from a joint across the river. Thought I shouldn't come empty-handed."

"You're a good thinker," she said with a warm smile. She got on the cycle behind him. "Straight that way, hang left at the blue sign."

"Yes, ma'am."

He took her back to the hovel, where a half-dozen of the kids were sitting around outside. Wenthi realized he had ridden plenty of patrol shifts where he had spotted a scene just like this, and had threatened the kids with arrest if they didn't "find somewhere to be." Which was ridiculous, and he couldn't think of a way to justify that.

"Look here," Tyeja said as she got off. "Our cityside kin brought us tacos."

The kids swarmed about and pulled tacos out of the bag.

"Make sure there's a couple for your uncle," Wenthi said. The kids savaged most of the contents of the bag, but did leave a few at the bottom. "All right if I go in?" he asked Tyeja.

"You bring tacos, kin, you can do whatever you need," she said with a wink. "I'm gonna sit on your ride in the meantime so no one tries to take it."

"Fair," he said, and went in. Ocullo was sitting in his chair, just like before.

"Didn't think I'd see you again so soon," he said.

"Brought you something," Wenthi said, handing him the remaining tacos.

"Quite kind of you, boy," Ocullo said. "I'm never so proud as not to take a free meal."

"So my father was some sort of mushroom genius?" Wenthi asked as Ocullo started eating.

Ocullo shrugged. "Not my place to say. I guess he fancied himself that. Not that it mattered."

"It matters to me," Wenthi said. "I think he . . . I think I might be . . . he might have made me more powerful than he could have guessed."

"Hmm," Ocullo said. "And what did you do with that power?"

"I—" Wenthi started. He hesitated, knowing how shameful it was. But he found himself unable to lie to this man. "I found the woman who was behind everything, got all the folks in the Fists arrested."

"I guess that's why there's been no fuel or food trucks in here of late," Ocullo said. "That's been a damned shame."

"You don't seem angry about that."

"After all I've lived through, it takes quite a bit to get angry. Shit is bad, shit has been bad, shit will continue to be bad. You didn't do anything that changed that situation significantly." He chuckled. "You think I should be mad. You think I should be angry at you."

"Maybe?"

"I've got too few years left to waste on that." He shook his head. "You came here for, what? Blame? Wisdom? I ain't got either for you. Looks like you're kicking yourself plenty."

"You knew about Varazina, right?"

"She that lady who gave orders over the radio? Not that we have radios here. Or current."

"She's the one. Like I said, I found her, turned her in. She's . . . not what I expected."

"How so?"

"She was a *llipe* woman, living in confinement in Intown."

The old man chuckled as he started his second taco. "Would not have guessed that."

"Here's the thing, she was—constructed to be a weapon. One that uses the mushroom, or the underlying power of it, and that was what she was made for. She didn't ask to be made, ask to be *llipe*, ask for any of it."

"What are you thinking?"

"That I might be just as much of a weapon as she was. Or at least I was made to be one."

"That wasn't what your father did," Ocullo said, for the first time with a bit of heat in his voice. "He did a lot of things I never understood. Talked about how the mushroom had levels of potential we don't understand. But I know this about him: He did not make weapons. He did not make you to be a weapon. He was about love, connection."

"Really?" Wenthi couldn't accept that. "How different am I from her?"

"I don't know. But . . . there she was, and she knew she had power, right? So what did she decide to do?"

"Sow chaos," Wenthi said. "Her words."

"And you?" Ocullo slowly stood up from his chair. He pointed a dark, withered finger at Wenthi's chest. "You're saying you've got power, too? Renzi made you into a weapon?"

"Maybe."

"Hmm," Ocullo said as he wiped his mouth on his sleeve. "I think the real question is, what do you want?"

"I just . . . I don't know. Justice? I always thought that was the point of the Civil Patrol, what I joined for, but now . . ."

"Son," Ocullo said, taking Wenthi by the shoulders. "I can't tell you who you are. Sorry if you think I can. You got to figure out who that is."

"Am I Wenthi Tungét, or Renzi Llionorco?"

"I wouldn't make it that simple," Ocullo said with an empty laugh. "But if that's a real question you're asking yourself, maybe you've got to make it that simple."

Wenthi nodded, not feeling any clearer, but glad he had come nonetheless. "Is there something I can do to help you all out here? I don't know, food, money? I can get Mother to—"

"You've got a good heart," Ocullo said. "Listen to that, and you'll be all right. Now you should get out of here. Sun'll go down soon, you don't want too much trouble getting back into the city."

Wenthi came out of the hovel, the sinking sun glaring in his eyes as he came up to the cycle.

"I look like I belong on this, huh?"

He knew it was Tyeja on the cycle, but for a moment, her voice, her face, everything was Nália.

Are you out there? he thought out.

He couldn't tell if he felt a faint hint of anger and fear at the edge of his senses, or if it was just his imagination.

"You look good," he said. "Next time I come out, I'll give you a proper run on him."

"Hold you to that, cousin," she said as she got off. He got on the cycle and made his way back to the city.

65

Wenthi had no urge to go to another brass club, especially a pricy one in the 3rd Senja filled with *llipe* swells and *rhique* posers, but with Lathéi leaving in a few days, he didn't want to miss his chance to see her. He could handle it.

He went on his own, once again riding Nália's 'goiz 960. He had grown attached to the cycle, enjoying it more than any other vehicle he'd ever ridden. He was going to miss it when he had to go back to the patrol issue Ungeke.

Crossing from the 9th to the 8th was no problem, but that changed when he crossed into the 3rd.

"What is this garbage?" the Alliance officer asked as he rode up to the checkpoint.

"What do you mean?"

The officer kicked the front tire of the 'goiz. "This junk you're riding. This is some *baniz* junk."

"It's a re-fit Puegoiz 960 with an inline four, and it can outrun whatever you might ride," Wenthi said.

"Is that attitude?" the officer asked. "Give me your cards."

Wenthi handed over his identity cards, which the officer took over to a lamp in the guard booth next to the checkpoint barrier. After scrutinizing it for a moment, he shouted, "What are you going to the 3rd for?"

"Going to a brass club called the Fire Chile," Wenthi said.

"Why?"

Wenthi sighed. This was one of those guys. "Meeting my sister."

The guard looked at the cards again, then looked at Wenthi. "Get over here."

Wenthi stopped the cycle and came over to the man. As soon as he got close, the man pulled out a baton and slammed it in Wenthi's chest, and then against his arm. Before Wenthi could react or recover, the officer swept his leg and knocked him to the ground. He got on top, pressing his knee into Wenthi's back.

"You try and pull this bullshit? You think you could pass as *rhique*, you *jifo* piece of shit, riding your *jifo* garbage cycle?"

"That's my card," Wenthi said.

"Right, you're just a dark *rhique* who rides a trash cycle that only a *jifo* would. And you're so fucking stupid you made a fake card with the name Tungét. Really? A Prime Family?"

"That's my name—"

"Your name is gonna be my boot, you're gonna get knocked with caste falsification, identity falsification, crossing incursion, and if you're lucky it'll just mean a train ride to Hanez."

"I'm a patrol officer," Wenthi said.

"Bullshit," he said, putting cuffs on Wenthi's wrists. He hauled him up and put him in the chair in the guard booth.

"Call the patrol headquarters in the 9th Senja," Wenthi said. "And then call my mother, the councilwoman."

That made the guard flinch for a moment. "You stay in that fucking chair. I'm going to call you in."

He went over to the outside of the guard booth and got on the phone. Wenthi felt a trickle of blood in his nose, but he couldn't do anything about that. All he could do was sit and wait, with the muffled conversation of the guard on the phone, his radio playing the news prop in the background.

"And local adjudicators have made rulings on the cases of the ringleaders in the riots, including the revolutionary leader they called Varazina and several other key agitators. We are proud to announce that all of them will be sentenced to a lifetime of hard labor at the Genzha Oil Fields in Upper Zian. They will drill for oil, a fitting punishment for people who stole petrol, destined for our war efforts overseas. They will work hard to replace the precious fuel they sought to steal. With these malefactors brought to justice and sentenced for their crimes, we look forward to a return to normalcy in our beautiful—"

The guard came in, scowling. "Your story appears to check out." He unlatched the cuffs and threw the identity cards at Wenthi's feet.

"You mean my cards were accurate and you made a stupid assumption," Wenthi said as he picked them up.

"Don't push it with the attitude," the guard said. Wenthi noted his name badge. Utnow. Wenthi would remember that.

"I'm free to go?" Wenthi asked.

"Get out of my sight," Utnow said. "Like we can even tell any of you apart."

"Charming," Wenthi said. He got on the cycle, gunning it as hard as he could as he tore out of the checkpoint. He whisked and wound through the curves of the 3rd, not slowing down a jot as he dodged the slow autos and parked sedans.

As his speed peaked, for a moment he felt a hint of them on the edge of his senses. Ajiñe, Gabrána, Nicalla, Fenito, Mensi. They were in cells at patrol headquarters with the others, waiting for the transfer. A train to take them away. In the morning.

And Nália. In the basement. Strapped to a gurney. Blood being drawn. Electrodes applied to her head. Doctor Shebiruht hovering over her.

Wenthi pulled his brakes and came to a hard stop, forcing the experience to fade. But while he wasn't living it, he still felt it. He understood. He was full of anger and rage, but more importantly, purpose and certainty.

He parked the cycle and strode into the club, heading up the spiral and pushing past the worker planning on impeding his path to his sister. She smiled at his approach—sitting with Oshnå in peach jumpsuits, which half the people on the dance floor had mimicked. Good. An idea was forming in his head, and seeing a club full of people copying Lathéi showed him exactly how it could work.

"I need you," he said as he sat down.

"Well, good," she said, waving off the two employees who had stormed over to the table. "Does that mean I can finally convince you to come to Dumamång with me?"

"No," he said. "I—I'm going to do something drastically stupid, and I need your help."

"Oh, my," Oshnå said.

"Intriguing," Lathéi said as she sipped her drink. "Will this irritate Mother?"

"Absolutely. To start."

She put her drink down and really looked at him. "This is something serious, isn't it? Not just to irritate Mother, but . . ."

She left it hanging.

"Drastically stupid," he said. "But it is right. And just. And I can't do it without you."

A tear formed at the corner of her eye. "I don't know if I . . . I know I don't understand what happened to you on this mission, how it changed you."

"Lath—"

"Let me finish," she said. "You asked before if I remember what happened during the war, and I can tell you I remember one thing very clearly. You were there for me. You kept me alive. So if you need something stupid, or irritating or—"

"Rebellious?" Oshnå asked. "Revolutionary?"

"Any of that," Lathéi confirmed, with a quick glance at her paramour that confirmed they were on the same page. "Anything you need, anything at all, I am there for you."

"I love you," Wenthi said.

"I know," she said. "So what do you need?"

"First, I need you to reach out to Enzúri Hwungko and get him over here."

66

Tungét, what are you doing here? I thought you were still on paid leave for another ten days."

Wenthi put on his best smile to the desk clerk at the garage entrance, whose name escaped him. "Oh, I absolutely am. I'm not formally here, so don't check me in or anything like that."

"Really?" the clerk asked. "That's kind of against protocol."

"Listen," Wenthi said, leaning in close, speaking like he was confiding. "They're about to ship out all those rebel shitheels I caught, and I'm, you know, not supposed be part of the team who takes them to the train and such. But I just want to see them get shuffled out."

"I hear you," the clerk said. "Just keep your head low."

Wenthi winked and went inside, keeping his face from showing how uncomfortable and out of sorts he was coming in the headquarters. He had taken a dose of mushroom, and while he was not synced with anyone, it pushed his senses to the edge. He tried to feel for Ajiñe, Nália, Mensi, anyone. Recapture that feeling he had last night. But he couldn't reach them.

Every member of the patrol put off that same spiky, static sensation, which helped him wind his way to the uniform room without otherwise being spotted. The fewer people who saw him right now, made note of him, the better. Not that he'd be able to go back to work once he did this. There was no going back. But every swipe was going to count, so anything that kept patrol off his trail for a few moments was going to be worth it.

No one was in the uniform room. Good. He quickly stripped out of his clothes and dressed in full cycle uniform: black coat buttoned up, gloves, helmet, and goggles on. He dug through the lockers, hoping that someone had been sloppy, and of course someone was: Cresai. One of the laziest riders on the night sweep, always leaving his gear anywhere. He found Cresai's badge and ident plate, pinned them to his coat. A glance in the mirror: perfect. No one would look twice at him. No one would note him as Wenthi Tungét.

He strode out of the uniform room, through the operations floor. He gave a glance at the assignment board, noting that several cycle patrol were escorting the transport trucks to the train platform. He checked the times and the clock.

Shit, he was already too late. They left twenty-five swipes ago. That's why he couldn't feel any of them.

He kept moving, making his way toward the main doors. Next part of the plan. He had anticipated this. It didn't matter. He needed to move on, to the most important part of his plan. The part that could only happen at the stationhouse. The rest would sort out. It had to.

He left the stationhouse, flashing Cresai's plate at the desk as he went, and went around the curve to the alley behind a fancy carbon shop. Enzúri Hwungko was waiting nervously there.

"Well?" he asked.

"Too late, plan two," Wenthi said. "Ready?"

"Not really," Enzúri said. "But I suppose we don't have time for me to be ready." He took a packet out of his pocket and deposited a bit of the mushroom on his tongue. Wenthi had gambled when he made this plan that not only would Enzúri be willing to join in, but that he still had a stash of the mushroom. He couldn't have done this without it.

Enzúri stroked Wenthi's cheek, and the contact confirmed them getting into sync with each other.

"Come on," Wenthi said. He slapped his tether cuffs on Enzúri and took him by the arm, leading him back to the headquarters. This time, using the bus doors on the side. This would have been where the prisoners were all unloaded into trucks, now long gone. Wenthi brought him through to the intake desks. Spiking static all around him, going over to the clerk who looked youngest and newest. Needed someone who he didn't know, and, hopefully, didn't know Cresai. He flashed the plate again.

"Got one for the cells?" the clerk asked. "He looks—"

"Yeah," Wenthi said, lowering his voice to a gruff whisper. "He's not just *llipe*, but from one of the Families, hear?"

"Spirits," the clerk said. "So are you—"

"He's also buzzing like anything on the *myco*. I already have orders and it's crucial that it's, you know, quiet. Not an embarrassment."

"When my aunt finds out I'll have your uniform," Enzúri said.

"Quiet," Wenthi said. "You deserve to be celled up for the rest of the season."

"So what do you need?" the clerk asked him.

"I need to take him to the ice rooms in the subbasement. That way we can cut off his buzz."

"Right," the clerk said, nodding with understanding. He produced a key from his desk. "Down that hall, take the lift, and use that key to get access to the sublevels."

"Thanks," Wenthi said. He pulled Enzúri along.

"That was too easy," Enzúri said as they reached the lift.

"I wonder if this happens more often than I realized," Wenthi said. They got inside, turned the key in the access panel, and started down.

"How will we find our way down there?" Enzúri asked. "Do you know what we're getting into?"

"Not entirely," Wenthi said as the doors opened to the sublevel. Pale, cold walls, unmarked doors. He would not normally be able to navigate his way through the place. But on the mushroom, synced with Enzúri, he could feel the spiky static coming off everyone down here.

Almost everyone.

There it was: the hint of the familiar connection of Nália Enapi. She was here.

"Got her," Wenthi said. "Let's go."

 67

As they moved closer to the source of Nália, static buzzed and flashed across Wenthi's brain, and he could tell Enzúri was feeling it as well. Like a streethammer to the skull, which each felt for themselves and in each other, feeding back like an angry microphone.

"What is that?" Enzúri asked. "It's not just the guards down here."

Wenthi remembered. "There's a different breed of the mushroom growing in the walls. We must be feeling that."

Enzúri nodded. "Yeah. It's stronger as we get closer to that room."

Which was exactly where he felt Nália. Wenthi tried the door. Locked. He took a chance and tried the elevator key. No luck.

"Well?" Enzúri asked.

"In for it all now," Wenthi said, and kicked hard at the door, knocking it open. He pulled Enzúri in and did his best to shut it behind them. "People heard that. Let's hurry."

This was the room Nália was in, as she was on a bed, hooked up to electrodes, drip bags connected to needles in her arms, strapped down to the table. Her eyes were shut, she was clearly unconscious. Despite that, this close, Wenthi could feel her faintly, struggling to push out of the dark. He pulled off the electrodes, undid the straps, pulled the needles out.

"Give me a dose," he told Enzúri. He handed over a packet of the mushroom, and Wenthi opened Nália's mouth and poured it in. He kept one hand on her chest, letting the connection spread out from there into her, feeling himself sink into her darkness and she lifted up into him. Both of them were together in a place that was neither body, deep into the space between them that was beyond the physical plane.

Wake up.

[What?]

Wake up.

[What are you doing here, asshole?]

Getting you out of here.

[This is a shitty trick you're trying to pull.]

No trick. Look.

That hint of her that pushed into him opened his eyes, looked down at her own body. And with that, like a radio tuning to the right station, there was a sudden lightning burst of energy flowing through him, into her, jolting her eyes open. And for a moment, they saw each other, saw themselves, were each other, completely and fully.

Then with a sharp crack, a sudden slam that hit Wenthi in body and spirit, they were pulled apart, on every level. Wenthi was knocked into the blackness, and then back into his body as he went flying down to the ground. Breath and sight and connection returned, to find Doctor Shebiruht standing over him, carrying a crusted baton. Six officers came into the room, a pair each grabbing him, Enzúri, and Nália.

"Officer Tungét, what a fascinating surprise to see you here. I had a feeling you were very special, and that your connection with Miss Enapi would yield incredible results, but I had no idea it would do something like this. Fascinating."

"You witch, you'll—" was all Wenthi managed to say before the baton slammed across his head, and with that, again, shocked him out of his body and tore through the connection he had with Nália. She screamed at the same moment he was struck.

As he snapped back into himself, Shebiruht ran her gloved finger across the encrusted baton. "An interesting crossbreed of the *mycopsilaria sehosi* and *ikusa*. The Iku apparently brew teas out of their *myco*, and with proper rituals, are able to briefly leave their bodies. Combined with the disruptive, blocking abilities of the *sehosi*, it makes for an effective blunt instrument."

Wenthi forced himself, through the disorienting haze of pain, to reconnect with Nália, reestablish that bond that was surely stronger than either of them had fully realized.

Help me.

The guards pulled his hands behind him, as the others worked to strap Nália back down to the table, despite her valiant efforts to fight them off. She was a wildcat, but she was still weak and woozy, and they had numbers and determination. Enzúri was pinned to the floor.

"But I'm very glad to have you here, Officer Tungét. I've been studying your blood, as well as Miss Enapi's, and there is something truly fascinating. I may have lost dear Penda to play with, but the two of you have opened up whole new avenues to explore. And I will enjoy learning everything your bodies have to teach me."

She pushed the baton against him again, holding it on his chest, and it forced everything that he was to fall out of his body, into an empty blackness. He fell deeper and deeper into that abyss, losing any sense that he had ever had a body.

Then a hard burst of light, like a rope thrown into the ocean, that he pulled himself back with. Nália, on the other end, dragging him back into the real world, still apart from his body, seizing on the floor. She was on the table, getting strapped down, one of the guards about to inject her with something.

But her phantom form was with his, holding his hand, fully connected.

"Remember Ajiñe on the highway?" she asked.

He understood. Despite the pain and disconnection that was coming from his own body, he drew strength from Nália, and channeled that into pushing his energy into the guards holding him. He and Nália took control of their bodies; what they had done on instinct with Ajiñe, they now did with intention.

They jumped on Doctor Shebiruht, pulling the baton from her hands and pulling her to the ground. He half snapped into his own body, while holding control over the guard. He and Nália expanded their control to the guards holding Enzúri. With the guards' own tether cuffs, they subdued the guards on Nália and locked them up. Shebiruht's face was an expression of horror as the four guards they held control over dragged her to the table while Nália got off it. Quickly she was strapped down, and then Nália used the syringe that they were about to inject her with to knock out the guards.

"Impossible," Doctor Shebiruht said.

"Not at all," Nália said. "You said we were extraordinary."

"You just had no idea how much," Wenthi said.

"You won't get away with this," Shebiruht said, struggling with her bonds.

"I don't care," Nália said, picking up the baton. She tore open Shebiruht's blouse. "You are an absolute monster. You will pay for what you did to me, to him, to Varazina, and the people of this country."

She ground the baton onto Shebiruht's bare, clammy flesh, and the woman screamed as her eyes rolled back. Then she froze in a rictus of open-mouthed agony. Nália left the baton on her chest. Wenthi hoped no one would ever take it off.

Nália turned to Wenthi, almost smiling at him. "Now what, asshole?"

68

First we get you out of the building," Wenthi said. "Then we've got a train to catch."

"Train?"

"Everyone else is being shipped to the oil derricks, sentenced to hard labor."

"And you care about that?" she asked. But they were fully connected, the same level of sync they had shared for over a season, even as they stood face to face. Emotion and thought and sensation were all one, like their two bodies were part of one person. "You do. You—" She shook her head. "Still an asshole, Wenthi, but at least your head isn't still wedged in yours."

"Thanks."

"So how do I get out?" she asked. She held out her arms and spun around, pointing out the medical gown she was wearing. "I can't exactly go out in this."

"Where I come in," Enzúri said, starting to take off his smartly styled suit. "You walk out wearing this."

"What?" she asked as he handed her his coat. "That's absurd. And what are you even doing here, you—"

"*Llipe* asshole?" he offered. "Setting it right." He gave her his slacks. She sighed and stripped off the gown.

"What are you going to do? Stay here in the gown?"

"Yeah," he said. "And in about a sweep, my aunt—the councilwoman—will get a call that I've been abducted and I'm down here. So I'll be fine."

She finished getting dressed, and while the suit wasn't a perfect fit, she looked pretty decent. "I still look like a *jifoz* playing dress up."

"Nothing we have time to do anything about," Wenthi said. "Just keep your head down while we walk."

Nália stopped and touched Enzúri's face. "Thank you. And thank you for . . . for being on the right side of things."

"There are more of us than you think," Enzúri said. "Now go."

Wenthi led her down the hall, back to the lift, and with the key, back to the main floor. He took her by the arm as they walked out, and he made a point to move with his head up, confidently.

He dropped the key back on the clerk's desk, keeping Nália positioned so her back was to them. "Bosses keep changing their mind. Now I've got to take him home."

"They do that, don't they?" the clerk said. "Good luck."

"You too," Wenthi said, and took her out the bus doors onto the street.

"That easy?" she asked.

"Probably not," he said. "We're out of the building, but any swipe now, one of those guards will wake up, and he'll sound an alert, and there will be an outcall for you."

"And then?"

"Every patrol on a cycle will be looking for you. Come on."

He went around a curve through a tight alley, up the steps to the indented niche between a paper shop and a clothing store, where Lathéi and Oshnå were waiting with the cycles.

"This is her?" Lathéi asked. She looked over Nália with approval. "I thought Enzúri looked a bit overdone in that outfit, but you? Rather spruce."

"Thank you?" Nália responded. "Who are these *llipe* minces? And why are they dressed like—"

"I'm not *llipe*, I'm Hemish," Oshnå said. "This is all very exciting."

"You know who she is," Wenthi said, nodding to Lathéi.

Nália looked back. "Oh, this is the famous sister. I should have guessed. You kept showing up in his dreams, you know."

"Really?" Lathéi asked. "Not improperly, I hope."

"Rarely," Nália said.

Wenthi started taking off his stolen uniform. "Get out of those clothes," he told her. "When the call comes, they'll be looking for that outfit."

"And wear what?" Nália asked.

"Oh, we've got that for you," Oshnå said, handing over a pair of bundles. Nália realized what she had been given: her raw denim coat and pants. Her own, which still fit perfectly despite Wenthi having worn them for days and days. Wenthi had his own set, though his didn't have the mileage of grease and wear like hers did.

"You got this back for me?" she asked.

"I knew how much those meant to you," he said. "Just like that does." He pointed to the 'goiz 960 in the niche.

"My baby," she said, caressing the machine. She looked it over. Wenthi had been taking good care of it. "And the tank is full."

Lathéi spoke up. "Well, I have this ridiculous petrol ration. I might as well use it for some good."

Nália got on her cycle, which felt so good to have beneath her. Not that she knew where she could go. "So, what now? If we ride out of here as denimed up cycle cats, we're definitely going to stand out."

"Oh, no," Lathéi said. "I've already taken care of that."

69

Wenthi had come to his sister with a crazy plan, but he had been truly amazed by how easily she had made her part work. She and Oshnå left the brass club, called on a clothier to open their doors for her—which they did without hesitation—changed into new outfits and returned to the brass club. They took to the floor, danced up a storm, chatted vivaciously with several acquaintances, and went home to make a few calls.

Shortly after zero on the naught, she and Oshnå strolled into the offices of ZV880, the preferred station for Lathéi's generation to hear the hot music, news, and gossip at all sweeps of the day. Among the crowds that danced at the brass clubs, followed the fashion trends, and paid close attention to the most notable of notables, ZV880 was the station to listen to. The announcer for the morning shift was enamored enough of Lathéi Tungét that with one call, he happily had her come on live air and talk about the fashion stir she had caused at the Fire Chile last night.

"It's very simple," Lathéi had said. "I was thinking to myself, you know who has it figured out? You know who understands a *look*? It's the *jifoz* cycle cats. That hard denim, cut clean, shining brass rivets. It's making a statement, and that statement is *hot*. They look good. They look like they can *do things*. They look *authentic*."

"But Miss Tungét," the announcer said, "you don't think that's a bit volatile, so shortly after the Outtown riots?"

"Style is about volatility. Being in style means embracing change. We have been stuck in a rut, my friend. Same broad-shouldered suits for years, same wide-brimmed hats for years. The colors changed, but did the style? No. I come back here with a few Hemish dresses and people go crazy. What this tells me is people are craving something new, and something of their own. And we're not going to find that by looking across the oceans to Hemish or Reloumene and *definitely* not to Sehosia. We're building a new nation here, we're going to be holding elections here, and part of that means looking about what makes us, *us*. And spirits help me, I think the look that will bring that is raw, it's hard, and it's real. It's who we are, friends. Just like the cycles that our streets were made for."

"I'll admit, Miss Tungét, you and your paramour do look smashing in your jackets and slacks."

"We absolutely do. And we're committed to embracing this look. Tell you what, friends. You get yourself this look. You get on your cycles, and you ride down to Circle Yendwei in the 9th Senja at three on the naught. If I see you there, and you look good, then the tacos are on me."

Wenthi had pulled Nália out of the patrol headquarters in the 9th Senja at two on the sixty, and by the time they were dressed in denims and riding their cycles, it was two on the eighty, and the streets were swarming with young overcaste folks on cycles, dressed in denim.

Wenthi and Nália delivered Lathéi and Oshnå to Circle Yendwei, where there was a whole crowd of people, all dressed the same way. None of them stood out at all, save Lathéi and Oshnå, who were expected as the hosts of this impromptu event.

"Are you going to be all right?" Lathéi asked Wenthi as she dismounted.

"Are you?" he responded. "That's a lot of tacos for you to buy."

"I'll manage," she said. "But you're—" She held her hand over his heart. "We're seeing each other again, yes?"

"I hope so," he told her. "I plan to survive this."

"And then?"

"Then . . . we'll see what happens."

"I love you so much, Wenthi."

"Love you more," he said. He looked to Oshnå. "You better be good to her, all right?"

"All my heart," Oshnå said. "See you soon, on this world or beyond."

The radio on Wenthi's Ungeke K'am crackled. "*All points, all points, be alert. We have an escaped fugitive from the 9th Senja headquarters. Be on the watch for Nália Enapi,* jifoz, *age twenty-three. She is possibly armed and has accomplices.*"

"Oh, accomplices," Lathéi said. "Very exciting. Time to do my part." She turned to the crowd. "Hello, my beauties! You look amazing!" She and Oshnå waded into the crowd.

Wenthi got on his radio, using Paulei's callsign. "Rider 309. Possible suspect spotted running north toward 8th Senja. In pursuit, send aid."

"*Confirmed 309.*"

"Now?"

"West, to Southwall, then out of town along the tracks. That train is surely out of the city already, and we need to run it down."

"Well then, asshole," she said with a wicked grin. "Try to keep up." She kicked up her 'goiz and gunned the throttle, rocketing through the circle, winding and weaving through the crowd until she jetted out the Northway exit. Wenthi was right behind, doing his best to keep up.

But she was already fire on that 'goiz.

"Damn right, I am," her phantom said in his ear. "Don't you forget it."

"Rider 193. Possible suspect—on cycle in denim outfit. North toward the Mixala Crossing."

"Rider 821. I've got one on cycle in jifo *denim."*

"Walker 032. Half the people in the shitting 9th are in jifo *denim. What the shit is this?"*

"Rider 309," Wenthi replied. "Can confirm many people dressed in denim. What was suspect last wearing?"

"I don't shitting know."

"Backup at the Mixala. This cycle is gunning hard at you!"

That was clearly someone on Nália's tail. As he closed the distance, he saw a cycle tory trying to get on her. She wasn't having it, weaving back and down, whipping into a narrow slope alley, and then whipping a half circle to fly at him. He swerved out of panic, and she whipped out to join Wenthi as they neared the crossing.

Several officers were congregating at the tunnel entrance, pulling out their handguns.

"That's a problem," Wenthi told Nália.

"Not at this speed," she said. "Feel me?"

He was on her wavelength, and as they accelerated, he let the part of him that was on her cycle, with her, slip forward and dive into one of the tories. Just as with the guards in the ice room, he was able to grab hold of the man's body and use him as a puppet. He threw the gun away, and then grabbed the next officer's gun and threw it away.

"What?" that tory asked, before another—the one Nália had jumped in to pilot—knocked him down with a punch.

"Faster, faster," she said as they buzzed past the brawling guards and down into the crossing tunnel. "When we catch up with that train, we'll be unstoppable."

"Don't get cocky," Wenthi said. "We're still learning."

They curved into a side tunnel in the crossing—one only authorized for patrol and other emergency vehicles, as if that mattered—and popped up in Southwall. Nália knew this area, and took the lead across a lot to the aqueduct drop. They twisted through the gully of the aqueduct, under another bend of access tunnels running the line through Southwall, and out in the sun again in the Ako Favel. The road parallel to the train tracks leading out of the city, toward the Genzha Oil Fields.

Between here and there was a train thundering along the tracks, filled with Fists of Zapi, and the hope for the future.

70

It was several kilos on the open plain before they could see the train, the hot sun glaring down on them. Nália had pushed the 'goiz up to fire gear, engine running hot but holding together. After uncounted days trapped in that ice room, feeling the world only through Wenthi, or being trapped in the darkness of whatever void the Witch had put her in, it felt glorious to be not only fully in her body, but in her own clothes, on her beautiful cycle. She had the open country in front of her, nearly a full tank of petrol, and felt like she could go forever.

Which was strange. Her body should have been a weak mess. But it was like Wenthi was somehow pouring strength into her. Like he could share that as much as they could share sensations and feelings.

She'd love to think more about that, but there was the train. Time to get to work.

"What are you feeling on there?" Wenthi asked her.

"Static," she said. "The whole thing. Am I imagining it or—"

"It's like the train is made of ice rooms," he said.

"Why would they do that?" They were pushing closer and closer; at this rate they would be right up next to it in a few swipes. But they had no sense of what was going on, where the Fists were, how many guards there were.

"Varazina," Wenthi said. "Penda probably doesn't even need to take mushroom—"

"And they want to contain her power."

It made sense. The last thing they needed was her calling out on the radio for hundreds of saviors. Maybe that's what took them this long to sentence them all and ship them out to the oil fields; they needed to get the train ready for the transfer.

"What's the plan?" she asked.

"I'd say stop the train, neutralize any guards, free everyone on the train."

"There's a big 'and after that?' question to be asked, you know."

"As in . . . where we stand?" he asked. "What do I do next? Can't go back to my old life."

"I was more thinking we'll be in the middle of nowhere and will probably need to use the train to get back to the city."

"Right," he said. They were coming up closer and closer to the train now. No sign of patrol on the outside, either riding in escort or taking guard posts along the top of the train.

"So however we stop the train, it can't be a permanent stop, you know?"

"Good point. You got an idea?"

"Spirits watch over me, because I do," she said. "Try to keep up."

She gunned her cycle into fire gear and went off. One-eighty. One-ninety-two. Two-hundred-four.

The burst of speed caused her senses to explode, like flowers unfolding in bloom. She could feel her way back to the city, to the oil derricks and the camps ahead—the pain and suffering of the people there, the ones who died in the fire, and the ones who lived—and the expanse of the mushroom beneath them. It was almost too intense for her to bear, except she had Wenthi to anchor her.

And the blaring, spiky static coming off of the train. What had Shebiruht said the ice room was made with? *Mycopsilaria sehosi.* The one from Sehosia. It blocked the other mushrooms. Blocked the signal. Blocked connection. It even felt . . . angry from the speed of the train. She couldn't push through that to the inside of the train cars. Every car of the train was laced with it.

But not the engine. Or the engineer running the train.

How easy it was now, especially at this speed, to slip herself into him, to take control of his arm, to pull from his memory how the controls worked. Pull the brake, the wheels screeched. Too hard, too fast. She had to ease up on the brake. Else the train would derail.

"You have it?" Wenthi asked, his phantom avatar appearing next to her in the engine room.

"I do," she said. "But it's going to take a few swipes to get us actually stopped. I need to keep focus on holding control over him while keeping pace on the cycle."

"Keep on it," he said. "But you'll probably have unwanted company."

She checked the engineer's body. Sidearm at his hip. "I can handle it."

"Then I'll find our friends."

"Are they, Wenthi?" she asked. "Our friends? They never met me, not really, or the real you. Are you going to be straight with them?"

"I'm going to have to be," he said. "Like I said, no going back."

His avatar vanished, and she could feel the engineer struggling to get control over himself. *Not today, friend.* She poured all she had to hold on to him for a few swipes more.

71

Wenthi pulled his awareness away from Nália, keeping her as just a buzz in the back of his mind. Her attention was already fully on two tasks; he didn't need to be another distraction.

He needed to get on the train.

Most of the petrol thefts, they jumped onto the train, using the aqueduct walls to ramp up. This was open scrubland. Nothing to ramp. So he needed another way.

He dropped back to match pace with the last train car, getting as close as he could while riding parallel with it. He brought the cycle as close as he dared, and carefully pulled his feet up onto the seat, keeping one hand on the handles, whispering to the spirits watching over him to keep it straight.

Deep breath.

Jump.

He landed hard on the rear platform, stumbling for a moment and grabbing the rail to keep from falling onto the tracks. As he took a moment to catch his breath, the riderless patrol-issued Ungeke K'am wobbled and swerved into the side of the train. It fell under the wheels, and with a hard jolt, was crushed.

The door of the last car opened up, and a day sweep patrol officer—someone Wenthi didn't know—stuck his head out. Wenthi grabbed him and yanked him, hurling him off the train. He didn't want to kill the man; he hoped he could avoid killing anyone today. But it might come to that.

He stepped into the rear car, and it was immediately like a static knife scraping across his skull, pushing against the senses and sensations awoken by mushroom and velocity. Now that he was inside the iced train, while its power pressed against him from all sides, it could no longer block him from feeling people inside. Two patrol were in the next car.

Along with something else, something so full of pain and static it made his eyes hurt.

He had a solid idea what that was. He had to push through.

Despite the pain, he pushed himself out, into the two patrol guards. Enrin and Thei. Two folks he knew, if not well. Folks he liked. He slipped into Thei, drew her sidearm, dropped it to the floor, and opened the car door. She tried to fight back as he made her step to the door—Enrin was shouting what in all faith was she doing—and he had her jump off the train.

Enrin's body tried to reject Wenthi as he strained to take control. The cold of the train walls made it harder than he had expected, taking almost all of his will and strength to push through. To make Enrin drop his gun, step to the door.

Enrin managed to turn his head. "Are you doing this, you witch?"

Through Enrin's eyes, Wenthi saw the cage, with fungal-encrusted bars, and inside it, Penda Rodiguen.

"Not at all," she said. "But I am enjoying it."

Wenthi pushed a bit more of himself into Enrin and forced him to jump.

The guards gone, Wenthi went into the next car.

Penda sat in a chair in her mushroom cage, a wry smile on her face.

"I wasn't expecting you at this point, I have to say."

"And why is that?"

"Because your story here was done. You played your role. I've not been able to go to the theater or the cinescope in some time, but usually when a character does their last scene, they don't come back again."

"My last scene?" Wenthi asked, moving closer to her. Her pale complexion was even more jaundiced and sallow than the last time. "This isn't some script."

"But it is, dear boy. Or at least, that was my intent."

"Your intent? Is this more of your—how did you say it—sowing chaos?"

She laughed, a dry, rasping laugh that degraded into hacking coughs. "You're not wrong," she said once she recovered. "But that was always with a purpose."

"Which was?"

"To align you and Miss Enapi," she said. "To make her feel angry enough, betrayed enough by an uncaring *llipe* she saw as a savior, that she would let you turn me in."

"What?"

"Are you this stupid, Officer Tungét? *Your betrayal was part of my plan.*"

The words hit him in the gut, but made a sick kind of sense. "Because you always knew I was an infiltrator."

"You think I didn't see you? You thought that 'mask' of melding your mind with Nália's worked on me? Who do you think put the idea in Shebiruht's twisted skull?"

"Why?" Wenthi asked. "Why me?"

"Well, the original plan was using that absurdly earnest Hwungko boy, but he got caught. And when that happened I discovered you. I learned how you were not unlike me."

"That I was made to be a mushroom weapon."

"Oh, Wenthi," she said, getting to her feet. "You have an affinity, and maybe that was unnaturally given to you—" He could feel hints of her pushing against his skull. "—but believe me, you were not made to be a weapon like I was. Open up this damn cage, though."

"Why should I?"

"Because I actually had a purpose to this." She sighed. "Varazina needs to be a martyr. But a martyr needs an apostate. I needed someone to betray me. What would rouse the people more than having someone turn me in?"

"Why would you want that?"

"To get the one thing I needed that I could never get while locked up in that apartment. The thing that unlocked everything in you and Nália."

"You had everything in there."

"Everything except speed. But now I have this train." She laughed again, then looked about. "Why are we slowing down?"

"Nália's stopping it."

"What the shit is wrong with you?" she asked. "Quick, get me out of here. This cage is holding me back, I need to get out of here, get up to speed again."

"Why?"

"Haven't you figured it out yet, Wenthi? I was made to be a weapon. I'm more than ready to show the world exactly what that means."

72

The train had stopped. Had they already made it to the slave camps? Ajiñe had no way to gauge the time or distance in the dimly lit cage.

"Something's not right," Nicalla said from the next cage. They were in boxes, too short to stand, too narrow to lie down, stacked on top of one another. Absurdly inhuman. Not that Ajiñe had expected anything less. Since the arrest, she had spent most of the time locked in small rooms, isolated from everyone she had been taken with. Everyone she loved. She was informed yesterday that she had been tried and sentenced to hard labor at a work camp.

The only comfort she could find was thinking that maybe her mother was there too.

Only when they had loaded her onto the truck to take her to the train had she seen anyone else. She rode with Mensi and Nicalla, and for some reason Isilla Henáca from Street Xaomico was with them as well.

"What are you doing here?" Ajiñe asked, but the only answer she got was the butt of a rifle across her chin. The tory asshole glared at her, telling her to stay quiet. She didn't fight it, not here.

On her truck, there were a few other faces she found familiar. Other members of the Fists that she had felt during the induction. She knew their souls if not their names.

And then, for a brief moment, there was daylight and fresh air as they were loaded onto the train. Ajiñe tried to savor it, drink in what she could, and glanced over to the next train car, loading from another truck.

Gabrána. Miss Dallatan.

Papa.

Why in any name was he here? Why had they arrested him? Just to punish her? Then she spotted other faces she knew. Gab's mother, side-mother, and aunt. Fenito's brother.

These shit-filled assholes. They had rounded up everyone they could, regardless of how they were involved in the Fists.

"Where's Renzi?" she had whispered to Mensi after they were shoved into the cages. "Or Fenito? Have you seen them?"

"They kept Fenito and me together for a while," he said. "But then he was taken to another cell, and . . . I don't know. Renzi I haven't seen since we were taken."

Now the train was stopped, and the silence was ominous. They must have made it to the camp. They must be there, and in a moment, the doors would open, and they would be led out to hard labor, torture, and death.

Then something familiar flitted over the edge of her senses. Like the memory of a mushroom sync.

The door flew open, the blinding glare of sunlight bursting in. Someone jumped into the train.

"Hey," she called. "Who wants to get out of here?"

With that came a flooding sense of sync connection, warm and familiar, but yet new and unknown. Ajiñe couldn't see what was happening until the woman—a young *jifoz* woman in hard denim—dropped in front of her cage.

"Ajiñe!" she shouted as she opened the cage. She grabbed Ajiñe's hand and pulled her out, kissing Ajiñe warmly and passionately as soon as she was on her feet. "Found you."

"Do I know you?" Ajiñe asked. Not that she minded the kiss, but she had never seen this woman before in her life. Except there was something familiar about the girl. Like she had met her in a dream.

"It's me, I—" She paused. "Sorry, it's complicated. Nália. Nália Enapi."

"Nália?" Nicalla called out. "How are you here? What's going on?"

Nicalla recognized her, so that was something. Wait, was this the girl who had been arrested? The one with the modified 960 that ended up in Renzi's possession. How was she here? And why did she know Ajiñe? Why did she kiss her . . .?

Kissed her like Renzi.

"Come on," Nália said, helping Nicalla out of her cage. "Let's get out of here. There are more prisoners on the train. Let's get everyone out."

Ajiñe jumped out of the train—they were in the middle of scrubland, well out of the city. Nothing but train tracks and dry bushes.

"Where are we?" she asked, not expecting a real answer from any of the others who were piling out of the train. Mensi grabbed her as soon as he was out, wrapping her up in his arms.

"Our spirits are watching over us," he said, clutching her tightly.

"I know, I know," she said.

"We'll get out or go down fighting," he said. "Who is that girl?"

"The one Nic recruited, who got caught on her first train job."

"Her?" He seemed shocked. He looked over to one side. "That's Renzi's cycle. The junkbashed 960."

"No," Ajiñe said. "That can't be." They went over together and looked it over. Even with just a quick glance, Ajiñe could tell it was the same cycle. A couple of the hoses still had the tape Ajiñe had wrapped them with.

"Hey, girl!" Ajiñe shouted as Nália came out of the train, leading the last of the prisoners—an older woman who seemed like she could barely walk—and helping them all out. "Why do you have Renzi's cycle?"

"My cycle," Nália said. "Like I said, complicated."

"Make it clear, then."

"Shouldn't we free everyone else—"

Ajiñe looked to Nic and Mensi. "Get it going. I'm talking to her. And find my father."

They scrambled off. She trusted them to handle it.

"Ajiñe—"

"Why do you think you know me?"

"Because I do," Nália said. "You were there for me in the truck, keeping it going so I could reach Varazina."

That made no sense. "That was Renzi."

"Renzi is complicated."

"How so?"

"Nália!"

Very familiar voice. Ajiñe turned, and Renzi was rushing over to them, half carrying a frail *llipe* woman.

"Renzi!" she called out, rushing over to him. "What is going on?"

"She's dying," he said.

"Who is she, and why the shit should we care if she's dying?"

"She's Varazina," Nália said, her voice dripping with contempt.

"This lady is Varazina? What are you even—Renzi, what are you talking about? How did you—what is—"

A wordless exchange passed between Renzi and Nália, like they were in sync with each other.

"You don't have to," Nália said.

"She deserves the truth," Renzi said. "She is Varazina, but she's also Penda Rodiguen, the granddaughter of the tyrant."

"What?" Ajiñe asked.

"And my name isn't Renzi Llionorco, not really. It's Wenthi Tungét."

That shook Ajiñe at the center of her being. She stumbled for a moment, and Nália caught her, her touch familiar and comforting. Electric sparks of sync and connection flew from her fingers, running through Ajiñe's body.

"That—" Ajiñe managed to say. "That's a very Sehosian name. Very *llipe.*" She stared at him in disbelief. "That's one of the Prime Families."

"All true," he said with his head down.

The old woman coughed and shuddered, but kept her eyes locked on Ajiñe. "We don't have time for this. Let's do this effectively."

She lashed out with a pale, bony hand and grabbed Ajiñe's face, and like a completed circuit, there was a full connection of touch from Renzi to Varazina to Ajiñe to Nália. Instead of their bodies coming together, though, Ajiñe felt herself being snapped out of her flesh, with such force her legs dropped out from under her.

73

Wenthi found himself at his mother's dining table, in her house, but with nothing but bright, white emptiness in the windows beyond. Penda Rodiguen sat at the head of the table, where Mother would always sit. Nália sat at his left, and Ajiñe across the table.

"How did we get here?" Ajiñe asked. "What is this?"

"There was too much to say, and every click of every swipe matters," Penda said. "Time has less meaning in this space with the mushroom, beyond our bodies, where we can stretch out the moment within the blink of an eye." As she said this, she slowly shifted into a fuller, healthier version of herself. Never losing the appearance of Penda Rodiguen, but somehow taking on the essence, the presence, that made Varazina.

"But why are we all in my bed?" Ajiñe asked.

"What do you mean?" Nália asked. "We're in my cousin's motor shop." She looked to Wenthi.

"My mother's dining room," he said.

"Your minds made this into something familiar, drawn from an uncomfortable memory. Wherever you are, it was likely a place where you were told something you didn't want to hear. You already know that's what's going to happen, and you're readying yourself for that hard truth."

Wenthi understood. This was where Mother made it clear that, due to his caste, he had to leave the house, and would no longer be welcome to come in without explicit invite, and never to stay the night.

This was where she had banished him.

"What is this hard truth?" Ajiñe asked.

"That you're going to have to fight for a free country. A country that exists on your terms, that you make."

"That's not a hard truth," Ajiñe said. "I've been in this fight."

"You've been in it, Ajiñe Osceba," Varazina said—and in many ways in this moment she *was* Varazina, in ways Wenthi couldn't describe but *understood* at his very core. "Why do you think I chose you? Why do you think I guided you to him in the first place?"

"And who is he? Is he Renzi or Wenthi or—and who is this Nália girl?"

Wenthi sighed. He had to tell her. "I'm a Civil Patrol officer who was assigned to infiltrate one of the cells of the Fists of Zapi and find my way to the Inner Circle and Varazina."

"What?" Ajiñe tried to get to her feet, but seemed to be unable to. Perhaps they were each experiencing this psychic space in different ways, and her experience and his couldn't interact properly. "What is this shit? That can't be true. We synced with him. We were united with him. We would have sensed he was there to betray us. It can't be true."

"It is," Nália said. "You didn't sense him because they had bonded us together, using me to make a mask for him. But the mask, our sync with each other, was more complicated than they expected."

"I don't understand," Ajiñe said.

"You know who Doctor Shebiruht is," Wenthi said. "We talked about her the other night."

"The Witch? So she is alive? And she's capable of . . . I don't even know what this is. I don't even know where we are."

Varazina spoke. "We're still standing outside the train, Ajiñe. The shock of this is making you fall to your knees. Right now, you're still falling."

"And you—"

"I'm still dying," Varazina said. "I was made to be a weapon, a weapon made by weaving the *myco* into my very physical being. To a lesser extent, so were Wenthi and Nália."

"What?" Nália asked. "How is that—"

"Your parents strove to alter themselves, and through that, altered you. But you two are so different than me. Your connection to the mushroom and your bodies and spirits are all in harmony. I was created in a far more vicious manner, and while it gave me power, the cost was my body."

"That's why you're dying," Wenthi said. "Shebiruht was keeping you alive, and without her care—"

"I can only last so long. And I want my death to matter."

"How?" Ajiñe asked.

"Because I was made to be a weapon, and I wasn't given a choice about that," Varazina said. "But I can choose where I aim that weapon. My grandfather wanted to use me against the world. The Sehosians and their Alliance the same."

"Really?" Wenthi asked.

"That was the only reason they kept me alive all this time. They told me pretty bullshit like they wanted to have me unite the Vailic, to heal Nemuspia, but . . . I could see the truth in their hearts. So I spent years putting together my fight, building my plan. Deciding who I wanted to be a weapon for. And it was clear that this place, this country I was born in—we all were born in—deserved to be its own nation. Deserved to be its own land. Deserved to no longer be infected by people who are not of this place."

"And how will you do that?" Ajiñe asked.

"I can't do it all. I can light the spark. You have to be my fire." She pointed to Ajiñe, Nália, and Wenthi in succession. "You need to be the mind, the voice, and the power behind this fight."

"You mean the Fists," Ajiñe said.

"I mean the three of you. Together. It has to be that way."

"That can't work," Wenthi said. "I—"

"If he's a stinking shithole tory, there's no way," Ajiñe said. "To think we welcomed him into our arms, out beds—"

"It wasn't just him," Nália said. "It was me. When we finished the induction, the effect on the two of us was beyond profound."

Ajiñe's face screwed up in thought. "The vision of the fires. Your insistence of pushing through to reach Varazina."

"That was me," Nália said. "The Renzi who you stood over and protected was me. Renzi was . . . the both of us. Together." She chuckled. "And that was the point, wasn't it, Varazina? You wanted Wenthi and me to melt into each other, to the point where we worked together now to rescue the others. To turn him to the cause, but also curb the edge of my anger."

Wenthi understood. "Because you want us to build a Pinogoz that's just. That's why you decided on us instead of the likes of Jendiscira or Hocnupec."

"Their hearts were in the right place, their passion extraordinary, but they . . . they petrified. Ultimately, they would have built something founded on toxic ideas. I can't . . . I can't see where the future goes, but I can see they would happily visit the oppression they suffered onto others. That Inner Circle, I couldn't trust them. But I think I can trust you, if you work together."

"Why would I need him?" Ajiñe said.

"Because his heart knows the truth," Varazina said. "And he is brimming with power, which you will need. And he can't do it alone because this fight will need a voice, a leader—"

Wenthi understood.

"And I'm just a tory spy, a spoiled *rhique* son of a *llipe* councilwoman. I can't be that voice, because the people won't follow."

"Exactly why I had to become Varazina," she said, her majestic persona melting away to the frail form of Penda. "Because no one would answer to a revolution from this woman."

"How can I trust any of this?" Ajiñe asked.

"The two of them are already deeply entwined, their spirits have tendrils like mycelium stretching between them. Reach out to them, feel the truth between them, share everything of yourself, and I will share what I can."

"What you can?" Nália asked.

"I mean my power," Varazina said. "I'll give you what I can, what you need, and you'll give it all to each other."

Wenthi took Nália's hand, a symbol more than anything in this space, since they were already so connected. He reached across the table to Ajiñe. "Believe in her, if you can't believe in me."

She took his hand, and her spirit, her pain, her anguish, her fire all flowed into him.

"Good," Varazina said, as the space they were in—this image of Mother's home—started to crack and crumble. "You'll be ready before your knees touch the ground. And then we'll have to hurry, because I don't have much time left."

74

Wenthi snapped back into awareness of his body as Ajiñe dropped to her knees.

"Spirits," he whispered. In the last moments of communion with each other, Varazina had touched each of them with just a portion of her knowledge, her power, and in that brief touch, Nália had felt the lifetime Varazina had known as Penda Rodiguen. The constant pain of her body, the needles, the tests, the apartment that had every amenity but was still very much a prison, all because the Alliance condemned her existence but still hoped to make use of her power.

Which made Varazina's intended use for that power all the sweeter. He needed to help her.

"She doesn't have much time," Wenthi said, pulling up Varazina as she gasped for air. "Let's unhitch the engine, get her on there and get her up to speed."

"Right," Ajiñe said, catching her own breath as she stood up. "I'm . . . I had no idea. We need to—"

"On the ground!" someone shouted. "Consider yourselves detained!"

Half a dozen Civil Patrol closed in on them all, guns drawn. Wenthi hadn't noticed them approach. Had they been in a different part of the train? Had they arrived separately just now? Why hadn't he felt them as the sharp static, like he had with the officers on the train?

Then he saw why.

Paulei was front and center in a group of officers: Minlei, Guand, Hwokó, Cinden, Peshka. The whole cadre, Wenthi's closest friends and lovers. His mushroom-activated senses didn't register them as a threat.

"Paulei, I—"

"Shut up!" Paulei shouted. "You drop your sidearm and get on the damned ground!"

But before Wenthi could react, Ajiñe grabbed his gun and got it up, and Nália did the same with hers. Wenthi quickly got his hands out and put himself in between them all.

"No, it doesn't have to be this way," he said. "Paulei—"

"How dare you, Wenthi," Paulei said. "What are you even doing?"

"The right thing for once," Wenthi said. "Just put down your guns, no one needs to get hurt—"

"People are already hurt!" Paulei said. "We found Enrin and Thei, a kilo back, both a mess of broken bones. What did you do?"

"Saved these people—"

"People you brought in!" Paulei shouted.

Gabrána and Fenito were to the side, hands up. "Is that true? Renzi, what is this?" Gab asked.

"Renzi?" Paulei asked. "Did you get in so damn deep you actually think you're Renzi?"

"He is Renzi," Ajiñe said. "He may have been one of you once, but he is Renzi Llionorco now. He is ours now."

"I'm not sure who you tricked more, Wenthi! These fools or yourself."

"These people are trying to make our country what it's supposed to be," Wenthi said. "You could be a part of that, too."

"I am a part of that," Paulei said. "I am an officer of the law, and I—"

Nália's hand shook, and Wenthi felt that, and saw Minlei's finger go to her trigger.

"No!" Wenthi shouted, pushing his will into Minlei. All he had time to do, taking control over her body, was throw her arm up wild, so the shot wouldn't hit anyone. All the other officers—all once dear friends, who he had shared everything with, responded by trying to shoot.

There were six of them, and Wenthi couldn't control all of their bodies at once. Not standing still. With no speed to fuel his power, all he could do was take hold over their trigger fingers, keep them from being able to shoot.

"What—why can't I—"

"Paulei," Wenthi begged. "Drop the guns. Stop this. We can all walk away."

"Wenthi," Varazina wheezed. "We don't have time."

"We need to end this," Nália said. She pushed her own control onto Paulei, bringing his gun up to his temple.

"What is this?" Paulei shouted. "What are you doing to us?"

"Please," Wenthi pleaded. "Drop the gun."

I'll do it, Nália thought at Wenthi. *We have to stop them.*

"No—" Wenthi said.

I know how much you love him. All of them. And us. I wish you didn't have to choose.

"If you don't drop the guns, you will die," Wenthi said.

"We can't let them live," Gabrána said.

"We have to be better," Wenthi said. "We have to give them a chance."

Mensi came up, a hand on Wenthi's shoulder. "A chance," he said quietly. "But only one."

Wenthi didn't have the strength to exert more control over their bodies, to fight them and Nália, who had brought all the guns to their temples. All he had was keeping their fingers from pulling the triggers. But maybe he could reach them.

He closed his eyes, dug into his memories, and pushed them into their minds. The story of this land from Varazina. The pain and degradation of the *baniz* in Gonetown. The radiant joy of Ziva Osceba's Spirit Dance. The constant fear in Miahez the people felt for patrol. The torture of the derrick labor camps. The dead and maimed in the name of taking Zapisian oil. The love shared between Ajiñe and Gabrána and Mensi and Fenito and Nicalla and Nália and himself and everyone who had been inducted under Varazina.

Tears formed in Paulei's eyes, and his hand spasmed, dropping the gun. The other officers did as well. Various Fists ran in, pulled the guns away, and starting tethering them with their own cuffs.

Paulei was on his knees, hands bound behind him, crying.

"I didn't know," he whispered. "I . . . I've been so cruel."

"Shh," Wenthi said, caressing Paulei's beautiful face. "You see it now. You can still change."

"This is the mushroom?" Paulei whispered. "This is what it lets you feel?"

"Yeah."

"No wonder they called it dangerous," he said. "It's full of truth."

"Will someone explain to me what's happening?" Gabrána asked. "Why is Renzi half making out with the tory, and why did they call him Wenthi and—"

"It's too much for right now," Ajiñe said. "We don't have time to—"

"You don't," Paulei said, looking back up. "We called for backup. The Alli nucks and the military are roaring in, just a few clicks away. You have to run—"

"No time," Varazina said. Nália holding her up was the only thing keeping her on her feet. "I don't have much strength left. I need . . . I need . . . the speed."

"Get her to the engine," Wenthi said. "We need to—"

"That'll take too long," Nália said. "The only thing that can get fast enough, quick enough—" Her eyes darted to the side.

Wenthi saw what she was looking to.

Her custom junkbashed Puegoiz 960.

75

Nália let Wenthi help her as they brought Varazina over to the cycle. "I've got to hurry," she told him.

"You've got to?" Wenthi asked. "No, I'm doing this."

"Who's doing what?" Ajiñe asked, coming over with the rest of the cell. "What's the plan?"

"My cycle. Like we told you at the track, this baby, on the flat open, can crack three hundred." Nália looked out to the barren scrubland, the tracks leading toward the derricks. "It doesn't get much more flat open than that."

Ajiñe hesitated. "But she can't drive the cycle in her condition, and if you take her—"

"You won't survive being next to me when I go," Varazina said weakly.

"Well, someone—" Nália started.

"It has to be me," Wenthi said firmly. "Like she said. Someone has to be the voice and the heart. That's you."

"But you—"

"I'm a tory, Nália. I am a *rhique* son of a *llipe* councilwoman from a Prime Family. My name is a Prime Family. I can't lead the charge that this will need. I can't be that voice. So I have to do this."

"It's my cycle—"

"It's your fight," Wenthi said, getting on the cycle, wrapping Varazina's weak arms around him. "Besides, you can build another one." He winked and kicked on the engine.

"But we need—" Nália started, but her words were drowned out by the engine as Wenthi tore off in a cloud of dust.

"What is he doing?" Gabrána asked. "Will someone please explain to me what is going on? Who was the *llipe* woman Renzi just rode off with, who is this girl, and is Renzi really a tory? Ajiñe, please?"

"That was Varazina," Ajiñe said. "She was made by the tyrant and the Witch of the War to be a weapon. Made from the mushroom, made to tear the world apart. But she chose to be our weapon. She's choosing to die, so she could save us."

"And you are?" Mensi asked Nália.

"The better version of the person you knew as Renzi Llionorco, Mensi," she said with a wink. Despite her outward cheek, her attention was still with Wenthi, her avatar on the cycle with him. Varazina was shuddering and seizing as he knocked the cycle up to passing gear, racing gear, fire gear, tearing the engine into the white. The speedometer was already past two hundred, almost to the limit of what it could read.

"Hey, asshole," she said. "How far do you need to go?"

"It's not the distance, it's the velocity," he said. "Do you feel what's coming out of her?"

"I do," she said. "I also feel a truck full of Alliance nucks racing up on us. And military tanks coming from the oil derricks. If this doesn't work—"

"It will," he said. "But maybe get people in the train."

The energy coming off of Varazina rose, building as a vibration that filled every gram of Nália's body, a song that came from the very earth beneath her feet.

"What's happening?" Ajiñe asked.

"Can you feel it?" Nália asked back.

"I can see it," Mensi said, pointing to the group of armored trucks coming over the horizon. "We can't run from that."

"Are there cycles or trucks we can grab?" Gabrána asked. "Get the train moving?"

"No time," Nicalla said.

"We just need to buy Wenthi a couple swipes," Nália said. "They're almost ready."

"Ready for what?" Gabrána asked.

"Her power," Nália said.

"Everyone in the train!" Ajiñe shouted. "Hurry, get inside!"

People scrambled to get inside, as Nic and Fenito helped rally them in. Even Paulei and the other patrol officers were dragged in.

"A few swipes?" Mensi asked. He picked up one of the guns left on the ground.

"I suppose it's a better way to go than slaving in the oil fields," Gabrána said, taking another. Nicalla and Fenito grabbed a pair each and took their place in front of the train car the rest of the prisoners were hiding in.

Ajiñe looked to Nália. "It's going to work?"

"It has to," Nália said. As the armored trucks raced up, soldiers and officers jumped out, rifles at the ready.

"Surrender or be fired upon!" one shouted. "You have no chance to resist!"

"Get ready," Ajiñe said.

Nália pushed herself to Wenthi one last time. The cycle's engine was blaring hot, white and gray smoke pouring from it, as he closed in at three hundred kilos. Varazina's eyes were rolled back in her head, a white glow emanating from her whole body. She could feel the heat from Wenthi's body, like he was on fire. It wouldn't be much longer.

"You did good," she whispered to him, kissing him on the cheek with her phantom form.

"Don't thank me yet," he said through strained teeth, even in his avatar. "There's still plenty of work for you to do. And it's going to be on you."

"Last warning!" the Alliance officers shouted. "We will open fire!"

"Give it to them first?" Gab asked.

"Get ready on my order," Ajiñe said.

"Light it up," Nália told Wenthi. "And thanks, asshole."

The last words came as a whisper that brushed against her spirit. "You're welcome."

Her sync with him snapped as a burst of white light erupted from the horizon, and a wave of light and power washed over the land.

76

Ajiñe was only on the edge of it—her sync with Nália and Wenthi and Varazina was muted, as if she had been sheltered from the brunt of it. But she felt the wave of Varazina's power. The moments of Wenthi's agony as his body was blown apart. Nália's joy as the song of the land, the song that Varazina had composed with her power, played through her body and spirit.

And the sky was blinding.

And then Wenthi—Renzi, in her heart he was Renzi, and that was how he should be honored—was gone.

The light washed over the world.

"What do we—" Gab asked. Ajiñe knew she was just a meter to her left, but in the blinding light, she couldn't see her.

"Wait," Ajiñe said. "Don't pull iron until you can see them."

The light faded, and Ajiñe's eyes adjusted, but the song still played in the back on her head, like a radio on the other side of a wall.

The other sounds were crying and retching.

When Ajiñe could make out the Alliance officers, they were all on the ground, on their knees. Thick black liquid—thick as blood, thick as oil—seeped from their mouths, noses, and eyes. They wailed, making sounds that more befit an animal being slaughtered than a human being.

"Are they dying?" Mensi asked.

"Don't know," Nicalla said. "But they look like they're suffering."

"Shame," Gab said. She strolled over and started taking their guns away. None of them—not one—was able to resist. "Do we put them out of their misery?"

"No."

That was Nália. She walked over, her face filled with peace and serenity.

"There's no need to kill them. They should live, live with the pain of what they've done to us, to our country. That's what they're going through."

"What *is* that?" Nicalla said, looking closely at the black gunk that was coming out of one officer's orifices, even as he weakly pleaded for help. "Is it oil?"

"It does look like it," Fenito said.

"They're feeling what the land felt," Nália said. "Feeling what they had done to it."

The train doors opened again, and Miss Dallatan—Ajiñe had no idea she was among the prisoners here—stuck her head out. "Is it safe?"

"It is," Ajiñe said. "Come out, come out." She watched the other prisoners as they came out, waiting to see her father. He came out, helped down by Isilla Henáca. Ajiñe went to him, wrapping her arms around him.

"Are you all right?" he asked her. "Did they hurt you?"

"I'm fine," she said. But his attention was on the Alliance officers on the ground.

"What happened here?"

"Varazina happened," Nália said. "She released the full weight of her power, pouring it out of her dying body, and with that she cursed the people who intrude upon this country. The pain they put upon the people and the land will be visited back upon them sevenfold."

Fenito and Mensi had collected the guns, dragged the officers into the train's prison cars, leaving them with the Civil Patrol officers who had already been locked up. Nicalla and Gabrána checked on the other survivors. Ajiñe held on to her father, never wanting to let go, while still the distant song vibrated in the back of her head.

"You're hearing it, aren't you?" Nália asked.

"What am I hearing?"

"Varazina was made to reach into an empty space—where the vibrations connect us, our spirits and minds to the mushroom, and the mushroom to the land. Through that power she discovered it resonated with the frequencies of the radio. All the transmissions, all the receivers. You're hearing the song she placed in there, the song that we can make our own. The song we can use to tune into those frequencies."

Ajiñe tried to wrap her mind around what Nália was saying.

Nicalla came up, putting her hand into Ajiñe's. "We can do it now. Take back this country. Teach the lessons of Varazina. Return Zapisia to what it was supposed to be."

"No," Nália said. "We're not going to do it that way. We're not going to stay mired in the past. We have to look toward tomorrow."

"And who are you to say?" Nicalla said with a sneer. "I brought you in. You haven't—"

"She's the one Varazina blessed," Ajiñe said, wrapping a protective arm around Nália. "And the one who rescued us here. She's the one with the power to lead us."

"You need to lead us," Nália told Ajiñe. "That's what she wanted. She trusted your vision. Your voice. She knew I could bring the power, but that you could be the just voice that Pinogoz needed."

Nicalla was still on it. "Pinogoz is a fake name, put upon us—"

"It's our country," Ajiñe said. "Pinogoz, Zapisia, whatever you call it. It should be ours. It's high time we made it ours, now that we have the tools and the power to do it."

"How do we have power now?" Miss Dallatan asked.

The radios in the armored trucks all sparked to life with a burst of static, and as Nália spoke, her voice came from all of them at once.

"Because we can be heard. And we can call everyone to our cause."

Miss Dallatan bowed her head and stepped back. Nicalla looked shocked, and then stepped forward, taking Nália's hand. "You are the one she blessed. I'll follow wherever you say." Many of the others stepped forward, bowing their heads. All ready to follow. All ready to fight.

"So now what?" Gabrána asked, curling one arm around Ajiñe's back. "Do we take those trucks and drive back to the city?"

"We do take those trucks," Ajiñe said, the smile coming to her mouth. "But they were expecting us at the work camps, and I think we shouldn't let them down. Let's go and show them what we think about that place."

Nália nodded. They would liberate the camps today. And then the country tomorrow.

REFUEL: DIRECTIVE

You're listening to Alliance Voice 930, coming to you with the sound of freedom. The time marks three mark zero, and it's the twentieth day of Tian. We hope you're having a very productive day. You may have heard disturbing news about the situations in Outtown or in the country work camps and outskirt villages, but we assure you that every situation is very well in hand. We want to assure you that these rumors are unfounded, exaggerations of a few acts of terrorism by a handful of malcontents. Everything is under control in the city—

Lies.

Where did that—no, everything is under control. And we are happy to announce that the Alliance overseers are quite pleased, despite these minor disruptions, and they have every confidence in maintaining the planned schedule to elections and self-rule. The people of Pinogoz will soon have voice—

They already have a voice.

What is that? Someone is—I don't know, find out. Listeners, we want to remind you that the Alliance is dedicated to building the country up so it can stand on its own feet—

You feed them lies. The Alliance is not building anything. The Alliance is only making its own coffers fat. Lining the pockets of the petty officials off the misery of the people who belong to this land.

I don't know who it is. Cut them off! Shut it down!

There is no cutting us off. There is no shutting us down. We are the voice of the people. We are the broadcasters of truth.

Who is this?

This is Ajiñe Osceba.

This is Nália Enapi.

We are the voice of resistance.

We are the voice of tomorrow.

And we have come with a message for all of you who have tried to plant your boot on the neck of this country.

Nix xisisa. We have paid too much.

Now your debts come due.

You may have noticed burning pain in your muscles, black tears from your eyes, dry bramble in your throat. This is the curse upon anyone who was not born here. This is Zapisia telling you, you are not welcome here.

We do not want you "building us up."

We do not want you deciding when we are ready.

You must leave.

Get on your steamer ships and your four-prop planes and leave this country, or you will be burned out, like a fever. We are humane, so we give you this chance to evacuate.

But let it be clear: If you stay, you will die.

And for the children of Zapisia, you who have been born to this land, no matter your heritage, join us. Baniz, jifoz, rhique, *and even* llipe. *Are you out there? Can you hear the call of Varazina? Her blood is soaked into the land. She bled and died for you, for your freedom.*

Do you feel the strength of Renzi Llionorco? He repented his sins, opened his heart to us all, and gave freely of the love he had for you. He can no longer ride for us, so we look to you.

Will you stand up, will you race out, will you fight back?

Will you follow us?

Will you fight with us?

Will you join us to reclaim your home?

Will you join us to reclaim tomorrow?

LAP OF HONOR:
THE BROADCASTS OF TOMORROW

77

Lathéi was not sick, but she seemed to be the only one getting on the steamer who wasn't. What should have been a leisurely cruise to Dumamång was now practically a steerage ship, packed to the rafters with people fleeing Ziaparr. People couldn't get out fast enough.

Oshnå was sick, but she seemed to have it mild. Her body ached, and she only occasionally had a black drop fall from her eye. Lathéi wondered if, when Wenthi did whatever he did—faith, that wild, stupid boy—he made a point of sparing Oshnå the worst of it out of love for Lathéi.

Though as she started to board the ship, she formed a new theory. She was familiar with quite a few of the Alliance Oversight ministers in the country—Mother did have to work with them, and some would come to the house—and she noticed many of them had drastic symptoms, especially in comparison to Oshnå. They were burning up, unable to stand, the black blood gushing from anywhere it could.

She had heard the broadcasts, the ones that Enapi girl was somehow making. She decided it stood to reason that the Alliance folks who had been more in power, who had caused more hurt and anguish, especially to the poor people who were waging this civil war, were hit with the Zoika Plague hardest.

That's what they called it, as it was only the *zoika* caste—the honored foreigners, all the Alliance overseers—who were getting sick. Even Mother and some of the other awful people in the Provisional Council, the rest of the Prime Families, they were all fine. Whatever this was—curse, plague, what have you—it seemed to target only those who weren't born here.

Even Oshnå, but for someone like Oshnå, who merely visited the country as a tourist, the effects were mild. Regardless, Oshnå had to leave. Some people in the Ministries of Control, the people in the upper echelons of authority, had died already.

No one else wanted to risk it. "Get out of this country and let those bastards be on their own."

Oshnå was more than happy to leave.

"We'll get back home, and forget all about this place," she said as they settled into their cabin. "I mean, it was a lovely city, and it was exciting to help your brother with the insurgency. But I'm happy to be returning to a civilized place so we can get on with our lives."

"A civilized place?" Lathéi asked.

"Of course," Oshnå said. That soured Lathéi's already bitter mood, and it must have shown on her face. "Oh, come now, Lathéi, it's not like you didn't say it yourself so many times. That Dumamång is the most modern and exciting city in the world, and you couldn't imagine wanting to live anywhere else."

"I did say that," Lathéi said quietly. "I'm sorry, I'm just quite out of sorts with all this."

"Of course you are," Oshnå said. She sat behind Lathéi, wrapping her arms around her body. "You have suffered here more than anyone. I know how much you loved your brother, and your grief needs to run its course. I will be here for you, every step, until you are ready to face anything."

You can face anything.

The voice came, faint and crackling, over the transistor radio in their cabin.

"What?" Lathéi asked.

"I said—" Oshnå started.

You can face anything, Lathéi, the voice said. A voice Lathéi knew like her own heart. ***And you don't have to go.***

"What is that?" Oshnå asked.

"It's Wenthi," Lathéi said.

Renzi.

The name he used in his mission. "Can you hear me? Are you . . . are you alive?"

In a fashion. The whole island is alive, it is connected to everyone and everything, including the frequencies of your radio. A part of me is everywhere.

"Not in Dumamång," Lathéi said.

That's true. But you could stay.

That hit her heart in ways she didn't know was possible. Wenthi was gone, but here was his voice. He was talking to her. He was somehow still here. As the voice on the radio continued, two other voices mixed in with his. Just hints of feminine voices, echoing and amplifying what he was saying, growing stronger with each word.

There's still a fight for this nation. For your nation, Lathéi. And that fight needs your voice, too. You are a daughter of Zapisia, and this revolution can also be yours. There's so much work left to do.

Lathéi stood up. She looked to her bag, sitting under the bunk.

Oshnå touched her face. "Tell me what you want."

Lathéi nodded. "My brother asked me to stay. I can't—I know it's crazy."

"It isn't," Oshnå said. "I want you in my life. I want you to spend your life with me in Dumamång. But I think . . . I never want to be a thing that stops you. It's all right if you need to stay."

"I think I do," Lathéi said, surprising herself how well she understood. "I would want to be with you, but . . . It's my brother. And he was there whenever I needed him. And if he says he needs me, my . . . my country needs me, then I will be there for him."

Oshnå kissed her briefly and pulled away. "I'll wire you when I'm home. Do what you have to."

Lathéi walked out of the cabin, part of her heart cracking. She was glad, at least, that Oshnå understood. That it made sense, in the center of her spirit, that she needed to stay. She needed to help.

She made her way through the throng of sick people, down the gangplank to a nearly deserted dock.

Nearly, but not entirely.

"Were you waiting for me, Paulei?" she asked after kissing her brother's closest friend and lover on the cheek.

"I was . . . told to be here for you."

"By a. . . . His voice?"

Paulei nodded. "I'm still not sure what's happening. Or what's going to happen. Or even what I think *should* happen, if I'm being honest. But I want to do something."

"There's so much work left to do," Lathéi said quietly.

He gestured to his cycle, parked on the curb. "You ready to go?"

She got on behind him, grabbing his waist. "So where are we going?"

The radio on his cycle sparked to life, and three voices spoke in perfect unison.

To join a better tomorrow.

ACKNOWLEDGMENTS

So this was a very different ride.

After writing twelve interbraided novels set in Maradaine, juggling four different series threads to come together into something resembling a finale, I had the idea that I should take a break.

Only I would define "a break" as "writing a completely different kind of fantasy novel, completely out of all my comfort zones, in a brand-new setting, doing all the new worldbuilding from scratch."

There's a reason I'm on a podcast called "Worldbuilding for Masochists."

That podcast proved to be such a critical catalyst in the creation of this book, and I have to give so much thanks and gratitude to my past and present co-hosts—Rowenna Miller, Cass Morris, and Alexandra Rowland—for being such absolute pillars of support and fountains of good ideas. Many of the conversations we've had on the podcast were reflected back into the work in this book, challenging my presumptions and driving me to more interesting choices. On top of that, we had a number of great guests who all provided insight and wisdom that I tried, to the best of my ability, to apply to the work here, including and not limited to Fonda Lee, Jenn Lyons, Tasha Suri, S. A. Chakraborty, K. A. Doore, Andrea Stewart, K. Tempest Bradford, Sarah Guan, K. S. Villoso, and several more. All of them helped me write a better book than I would have written a year ago.

And the year I was writing this, well . . . most of the writing took place in 2020, which hopefully will go down in the history books as "that terrible year" as opposed to "The Beginning of the Aftertimes." But continuing to write in 2020 required patience and support, and I was very fortunate to have quite a lot of both. Some of that support came from patrons and fans, like Victoria Luther and Ember Randall. Some came from dear old friends like Nilda de la Llata, who was so kind as to host me for a mini-retreat (well before the pandemic) in Guanajuato, a city that provided a lot of insight and inspiration for Ziaparr.

Of course, as usual, I relied heavily on my publishing team, including my agent Mike Kabongo (who was **all in** when I said I had a weird idea with motorcycles and psychic mushrooms), my editor Sheila Gilbert, and everyone at DAW and Penguin Random House: Betsy, Katie, Josh, Leah, Alexis, and Stephanie, plus countless others whose names I don't know. Artist Matt Griffin created a gorgeous cover which I just adored the moment I saw it.

Daniel J. Fawcett, as usual, has been the best sounding board for Big Ideas that someone could ask for, and Miriam Robinson Gould went above and beyond as first reader, helping me shape this book into something tighter and stronger, and helping me see what, exactly, the book I wrote actually was.

On top of that, my family remains a source of strength and inspiration. This includes my parents Nancy and Lou, and my mother-in-law Kateri. And, of course, my wife Deidre, who dove deep into this project, more than any other one, helping with research and concepts, being my guide through Guanajuato, Mexico City, and all her home country.

And finally, my son Nicholas, who provided the initial spark that set this story ablaze. I had gone with him to a specialty shop to buy a pair of raw denim jeans, and in the middle of the shop was a vintage motorcycle, seemingly built out of spare parts, with a denim-clad mannikin on it. He pointed it out and said, "Hey, why can't fantasy look like *that*?"

Yeah, why can't it?

So I made it look like that. For him. And hopefully for you as well.